AGAINST THE TIDE

Recent Titles set in Cornwall by Rosemary Aitken

CORNISH HARVEST
THE GIRL FROM PENVARRIS
THE TINNER'S DAUGHTER

AGAINST THE TIDE *
THE SILENT SHORE *
STORMY WATERS *

* *available from Severn House*

AGAINST THE TIDE

Rosemary Aitken

severn House

This first world edition published in Great Britain 2004 by
SEVERN HOUSE PUBLISHERS LTD of
9–15 High Street, Sutton, Surrey SM1 1DF.
This first world edition published in the USA 2004 by
SEVERN HOUSE PUBLISHERS INC of
595 Madison Avenue, New York, N.Y. 10022.

British Library Cataloguing in Publication Data

Aitken,   Rosemary
    Against the tide
    1.   Sisters - Cornwall - England - Fiction
    2.   Cornwall (England) - Social conditions - 20th century - Fiction
    3.   Domestic fiction
    I.   Title
    823.9'14 [F]

    ISBN 0-7278-6029-1

Typeset by Palimpsest Book Production Ltd.,
Polmont, Stirlingshire, Scotland.
Printed and bound in Great Britain by
MPG Books Ltd., Bodmin, Cornwall.

To Betty, with love

Part One

Summer 1909

One

As soon as the two girls turned the corner of the lane late that gusty, Cornish summer afternoon, they could see that the men were there again, leaning on the granite wall beside the gate.

Dora knew some of them by sight – the Pollock brothers, from the *Silver Gull*, red-haired and squat, somehow menacing in their thick jumpers and their trousers stained with salt; and also Dan Taylor and Marty Olds who worked the *Cormorant*, like as two haddocks on a plate, with their grizzled hair and beards, and faces tanned like old oak by the wind and sea. There were others that she didn't recognize, but you didn't need to know their names or boats to see that they were fisherman as well. Their fishing smocks and sea boots told you that.

They were angry fishermen at that. Dora sighed. Why was it Father could never do anything the simple way and keep the peace? He'd been off-sides with everyone for years because he would insist on fishing on the Sabbath, when others in the Cove preferred to keep the day. 'Why should they beggars from up east have all the catch?' he used to say. He'd braved it out too, though he'd often had to sail right round to Newlyn to land the catch. He'd caught a good shoal once or twice that way, which had earned him money, certainly, but it had earned him the resentment of his neighbours too.

All that was when the twins were very small, though Dora could still remember – just. And then, when that had simmered down (other men went out on Sundays too, these days) he'd fitted out the *Cornish Rose* again and caused another outcry in the Cove. The deep-trawl nets were bad enough – men said they picked up everything and spoiled the catch – but this new-fangled petroleum engine was the final straw.

3

She had heard the row that morning, when the *Cornish Rose* came home from sea and the men marched up to the door demanding to see Father face to face. She didn't understand it very well – he never discussed his business with the girls – but she'd huddled with Winnie and their brother in the hall while a lot of shouting and bad-temperedness and threats went on. 'Worse than they steam buggers for ruining the sea,' someone had roared. 'And snatching our livelihood from under us, besides. Mind we don't set fire to you, and all – there's more than one way to use that paraffin you have to start that wretched engine with.'

Father had gone out to them at that, and after a little the shouts and jeers had stopped, though Father hadn't come back in again, not all the afternoon. Dora had been still half afraid to go into the lane when it was time to leave for chapel tea, but to her relief there was nobody about. Not then.

But now here they were again, lurching upright as they saw the girls approach. The oldest Pollock boy pushed back his cap and took a step towards them. He was twice as broad as Father – it was said he could pull in a net of herring on his own – and his work-hardened hands were the size of mutton joints. He had that horrid swaggering look as well, the way he always did when Winnie was about. He stood straddled in the middle of the lane and leered.

Dora drew back instinctively. She hated this. She clutched at Winifred to make her stop. 'They're going to call things after us. Let's go round the back way, by the stile.'

But it was no use – it never was. 'And let them know we're scared! Don't be so daft!' Winnie lifted up her head, in that pert, self-conscious way she had, and marched on towards the gate as bold as brass. Joe Pollock eyed her up and down, as if she was a mannequin in the Co-op window in Penzance.

He stood deliberately in her path and said, 'What's all the rush, me darlin'?' in a sneering way.

One of the younger men – Dora recognized him as from Penvarris Cove – said, in whisper that would have carried to the town, 'Look at 'er, nose in the air like a dead herring. More push'n her father's engine-boat, that one.'

'Wouldn't mind finding out what makes her go!' Joe Pollock said.

There was a lot of laughing and nudging at that, and someone

4

shouted, 'Here, Joe, bet you don't need paraffin to make her start!' Even Winnie's cheeks blazed, but she just shrugged past him and walked on with only the faintest flounce of her gold curls to show him that she'd heard.

That left Dora stranded on her own. There was nothing for it. To turn and flee now would make things worse. She took a deep breath and hurried after Winnie – as, in the end, she always did. Her sister was the older by only half an hour, but Dora seemed to have followed her twin ever since.

Except in looks and personality, she thought, trying to keep her eyes in front and occupy her mind with other things. She didn't follow Winnie there at all. She and Winifred might be twins, but they were so different that people who didn't know them were sometimes quite surprised when they found out. Winnie was blonde and bouncy and self-confident, while Dora was more mousy, gentler and pale. 'Back of the queue when looks were given out,' Father used to say, looking at Dora with a laugh.

Well, sometimes there was security in that. These lolling fishermen weren't interested in her. Joe Pollock made no move to molest her as she passed, and the other men just followed with their eyes – sunburned wrinkles squinting in the sun – as Dora half-ran up the path, so flustered that she almost dropped her bible on the way. Then she was inside and safe, in the welcome shadows of the hall, and she untied her bonnet with fingers that still shook, while Winnie closed the front door with a slam.

'Silly beggars,' Winnie said lightly, dragging off her own hat with a single tug, without even stopping to undo the bow. 'Laugh on the other side of their silly faces, one day soon.' She looked at her sister. 'Don't look so stricken, Dora. What d'you think they're going to do? Not attack you in the street, I don't suppose.'

Dora made no reply to that. She wasn't quite sure what she'd feared, but being mocked and jeered at was enough. She changed the subject, 'Better go up and see Mother, now we're home. I wonder how she is this afternoon.'

'Much the same as ever, I should think.' Winnie could be heartless when she tried. 'It isn't as if we've been out very long. It was only a missionary tea, for heaven's sake – and she had James and Gan for company.'

5

James was their younger brother, excused attendance at the chapel do because he, like mother, was deemed 'delicate'. Gan was Father's mother, steely and unbending as the four busy little knitting needles that were always in her hands whenever she snatched a minute in a chair. Even on a Sunday, like today. No nonsense about Sabbath days with Gan. 'Devil still finds work for idle hands,' she used to say, pinching her thin lips and hugging her bony elbows to her sides as another lumpy woollen sock grew longer by the hour.

She was knitting fiercely now, sitting in the chair by Mother's bed – quick, tight, grey stitches that would one day pinch your toes and leave red rings round underneath your knees. Gan knew how to knit impatience even into socks. She looked up as the twins came in and sighed.

'Well, there you are. And long enough you've been about it, too. How it can take you half an hour to walk a dozen steps, I'll never know. Still, I hope you enjoyed your afternoon teas and magic lantern slides and everything while James and I have stayed indoors watching over your poor mother here.'

Dora made a sullen face, hurt by the injustice of the jibe, but Winnie, as usual, was blithe. 'Pity you didn't say before. We'd have stayed here and you could have gone. I never knew you were so keen on magic lantern slides.'

That was saucy. Eli Westrill's missionary teas were famously tedious affairs and Gan was an expert at finding reasons not to go – though attendance was expected of the twins.

Dora would have given something not to go herself. When there was no visitor from the mission field, Eli always 'stepped into the breach' himself and gave the talk. Always the same talk, more or less – 'Taking the light to darkest Africa' – delivered in a high-pitched, rasping and peculiarly emphatic voice, quite unlike his normal tone, and one which he reserved especially for his lantern show. That had been quite interesting at first, but once the novelty had passed there was little pleasure in looking at the same old slides of whitewashed leper hospitals and rows of solemn bowler-hatted men. But there was small hope of relief. Eli was very cautious about lantern shows, and had been ever since an overzealous visitor from overseas caused a scandal out Bollogis way by showing

6

a slide of starving female Africans with very little on.

Gan was looking daggers at Winnie's impudence, and there might have been words, but Mother sat up on her bed and said, 'Isn't that your father coming in? He'll be vexed if he finds me lying here, and nothing on the table for a man to eat. Time I got up and went downstairs for a bit; my headache's nothing like so bad tonight. Winnie, you can stop and help me down. Dora, you go down and make a cup of tea.'

And there was nothing for it but to obey.

Stan Hunkin stuck his face around the kitchen door and scowled. Nobody there but Jamie, and he was curled up on the settle, reading one of his confounded books as usual.

The boy glanced up at him and flushed, putting the volume guiltily away. 'Hello, Father. Didn't hear you come. It's only the prize I got from Sunday school. Gan told me to sit down here and rest.'

Stan gave an infuriated sigh. He was a reasonable soul. Surely it wasn't too much to expect that a son of his should be a proper man with a bit of grit and backbone, and a proper interest in the world, who could take over the boats and business one day. But instead, what had the Fates decreed? First twin daughters – strapping enough, but what was the use of that? And then – after several false attempts – this pale, weedy child, always with a hacking cough and weak, short-sighted eyes. For that they'd lost the hope of any other son: the wretched infant had almost killed his mother at the time and any more births would be the death of her, they'd said, so she wouldn't let him near her any more. He had insisted, once or twice, but anyway, she'd lost her looks – gone all strained and yellow – so that was the end of that. He sighed again. Was any man so put upon by fate?

'Gan told me to . . .' the boy began again.

Stan looked at him – just like Sybil, the same skinny frame and mousy hair. He knew what his own mother, Gan, would say. 'Serves you right, it's your own fault for marrying a Jenkins instead of choosing someone from the Cove.'

'All the same, those Jenkinses,' she'd grumbled when Stan first courted Sybil. 'All top-show and no knickers, giving themselves airs – just because one of the family had some money once, and had a housemaid and a cook and all.'

But he'd ignored her. It had seemed a good match at the time – Jenkins with his only daughter and his baker's shop. It *had* worked out well, too, as far as money went – not even Gan could argue against that. Not many fishermen round Penvarris had their own boat by the time they were twenty-one, and fewer still had a share in a fish store in the town, so as to cut out the middleman and always have a market for the catch. Course, her father hadn't thought a right lot of the match, but he'd come around – Sybil was twenty-five by then and on the shelf, and he'd have married her to a Hindu by that time. When the old man overturned his cart and broke his neck at last, the sale of the bakery had served them well. Enough to buy this house at any rate – three-up, three-down, and all their very own. Envy of all the other fishermen, that was.

But Sybil herself, that was another thing. Never was a proper sort of wife. Couldn't cutch a net, or skin a fish, or even darn a sock to save her life. 'Wasn't raised to it,' she always said and was forever bursting into helpless tears as soon as anyone raised their voice to her. It was enough to drive a man to drink. Thank heaven Gan had come to stay the day that James was born. Came for a fortnight, at the time, and hadn't ever left. Sybil didn't think very much of that, he knew – sometimes he thought his mother made an invalid of her, and Sybil could have done more if she tried – but that was her lookout. Wouldn't have been necessary if she could have coped. As long as he had his clothes washed and his house kept clean and his meals on the table when he wanted them, he didn't interfere.

But there wasn't any meal on the table now. 'Where is everyone?' he asked. Jamie flinched. Dear God, couldn't the boy answer a civil question without starting like a hare? 'Where is everyone?' Stan said again, banging the table with his fist.

'I'm here, Father,' said Dora, coming in from the hall. 'We didn't hear you come. Mother sent me down to set the kettle on – she and Gan and Win will be down in a tick.' She busied herself filling the kettle from the pail, and setting it on the trivet on the fire.

Stan said nothing. He loosened his shirt and braces and sat down glowering on a chair. Dora was another one, he thought. Wispy sort of creature, afraid of her own shadow – a Jenkins to the core. Dopey Dora, he had nicknamed her, and she deserved it too, always dreaming with her head stuck in a book. Her sister now, that was something else. If Winnie had been born a boy, there might have been a chance. She had the Hunkin spirit and the Hunkin looks. He called her Wilful Winnie, because she answered back, but she was worth half a dozen of her twin.

Winifred and Theodora – what a pair of names! That was Sybil's doing too, of course. Why couldn't she call her daughters something plain – Millie or Annie – like anybody else? But no, Sybil wanted the twins called after her own two maiden aunts – Jenkinses, the pair of them, of course. So Stan had gone reluctantly along with it – thought it might have done some good when it came to the estate – but if old George Jenkins was pleased by it, he never said a word, and the two old girls left everything to the Church. But Winifred and Theodora Hunkin the two girls remained.

The others had come downstairs by now, and were taking their places at the table too, Winnie helping her mother to her seat. Stan said nothing to them, and they said nothing back. Dora cut some bread and put it on a plate while Gan stirred up some fish stew that had been warming on the hob.

Mind, Stan thought, absently taking up a piece of bread and dipping it into his bowl of stew, the girls were growing up now – sixteen gone – and he could think of finding them a husband pretty soon. Have their feet under someone else's table then. Someone with a bit of class and clout – that was one thing he did agree with Sybil about. He wasn't having his girls working at the mine, or going into service, or anything like that. The Hunkins were above that sort of thing.

He mopped up his plate and wiped his hand thoughtfully across his mouth. It had not been easy, finding them a place, but you couldn't have four women in the house all day – it was bad enough with two. Besides, even for a Hunkin, an extra bob or two a week wasn't to be sneezed at. It had worked out quite nicely in the end for Win – going up each day to read to Mrs Zeal, a sort of female companion in a way – not the same as going into ordinary service, not at all. Dora was a worry though, as usual. In the end he'd had to let her go up as monitress at the school. He wasn't very keen on that, if truth were told – for one thing it didn't pay a proper wage, and for another it was giving her ideas. She'd talked once about going up to Truro and training properly, if you ever heard the like, but he'd soon put a stop to that, and started looking out for something else. But in the meantime it would have to do. It kept her out from under Gan's feet anyway.

She handed him a cup of tea and he drank it noisily then pushed his cup away. 'Well,' he said. 'How was this missionary tea? Eli Westrill bore you all to tears as usual?'

You could feel the tension ease around the room. Everyone began to talk at once. Gan sat down with her bowl, and Sybil and Jamie – who had been sitting frozen up to now – took up their spoons and started sipping at their stew. Dora poured herself a cup of tea, while Winnie wittered on with an account of what had apparently happened in the lane.

Silly, spineless idiots, Stan thought contemptuously. The lot of them. Think I was a tyrant, the way they carry on. But the thought did not altogether displease him, all the same.

When Winnie went to Mrs Zeal's next day she didn't mention anything about the trouble in the lane, although the story, with embellishments, was burning on her lips. Old Mrs Zeal, plump as a pouter pigeon in her embroidered black, was rather prim. She didn't approve of things that weren't 'respectable', and it mattered to Winnie very much what her employer thought. Not for its own sake, naturally – Winnie didn't give a hoot about that – but because of Mr Nathan, the old lady's son.

The thought of Mr Nathan made her smile. He was no longer all that young himself – he must be all of thirty-three or four – but he was still good-looking in a dark-haired, smooth, pomaded sort of way. A man of careful habits: most of the time you would not know that he was in the house. He was fond of rather old-fashioned collars and cravats, but other-wise he dressed so carefully, neat as pink plump tin-tack in his pressed black trousers and the cutaway jacket that he wore each day to his undertaking business in Penzance. With his signet ring, cravat pin and his gold-topped cane, Winnie thought he looked as smart as paint.

He had his own horse and carriage too. Not the hearse – he kept that in the town – but a proper little gig with a smart black horse to pull it, which he drove about himself. Invaluable, he said, when he wanted to go out and visit the bereaved.

Made the right impression, and that mattered a great deal when you were dealing with the wealthy, as Mr Nathan was. Not for him the simple funeral cart with a brass band and chapel choir like they used round here. Like his father before him, he had sent off some of the biggest names in all Penwith – six or eight black horses if you wanted them, with plumes, and flowers and matching coffin bearers in their tall black hats. Mahogany coffins with brass handles, a black wreath for the door, and straw to muffle the hoof-beats in the street. Mr Nathan could arrange it all.

Winnie had dared to ask him once if he enjoyed his work. He'd looked at her with some surprise – as if not many people talked to him, except about themselves – but when he saw she wasn't making fun of him he'd said, 'It's no worse than any other job, and a good deal more agreeable than some. Someone has to do it, and it fills a need. It's steady – there'll always be a call for us, no matter what – and there's money in it too.' He saw her face and gave a sober smile. 'Don't look so shocked, my dear. It's truer than you think. People are always trying to make up to others when they're dead for things they failed to do for them while they were alive. Oh, there's money in funerals all right.'

He had a nice voice, sort of hushed and grave – though that wasn't a word that you could use when you were talking about an undertaker, she thought with an inward grin. Not that he would have seen the joke of it – Mr Nathan didn't have a sense of humour, much.

So she composed her face and nodded sympathetically. 'You must meet all kinds of people in your line of work.'

He looked at her with serious grey eyes. 'Indeed. Though, it is true, not many young ladies like yourself. One doesn't, you know, in the circumstances.'

Winnie nodded sympathetically. When you came to think of it, perhaps not so many girls would want to marry some-body who spent their whole life working with the dead.

Since then, she was almost sure, he had sought her out whenever both of them were in the house. He had always come home if he was in the area, to look in on his mother and have a cup of tea – Mrs Z. expected it, and he was good like that – but he was starting to do it more often nowadays. And then this morning, there he was, sitting in the gig at the front gate almost as if he had been waiting till she came, though he only said, 'Good morning, Winifred,' before he twitched the reins and bowled away.

Winnie flounced her fair curls in delight. Nathan Zeal! Now there was a catch! It wasn't outside of possibility. His great-grandmother had been a Jenkins too. That was how Winnie had been thought of for this job. And Winnie had been working hard to get his mother on her side. Mrs Zeal had confided once that she was worried about Nathan growing old alone and how there was nobody to carry on the name.

Winnie had striven ever since to make herself indispensable to the old lady. There had been an upstairs maid when she first came – a gawky girl with spots – but Winnie had volunteered to take over many of her duties bit by bit, until Alice was finally 'let go'. Mrs Zeal kept another maid, of course, as well as the cook and outside boy, so there was nothing too menial to be done, and sponging the old lady's hems or mending pillowslips was a small price to pay for future happiness.

Winnie allowed herself to dream. That big house and all that lovely furniture. Embroidered sheets and bowls of pot-pourri. That would show Joe Pollock what was what. Always after her, he was, just because they'd been sweethearts long ago, when they were children walking home from school. Never when Dora was about, of course – she would have gone home telling tales, for sure – but on the days when Dora stayed back after class, borrowing her wretched books and fidgeting about. She had been keen on reading, even then.

Not that Winnie had minded, at the time, as it meant Joe Pollock could walk home with her. Exciting walks they'd been as well – across the fields instead of down the lane, keeping out of sight in case Dora came along and caught them up. It was Joe who first taught her to catch minnows in the stream, and shown her where the best wild blackberries and mushrooms could be had, and dared her that day to climb the hollow tree looking for eggs in the blackbird's nest. And when she tumbled down and grazed her knee, it was Joe who picked her up and dusted her down and, greatly daring, planted a kiss upon her lips.

But that was years ago, and this was now, and she'd learned to hope for something better than a fisherman. 'There's money

12

in funerals,' she repeated to herself. Enough for fine dresses and a milliner.

Of course, bright colours wouldn't be the thing if you were an undertaker's wife, but there were handsome violets, dove-greys and muted blues. Even Mrs Z. herself, though she wore mourning all the time, permitted herself what Dora called a 'sparkling black', adorned with dark lace, jet beads or silk embroidery. With a little imagination, Winnie thought, one could look quite fetching in these sombre hues, especially if one had blonde hair and sparkling eyes. A sweet two-piece costume in lavender, perhaps, trimmed in deep aubergine . . .

Mrs Z.'s sharp voice recalled her to herself. 'If you've quite finished dawdling over those pillowslips, Winifred, it is time to read.'

Two

'Sit up straight. Hands on heads. When you're completely quiet you may go!' Miss Blewitt's voice was firm, but not unkind. 'I'm waiting till you stop fidgeting, Harvey Pierce!'

Dora looked round the schoolroom with a smile. The children were thrusting out their chests, straining and red-faced in their attempts to sit upright, all of them wanting to be most erect, and therefore the first to be released into the warm and shining afternoon.

They were a very mixed group – from little Amy Taylor, shining and polished from the top of her neatly coiled plaits to the soles of her tiny buttoned boots, to great, shambling Harvey Pierce with his rebellious hair, already bursting out of his father's cut-down shirt and pants – but Dora had a soft spot for them all.

She would have liked to have done this properly, and applied to be a pupil-teacher at the school, working as an apprentice in the day and studying with the headmistress at night, until at eighteen she could go to Truro and take the examination for the Certificate. She could have done it – Miss Blewitt thought so and Miss Blewitt ought to know. But Father would never have permitted that. No man wanted a bluestocking, he said, and though the twins had both stayed on at school until they were fourteen, that was not because he wanted education for his girls, but simply to show the world that Stanley Hunkin could afford to keep them there.

So she was fortunate, extremely fortunate, that he had allowed her to come up to the school as monitress. It was Gan's doing, oddly, that she was here at all. Gan had heard tales, years ago, of some widower up east who'd married his daughter's monitress from school, because the child was very fond of her and needed a mother to look after her.

14

'I should let Dora go there, Stan, if it's what she wants to do. You never know. She might meet up with somebody herself. There are men who like that dreamy, bookish sort of girl. Even a parson, or a schoolmaster, perhaps. Think of that! Where else is she going to meet that class of man? Better than her moping round the house under my feet all day. And she can keep an eye out for our Jamie, too.' That had been the clinching argument, and Father had eventually agreed.

That was two years ago, and here she was, teaching the babies and even helping the older girls with needlework, now that the sewing mistress had resigned. Dora was handy with a needle, and she'd jumped at the chance. In fact, she did much of the work a pupil-teacher would have done, though of course she was still paid only 1s 3d a week. 'You ought to speak to your papa again,' Miss Blewitt often urged, but Dora never dared. The one time she had attempted it he'd been so furious he broke a dinner plate, and she knew better than to speak of it again.

'Very well.' Miss Blewitt's voice cut across her thoughts. 'Front row, you may go.' And with a great scraping and clattering of desks and boots, they went. The classroom was empty in no time at all. Miss Blewitt closed the windows carefully – thirty-two children of all ages in a smallish room have a distinctive smell – while Dora collected up the writing slates. She had been helping the infants to write their alphabet, and they were deemed too small for copybooks.

Harvey Pierce, the fidget, had been in the group as well. Despite his fancy name, he was a ragged child, more often out of class than in it, and he'd been kept back for a second year because he still hadn't mastered his letters properly. Poor Harvey, he screwed his face up manfully and made his slate pencil squeak like forty cats, but what should have been a neat row of Cs today still looked like a haphazard field of wispy grass – though if waggling your tongue about while you wrote could help, Harvey would be the greatest scholar in Penwith.

'Well, Dora,' the headmistress said, in her calm, efficient way, 'you have your object lesson for tomorrow planned?'

'Yes, Miss Blewitt, this week it's the cat.' She nodded towards a coloured chart picture of a cat which she had pinned on the wall in readiness. 'I've chosen the topics: Useful Words,

Hunting and Habits, and What it Eats and Dri—' She broke off as a piercing cry reached them from the boys' playground just outside the door. The shriek was followed by a sobbing sound.

'It's that Harvey Pierce!' Miss Blewitt said before she'd even looked. 'Playing on the wretched ash pile again, I expect. I wish the Board would see to it. The inspectors have complained that it was dangerous ever since the new stove was installed, and I've put it in the yearly report book twice myself, but nothing has been done. It's like a magnet for that dratted boy.'

The new classroom stove had been greeted with delight, since the school building in the winter could be very cold. Dora could remember days, when she was a pupil here herself, when the whole class had to be dismissed because it was simply far too cold to work, when not even flag drill or running on the spot could bring warmth to skinny limbs, and even the water for the paint pots froze. The small pot-bellied stove had spelled an end to that. Not only did it warm the classroom, but now the children could dry their sodden boots and coats nearby, and lunchtime pasties could be reheated on a shovel on the top. The problem had been where to put the ash. No one had made any plans for that, and so it was simply piled up against the boys' playground wall outside, where – together with the clinker and bits of unburned coal – it formed an unholy climbing place in summer and a grey, slushy sliding rink when it rained. Playing on the ash heap was forbidden, naturally, but that only added to the attraction of the game.

Jamie – their Jamie – appeared in the doorway, with Harvey Pierce limping painfully behind. Harvey's ragged coat was more bedraggled than ever, smeared with black soot and covered with grey ash, and his grimy knees were bleeding copiously.

'It's Harvey, Miss Blewitt,' Jamie said unnecessarily. 'Fell over on the heap. He's cut his knees and he's got stones in him and something's the matter with his foot.' He didn't look at Dora. There was a kind of unspoken understanding between them that he didn't speak to her in school if he could help it, and he called her Miss Hunkin when he did.

Dora looked down at Harvey's foot. Something was the matter, certainly. Harvey's boots were far too small for him

16

and he always wore them unlaced to loosen them. The sole of the left one was half hanging off, and over the top of the boot his ankle was turning black and blue and swelling visibly. It was obviously painful, but Harvey was more concerned with avoiding punishment for disobeying rules.

'Weren't sliding on the ash heap, Miss. Fell over me own feet,' he managed between sobs.

It was so obviously a lie that even Miss Blewitt smiled. 'Well, sit down over there,' she said. 'Miss Hunkin and I will have a look.'

The boot was taken off. Harvey had no socks on and his toes were rubbed and sore. The new damage though, was obvious. The swelling was severe, but though Harvey sucked his breath in hard when his foot was touched, he could still move his toes.

'Not broken, but it is a nasty sprain,' Miss Blewitt said with the authority of experience. Jamie was dispatched to the boys' toilet block outside to wet a clean cloth at the tap, and with the aid of this makeshift cold compress the ankle was bound up, though it would not go back into the boot again.

'Now,' Miss Blewitt said, surveying her handiwork, 'how are we going to get you home again?'

'I'll help him,' Jamie volunteered.

'No, Jamie, I'll go with him,' Dora said. 'Your father will be vexed if you are late. It's different for me – it's all part of my job. You run along.' Jamie bit his lip – he knew as well as anyone what would await him if he got home late. He looked up, smiled and nodded and ran off.

Miss Blewitt looked at her. 'You're sure, Miss Hunkin?' She always called Dora Miss Hunkin when the children were about.

Dora nodded. 'The walk will do me good. It isn't more than a mile or two down to Penvarris Row, and it's a lovely afternoon.'

'Well, if you're quite sure.' Miss Blewitt sounded so grateful that Dora glanced at her, and was surprised to see the other woman blush. There was a rumour that Miss Blewitt had a beau, though Dora had dismissed this privately – you couldn't be a teacher if you wed. Now, though, she wondered if the story might be true. No one had ever seen the man, of course, but a teacher had to be discreet.

17

'A pleasure,' she said briskly, and put her bonnet on. Harvey Pierce slipped his grimy paw into her hand and gave her a tearful smile.

'I aren't going home, 'zactly,' Harvey confided as he half-limped, half-hopped beside her down the lane. 'Me mam's took bad again. That's why I wanted to stay behind a bit and play on the ash p— That is . . .' The round, freckled, tear-stained, grubby face coloured as he realized his slip. 'In the schoolyard.'

She ignored it. 'Where are you staying then?'

'Next door, with the Trewins. They're quite nice, they always have me, but there isn't any – you know . . .' He shrugged. 'Laughin', comfy-like. Nobody to talk to. And they have funny things for tea – eggs and that – 'stead of bread and dripping like we b'long to do.'

She squeezed his hand and he held her fingers tight. 'Show me when we get there,' she said, and smiled down at him.

'Yes, Miss.' He gave her a confidential smile. 'Supposing we ever get there, with me foot like this.'

He was trying to hobble a little faster now but it was clear his ankle pained him dreadfully. His face was getting ashen, though he did not complain, and it was almost a whole, painful hour before they reached the Row.

Tom Trewin stood on the doorstep of his home and watched them come. Harvey he recognized at once – he would have known that scruffy form anywhere – but it took him a moment to take in the young woman by his side. When he did, it made him feel a bit awkward and uncomfortable, and he turned to action to disguise the fact.

'Harvey!' he said warmly, bending to tousle the boy's wayward hair. 'What's been happening to you? Hurt your foot, is that it? Ma and I were starting to get worried – you should have been here half an hour ago.' Only then did he look up and turn towards the girl. 'And you saw him home. That's kind of you.' And then, as if the realization had just come to him, he added, 'Dora Hunkin, isn't it? I remember you from school.'

She looked at him and he was forced to meet her eyes. Pretty eyes – grey and sort of luminous. In fact, she was a pretty girl altogether – always was, though most of the boys at school preferred the blonde and bouncy one. Tom had always admired Dora more, although he'd hardly spoken to her even then. The big boys didn't talk much to the younger pupils – especially not to girls.

'Don't suppose you remember me,' he mumbled awkwardly.

She smiled then, showing little dimples in her cheeks, though she didn't look as if she often smiled. In repose she had a sad and patient look. 'Of course I do. You're Tom Trewin. Always came top in arithmetic, and won the scale drawing prize.'

He laughed, pleased that she remembered him for that. 'Well, you weren't so bad yourself. I know you recited for the inspectors once, and had your writing book held up to all the rest of us to show how good it was.'

'Miss Hunkin's learning me to write,' young Harvey put in importantly. 'She's one of the teachers up the schoolhouse now.'

Tom looked guiltily at him. He'd almost forgotten that the boy was there. 'Well now, you're a lucky lad,' he said. 'But come on, you're to come inside with me. Your mam isn't ready for you yet.'

'Is she very . . .' the young woman started, but even as she spoke a shuddering moan came from the bedroom of the next-door house.

'Having her sixth,' Tom said. And then, for no reason that he could explain except that he was so embarrassed that he wasn't thinking straight, he said what his mother had confided earlier. 'Coming wrong way round again, it seems. Thought she'd have got the hang of it by now.'

It was unforgivable – and to a young lady too! The minute the words were out, Tom wished he could bite out his tongue. He felt himself blush up to his ears. Miss Hunkin coloured too, and looked away. Tom longed for the ground to open up so he could fall to the bottom level of the mine and stay there for a week.

Harvey saved the day. 'I'm seven. I'm the oldest one. Then there was two other boys that died, and then there's Poppy – rising four, she is – and there's Daisy and then there's this one. Ma's hoping it will be a girl again, but I aren't so keen. If there's two boys we can hand things down a bit, and I might get new boots from the Provident.'

19

'He fell over the sole of that one in the yard,' Dora said quickly. 'I think he's sprained his foot. He ought to stay off school a day or two.'

Tom nodded. 'They'll keep him home in any case, most like, once the baby's here.'

Harvey's people always kept him home if there were extra jobs to do, like cleaning the copper or whitewashing the walls. And not just at home either. Like many pupils in the area, Harvey was always missing school when there were potatoes to be lifted from the fields, or fruit to pick, or hay to stook. Tom had done the very same himself. A few pence extra here and there could make a big difference to a family.

Another long, shuddering moan reached them from next door. Harvey looked anxiously at the window, but the curtains had been drawn. 'Best come inside,' Tom said. 'Mother's got your tea for you.' The boy nodded, and it might have ended there, but Tom was suddenly reluctant to let Dora go.

'Want to come in yourself a minute, do you? Mother will have the kettle on, and you've got a long walk home. Daresay you'd like a cup of tea?' She was hesitating, he could see, so he added quickly, 'Harvey'd like it, too.'

She looked down at the boy, who was gazing up at her with shining eyes. 'A quick one, then,' she said and smiled. 'I mustn't be too long. My family will be wondering where I am.' And to Tom's delight, she turned and followed Harvey and himself into the house.

Mother was in the kitchen, cooking sprats for tea. She got all flustered when she saw the visitor, wiping both hands on her pinafore and straightening her hair. 'My dear life!' she exclaimed, giving an embarrassed little bob. 'Whatever's this? Lady from up the school, isn't it? Come about Harvey, have you? And me in the kitchen in me pinny, too. Well, this is an honour, Miss.' She shot Tom a panic-stricken glance and said, 'How don't you take her in the front room, Tom?'

He said quickly. 'It's all right, Mother. I just asked her in to have a cup of tea. She's brought Harvey home. He's hurt himself. Miss Dora was at school with me, one time.' He pulled out a kitchen chair and offered it to Dora as he spoke. He meant to calm things, but his mother gave him such a look it would have killed a weaker man.

Dora seemed to realize something of all this. She didn't sit

20

at once. 'I'm sorry, Mrs Trewin, Tom asked me in. I didn't mean to interrupt your meal. It's only that Harvey sprained his ankle, and I thought I should see him home. Please, I don't want to trouble you . . .'

'No trouble,' Tom's mother said, getting the best tea set from the shelf. She prided herself on hospitality, though she was still looking daggers at Tom. But Dora Hunkin sat down by the fire, and Mother gave her the rose china and a piece of fresh jam tart.

'Quite delicious!' Dora said, and that helped a little bit. Mother was fond of baking and it made her preen. Then, while Tom and Harvey sat down to their sprats, Dora went on, 'So, Tom, what have you been doing since I saw you last?'

She seemed so genuinely interested that he found himself telling her everything, how he'd followed his father and brothers down the mine. 'Only a kettle boy at first, of course, like everybody is. Fetching and carrying, or moving spoil, or holding the bore end in the hole while the other men take turns to whack at it. Beast of a job, that is – nobody can stand it more than half an hour. Vibrations go up your arms till you're shaken to your bones, and your ears ring till you can hardly think.'

'Didn't last long,' Mother put in proudly, coming to sit down and eat some sprats herself. 'Captain Maddern, the head one down there, got to hear of Tom – how he was so reliable and quick at sums and that, and handy with anything mechanical – and he sent his man up here to ask would we like for him to come up to ground and go as apprentice to the engine man. Course, it meant a struggle just at first, with apprentice wages, but his dad was agreeable so that's what Tommy did. Isn't down underground like most of them. Making a good job of it as well. Be chief engine man himself one day, I shouldn't be surprised.'

Dora smiled at him. 'That sounds like an important sort of job. And you enjoy the work?'

Tom was surprised. It wasn't a question people asked you much. Work was just something you got on and did, waiting for pay day to come round again. 'Like it?' he said thoughtfully. 'Yes, I suppose I do.'

Mother, though, was anxious to impress. 'Important? I should think it is!' she said, plonking the teapot down for emphasis.

21

'If it wasn't for the engine man, there'd be no tin mined at all. They've got steam engines for the pumps and whims, another one that drives the stamps, and there's a locomotive one as well that you can move about. Somebody has to look after all the boilers, keep the steam up, check the pressure and all that kind of thing. Well, that'll be our Tom before so long. Be a time-served boilerman, he will. And not content with that, he's up the Institute three nights a week, trying to improve himself. Reading here till all hours every night.'

Dora latched on to that at once. Tom guessed that all this talk of steam engines hadn't meant much to her, but this was something she could understand. 'What are you studying?' she asked with interest.

'Technical drawing and mechanics,' Tom said, trying to sound as if he didn't care.

'He's marvellous with engines,' Mother said. 'All different, like as if they have personalities, he says. Like people, almost. Why, there's one pumping engine up Penvarris mine . . .'

She would have gone on boasting about him like this all night if Tom hadn't said, 'I'm sure Miss Hunkin isn't interested in my old boilers.'

Mother flushed. 'Well, maybe so. Anyway, if you don't hurry up and eat your sprats, your father and your brother will be home, and you won't get to that evening class on time. And after Captain Maddern let you go off early, specially!'

But Dora was already on her feet. 'And I must go as well. I'm—' This time the roaring from next door was so loud that it came straight through the wall, and everybody stopped and froze, stock-still. There was a silence. Then Harvey, who had been toying with his fish, pushed back his plate. His face was white and Tom thought he looked as if he might burst into tears.

Then, thin and distinct, there came a baby's wail. You could almost feel the atmosphere relax. They heard a door slam somewhere through the wall, and then a clatter on the next-door stairs, followed a moment later by an insistent pounding on their own front door.

'I'll get it,' Mother said, and there stood Mr Pierce, looking pink and flustered in his working clothes. Tom could see him through the passageway, standing on the step, still all red and dirty from the mine. His eyes and mouth were little pits of pink flesh in the mask of dust. 'Just thought I'd let 'ee know,' the man said breathlessly, and his teeth flashed briefly in a smile, 'Liza's had a little girl – no bigger 'n a shoe box, but they say she'll do, so Harvey can come home now if he likes.'

Mother said quickly, 'No, that's quite all right. Boy's hurt his foot. You get home to Liza; we'll look after him.' She came back into the kitchen. 'Hear that did you, Harv?'

The boy nodded. His eyes were bright with tears.

Dora said brightly, 'Come on, Harvey, you should eat your tea. Get your strength up for when you get home. Your ma is going to need you, seems to me.'

Harvey looked down at his plate again. 'Don't know what they are,' he muttered, poking at a sprat.

'They're little fishes,' Dora said. 'You know, like Jesus had. We had the story about it in school. I hear they're splendid for sprained ankles, too.'

'You sure?' He put a reluctant forkful in his mouth.

'You eat that up,' Mother said, 'and you can have some jam tart afterwards.' She turned to Dora, who was on her feet to leave, and gave her a warm smile. 'Well, thank you, Miss. You've been very good. It's clear that Harvey thinks a lot of you. Tommy, you show Miss Hunkin to the door.'

He did so gladly, smiling as he watched the trim figure move down the street. But when he came back into the kitchen, Mother didn't half give him what for.

'Tommy Trewin, what are you thinking of! Bringing young ladies to the house – into the kitchen, too – when everything's up in heaps like Bodmin Fair, and me in my old pinny with my hair not done. And her a teacher up there at the school! Whatever must she think?' She kept on so much that Tom was quite glad to finish up his sprats and go.

When Dora got home, she went into the hall with excuses ready on her lips. She was late. Father was liable to be furious and though she could rely on Jamie to explain, it wasn't likely to help her much. They would all be sitting at the table now. She took off her bonnet and went in to tea, fully expecting to be shouted at.

She was lucky. Father was in a cheerful mood. He did look up as she came in, and growl, 'What time do you call this?'

But that was all. Perhaps the *Cornish Rose* had brought home a good catch.

She sat down at the table and helped herself to ham. Poor little Harvey Pierce, she thought – what would he make of a teatime spread like this? Whatever you might say about Father, he saw that they were fed – and not just with fish, though that was what he dealt in and they always had the best. Tonight, besides the ham and pickles, there was cake and bread, and jam or butter if you wanted it. Either jam *or* butter was the rule, though you could spread one piece of bread with each and make a sort of sandwich out of it.

Winnie was doing that right now, and tucking into it, pretending not to notice that Mother was picking at her food, and Jamie – who was very fond of cake – had left his slice untouched. Dora stole a glance at Father but he was spooning sugar into his tea with every sign of being satisfied – pleased with himself, if anything.

Dora ate her ham. Something was obviously happening, but she knew better than to ask outright. If Jamie was in trouble she'd discover soon enough.

She got her answer a little later on. Ma suddenly put down her knife and murmured meekly, 'Stan, I do wish you'd think again. The lad's got to go to school tomorrow. It isn't fair to keep him out all night. Besides, it's cold out there. He'll only get an infection on his chest and we'll have to have the doctor here again.'

'For Pete's sake woman, can't you let it rest? You'd think I was going to take him halfway across the Atlantic, the way that you go on. We're only going out for an hour or two – try the engines out. Might set the trawl and see, to make sure it doesn't foul, but we won't be fishing properly. Just want to go and try it out, that's all. Scarcely be dark before we're home again.'

When Father was in this mood it was best to let things be, but Mother had courage where Jamie was concerned. 'I don't know why you want to go at all, you haven't been out on the boat yourself for months. Why can't Charlie and the boys do it, the same as usual? You pay them to be crew. It isn't fair on Jamie. You forget, he's delicate.'

Then, of course, Father did get mad. 'Forget! My dear woman, how could I forget?' He slammed down his cup.

'Every blooming time I walk in the house, there he is, white and wet and useless as a ling. Well, I won't have it, do you hear? He's my son, and if I say he comes with me, he comes. Do him good to have a bit of exercise – get a bit of salt air in his lungs.' He was shouting, but he seemed to recollect himself, and said more quietly, 'For God's sake, woman, don't you see, it's all for his own good in the end. It will all be his one day – boat, nets, fish store, everything! He's got to understand the ins and outs. Besides, he's looking forward to it, aren't you, boy?'

There was an awful silence. Dora – who knew that for James the prospect of tossing about in a fishing boat for hours was nothing but cold, wretched misery – glanced at Winnie, but she looked away and they both stared in silence at their plates.

'Well, I'm waiting,' Father said to James. 'You're looking forward to it, yes or no?'

Another pause, and then Jamie said, 'Yes, Father,' through white lips. Gan snorted. Ma began to cry.

'There you are then,' Father said triumphantly. 'What did I tell you? You heard the boy. He wants to go with me. Now, will you stop that snivelling and pour a man some tea?' The little victory had restored his self-regard, and he turned to Dora with a smile. 'What's all this I hear about a boy who broke his leg? Pay you to walk home with pupils, now, do they?'

So Dora told her story, though she didn't mention Tom. Not in particular. She just talked about 'one of the Trewin boys' as if he was just anybody, and not a singularly nice young man with deep, blue-green eyes and a face that crinkled when he smiled. She wanted to keep that memory to herself.

She told them about Harvey and the ash heap though. She spun out the story as long as she dared, but it didn't rescue Jamie all the same. Father interrupted suddenly.

'Have to hear the rest some other time. Promised to meet Charlie at the boat at eight. Come on, Jamie, get your sea things on.' A few minutes later they were gone, Father striding briskly down the path, with Jamie, in pullover and boots that were too big for him, trailing after him like a reluctant ghost.

'Shan't be long,' Father called behind him as they went,

25

but it was almost one o'clock next morning before they came back. Dora heard the door. There were muted mutterings, then footsteps and a flickering candle on the stairs.

Mother had obviously been wakeful too. Dora heard her whisper, 'You safe home? How's Jamie, then?'

'Wretched child did nothing but be sick,' Father grumbled in a scornful voice. She heard the creak as he got into bed. 'Shan't be so soft on him another time.'

Then he blew out the candle and the house was still.

Three

Breakfast was an uncomfortable affair. Stan ate his in silence and was glad when it was time to leave the house. How could a man enjoy his bit of bread and jam with his wife darting him reproachful looks and that boy sitting opposite like a wet weekend, all snivelling and wan?

Stan pulled on his coat and went down to the Cove. Charlie and the Stephens boys were there, already hard at work. Even the younger one was busy baiting hooks. Stan felt a stab of anger at the sight. Why couldn't his son be like this – manly, useful and robust? The memory of the night before, with Jamie retching and clutching at the side of the boat, was raw and bitter in his mind. Wasn't even as if there had been any sort of sea running, just a bit of fetch across the bay, but his son – his son! – was as useless as a woman the minute they were half a yard from land. He spat into the water in disgust.

Charlie looked up from his task, his lean, lined face screwed into a squint against the morning sun. 'Morning, Cap'n.' None of the crew aboard the *Cornish Rose* ever called the skipper by his name, the way men did on some other boats. 'How's the boy today?'

'Got over it,' Stan said curtly. He didn't welcome Charlie's sympathy. It wasn't often given, and that made it worse. Charlie Cox was the sort of man he liked; a bit surly and unsmiling, but first-class at his job. People didn't care for him round here – he'd been a fisherman up east and nobody knew quite why he'd come away – but he suited Stan. Charlie wasn't a big man but he was wiry and strong, and he could read the weather like a book. And he didn't think chattering and yammering was all part of the job, like half the other fellows in the Cove. Found a job to do and did it, that was Charlie's way.

Charlie nodded towards the Stephens boys. 'Baiting up the short-lines for tonight. We'll give that a try this evening, rather than the trawl – if that's all right with you, Cap'n? Shan't take her very far, a time or two, till the engine settles in, and there won't be many deep shoals about unless you're well offshore.'

Stan nodded. He was content to let Charlie make decisions of that kind. The old man knew what he was doing, how to read the sea, what kind of fishing would yield the best results. Besides, if Charlie got it right, Stan got the benefit, while if he was wrong it was only Charlie's fault.

'All right, Charlie, anything you think. I shan't be going with you in any case. Only went out last night to try the trawl now that we've got the engine in the boat. Though you can't judge anything by that. Hardly had time to shoot the damty nets before we had to haul them in again.' Pity I ever was persuaded to bring that wretched child, he thought to himself. Might have had a proper night out, otherwise.

Charlie flashed one of his rare smiles, showing a broken tooth. 'Don't you fret about that, Cap'n. Trawl was a lot better'n you might suppose. Must have caught two thousand fish all told. Davy took them down the store first thing when you'd gone, soon as we'd washed down and sorted out – cod and ling mostly, but there were a few skate and turbot in there too.'

Stan grunted. That was good news. Turbot always fetched top prices in Penzance. Two thousand fish for three hours' work – that was a fair return. You could be out all night and not bring home more than that, though there had been some occasions – when the pilchards ran – when they'd landed twenty thousand fish. He kicked at a bollard. 'What you want to try the lines for, then?'

Charlie gave him a sideways look. 'Well, Cap'n, I want to try her out. I figure with this engine we can run more hooks, and longer lengths, if we go right offshore. Maybe manage two mile on the long-lines – that's nigh on two thousand hooks – if we get mid-channel before we shoot them out. Got the power, see, to get out there and back, and not miss the markets with the fish. And we can get home, never mind the wind. Then we'll show these sailing boats a thing or two.'

Stan nodded. 'Right. I see the force of that. But that's the long-lines that you're talking of. I thought you were only short-lining tonight?'

'Well, so we are. T'isn't the right time of year for the others yet – they're better in the spring. But even on the shorter ones we've spliced on extra hooks, see? Show him, Davy.'

Davy Stephens grinned and lifted up a length of baited line for him to see, now with a triple row of barbed hooks hanging from it, each bristling row set at a different length, so as to fish several depths at once.

Stan grunted approvingly. 'What time are you going?'

Charlie looked towards the sky. 'Set fair,' he said. 'Set off round five o'clock, most like – still helps to catch the tide, engine or no engine. We'll go home when we've finished here and get a few hours' sleep. If we go out at teatime, more or less, there'll still be hours of daylight left.'

Stan nodded. These men had been up working half the night – scrubbing decks, re-stowing nets and landing all the fish, while he, the owner of the boat, had been forced to slink off with his miserable son as soon as they were tied up at the quay.

'I'll get up to the fish store right away,' he said, 'and let you know how much your share comes out at.' The money earned from every catch was divided into fifths. Stan, as boat-owner, was entitled to two shares, one for himself (whether he was in the crew or not) and the other for the boat. Each of the three others got a single share. Of course, since Stan controlled the fish store, he controlled the price, but he was always very careful about that. He bought fish from the other crews as well, to distribute to fish shops in the towns, and if he didn't give a reasonable price there were other dealers round about who would. If he didn't pay his own men what he paid the rest, he lost out on his own shares in their catch and there was a danger they would cease to work for him. It was always a shifting tidemark between turning a decent profit and losing his supply.

Still, he enjoyed the fish store. He loved the rush and the bustle when the boats came home, and the boys came in with tottering loads of fish – baskets and boxes of the things to be cleaned and sorted. Then they would either be sold to the pressers and the jousters and the wet fishmongers, or passed to the skinners – who could put a hook through a fish and

29

have the skin off in a single movement – and then the filleters who cut it into gleaming steaks for the convenience of the fish and chip shop trade. Then the offal would be taken out and thrown back in the sea, while the gulls whooped and circled overhead and buxom women scrubbed down the blood and scales and sent little rivulets out into the street. Stan enjoyed it all. He didn't even mind the smell – it was the smell of money, he told Dora once when she wrinkled up her nose against the stench.

Certainly the gulls enjoyed the smell. There was a wheeling flock of them, as usual, as he walked up the street towards the store. A couple of fish carts had just been loaded up, but the birds' cries almost drowned out the sound of hooves.

Someone was waiting for him by the big open door – that young limb, Joe Pollock, by the look of it. Stan knew what he wanted. Come up here to sell his fish, had he, as though nothing had happened and he hadn't taken part in that disturbance in the lane? Well, if that's what he expected, he'd have to think again. Stan was grinning inwardly, though he didn't let it show.

'Well?' he said, as soon as he'd got close enough to be heard over the squawking gulls. 'What is it now? Come to complain about my boat again?'

Joe Pollock shifted uncomfortably from foot to foot. 'Fact is, we've just come back from sea,' he said. 'Heard you were paying a good price for skate.'

'That so?' said Stan, although of course it was. He had left instructions with his man to pay his regulars a full halfpenny higher than the market rate – precisely in the hope of luring Pollock here.

There was a silence. Stan wasn't going to make it easy for Pollock by saying anything.

'I wondered . . . That is . . . We wondered if you were buying now,' the young man said. 'We've come in with skate.'

Stan leaned back on his heels and looked at him. 'And what makes you think that I'd be interested in buying fish from you? After all the fuss you and your pals have made?'

Pollock flushed, but he stood his ground. 'Fish is fish, mister. The men heard that you were buying skate, and asked for me to come. Some of them have got young mouths to feed, and that bit extra would have meant a lot.'

Stan was calculating mentally. Pollock had delayed to come up here, which meant he and his cronies hadn't had the chance to sell their fish elsewhere. The other dealers would have been down at the quay and filled their orders from the rival boats. His original intention was to turn young Pollock down, but how much more satisfying it would be to buy the catch and force a lower price!

'You come here to apologize then, have you, and beg me to help you out?' he began. 'I daresay we could manage something . . .'

Pollock squared his shoulders and interrupted him. 'I haven't, Mr Hunkin, and I can see you're right. I don't approve of your methods and I shouldn't take your cash. We've got an offer on the remainder of the catch from Edward's fish store in Penzance, and I'll go back and tell them they can have the skate as well.' He turned to go.

'Won't be getting my price,' Stan called after him, suddenly willing to dangle the offer again.

Pollock looked back over his shoulder as he went. 'Your price is too high, Mr Hunkin, and that's the truth of it. You brought me here to make me beg – I can see that plain as pike. Well, I shan't give you the pleasure. And I'll tell you this: if it wasn't for the men, I never would have come. You say that you aren't keen on buying fish from me, and sure as sprats are sprats, I don't want to sell my fish to you. In fact, I wouldn't sell you my skate now if you was to offer me a shilling each for them. Good day.' And he crammed his cap upon his head and went.

It made Stan feel out of sorts for the remainder of the day. Cheated of natural justice he had been, that's what, and not even a good market price for cod could cheer him up.

Tom was still thinking about Dora Hunkin when he got to work the next day. His feelings must have been showing on his face, because no sooner had he gone inside the dry to change, than he found Jack Maddern, the senior engine man, waiting for him with a grin.

'Morning, Cap'n,' Tom said respectfully. The leader of any group of men was always 'Cap'n' at all the workings hereabouts, whether he was a tinner or a carpenter, or even the man who supervised the dry. Some of the underground men poked fun at it, and quoted the old rhyme – 'Cappen Oats and Cappen Ralph, too many Cappens by a half' – but if any man alive deserved the title, it was Jack. Knew more about engines than anyone, from setting them up – and that was a performance in itself, with the bob weighing nearly fifty tons – to stoking the fireboxes and driving the machine itself. He could even tell, just from the feel of the pumping engine on the surface, which water valve, or 'clack', needed to be changed in the pitwork underground. If he was ever engine captain one day himself, Tom thought, he'd like to be the sort of man Jack Maddern was. Perhaps even Dora Hunkin would look twice at him then.

'What you looking so gone-out about?' Jack mocked, his thin face already smeared with oil and soot. Obviously he'd been in the boilerhouse today – usually the cap'n was neater than a pin. He gave Tom a sharp nudge and bared his broken tooth stumps in a smile. 'Never fallen for some soppy maid, have 'ee? Heard tell you 'ad one calling at the house last night.'

Tom mentally cursed the cheerful gossip of the mine. Couldn't so much as blow your nose round here without half of Penvarris knowing it the next day.

'Don't be so daft,' he said, stripping off his shirt and putting on his grey cotton overall instead. It was always warm inside the engine room – comfortable in winter, but on a summer day like this it could get very hot, and then anything you wore got soaked through in a trice. 'Schoolteacher came up with Harvey Pierce, that's all. I aren't fixing to be wedded yet – I got a bit more sense.'

Jack dragged a grimy hand across his face and gave a rueful grin. He was a scrawny man himself, but his wife was built like a standing engine and was rumoured to rule him with a rod of iron. 'Well, I hope you got a bit o' sense, and all,' he said. 'Tell you for why. That new boiler's coming in today for the compressor house – that means getting the traction engine up to steam, to get her here and move her into place . . .'

Tom nodded. This was hardly news. The operation had been planned for months. The road to Penvarris Mine was not in good repair, and though waggons and horses were gener-ally employed to shift the tin, there was a big steam traction engine too, which could be used to move the heaviest loads.

This new compressor boiler would be very big – the one in operation now was large enough – but the mine owners had decided that more capacity would drive the compressed air drill at greater depth and permit them to open up another seam.

'Thing is,' Cap'n said, 'I'm short a man. Bill Handiman fell over stairs and broke his leg last night. That means I haven't got an extra engineer on hand, in case there's any trouble with the bob. Manage the Duchess on your own, can you? I'll come up when I can to keep an eye on things, but I'll be needed down the compressor house all day while they're getting this new boiler in.'

Tom stared. This was a compliment, of sorts, but an alarming one. The Duchess was the pump engine for the middle shaft – an enormous, awesome thing, so big that she could be coupled up to drive a stone-hauling whim at the same time as powering the pumps, and still she had never been steamed up to capacity. She wasn't likely to be either, with ninety inches bore – at least until the lower stopes were opened up. She was officially named Higher Engine (all new engines on the mine were christened with a bottle – just like ships) but she was always called the Duchess, or the '90', in tribute to her dignity and size. Tom had handled her several times before, though never entirely on his own without Bill Handiman or Jack close by. But this was a chance to prove himself, he knew. 'S'pect so, Cap'n,' he said, trying to disguise his nervousness. 'If you think I can.'

'Wouldn't ask you if I didn't,' Cap'n grunted, laying a hand on Tom's shoulder as he spoke. 'Don't want a stranger driving her if we can help it.'

Tom nodded. Most drivers at Penvarris stuck to their own engines, more or less. It was true what Mother had said to Dora yesterday. The engines did have personalities. The Duchess was a grand old lady, three storeys tall, always softly hissing steam, while the flywheel turned majestically and the great bob outside thudded up and down. Some of the smaller engines elsewhere on the mine needed all a man's strength to press down the bottom handle, but the 90 was so well balanced that even Tom could manage her with ease. 'Leave her to me, Cap'n,' he said with more confidence.

Jack gave him a wink. 'You got a new boy started in the

33

boilerhouse as well.' He held out his grimy hands to show. 'Been down there showing him how to stoke the fire. Just keep an eye on him for me.' And with that he turned and walked away.

Tom's heart was thudding as he left the dry and walked down towards the engine room. Already he could see the outside nose – the main rod lifting and falling as it moved the rams, pumping the water from the shaft below. The drive shaft which could be used to connect all this to the whim machinery next door had been declutched, he was relieved to see. Because of the new compressor, probably – a lot of men would be on surface work today, so the extra hoisting whim would not be needed. That could be a proper headache sometimes, making sure the crank stopped dead centre when you made a lift, so that it was easy to start it off again. Well, that was one less thing to think about. He squared his shoulders and approached the door.

He looked into the boilerhouse first of all. The boy was in there at the firebox, with the doors open and a shovel in his hand. Tom ran an appraising eye around the fire – he'd done a few weeks as a stoker too. Jack Maddern saw that all his drivers did that, he always said, a good engine man had to be a fireman too. This one was burning well. The clinker had been cleaned out for the change of shift and the fresh coals were glowing fiery hot – though there had obviously been a blowback earlier: it was very hot and smoky, and when the boy turned round his eyes were just white patches in a sea of soot.

Tom remembered his first day at this, and nodded towards the kettle on the floor nearby. 'You can fill that up directly and make a cup of tea. Put it in the firebox, at the back. You'll find a little bridge there, see? Use that long poker with the hook on it. Oh, and you can bring me a cup as well. And make sure you clean your boots before you come.'

The middle chamber upstairs, where the levers were, was kept like a proper home from home, with spotless levers, holy-stoned floors and a wooden settle for the engine man. Drivers were generally envied for their lot.

'Yes, Cap'n,' the boy said in awe.

'I aren't a captain yet,' Tom said, but he walked up the stairs into the engine room with a swagger in his step to take the handles and assume control.

34

Everything – the cylinder, the crank, the massive beams – gave him a sense of purpose and delight that day, and when, just before the change of shift that afternoon, he was obliged to stop the engine for a time because of some trouble with a valve, he did so expertly, opening the dampers and the safety valve and bringing the great wheel to a halt as smoothly as Bill Handiman could have done.

Cap'n Maddern said as much himself. Turned out he'd been out there watching at the time.

Winnie hurried up to the top road with the post – one of the extra duties for which she'd volunteered, partly because she wanted Mrs Z. to think her indispensable, and partly because she knew there was a chance she'd run into Mr Nathan on the road. He'd said last night that he'd be in the area because there was a funeral in St Evan church today. He might even have said it purposely, she thought. He'd been looking straight at her, as if suggesting she'd be interested.

She coloured at the notion, rehearsing in her mind what she would do if she did encounter him. Head on one side, a charming smile – nothing too forward – and a little nod. 'Morning, Mr Nathan! Fancy seeing you!' she'd say, and then she'd look away. She knew that she looked fetching when she dropped her eyes just so, and glanced up underneath her lids. She had a little practice – there was nobody about – and when she was pleased with the effect, walked on again, holding herself more perkily upright and making her blonde curls bounce against her cheek. She hadn't taken half a dozen steps before a voice behind her made her pause.

'Winnie? Winnie Hunkin?'

That wasn't Mr Nathan's voice. She turned and sighed. Joe Pollock was striding up the road, an idiotic smile on his face. 'What you doing out here, this time of day?' he said companionably as he came up to her. His glance fell on the letters in her hand. 'Going up to the post? Well, I'll come with you then.'

It wasn't what she had in mind at all. 'It's a free country,' she said disagreeably. 'I can't stop you, if that's what you want to do.' She shot him a look. He must be eighteen or nineteen now, and better-looking than ever, in that bold sort of way, with broad shoulders and dark eyes and his skin all tanned and weathered by the sun. And he still looked at her in that smouldering fashion that made her heart beat fast. 'You got a cheek, you have, going on like this after that performance in the lane.'

'Winnie?' Joe said and put out a hand to her. 'You know that wasn't meant. Never would have done it if you'd stop to talk to me. It's your father I've a quarrel with, not you.'

'Well, go and talk to him then.' She snatched her wrist away.

'What is it?' he demanded. 'What's the matter, Win? Why won't you even look at me these days?'

She stopped and turned to face him. 'You know quite well why not. Because . . .' She couldn't say 'because you're just a fisherman with nothing to your name.' 'Because my family wouldn't like it, that's why not.'

He grinned at her. 'Didn't stop you when we were bird's-nesting and walking in the woods. You were happy enough to do that, as I recall – though your father would have had ten fits if he'd known.' He bent over and snapped off a late foxglove from the hedge. 'Didn't it mean anything to you at all?'

Winnie felt the colour rising to her face. 'Joe Pollock, don't be so absurd. We were just children then. It's different now.'

'It isn't different to me,' Joe said. 'I meant it when I said it, and I mean it now. I like you, Winnie Hunkin, that's the truth. More stuck up than a heron with a fish, but you're the prettiest thing in Penwith, always were. Whole of Cornwall, maybe, for anything I know. Oh, I know your father wouldn't have it – we don't see eye to eye – and after yesterday he'd like it even less. But you've got the spirit to stand up to him. One day you'll be twenty-one and then you can please yourself. I'll wait.' He had a bunch of foxgloves now, and he thrust them in her hand.

Winnie threw them from her, horrified. 'Wait?' she repeated. 'Wait? What for? Do you suppose I'm going to marry somebody like you, when you're just a blinking fisherman and haven't got three ha'pennies to bless yourself? Well, if you think that, Joe Pollock, you can think again.'

Joe looked stung. 'All right, Miss hoity-toity. I understand. I'm nobody, and you're too good for me. I don't need sema-phore. But I don't know for the life of me what there is to get so high and mighty about. Your father was "just a fisher-man" himself once.'

'So he might have been,' she answered. 'But he married well. And I'm going to do the same. So there. Horses and carriages, and servants too. Nice dresses and somebody to look after me instead of having a brood of children and slaving every hour over a hot stove until I'm worn out and old at twenty-five.' She had begun by speaking with some dignity, but she could feel herself getting emotional by now, and she added, spitefully, 'So put that in your lobster pot and sink it.'

He seemed to know that she was secretly in turmoil inside. He reached his hands out again and grasped both of hers. 'Winnie, I swear to you . . .' He moved closer, looking deep into her eyes. 'I'll make something of myself. I'll . . .'

He was interrupted by the clatter of hooves along the lane as a neat black gig appeared round the corner, and Mr Nathan Zeal trotted past. Winnie caught a glance of his startled-looking face as he drew parallel, and then he looked away and flicked the reins. The pony moved on at a brisker pace.

Winnie broke away from Joe impatiently. She almost stamped her foot. 'Now look what you've done! After all the trouble I've taken to be here. Mr Nathan saw us. Whatever will he think?' Tears of disappointment stung in her eyes.

Joe stared at her. 'Mr Nathan?' he said disbelievingly. 'Him? That greasy little undertaker? A man who spends his life working with the dead and looks like a waxwork himself? You're interested in him? Just because he's got a house and carriages? Why, he must be twice your age!'

She tossed her head. 'Mr Nathan is a gentleman!' she retorted, irritated. 'And what if I do decide I want a few nice things? Is that so terrible?'

Joe looked at her. 'It's seems I misjudged you after all. There's more of your father in you than I thought.' His voice had taken on a harder edge 'Well, Miss Hunkin, I apologize. Obviously I can't offer you the things you want – money and coffins and a gloomy house. I wish you well of it.'

'You needn't trouble to wish anything. After this, I don't suppose Mr Nathan will even look at me.' She was furious, and she could hear her voice shaking as she added, 'Just when I thought I'd got him interested!'

Joe took a step backwards. 'Oh, I'm sure you'll manage

something. Bat your eyelids at him. He won't be able to resist. No one ever could.' He sounded bitter. 'But I'm richer than you are, Winnie Hunkin, in one way at least. I only sell fish. I don't sell myself.'

He turned and walked away without a backward glance, leaving the foxgloves scattered in the lane.

Four

Harvey Pierce didn't come to school the next day or the day after, and when he did turn up at last he was so sleepy that even in the morning he was slow, and by lunchtime he was struggling to keep his eyes open at all. When the bell went for classes in the afternoon (little Amy Taylor ringing it with pride, though it was nearly as big as she was) Harvey did not line up with the others in the yard, and was finally discovered curled up just outside the boys' gate, fast asleep.

When he was shaken into wakefulness and summoned to the teacher's desk, he looked abashed. 'It's that dratted baby, Miss. Wants feedin' every whip and while, and Ma can't do it every time – she hasn't got the milk – so I got to give it a feeding bottle now and then with sweetened tea in it. Let Ma and the others get a bit of sleep, and stop the child disturbing Pa – he's got to go to work.'

Dora wished that, far from giving him the strap, she had the authority to send him home again, but Miss Blewitt gave him a tap on either hand and then said, 'Go into the toilet block and put your head under the tap. Cold water will help you keep awake.'

Harvey came back dripping wet, but no more lively than he'd been before, and when the time came to go home he set off so slowly, and with such dragging steps, that he was still in sight when Dora came to leave. She stood at the school gate and watched him for a moment.

'Poor little mite,' she murmured to herself.

'Not so little,' said a soft voice by her side. She whirled round to find Tom Trewin standing there.

He grinned at her. 'Quite a big boy, that one, I'd have said. Growing away faster than Dolly Whidden's leeks.'

In spite of herself, Dora laughed aloud. Dolly Whidden was

39

famous for her leeks – or 'licks' as people called them here-abouts – and still more famous for boasting loudly that she fed them with the contents of her privy. She hawked the biggest vegetables for miles, but some people wouldn't buy them when she called, because of the fertilizer she used.

'All the same,' she said, 'what future has he got? He isn't stupid, though he thinks he is. He simply never has a chance to learn.'

Tom made a face. 'What chance has anybody got round here? They're talking down the mine about the price of tin – it's got so low they're closing down Wheal Kate, by all accounts, and capping her. Can't make a profit, the mine-owners say. It's not the first time either. If this goes on they'll be turning men off down Penvarris next, and all the time there's more folk out of work and jostling for whatever jobs there are.'

Dora looked at him. 'But you'll be all right, surely? Learning to be an engineer, and everything.'

He gave her that slow smile that lit his face. 'Oh, I daresay. Won't be my turn for a while at least. Though sometimes I think I should do what my brother Jimmy did and go abroad. He's in Australia. Plenty of work out there, he says. Been sending money to Mother every month – that's how we can afford for me to do this evening course. Now, that would be something, wouldn't it? Support your family, do a bit of good – and see the world, besides.'

She found she was looking at him with dismay. 'And you would think of it? Going all that way?'

He grinned at her. 'Not for a minute, anyway. Got to finish all these classes yet. But after that – who knows.' He met her eyes. 'Of course, I might have other plans by then.'

He said it lightly, but it made her blush.

She looked away, confused. 'Well, I wish you luck with it. Now, I must go and catch up Jamie if I can. Father will be vexed if I am late.'

He didn't move, just stood there leaning on the wall, dangling a parcel of two books tied up with string. She could see the name of one of them. *Mechanical Drawing – Intermediate*. 'That looks dry and difficult. You're going to night school then?'

He nodded. 'Wondered if I could walk part of the way with

you.' He had gone bright-red around the collar of his shirt, and was swinging his foot to kick the daisy heads. 'If you've got nothing else to do, that is?'

'I've got to . . .' Dora began, then broke off short. Somehow with Tom she could not be shy, the way she would have been with other men. 'That'd be very nice. Better be careful, though, in case we're seen – any scandal and they'll throw me out.'

He laughed. 'What do you think I'm going to do? Start to kiss you in the lane?'

'Oh, Tom!' Dora coloured. 'Don't be daft.'

And of course he did nothing of the kind. But as they walked quietly along – talking about Harvey and Jamie and the mine – somehow she couldn't help wishing that he would, and wondering what it would feel like if he did.

Winnie had been expecting a dressing down ever since that disastrous encounter in the lane, and sure enough it arrived the next day. Mr Nathan must have stayed home especially to deliver it, because as soon as she got to the house that morning she was summoned to see him in the drawing room.

It was an imposing room, with its heavy curtains and brocaded furniture. It was crammed full of ornaments, all of them rather forbidding, from the bad-tempered-looking china cats that framed the mantle-clock, through the glass domes containing stuffed birds and artificial flowers, to the framed texts and samplers on the wall and Mr Nathan's father frowning stiffly down from his self-important portrait. It was enough to make anyone feel uneasy as soon as they came in, and today was even worse than usual. Mr Nathan was sitting in a wing chair by the fireplace, and he did not rise, as he would normally have done, but motioned her to come and stand before him as though she were no better than a parlour-maid.

'Well, Winifred.' His voice was as unsmiling as his face. 'I imagine you know why I've called you here. You have been welcomed, almost as a member of the family, to read and generally be a companion to Mamma. Do you imagine that in the circumstances we can tolerate the kind of exhibition which I witnessed yesterday?'

Winnie swallowed. This was even more serious than she'd supposed. Mrs Zeal was a real stickler for appearances and had once famously dismissed a cook for 'enticing followers'. The same thing could easily occur again.

She glanced up underneath her lashes, and gave Mr Nathan her most devastating smile. 'Of course not, Mr Nathan. I . . .'

He interrupted her, so firmly that she felt ashamed. 'Of course I can't ignore it – as you rightly say. What you do in private is your own affair, but your public behaviour reflects on all of us. So let it be clearly understood that if anything of the sort occurs again – if so much as a whisper reaches me – I shall be obliged to tell Mamma at once, and that will be the end of your employ. Do I make myself clear?'

'Yes, Mr Nathan.' Winnie felt herself breathe out. He had snubbed her brutally, but at least he hadn't told his mother anything. That was something to be grateful for. 'It won't occur again.' She tried to hide her chagrin and relief and sound appropriately penitent.

But Mr Nathan had not finished yet. 'I should hope not indeed. I am surprised at you. Cavorting openly in that unseemly way, and with a young man of that sort as well. What do you suppose that your papa would say if he learned of it? And your poor mother too?'

Winnie said desperately, 'I wasn't cavorting with anyone. It isn't what it looked like – it was just—'

He held up a hand. 'That's enough, Winifred. I know what I saw. I've said what I had to say. Let that be an end to it. I've made my position very clear, I think.'

'But . . .'

'No buts, Winifred. The matter is closed. I do not want to speak or hear of it again. Now, Mamma will be waiting for you in her room.'

He turned his attention to his newspaper, and there was nothing for it but to go. Winnie went upstairs, raging inwardly Drat that Joe Pollock! This was all his fault. She'd been told off properly, was lucky to retain her job, and Mr Nathan had gone all curt and cold. Just when she'd been sure that he was getting interested. It was mortifying to think he might have changed his mind, especially after all the things she'd said to Joe.

If only she'd been able to explain. She hadn't wanted Joe to take her hands, he'd simply forced it on her. Her face blazed with the unfairness of it all. Well, she would just have to make an opportunity to put it right, that's all. She tapped on Mrs Zeal's door and went inside. To crown it all the old lady scolded her for being late.

All morning as she went about her tasks – Mrs Zeal depended on her more and more these days – the memory of that interview stayed with her like an ache. Even when she picked up the *Ecclesiatical Magazine* and began to read the story they'd started earlier, her mind was not fully on the task.

'Winifred?' The old lady's sharp voice cut across her thoughts.

'Yes, Mrs Zeal?'

'Do you think me quite an idiot? That's the second time you've read that paragraph.'

'Sorry, Mrs Zeal. I lost my place.' In fact, she had been mentally rehearsing a dozen different ways to justify herself to Mr Nathan when she could. She forced her thoughts back to the printed page. 'Let me see, where were we? Ah, yes. "The long cold winter had gone by and spring once more smiled brightly . . ."'

By the time she came downstairs again, he'd gone.

Nathan was later than he meant to be arriving at Zeal's Funeral Parlour: Interments of Discretion and Integrity. The events of the morning had upset him – he always hated disciplinary confrontations of that kind, and this one had disturbed him more than most. He was disappointed in the girl as well. Severely disappointed. To think that he had actually begun to entertain notions of courting her himself!

Well, that was clearly a mistake. He should never have countenanced the scheme of bringing the young woman to the house at all. It had been Mamma who thought of it, of course.

She'd come up with the idea quite suddenly one day when she was answering the mail. Cousin Zachariah, who had been widowed twice, wrote that he was looking for another wife, and his letter seemed to spur her into thought.

'You should think of getting wed yourself,' she had said, turning her own letter over to blot the ink. 'If you're not quick about it, it will be too late and there will never be another Zeal to carry on the trade.'

Nathan had heard it all a dozen times, and muttered his

43

usual excuse. 'You don't get much chance for walking out in this line of work.' He hated it when Mamma went on like this. He'd never been any good with girls – not that he'd had much to do with them. His sober manner – so perfect for his job – had drawbacks when it came to lady-friends. The last young woman that he'd dared approach, merely inviting her to dance at Cousin Zachariah's Christmas ball, had not only made a swift excuse, but had been overheard asking loudly afterwards who that 'lugubrious, creepy fellow' was.

'You're not getting any younger, Nathan,' Mamma had said.

Nathan scowled. What did getting older have to do with it? Even years ago, when he was a boy, it was the same. He'd hardly had a conversation with a girl. Of course, he'd never been permitted to play with the other children of his age. It was his job to sit beside the driver of the hearse at funerals, dressed in a miniature black top hat and morning coat, ostensibly to hold the horses while the coffin was brought out, but really to be a kind of live advertisement for Father's trade when men stood respectful in the street and took off their hats to let the cortège pass. The sight of a little boy in mourning dress was eye-catching but – Father said – people didn't want to see the same lad playing tag or making mud pies by the stream. In any case, in those days you didn't go to school and meet girls and boys to be your friends, the way the young did now. He'd had a bit of tutoring at home, that's all, and then he'd turned his hand to learn the trade.

For answer, Mamma sighed, blew on the paper and folded it – with emphasis. 'Cousin Zachariah tries, at least.'

Nathan knew exactly what she was getting at. Both Zachariah's wives had died while giving birth, though neither baby had survived, so even the family name might not survive. It was one of Mamma's favourite themes these days. 'Time enough for that,' he'd said, as usual.

But this time Mamma hadn't given up. 'Those twins of Sybil's are of marriageable age. Perhaps I could arrange for one of them to come up here somehow. To come and read to me, perhaps. Yes, that would do. My eyes are failing, and it would not be inappropriate. The family is not wealthy, but it's respectable, and they are relations of a kind.' Mamma was getting more enthusiastic as she spoke. 'I'll have the eldest one, if she's available. She's got a bit more drive by all accounts. No need to look so nervous, Nathan. You're not bound to anything. We can simply have a look at her and see. It can't do any harm. If you like her, and she is suitable, I should think she'd jump at you – she wouldn't make a better marriage anywhere else. Oh, don't scowl so, Nathan. Shall I put the thing in hand?'

'Oh, very well,' he said ungraciously, though secretly the thought quite excited him.

So Winifred had come, and up to now it had all gone swimmingly. Even Mother was inclined to think she'd do.

'Not the class of girl I would have chosen, Nathan, but one can't be choosy at your time of life. Winifred's a little flighty, but she's neat and quick and not afraid to turn her hand to things.' And, thus emboldened, he'd begun to hope.

He almost thought she liked him. Always a smile when he ran into her. She listened to him with interest when, once or twice, he'd stopped to talk to her. He'd paid her a compliment last week, though he'd never been much good at that sort of thing, and she'd seemed to like it well enough.

And then this. Coming upon her in the lane hand in hand with some young ruffian almost young enough to be his son, all pink-faced and embarrassed when she knew that she had been seen. Well, that was the end of that. Mother thought her flighty and it was clearly true. Not at all a suitable person for an undertaker's wife.

The sharpness of his disappointment irked him so that not even the business of the day could quite distract his mind. Mrs Conley: quite a big affair. He mentally ran down the list of everything required. Large casket – best quality, with brass accoutrements. Sammy had already gone to measure up. Eight plumed horses were wanted for the hearse. Six professional coffin bearers, matched – tall hats, crêpe ribbon and tailcoats for these. Half a dozen following carriages, all draped. One black wreath with a white bow for the door and two loads of muffling rushes for the street outside. Oh, and flowers for inside the coffin around the face. The family didn't want her screwed down right away, so that meant bringing her here to the embalming room where he and Sammy could discreetly get to work – preservatives to mould the features into shape, a wash and hairdo and a little touch of carmine on the cheeks and lips, then into the clothes the family had sent, and back she'd go to be laid out in the best room until the funeral.

He was still engaged in checking off the items in his head when he heard the front bell ring. He put on his morning coat again and went out to the parlour room – discreet dark furnishings and lilies in a vase – composing his features into an appropriate expression of solemnity. Some new customer, perhaps, or Mr Conley coming to change his mind again about the white. White bow and armbands when a lady died, that was the old-fashioned way, but a lot of people just had black these days.

But this was not a grieving relative. This was a sleek and smiling man with hat and gloves in hand.

'Cousin Zachariah!' Nathan was amazed. He had been thinking of his cousin not a minute since, and here he was in person, as if thoughts had conjured him. 'What brings you to Penzance?' He forced a smile. His visitor, as usual, looked prosperous: resplendent in a fashionable tailored coat, smart trousers and what were, even to Nathan's untutored eyes, obviously expensive, handmade polished boots.

Zachariah grinned. 'Oh, business. Business.' That meant a woman, probably, Nathan thought. Zac had invested shrewdly long ago, and now had financial interests in a score of things – from gas to shipping – but something in his manner suggested that this 'business' was of quite another kind. He was older than Nathan by a year or so and his hair was already touched with grey, yet with his little pointed beard and piercing eyes he still contrived to have a youthful, dapper look. No wonder women always fell for him. Nathan felt a little surge of envy at the thought.

'I am in Penzance for a week or so, staying with my late wife's relatives, and thought I'd call by and pay you my respects.' Zachariah gazed around. Suddenly to Nathan the little room seemed dusty and depressed. 'How's the undertaking business? Flourishing?'

'Always busy in our line of work,' Nathan said and frowned, irked with himself for making this traditional response. Zachariah always made him feel inadequate.

Zachariah smiled. 'Too busy to spare an hour for a relative? I wondered if I might impose on you, and beg an invitation to the house sometime? Early next week, if that would suit you both. I haven't seen Aunt Millicent since you came to us – the Christmas before last, it must have been, when Anna was alive. We held a ball. You might remember that.'

Nathan remembered it all right. That dreadful girl who had humiliated him. The recollection made him squirm but he recovered himself quickly. 'Of course, Cousin. You must come to tea. On Tuesday, perhaps? I have no funeral that afternoon and Mamma would be delighted, I am sure.' That was true. Even Mamma came all over fluttery where Zachariah was concerned.

'How is Aunt Millicent? Keeping well?'

'Very well indeed, thank you. She has a young companion now, who comes and reads to her. A sort of relative . . .' He stopped, seeing Zachariah's knowing grin. 'Perhaps you've heard?'

'I believe she did mention it in her letters once or twice,' his cousin said. 'A very pretty girl by all accounts. Well, I shall look forward to making her acquaintance soon. Ah, there's someone coming in the back. That will be your assistant, I suppose. Tuesday would be excellent – I'll see you then. Don't trouble to escort me out.' He gave a courteous but mocking little bow and left.

Nathan hurried through to the workroom at the back, just as Sammy Pengally scuttled in. Nathan put his hands behind his back and assumed his normal, measured, more becoming pace.

'When we go to fetch Mrs Conley to the room of rest, we'll have to take some help,' Sammy informed him in his mournful voice. 'The two of us can't manage her alone, not even with the driver there to give a hand. My word, she is a weight.' He was already eyeing up the stock – 'a wide selection of wooden and metallic caskets always kept in store' as the advertisement proclaimed. 'Who's the swell you were talking to?' he added, nodding toward the door. 'Someone looking for a funeral?'

'No,' Nathan said shortly. 'Bit of family business, that was all.' He was still smarting from Zachariah's last remarks. He would not have put it past his cousin to have engineered this whole visit to Penzance simply to inspect this 'pretty girl'. No doubt he would charm her off her feet – he always did. Nathan felt unreasonably irritated by the thought.

'Nothing here that's suitable,' he said to Sammy, to the

47

man's surprise. 'Mrs Conley's a big woman, as you say, and they're having her on view. Can't go tucking her up inside the box to make her fit. Have to do one custom-made. I'll see to it myself.'

And so he did. It was a job he hadn't done for years, but he took a savage satisfaction in the task, hammering each nail firmly home as though Mr Zachariah Zeal were under it.

Five

Who should turn up at chapel the following Sunday but Tom Trewin – though up till then he hadn't been for years. Winnie was the one to see him first, because she'd been gazing round during the sermon as she often did. She gave Dora a sharp little nudge and signalled with her eyes, then dropped her hymn book accidentally-on-purpose on the floor.

Dora bent down to pick it up so that she could have a quick look round her as she straightened up – it was a trick they had developed when they were very young. And there he was, sitting at the back, looking smart as ninepence in his Sunday suit, even if it was a bit tight round the chest. To her confusion he was looking straight at her.

She knew she must be turning scarlet as she turned to face the front again. She concentrated a rapt gaze on the preacher for the rest of his address, though she was more aware of Tom Trewin's eyes upon her back than of anything the speaker said.

'Who is it?' Winnie murmured, under cover of the collection hymn. 'I'm sure I know the face.'

Dora attempted to ignore her and went on singing about angels casting down their crowns.

'Thinks he's somebody, whatever else.' Winnie's whisper was so loud that Dora was sure everyone must hear. 'Keeps on staring at us all the time.'

Dora mouthed, 'Tom Trewin, you know. In school with us.' Winnie turned around to have another look. Dora kept her own eyes steadfastly ahead, but she couldn't keep the colour from her cheeks. A woman in the row in front turned round and glared at them.

Winnie was about to whisper something else, but Dora gave

49

a warning 'Sssh!' and refused to look towards her twin again until the service was over and everyone was starting to file out.

'Well, if that's Tom Trewin, he's turned out better-looking than I thought,' Winnie said as they emerged on to the step and saw him standing awkwardly beside the wall. 'Look at him staring! I do believe he's smitten.' She tossed her curls and flashed a smile at him. 'Here!' she said suddenly, looking into Dora's face. 'What's the matter? Why have you turned redder than a cooked crab suddenly? I do believe it's you he's looking at! You're not . . . Oh, come on Dora, surely you can't be thinking of walking out with him. He's just a working boy. The Trewins are one of those miner's families, surely, down Treventon way.'

'Of course I'm not walking out with him,' Dora protested. 'I'm not walking out with anyone. I've only spoken to him once or twice since we left school.' Exactly three times more, in fact, since she took Harvey home. 'And anyway, he isn't down the mine. Training to be an engine man, he is. Ran the pumps himself, all shift, the other day.'

Winnie made a mocking face. 'You know a lot about him, for somebody you've never spoken to.'

Dora flounced. 'I run into him occasionally when I'm coming home from school, that's all. He walks that way down to the Institute – he goes there to evening class three times a week.'

Winnie gave a derisive snort. 'He must be fond of walking then, that's all I can say. Puts half a mile on the journey easily, to go up round the school.'

Dora for some reason hadn't thought of that, but now she came to work it out, it was of course true. She said crossly, 'Well, what if it does? He's a nice enough young man, and I like to talk to him.'

'You make sure Gan and Father don't find out, that's all. You and a miner's boy! Whatever would they say?' She was teasing, Dora saw, not thinking there was any truth in this.

'Who's going to tell them?' Dora said, and added quickly, 'Not that there's anything to tell.'

'What about Jamie?' Winnie wouldn't let it drop. 'What if he waits after school for you and sees you meeting Tom Trewin in the street? Soon get about that you've got a young man then.'

Dora forbore to point out that she met Tom only in the lane, precisely to be away from prying eyes, and that anyway, Jamie already knew. He had promised to say nothing to anyone at home, and he'd clearly kept his word. 'Well, he isn't my young man, so there's an end to it. But, speaking of young men, there's Joe Pollock over there. Hoping to find you, by the looks of it.'

That was unkind, but it was Winnie's turn to blush. Dora rather wished she hadn't said it though, because her sister cried out at once, 'Oh, my dear life! So it is. We had words the other day, and I don't want to speak to him. Come on, let's get on home!'

She shook hands with the preacher, who was waiting at the gate as usual, and began to hurry off. There was nothing Dora could do but follow her. There was only time to glance towards Tom Trewin once, and throw him a secret, apologetic smile.

'My nephew's such a cultured man!' Mrs Zeal said again, rejecting yet another beaded dress. 'I wonder if he's keeping full mourning for his wife, or whether I dare wear embroidery.' She had been in a flutter all morning, trying to decide what gown to wear for tea. Winnie had almost had enough of it, though she was bursting with curiosity to see what this paragon might be like.

She did not seem likely to find out, because her employer had promised her a rare few hours off – as though to keep Mr Zachariah to herself. But when, in the early afternoon, the sound of hoofbeats reached them from the gate, Mrs Zeal seemed to change her mind.

'That will be my nephew now,' she said, forgetting herself sufficiently to lift the corner of the curtain and peep out. They were in Mrs Zeal's dressing room upstairs, so the gesture was unlikely to be seen. 'Yes, so it is. Come in a hansom cab, no less. And here am I, not ready to receive him yet. I can see nothing of him but his cape and hat. Winifred, you go downstairs. Then come and tell me if he's got an armband on, or whether he is still in proper crêpe. Then I shall know better what to wear.'

Winnie stared at her. 'But, Mrs Zeal, I can hardly . . .' She tailed off. It was clearly not her place to go down and inspect the visitor.

The older woman made an impatient clucking sound. 'Of course not, Winifred. A little tact is obviously required. Tell them I've sent you down to fetch my book. Mr Nathan will show him to the drawing room, no doubt, and I think there's one there on the window seat. Well go on, girl, don't stand there staring like an owl.'

So Winnie went down, reluctantly. She was in a proper pickle now. Mr Nathan hated to be disturbed, especially when he had a visitor, and was already cold and curt to her. However, she must do as she was told. She tapped softly on the door to the drawing room.

Mr Nathan's voice, not pleased, called. 'Come in!'

She pushed the door open but did not venture in. The two men were standing by the fire – obviously they had not had time to sit.

'Begging your pardon, Mr Nathan, I didn't know that you had visitors.' A blatant lie, delivered with a smile, but his face did not relax a single inch. 'I'm sorry to disturb you, gentlemen, but Mrs Zeal has sent me down to find her reading book.' There was a volume on the window seat, she was relieved to see. It would not have surprised her to find that there was no such book at all. 'But if it is inconvenient . . .'

Mr Nathan was about to grumble that it was, she would have bet half a crown on it, but instead the stranger spoke. 'Not at all. Come and find your book.' A bit older than Mr Nathan, perhaps, since he was turning grey, but my word what a handsome man. Smarter than a fashion plate as well – in fact he looked quite like one, standing there. She took in all the details to relay to Mrs Zeal. Black coat, dove-grey waistcoat, sombre tie. No armband, but a single diamond pin, gold cufflinks, highly polished shoes. Neat little beard and whiskers, like the King, and a pair of strikingly green-grey, piercing eyes. Nothing flamboyant, but he looked elegant. He smelled very nice as well – of leather, soap, bay rum and brilliantine. The smell of money, she thought approvingly.

He returned her smile. 'You must be this companion of Aunt Millicent's I've heard so much about. I'm Zachariah Zeal, by the way.'

She glanced at Mr Nathan in surprise, but he just scowled and made no attempt to introduce her in return. 'I'm Winnie, sir. Winifred Hunkin, from the village here.'

Zachariah's eyes twinkled at her. 'Some sort of relation of the family, I understand.'

'Mother was a Jenkins,' Mr Nathan said, for all the world as if she were a horse that he was trying to sell by demonstrating her bloodstock.

'My father owns a fish store in the town,' she said, stung into defence. 'And he's got a fishing boat as well.'

'He's been quite enterprising in his way,' Mr Nathan said, and all at once she saw the opportunity that she had been waiting for all week.

She seized it.

'He's put a little engine in it now – says that all boats will be engine-driven one day. Though folks round here don't like it very much. There's been a bit of trouble, actually – people accosting my family in the street.' Mr Nathan was looking daggers, as if she was disgracing him with this account, but she was not about to be deflected now. 'First it was my sister who was alarmed by them and then, the other day, one of the local fisherman met me on the road. He grabbed hold of me and started saying all sorts of horrid things to me. It was terrible. If it hadn't been for Mr Nathan turning up and making it clear he'd seen, I don't know what might have happened.'

She had the satisfaction of seeing the alteration in his face. 'My dear girl, I had no idea. I realized that there was some sort of scene, of course, and I'm glad I managed to put a stop to it. But had I known the ruffian was threatening you, I'd have laid about him with my whip.'

He looked so puffy-faced and solemn as he uttered this, that suddenly Winnie was hard put not to laugh. He was exactly like the penguin in a picture book at school – all black and shiny, self-important and absurd.

Mr Zachariah must have seen the laughter in her eyes. 'So my cousin Nathan rescued you – quite a knight errant, isn't he? I trust that you yourself sustained no harm.'

He was teasing her, she knew it. She lifted her head and smiled into his face. 'Fortunately I was perfectly all right, thank you. A little shaken at the time, that's all. And now, if you'll excuse me, gentlemen, I must collect the book.'

'Of course.' Mr Zachariah stood back to let her pass. 'Do give Aunt Millicent my best regards, and tell her that I look forward to her company.'

'I will,' Winnie promised and picked up the book. But as she went to leave, Mr Nathan accompanied her discreetly to the door.

'I'm sorry about – you know – all that,' he muttered, so that only she could hear. 'Should have known better, a nice girl like you.' And he actually reached out and squeezed her arm.

She gave him a quick smile. 'I'm just glad I was able to explain.' Though she did have the grace to feel abashed.

She had not lied exactly, she told herself as she went upstairs. Joe *had* said horrid things to her. Was it her fault if Mr Nathan drew his own conclusions from her words?

And it had turned out better than she could have dreamed. He had spoken warmly to her, and he'd squeezed her arm. Just what she had always hoped he'd do some day.

Why then did she feel slightly discontented?

'Winnie, what's got into you? You've been looking like a thundercloud all night.'

They were sitting together on the bed – the one they shared. (Gan had a second bed beside the wall, but neither of them ever sat on that.) They were sewing as they talked, taking advantage of the evening light that still streamed in through the window, though it was almost eight o'clock. Dora was making over an old dress of Mother's to make an autumn skirt for school – fortunately she was a good hand with a needle, and the material inside-out was good as new – while Winnie was adding new trimmings to a blouse to give it a fly-away lace collar like the new queen had.

'Mrs Zeal been finding fault again?' Dora continued, biting off her thread. However, when she glanced towards her twin it was obvious that Winnie was severely out of sorts. She was sighing and snapping threads impatiently, until at last she buried the needle in the cloth and bundled it away.

'It's not the slightest bit of use,' she said. 'I'm all thumbs tonight and it will have to be unpicked. Nothing's gone right for me today. And no, it isn't Mrs Zeal – or no more than usual. I got a wigging from Mr Nathan the other day, that's all. It's blown over now, but you know how upsetting it can be.'

Dora made a sympathetic face. 'What did you get a wigging

54

for? Strikes me you do a great deal more than read, though that's supposed to be what they pay you for.'

'Just that Joe Pollock. You know what he's like. Accosted me in the street again and made me look a proper idiot.'

She had gone bright pink and flustered, and Dora thought she understood the signs. She said wickedly, 'I thought you didn't mind him? That's what you told me. I do believe he's sweet on you, you know.'

Winnie got up from the bed and went across to gaze into the mirror on the washstand by the wall. 'Don't talk so daft.' She'd turned her back, but Dora could just see the reflection in the glass as Winnie pursed her lips up at herself and pushed her curls up with her fingertips. For all her pretence at flouncing, she had not managed to quite hide the ghost of a self-satisfied smile.

'What's so daft about it?' Dora said. 'I know he was keen on you at school. Forever giving me a sweet, he was, to stay behind and keep out the way so he could walk across the fields with you. You didn't seem to mind, as I recall. You didn't think he was so awful then.'

Winnie whirled on her with a snappishness that took Dora aback. 'All right, so I quite liked him. What difference does it make? I liked playing hoops and mumbly-pegs as well. I was a child then, don't you understand? Or perhaps you don't. You've never had a beau.' She said it nastily, but obviously thought better of it, because she caught Dora's glance and added with a smile, 'Unless you count that fellow who was making eyes at you in chapel, Sunday morning gone.'

That was the thing with Winnie. She could flare up at nothing just like Father did, especially when she was angry or worried or upset, but a moment later it passed and she was her normal self again.

Dora thought about Tom Trewin and went pink herself. 'No, of course I don't. And I don't want Joe Pollock either, thank you very much.'

'No more do I,' Winnie said ruefully, plumping herself down on the bed again. She looked at her sister with a rueful grin. 'Is that true what you said about the sweets? I never knew.'

'Course you didn't,' Dora said, glad that her sister had

cheered up a bit. 'Wasn't going to tell you, was I? Wouldn't have got my sweeties if I had. Anyway, did you confide in me?'

'Don't have to tell you everything.'

Dora chuckled. 'And no more do I. So I shan't say a single word about my secret beau, who's tall and handsome with amazing eyes and talks of whisking me off to the colonies some day.' It was wicked, but it did give her a thrill.

Winnie obviously didn't see Tom Trewin in that light. 'Oh, don't be dopey, Dora.' She picked up a feather pillow from Gan's bed and tossed it at her sister playfully. Dora picked it up and threw it back and in an instant they were in a cushion fight, squealing with laughter and rolling on the bed as if they were little girls again.

'What in pity's name is going on here?' That was Gan, glowering at them from the door. 'What do you two think you're playing at, making a racket at this time of night? Don't you know your mother isn't well? She has a headache, and your father wants to rest. And what have you been doing to that pillow, may I ask? You've got feathers everywhere. I want them picked up and put back, every single one. And when you've done that, you can come downstairs. There's wood to chop and water to be fetched. Plenty of work for idle hands if you've got nothing else to do than make a row up here. Thought you were sewing – or supposed to be!' And, still grumbling, she turned away.

Winnie made a face at her retreating back. '"Water to be fetched and wood to chop",' she mimicked, adding in her ordinary tone, 'Three times today I've been out to the barrel. Can't someone else fetch water for a change?'

'Oh come on, Win, it's not as bad as that.' Dora was picking up the feathers as she spoke. 'Who else is going to do it? Gan's too busy, Mother can't, Jamie would do it if he could but he's not well enough, and Father has been out at work all day.'

'Well, so have I been too. And so have you. It isn't fair. Why should some folk have everything, while others fetch and carry all day long? Look at Mrs Zeal now – nothing to do but worry about what to wear when Mr Zachariah comes to tea, while somebody else does all the work.'

Dora paused in the act of bending to pick up the feathers

56

from the floor. 'I wouldn't want to be her, though, would you? A frazzled-up old thing like that, with nothing to think about but her precious son.'

Winnie tossed her head. 'Well, if I was Mrs Nathan Zeal I could. And I could have new blouses if I liked, as well, instead of having to re-trim this beastly thing.'

Dora looked at her, shocked. 'Win, you wouldn't! Not that awful oily man?'

Winnie scowled. 'Why not, if he would have me? And he's not so bad. He's gentle and polite at any rate. Bad as Joe Pollock you are, finding fault. Though . . .'

'Though what?'

'Though nothing!' her twin said peevishly. 'Now, are we going to pick these feathers up, or sit and talk all day? Gan will have found more jobs for us by now.' She got on her hands and, for once, did more than Dora did.

By the time they had finished and gone back down the stairs, Gan had a dozen chores awaiting them.

Part Two

Autumn 1909

One

Nathan was planning his strategy with care, in stages, much as he would have planned a funeral. He had been heartened, the day of Zachariah's visit, to learn that Winifred was neither as flighty as he'd feared nor already spoken for. But, although that left the field open for himself, paying court to a young woman was not as easy as Mamma supposed, especially when you were not used to it.

Stage one in this process had passed off well enough – ensuring that he met Winifred in the house sometimes, and loitering to have a word with her. In fact he was pleased with his progress in that respect. At first he had found it very difficult to think of anything to say, once the 'good morning' or 'good afternoon' had been dispensed with. Instructions to a servant or the bereaved, he was familiar with, but he was not accustomed to idle social conversation with a girl, and some early exchanges had been very short. However, he had invested in a little book on etiquette, which gave suggestions for 'beginning small talk with a guest' and that had helped. While openings like 'Do you know everybody here?' and 'Do you like to ride?' were obviously not applicable, he had – with a bold leap of imagination – adapted some of them.

His first attempt was a hesitant 'Do you like to read?', inspired by the fact that Winifred was carrying a book. That had been a great success and next time he met her he had been emboldened to try a variation on the theme: 'Do you like to paint?'

By now he'd used a dozen opening gambits of the kind and was extremely grateful to the book. Winifred was always delighted to talk about herself, and he was learning more about her all the time. She'd even started asking him about himself, and conversations were far easier.

Today, when he met her in the hall as she was preparing to go home, he was unprepared. He had no question ready, but while they were exchanging the usual greetings he came up with one: 'Do you care for walking by the sea?'

To his amazement, she seized upon his words. 'Why, Mr Nathan!' she said, colouring. 'That would be delightful. What did you have in mind?'

That stumped him for a minute. Invitations were supposed to be stage two. He'd been thinking about working up to one, but here he had suddenly embarked on it, without having time to plan the thing at all.

He rallied. 'One evening when you've finished work, perhaps.' He had a sudden worry about impropriety, since he hadn't had time to consult his book on this, and was about to add, 'You might allow me to escort you home,' but Winifred was too quick for him.

'It's getting pretty dark, these evenings,' she observed. 'It might be better on Sunday afternoon. Where did you think of going?'

He hadn't thought at all. If he had chosen an activity, it would never have been this. He was not given to physical exertion, and did not greatly like the open air. Suppose she thought of walking on the cliffs? It was not seemly for a man in his walk of life, and the weather was inclement at this time of year. Yet now he had the opening he could not let it slip by. He hastened to think of something suitable.

'We could walk down the hill to Penvarris Cove, perhaps, if the weather's fine. It's quite steep but it's solid underfoot.'

He thought she looked a little disconcerted for an instant, but she smiled. 'This Sunday then, provided that it's fine. Perhaps you would be good enough to call for me?'

He said, 'With pleasure.'

And there it was. The thing was done. Mr Nathan Zeal had an assignation with a girl. He was inwardly delighted with himself, and when Winifred had put on her cape and gone he went upstairs and looked into the full-length mirror in his room.

'So kind of you to consent to come, Winifred,' he said to his reflection, practising a warmly courteous smile. So much for Mr Zachariah Zeal! Nathan could escort a lady too. He cut a reasonable figure, he told himself, if he stood up straight and held his stomach in.

He was a little nervous of going to tell Mamma, but all she said was, 'And about time too. I told you she would jump at the opportunity. Though I must say, Nathan, you might have chosen something a little more appropriate – a concert perhaps, or something of the kind – rather than walking down a public road she's walked a hundred times, going nowhere in particular, under the eye of everyone for miles. Still, it is a beginning, I suppose. I presume she does not propose to bring a chaperone?'

Nathan had to murmur that he didn't know.

'She might bring her sister, I suppose,' Mamma went on. 'Though since you're related, it doesn't signify. Well, I'm glad you've taken the initiative at last. I was beginning to think you never would.'

He never did tell her how it came about.

Harvey Pierce was predictably absent from school for the whole of harvest time. Miss Blewitt was fretting that he would turn up again just in time for the inspectors' annual autumn visit to the school, but he didn't. The inspectors noted his absence record with a frown, but that was better, Miss Blewitt said, than questions about why his progress was so poor.

In general the report was good. The ash pile was criticized again; senior mental arithmetic 'would repay additional attention', and there was some disquiet about recitation work – 'memorized poetry was satisfactory, though it was rendered in sing-song fashion and without regard to rhythm or common standards of pronunciation' – meaning that the Cornish accent was too strong.

Dora had to smile ruefully at that. She had spent much effort on elocution with the younger ones, but no amount of chorusing ''Arry 'ad a 'addock at 'enrietta's 'ouse,' could make these country children learn to aspirate an 'h'. Flat-seam work, infant behaviour and junior reading had all been commended, and that gave her a little glow of pride. But the inspectors did note with concern a 'lack of properly certificated staff', and that had started Miss Blewitt off at Dora again, fussing about her training properly.

If only she could, Dora thought, but it was useless talking to Father about it – worse than useless when he was in this sort of mood. Just as the weather was turning for the worse with autumn squalls and rising winds, when the new petroleum engine should have come into its own, it had begun to give all sorts of trouble – sea water in the system, or something of the kind. Several times the other boats had all put out to sea while Charlie and the crew were stuck beside the harbour wall, wrestling to start the *Cornish Rose*. They had actually twice resorted to fishing under sail, which infuriated Father, since it was an admission of defeat, and even then Charlie had been heard to mutter that the engine weighed a ton and made the boat a pig to handle in a storm. It all made Father crosser than two sticks, and the jeers of the likes of Joe Pollock didn't help.

Emphatically *not* a time to raise the subject of educating girls.

Dora sighed, and turned her attention to the classroom stove. The caretaker and cleaner, Mrs Bates, had cleared the ashes to the pit and set and lit the fire for the day, but it was Dora's task to keep an eye on it and feed it with a shovelful of coal from time to time. It was raining like the seven seas outside, and when the children came in from the yard they would be soaked through to their skins, and the iron rail that ran around the stove would soon be draped with steaming coats and socks, while sodden boots were turned soles-up and set to dry nearby. The stove would have to be well stoked today.

She was in the act of lifting up the lid with the hooked iron poker to inspect the fire, when the classroom door opened and a child came in, dragging a smaller infant by the hand. Their faces, clothes and hair were streaming wet with rain, so that they dripped little pools of moisture where they stood.

Dora opened her mouth to issue a rebuke. Pupils were not permitted inside the school until the bell had rung – there was a roofed shelter by the toilet blocks where they could line up and wait until the summons came.

'What are you . . .' she began, and then saw who it was under the uncharacteristically flat and plastered hair. 'Harvey Pierce!'

The boy framed his shivering lips into a smile. 'Yes, Miss. It's me and Poppy. Ma says is she big enough to come?'

'Well . . .' Dora hesitated. 'That all depends. What age is Poppy, then?' She looked at the infant, who was regarding her with big, suspicious eyes. A tiny, solemn scrap, with a running nose, tangled auburn hair and outsize boots and pinafore – so small she looked hardly three years old, let alone the four that was the accepted minimum.

Harvey's grin faded on his lips. 'She's almost four, Miss. Honest. Do let her stay, Miss, then I can come meself. Ma can't manage on her own with they three babies all at home.' He was blinking back the tears, she realized.

Poppy, perhaps perceiving this, began to cry. She made no move to wipe her eyes or nose, but simply stood there, howling noisily, tears mingling with the shining moisture on her face.

'Here, Poppy! Shut that up or they'll send you 'ome for sure,' Harvey muttered fiercely, giving his sister's hand a sharp little tug. 'You'll get to like it by and by. And, see what I told you, it's nice and warm in 'ere.'

Too late. Miss Blewitt had already heard the noise as she came bustling in from the schoolhouse opposite.

'Harvey Pierce! Whatever is all this?' she demanded briskly. She took off her cape, which was already glistening with the rain, and hung it on the hook behind the door. 'And who is this apparition?'

'It's his sister, Poppy,' Dora said, suddenly appointing herself the children's champion.

Miss Blewitt met Dora's eyes and raised her brows. She turned to Harvey. 'She really isn't old enough to come. I'm sorry, Harvey, I don't make the rules.'

'But . . .' Harvey blurted. He looked close to tears. 'Please . . .'

Dora bit her lip and looked at the headmistress beseechingly. The children were both shivering, she saw.

Even Miss Blewitt seemed to hesitate. She sighed. 'Very well, Harvey,' she said at last. 'Poppy can stay here for the day. As for the future, we'll just have to see. Now, you leave her here with us, while you go outside and ring the bell for me.'

'Me, Miss?' Harvey said, his grubby face alight with pleasure at this unexpected dignity. Ringing the bell was generally a sought-after privilege, awarded only for neat work and good behaviour.

'Quickly, before I change my mind,' Miss Blewitt said. She shook her head and added in an undertone, 'They're all the same, these mothers, send the children here when they are really far too young to learn, and just disrupt the class, because they can't look after them at home . . . Now, stop that noise!' This last was to Poppy who had set up a wail again, but who lapsed into obedient silence instantly.

Miss Blewitt fetched a piece of rag and wiped the child's nose and face, while Dora did her best to dry the hair. Outside in the playground, streaming wet but suffused with pride, Harvey was ringing the bell with all his might, as if the future of the realm depended on the sound.

Tom knew that something was amiss the minute he walked through the door. The table not laid and the fire gone out, a pail and scrubbing brush abandoned on the floor – that was not like Mother, not at all. He took off his cap and coat to hang them up and frowned. No sign of Father's jacket on the peg, or of Lenny's either. No working boots in the box beside the door, as there should have been if anyone was in. Tom had been working a double shift, but the others should have been home hours ago.

And where was Mother at this time of night?

'Ma?' Tom stood at the bottom of the stairs and called. No answer. It was strange. Only twice before in all his eighteen years had he ever come home to a wholly empty house, and that was when Gran and Grandfather had died.

'Mother?' he hollered with more urgency. And then, mercifully, she came bustling in, wiping wet hands on her pinny as she came. She was unhurt as far as he could see, but she looked flustered, pale and grim, and her hair was escaping from its pins and hanging in untidy streaks around her face.

'Where is everyone?' he enquired at once. 'What's happening? Is everything all right.'

'I'm some sorry, Tom, I didn't mean for you to get home to find the house in uproar and your tea not made,' she said. The kettle was already on the hearth and she put it on to boil. 'It's just that child next door has been taken bad. Come out in an awful rash again, but hotter'n a furnace with it this time, too. Mrs Pierce sent the eldest boy around to ask me could I come and keep an eye, while she went round the village to see if anybody had some camomile. Well, course I went. What could I say, poor soul?'

Tom raised his eyebrows in a gesture of despair. 'Let's hope it isn't something catching then, that's all.'

'Isn't likely,' Mother said. 'That child's been allergical ever since it was born. Ought to have the doctor to her really, she gets that bad, but the fact is, Tom, they can't afford to have the doctor call. The poor woman does the best she can, but it's hard enough to put food on the table for them all.' She began to busy herself fetching plates and knives, a loaf, pickles and an end of cheese. 'Truth is, son, I felt that sorry for those mites, I took the bit of stew I'd put aside for you. Was going to scramble you an egg when you got home but here you are ahead of me. You eat this up, and I'll fix that egg for you in less time than it takes to tell.'

'It's all right, Mother, this'll do me fine. I had my bit of crowst at dinnertime. So, how's the baby now?' He took the breadknife from her and cut himself a hefty round of bread.

Mother fetched a breathy sigh. 'Sleeping peacefully, thank heaven – though whether that's the camomile or whether she just cried herself to sleep, I couldn't say. But anyway, here I am at last. I'm some sorry you had to come home hungry to an empty house.'

'It doesn't matter, Mother, so long as everything's all right.' He made himself a sandwich, and fell on it greedily. 'What about Father and Lenny, where are they?' he added, swallowing.

Ma made a face. 'Gone down this evening to the Miner's Arms. Hear this union fellow, if you heard the like. Course, Lenny's all for it, you know what he's like. Nothing would do but that he should go down the public house and listen to that tripe.' She poured a cup of tea for Tom, and plonked the milk jug down with extra force. 'Making an exhibition of himself!'

'Father's gone down there too?' That was a surprise. Father usually wouldn't hear a word of union talk.

'Gone there to keep an eye on Len, or so he says. I wish he wouldn't, but I can't change his mind. Gone to heckle, if you ask me. God help us, if Lenny catches him! Almost came to blows before they set off as it was. And what for, that's what I want to know. All very fine, this talk of unionism and extra pay, but where's it going to come from, with the price of tin so low?'

It was a long speech for Mother and her cheeks were flushed. Tom nodded. She didn't like this, and it was easy to see why. There had been several walkouts down Penvarris years ago, when the standard price of tin was dropped, and once over the price of candles in the tally shop where the men were forced to go to buy their own. But it always ended up the same way, with everyone going back in a week or so, when times got hard. And when there was nothing coming in, it was always the womenfolk who bore the brunt of it. Everyone had heard the stories of those times: wives begging for credit at the village store, pawning what few objects they possessed to buy a bag of flour, or trying to conjure food from hedgerows to feed their families, even if they scarcely ate themselves.

'All the same, Ma, it does a bit of good sometimes. They won their argument about the candles, didn't they? Or at least they forced the shareholders to listen to their case and give them candles cheap.'

Mother snorted. 'And the next time the price of tin dropped and they laid off men, who do you think were the first to go? The ones who led the strike, of course! Up in the workhouse after, some of them. I'm not so young I don't remember that. I told your father straight. Don't think that the mine-owners won't know who was at the Miner's Arms tonight, because they will. And it won't matter a hoot if you just went to jeer. They won't be in the meeting taking notes. They'll just know that you were up there. They'll be making lists, same as they always do. But would he listen? No, not him, of course.'

Tom avoided looking her in the eye, and turned his attention to his tea instead. He was glad he hadn't gone to tonight's gathering himself. The union representative had come into the engine house that day, urging everyone to come and listen to the talk, but he'd been so busy with getting the Duchess up to steam that he hadn't given it another thought.

Of course, he'd heard all the arguments from Len. 'It isn't like it used to be, last century,' he always said. 'The working man has got the vote. They've got to listen to us now, or we'll have Lloyd George out of parliament and put our own man in.'

Now that would be something, wouldn't it? Choosing the government. He might have gone and listened if there hadn't been a crisis at the pit.

The pump engine at North Shaft had sheered a pin and lost a counterweight. Jack Maddern ordered her stopped from steam at once – though she almost shook herself to pieces as it was. Course, that meant every other pump was working twice as hard. Bill Handiman still wasn't back to help, and Jack Maddern needed every man he had to keep the levels drained, or half the miners would have had to go back home and gone short for the week – their wages depended on the weight of the tin they won. So Tom had driven the Duchess sixteen hours straight through, up to full steam as well, doing his own stoking half the time till his head rang and his arms and shoulders ached.

Mind, he would be paid for it or get time off in lieu, and he'd managed to snatch an hour or so of rest – if you could call it that, lying on a wooden settle with one ear open for any change of engine note. But it had been worth the effort in the end. Cap'n Maddern had made a point of coming up to him, saying, 'Well done, lad! We'll make a proper engine man of you yet!'

Tom smiled at the memory. Better than the extra pay, that was. He grinned, thinking what his brother Len would say if he heard him talk like that. 'Some unionist you'd make!' He could just imagine it.

''Tisn't funny,' Mother said, misinterpreting the grin. 'If it wasn't for that bit of money your brother sends me from Australia, I don't know how I'd manage sometimes as it is.'

'I know, Ma,' he said placatingly. 'I was thinking about something else, that's all.'

'Mooning about that stuck-up schoolmistress of yours, I suppose.' She cleared away the tea things with an affronted air.

'Of course I wasn't, Mother!' he called as she went out into the scullery. But naturally after that he could think of little else, until Lenny and Father came home arguing and he was forced to turn his mind to other things.

Two

Poppy Pierce was not really settling down at school. She was as much a fidget as Harvey himself had been, and though she did her best, doing more or less as she was told and joining in the lessons when she could, she was nevertheless a disturbance to the class. She scribbled on the blackboard with the teacher's chalk, cried whenever Dora spoke to her, and kept having to be escorted to the toilet block – invariably not in time.

Harvey, though, had become a different boy. The fact of having a younger sister in the class seemed to give him a sense of responsibility. It didn't stop him playing on the ash pit or making whistles out of bits of grass, but he was now often first to put his hand up – whether he got the answer right or not – and he'd been chosen several times to ring the bell. He was even making progress in his number work. His writing was as wayward as it had ever been, but Dora had moved him up a level in his letters, too, to save him the shame of being in the same group as Poppy. Harvey was responding splendidly.

Perhaps that was why Miss Blewitt had still not carried out her threat. No letters had been written to the parents or the Board, and Poppy continued to attend, though the headmistress muttered to Dora every day that something must be done soon to regulate affairs.

It was the spots that brought matters to a head. Dora didn't notice them at first. Poppy often had a rash around her mouth. Her face was never particularly clean, even when she had been sent outside with a bar of soap and told to wash it in the handbasin. She would come in looking a little more respectable, but half an hour later the combination of a runny nose and grimy sleeve would have contrived to return the situation to where it started.

This morning, though, even the cold wash had no effect and Poppy, far from fidgeting about, seemed increasingly list-less as the hours passed. Dora went across to speak to her and noticed that the flush of red was now not only round the child's mouth, but up her neck and spreading down her arms and legs as well.

Dora knew from her own schooldays what to do. An outbreak of scarletina had killed two children in her class. She stopped the lesson instantly and fetched the headmistress.

Miss Blewitt's reaction was immediate. 'Harvey, I'm sorry, you'll have to take your sister home. Tell your mother she's to keep her there until the spots have gone. You too. I think these are the measles, and you can't come here with those. You'll have the whole school off sick otherwise – though where she caught them from, I've no idea. Is anybody else in the family sick?'

'Only the baby,' Harvey muttered. 'It's always ill. And Ma isn't very well today.'

'Well there you are then,' Miss Blewitt said. 'Go on. You get your hats and coats and go off now.'

'But I aren't spotty,' Harvey wailed.

'I'm sorry, Harvey, there's no argument. It's in the rules. Now, are you going, or do I have call the doctor here?'

'No, Miss Blewitt,' Harvey said, and off he went, dragging his little sister by the hand. By this time the child looked so flushed and unsteady on her feet that Dora worried she might pass out before she got home, so twenty minutes later, when it was dinner-hour, with Miss Blewitt's blessing she forwent her lunch and followed the children's route herself, just to make sure they'd got there safe and sound.

She didn't have Harvey's hobbling to slow her down today, and she made good progress. She calculated that she just had time to walk the mile or so each way and still arrive back at school at one to take the senior girls for sewing class.

It was a breezy afternoon, but fine, and she enjoyed the walk. It was not often she had the freedom to do this, listening to the seagulls wheeling overhead and watching the workers on a distant farm expertly forking up the sheaves of hay to make a stack – or 'mow' as they called it hereabouts.

There was no sign of Harvey and his sister on the road, nor on the path across the fields, and she had almost decided

71

to give up when she saw them – two tiny figures squatting on a stile near Farmer Crowdie's barn, perhaps a quarter of a mile ahead.

Poppy was evidently being sick, and Harvey had his arm protectively around her back. Dora began hurrying towards them to assist when she realized that the farmer himself was clopping down the lane. Perhaps he had noticed their distress because he'd saddled up his horse and cart, and was stopping by the stile to pick them up.

Dora let out a little heartfelt sigh as she watched the children clamber up and saw the cart go rattling up the hill. There was nothing to worry about; they'd be all right now. She was about to turn back and retrace her steps when a familiar voice shouted, 'Dora? Miss Hunkin? Wait for me!'

She turned, feeling her heart lift and a smile rising to her lips.

'Tom?' she cried with undisguised delight. 'Whatever are you doing here, this time of day?'

He hurried down the field path to the road. The day had felt bleak and depressing up to now, despite the clear skies and autumn sun, but it suddenly seemed brighter at the sight of her. Nettles and brambles clutched at him as he passed, as if determined to impede his path. He didn't stop to look where he was going, and once he almost slipped and lost his cap, but at last he had reached the lower gate and skiddle-skaddled through the mud to reach her side.

'Never thought I'd see you here,' she said as he stumbled up, panting and breathless. 'Thought you'd be working, half past twelve.' She didn't look as if she minded, though.

'Might say the same thing about you.' He grinned. 'Fact is, I worked a double shift the other day, when one of the other engines shed a rod, and this is time that I've got off in lieu.'

'You don't look very pleased about it,' Dora said.

Tom made a face. 'I was hoping for a bit extra in my pay, but no such luck.' He felt like telling someone of his woes, so he poured it out to her. 'But that's not the worst of it. They patched up the broken engine and got her up to steam, but she isn't right, and there's some damage to the beam as well. All cost a fortune to repair. Seems they might even have to seal off that shaft, with the price of tin the way it is. Then,

72

of course, they'll have more drivers than they need. Course, I might be lucky, but it isn't good. They'll be turning underground men off, as well.'

She nodded sympathetically, but he could see that she didn't understand the half of it. He was tempted to tell her what was really on his mind – how the union men were urging stoppages, and how Father and Lenny were at loggerheads at home – but instead he finished lamely, 'Well, that's me accounted for. Now it's your turn. What are you doing up here, dinnertime?'

He saw a shadow flit across her face. 'Oh, Poppy Pierce came to school with spots, that's all. Miss Blewitt sent her and Harvey home. I just came out to make sure they'd got there all right.'

He looked at her with admiration. 'You're some good to those children that you teach. I'm damty sure my teachers never thought so much of me.'

She frowned. 'Tom! Language!' But it only made him laugh.

'Well, it's true. But then, I never had a teacher that I cared about.' He looked at her. 'Not till now, at any rate,' he added daringly. She was so pretty when she blushed, he had to thrust his hands into his coat so that he didn't reach out and hold her there and then. 'I mean it,' he said. 'You know I do. I think an awful lot of you.'

'I know you do, Tom.' She was pinker than the geraniums by Crowdie's garden wall. She looked away. 'I think a lot about you, too.'

'Here, Dora, look at me.' Her turned her to face him, and took her hand. She didn't draw it back. 'Could you, you know, think of me that way?' He saw the trouble in her eyes and added quickly, 'Not just now perhaps, but one day? You know I'd do anything for you.'

She said nothing, but her hand was still in his.

He raised her fingers and touched them to his lips. 'Then why won't you say yes? Or do you only want me as a friend? Is that it?'

She shook her head. ''Tisn't as simple as all that, Tom. Do you know what my father would have to say if he caught me standing here with you?'

'He wouldn't approve of you talking to young men? Doesn't he want for you to wed some day?' He was anxious to impress

73

her suddenly, and regretted what he's said about the broken pump. 'I got prospects, Dora. I know I said there was a bit of worry down the mine just now, but there's got to be good prospects in the end for a man who works with steam. I could go on the railways if it gets too bad – or go off to Australia, like I said before. I got a brother out there, and he's doing well. I'd go, and make a life for us, and when you were ready you could come to me. If you'd have me, Dora? Surely even your father couldn't disapprove of that.'

She laughed, a laugh of such bitterness that it startled him. 'Disapprove? You don't know him, Tom. Father could disapprove of anything, unless he thought it up himself. He'll turn up at the Pearly Gates one day and find fault with how they're kept.'

He shook his head. It occurred to him with some astonishment that he seemed to have just proposed to her. 'So you don't want even to consider it?'

She turned to him, and he could see that tears were shining in her eyes. 'It isn't that I don't want to, Tom. It's that I can't. You don't know Father – I keep telling you. He'll shout and storm and stamp and make everyone's life a misery – more of a misery than it already is. He won't only take it out on me, he'll take it out on Mother, and Jamie most of all, and I can't stand that, Tom, I really can't. He gets so violent sometimes, you can't imagine it.'

Tom, whose father would walk a mile to miss an argument – unless it was a matter of moral principle, like the union thing of Len's – gazed at her in astonishment. 'You mean he hits you?'

Dora went scarlet and turned her head away. 'No, it isn't that exactly, though he has laid into Jamie once or twice. It's more . . . Oh, I don't know. I just know he'd put a stop to it, that's all.'

'I'll go and talk to him. I'll explain . . .'

'No, Tom! Can't you understand? Better that he doesn't even know that you exist. If you were wealthy, with a fish shop in the town, it would be a different thing. It wouldn't matter then if you were fifty-five and had a warty nose, he'd probably decide that you were just the man. But as it is, it's hopeless. He thinks we're a cut above, because he's trade.'

74

'I'm not good enough for you, you mean?'

'It's not me saying that, Tom! I'm telling you what answer you would get. You're a man, you don't know what it's like for me. He'd only forbid me to talk to you at all, and that's the very last thing I'd want.' Tom was a little cheered by that, and was about to tell her so, but she added tearfully, 'He'd probably make me leave the school as well.'

It was obvious she meant it and he would have dropped her hand, but she wound her fingers round his and would not let go.

'Don't be upset, Tom. It isn't that I don't like you. Course I do. If it was down to me I'd . . .' She tailed off.

He twirled her round to look at him again. 'You'd what?'

She shook her head and looked away. 'I'd . . . Nothing. I don't know. I wouldn't have to say these things.' She sighed. 'It's hopeless, isn't it?'

'It's not hopeless if you love me, and I think you do. Don't you?'

She still wouldn't look him in the eyes. 'Tom, don't go on so much. I don't know. Perhaps.' Now she did snatch her hand away from him and began to walk away.

He caught her up and took her by the waist. 'No, Dora. Stop and listen to me, please. Of course I can't ask you for an answer yet. You're – what – almost seventeen?'

She nodded.

'In four or five years you will come of age, and it won't matter what your father thinks.'

She raised her head to him. 'Four and a half years is a long time,' she said in a strained little voice. 'You mightn't want me then.'

'You let me worry about that,' he said. 'What do you say?'

'Tom, I can't promise anything out of the blue like this. I need time to think. And I've got to be getting back to school – I only came out for half an hour.'

He was immediately penitent. 'Course you have. It isn't fair to spring all this on you. I didn't mean to do it, but you look so beautiful. I wish that you'd just tell me I could hope, that's all.' He looked down at her, and in an instant she was in his arms and he was pressing kisses on her cheeks and lips.

For a breath-stopping moment she returned his kiss, and then she pulled away. 'Tom, you are a caution, honestly! Out

75

here on the road! Suppose someone had seen us?' But her cheeks were flushed and she was smiling helplessly.

'I don't care if the whole world knows,' Tom said, half-drunk with happiness, and went to take her in his arms again.

This time she was more sober. 'Oh, Tom, don't. What if somebody tells Father? Where are we then?' She pulled away. 'And it really is important that I go.'

He tried to hold her back. 'You're mad with me?'

She smiled. 'Of course I'm not. And I enjoyed the kiss. Only I'm going to be late for the bell otherwise.'

'I'll see you Sunday then.' He didn't try to stop her after that, or walk with her on the public road. He simply went down to the stile and stood on it so that he could watch her hurrying out of sight. She hadn't given him encouragement exactly, but her warmth was so much more than he had dared to hope that he walked home fairly floating on delight. Not even Father and Lenny squabbling could ruin his evening after that.

Dora didn't see him again all week, and that bothered her. Perhaps it was only that he was working late, but though she looked out for him every afternoon, he didn't come, not even on the evenings of the Institute class. But on Sunday morning, there he was, waiting for her on the chapel steps as usual.

She went over to him, feeling her cheeks turn scarlet as she went, conscious of the eyes of the old women in the congregation watching her. Surely they must realize what was happening. She felt as if the evidence of that kiss must be imprinted on her for the world to see.

Tom seemed a little awkward too, and after a stiff 'Good morning' the conversation flagged.

She looked around for a neutral topic. 'And how are Harvey and Poppy and the little ones?' She said it partly for the benefit of old Mrs Johnson, who was standing close by.

He seized on the subject gratefully. 'Still pretty poorly, I'm afraid. You and Miss Blewitt were quite right to send the children home. All the family is down with spots and fever now – even Mother won't go in there without she scrubs herself with carbolic afterwards.'

'Poor things,' she said with feeling. Her instincts had been right. Mrs Johnson had lost interest now and moved away.

76

Tom met her eyes. 'And how are you?' he murmured, softly enough that no one else could hear. 'Have you forgiven me for what I did?'

'There's nothing to forgive.' She turned pink again.

He took her elbow and walked beside her down towards the gate, talking in an undertone all the while. 'I've cursed myself all week for being such a fool. Just to blurt out with it like that! No wonder you were flustered. It wasn't what I meant to do at all. I've thought about telling you how I felt, scores of times, but not like that. I meant to be more gentle, hold your hand, put my arm around you once or twice – but somehow when I saw you standing there like that, I just came out with it. Please God I haven't spoiled everything.'

She looked at him. 'I wondered if you'd thought better of it when I hadn't seen you all the week.'

He grinned. 'I was working late shift every afternoon. Couldn't get out of it nohow. Though I confess I was a bit nervous about meeting you again, after what I said and did last time.'

She laughed. 'And here I was afraid you'd changed your mind.'

'Change my mind? I meant it. You remember what I said.'

Suddenly her embarrassment had fled. 'As if I'm likely to forget! Truly, Tom, I'm flattered – and I do care for you. But I told you, I need more time to think.' She was still speaking in an undertone as he had done, and she might have said more, but then she looked up and Winnie was coming towards them. She went on quickly in an ordinary voice, 'Do tell Harvey and Poppy that I hope they're better soon.'

It wasn't often that she kept secrets from her twin, but something told her that this time she must. Tom Trewin was too precious to be teased about.

Winnie, mercifully, was too busy thinking of her own concerns to worry about her sister's possible romance. 'Come on, Dora,' she cried impatiently. 'You know I'm in a hurry to get home. I've got to go out for a walk this afternoon.'

Three

So the Sunday of the promised walk had come. Winnie had been twitchy all the way through chapel, with her mind not on the service in the least.

Suddenly she wasn't at all sure that she was looking forward to the afternoon, but since she had been boasting of nothing else for days, there was no way of avoiding the assignation now. She gave herself a little shake – she was being silly, that was all. This was exactly what she'd wanted, wasn't it? And Mother had been so delighted when she heard, it brought a little colour to her cheeks. 'Think of it, Winnie – what a chance for you.' And Father, for once, had agreed with her.

Whatever should she wear? Her going-to-chapel costume was a bit severe, even with her best blue bonnet and the blouse that she had trimmed. If she was to be seen in genteel company she must look the part. Perhaps if she wore just the skirt and blouse with her short cape over it, that would be better and more feminine – a bit chilly if there was a breeze, but it shouldn't be too bad provided that the wind did not turn easterly, as Father had said earlier that it might. And if . . .

'Winnie!' Dora had had to dig her sharply in the rib to bring her to herself, and Winnie rose sheepishly to her feet to join in the closing hymn.

Now that the service was over she was eager to be off, but when she turned around to look, her twin was loitering to talk to that Trewin boy again. And Joe Pollock, of course, was hanging round the way he always did.

Winnie looked around for an escape, but could only find big fat Ruby White, a red-faced girl who scrubbed out the fish-store floor. Winnie went across to her, and asked her how she did, and then had to listen to her tedious tales about her wretched children and how the littlest one could nearly walk until Joe gave up in disgust and went away.

'What was all that about?' she challenged Dora when at last her sister broke away, and they were walking home along the lane. 'Think you two hadn't met for years, the way you were jawing on.'

Dora turned pink. 'Just talking about those children who live next door to him. They're off with measles, and I wondered how they were.'

Winnie sighed. And all this while she was waiting to go home and get ready to go out! She couldn't keep her exasperation to herself. 'Dear heaven, Dora! Isn't it enough to be teaching all the week, without dragging your work into the weekends too?'

Dora, for once, was unrepentant. 'Well if you wanted to go earlier, you should have said. Anyway you don't have to be so cross. You're going out with your beau this afternoon, so why are you suddenly snappier than a crab?'

That reduced Winnie to a sulking silence, and her restless mood lasted all through dinnertime, when the whole family conspired to tease her wretchedly. Every reference to the coming walk made her crosser than before, and as soon as she could decently escape – Gan had let her off washing the dishes in honour of the day – she rushed upstairs. She spent so long titivating herself (as Dora would have said) in front of the bedroom mirror and arranging her bonnet in the most becoming way, that she almost wasn't ready when Mr Nathan called.

He was dressed in the same way that he always was, in faded black, although he had honoured the occasion with a new maroon cravat. It made him look more funereal than ever, Winnie thought, though she went out to greet him with a smile.

Mother, with unaccustomed energy, came out to greet him in the hall and was obviously impressed and overawed – you could tell from the nervous way she screwed up her handkerchief and put on what Father called her 'Jenkins voice'. Father himself had gone out to the boat, but Mr Nathan was invited into the front room, which smelled of dust and polish and disuse, and was even asked if he would like a drink.

He looked a little startled, but said, 'Perhaps a very small one, then. I sometimes have a glass of something with my customers.'

That caused a slight embarrassment, since Mother, being Methodist, was only thinking of a cup of tea and wouldn't even have a drop of Christmas sherry in the house. Of course Father grumbled and ranted about that, and sometimes went off down the public house to have a pint or two, but Gan sided with Mother over this, and so she had her way. There was no 'glass of something' to be had.

Mr Nathan passed the moment off by saying that he rarely drank himself, except in the course of business, while Mother murmured that it was quite all right.

'And how is your dear mother keeping now?' she added, and the conversation turned to other things. All the same, Winnie was relieved when the courtesies were over and the two of them were free to take their walk at last.

It wasn't altogether comfortable. Mr Nathan offered her his arm, and although Winnie felt quite the lady as they strolled down the lane and out towards the harbour, it was all rather stilted and peculiar. Mr Nathan seemed to have nothing much to say, and when she ventured an occasional remark, about the season or the weather or the view, he only answered in a word or two and gave her his solemn little smile.

Perhaps this is what it was like to be a lady, Winnie thought. It was all very different from those long, laughing wanders through the fields with Joe . . . But no! She brought herself up short. She would not allow herself to dwell on that. Somehow she must find a way to break the ice. Mr Nathan, she was almost sure from the stiff way in which he held himself, was finding this as difficult as she was herself.

What was he interested in, she wondered. She had tried asking questions about his family, but that hadn't worked. Funerals, that was the only other thing. Almost in desperation, she asked a question about a burial in Pendeen the week before and, rather to her surprise, it did the trick. He told her all about it – more, indeed, than she had wished to know – but he squeezed her hand against him as she held his arm, and talked as if it really mattered that she understood.

He was still talking to her in this way, leaning towards her with his face aglow, when Joe Pollock and his brothers sauntered by, going down to the *Silver Gull* no doubt. Joe, in his sea boots and oilies, looked three times the man that Nathan was, but when he glanced across and realized who she was and who was walking with her, he almost seemed to shrink. His swagger vanished and he clenched his fists and scowled, like a little boy deprived of treats, she thought.

Winnie felt a little surge of power, and she turned back to Nathan with a winning air, smiling and nodding warmly as if he were the most fascinating man alive, as he told her about glass coffins and white ribbons and the use of ice.

Stan was not having a successful day.

First there was Sybil simpering like a fool because that undertaker fellow was about to call. All right, so it was a good match for Winnie – he accepted that – but was that a reason why a man should have to wait ten minutes for his cup of tea, because his wife had suddenly decided to start fussing with her hair?

He had intended to meet the man himself – it was a father's duty, after all – and he would have done if Sybil hadn't started nagging him. Wanted him to put on his good shirt, no less, as if it was a wedding or a funeral, if you ever heard such nonsense in your life.

'Dress up like a prize turkey, and for what? If Nathan Zeal is coming, well and good, but he's paying court to Winnie, not the other way about. Think it was the King coming, the way that you're going on.'

'But, Stan ...' Sybil had become all white and whining like she sometimes did. 'It's Sunday after all. And it means a lot to Winnie, can't you see? Do it for her sake, if you won't for mine.'

In general he could count on his own mother for support, but she was on Sybil's side for once. 'Perhaps you really ought to, Stan. Isn't this what you were hoping for when you let the girl go up to Mrs Zeal in the first place?'

Well, of course, that put the lid on it. He wasn't going to put up with that. Wasn't a man master in his own home any more? It was a wonder he hadn't smashed the tea cup in his hand. 'Can't you two bloody women learn to hold your peace, and stop nagging a man to death in his own house? Anyway,

81

I shan't be here, shall I? Told you I was going down to the boat this afternoon.'

Of course, he hadn't said anything of the kind. In fact he'd just decided on it then. It ought to be all right, although Charlie wouldn't be expecting him. The *Cornish Rose* had come in very late – not until yesterday afternoon – full to the gunnels with a great load of fish. He'd had to have the fish store working late to cope with it, and all the jousters and fish hawkers had been down the jetty too, buying off the boat as she came in. Always on the watch, they were, for any boat that came in loaded down. You could tell a decent catch from how high she was riding on the sea.

So by the time they'd got her all hosed down and cleaned, and the men had gone home to have a bit of sleep, they wouldn't be putting out again till late. Well, if he'd missed her, he'd come home again. He was master of his ship, so he could do what he liked – he didn't have to tell the women in advance, though they were both staring at him now.

'So, you getting me my 'lowance bag or not?' he barked, referring to the canvas pouch containing bread and meat and cheese that every fisherman took with him when he went out overnight. 'I'll want to eat, besides. Got to get down in time to catch the tide.'

Then, of course, nothing more was said. Trying to make him out to be unreasonable. Well, he knew their tricks. Stan drank his tea in silence while the women fetched the Sunday cold meat and potato to the table and that wretched boy cowered in the corner like the hopeless thing he was. There was still an atmosphere when the girls came home from chapel and sat down to have their meal.

And then Winnie wanted to start on about her visitor, until her mother silenced her with a warning look. It was enough to drive a man to drink. In the end he'd bolted down his food as fast as possible and had come down to the boat to have a bit of peace.

But there was no peace to be had this afternoon. He could tell there was something wrong as soon as he arrived. Far from being ready to put out to sea (many of the other boats had gone) Charlie and the boys were kneeling on the deck with the cover off the engine while the nets, which had been drying on the wall and should have been neatly stowed by now, were heaped up beside them in untidy piles.

Charlie looked up at Stan as he approached, his face furrowed in a worried frown.

'What's going on here then, Charlie?' Stan enquired. 'Hope you aren't going to tell me that the damty thing won't start?'

Charlie shook his head. 'Be a wonder if she did, the way things are. Just going to send for you, we were, Cap'n. But here you are, and saved the boys a trip. Something's been going on here, and I don't know what. Somebody's got it in for you, by the looks of things. Slashed the big nets, for one thing – look at them! It's taken the boys half an hour just to sort out where the damage is.'

Stan scowled. 'Who'd do a dastard thing like that?' Despite the general feeling in the area about him and the *Cornish Rose*, he couldn't credit this. It was unheard of for any local fisherman to interfere with someone else's gear – though, admittedly there had been incidents years ago with some of the east coast skippers who came down and poached the catch. 'Snagged them on something last time you were out, more like.'

Any other man might have bridled at his words, but Charlie simply pursed his lips and spat expertly into the harbour. 'They were all right when we left them there last night, and this morning they were damaged, that's all I know. Clean cuts too, all in a little row just where they gather to the rope. Like as if somebody'd hacked them with a knife. Good job the boys noticed it before we went, or next time we shot the nets we'd have lost a half of them. We'll have to make do with the smaller ones tonight.'

Stan's mood darkened further. The new nets were part of his refitting of the boat, and they had been a considerable cost. None of your second-hand nets or do-it-yourself curing by boiling up the nets in a pot of steaming bark above the fire for him. He'd had these made especially for him, by a factory that had a net machine and bark house over towards Mevagissey, and they'd only just had their first six-weekly wash and redipping in tar and Burma cutch. And now they would have to be repaired – which meant more days and nights without using them at sea – and he had lost the advantage of the deep nets besides.

'You wait till I catch the blighter who did this to me! Must have been somebody around who saw.'

Charlie looked doubtful. 'I don't know who or when it can have been. We didn't leave last night till after five o'clock, and this morning I was back down here by nine. Doesn't leave a lot of time, and there were boats about. You'd think someone would have seen, but no one did – at least to hear them tell it.'

'I don't need to see it,' Stan said bitterly. 'I've got a pretty good idea who did it, anyhow. It'll be that Joe Pollock and his crew, you mark my words.'

Charlie put his empty pipe into his mouth and began to suck on it. That was a sign that he was about to say something he knew Stan wouldn't like. Sure enough, he said, 'Careful who hears you saying that, Cap'n, or there'll be more trouble than there already is. Joe Pollock's got a lot of friends round here. Any case, I aren't so sure that it was him at all. Wouldn't have had time that I can see. He was all moored up and gone long before we came in last night, and I know for a fact he was at chapel all morning.'

Stan wasn't in the mood for logic, especially where Joe Pollock was concerned. 'Who else round here would have the gall to cut my nets like that?'

Charlie bit on the stem-end of his pipe. 'And that's not the worst of it. When we got here, the engine wouldn't start. Bit of a mystery, since yesterday she was running like a dream. And when young Davy there went to investigate, he found that the pipe to the fuel reservoir was hanging loose – as if someone had undone it purposely – and it looks like we've got sea water in the tank again.' He sighed. 'We've had to strip her down and clean her out. Had to tip out the fuel and start again.'

Stan was filled with a sudden fury that he found difficult to control. Fuel was expensive and hard to get. Every drop had to be fetched and carried from Penzance in special cans and then locked into a storeroom on the dock, which cost him rent. The idea of tipping half a tank away because someone had contaminated it with sea water made a red mist descend before his eyes.

'Damn them!' He brought his fist down on the jetty capstan with such force that he almost brought tears to his own eyes. His thumb turned purple and swelled up at once, so much so that he feared he might have broken it, though he jammed it in his pocket so that Charlie wouldn't see.

It would be hours before the *Cornish Rose* was ready for the sea. And, like his stinging thumb, it was all Joe Pollock's fault. He was convinced of that, though Charlie was obviously right. Most of the other fishermen where thick as thieves round here and an attack on any one of them, without proof that a man had reasonable cause, would only bring retaliation from them all.

So when, a little later, he saw the Pollock boys sauntering down to the harbour-side like kings and putting off under sail in no time at all, he felt such a fury that he was obliged to look away. Otherwise he might have jumped aboard *Silver Gull* as she went past, and knocked the pair of them into the sea.

Nathan went home delighted with his day. It was a new experience for him, that kind of social interaction with a girl, and it had all gone off much better than he'd dared to hope. A little sticky with her folk perhaps – he had found himself extremely ill at ease in that cramped, wretched little house, being stared at like an exhibit on a tray. But as for Winifred herself, she had been charming. Simply charming. And so interested in what he had to say. Nathan allowed himself to preen. So much for Cousin Zachariah's taunts.

While they were out strolling, some youths had passed them on the road, going down to the harbour by the look of it, and they had actually been jealous, he was sure. Jealous of him, Nathan Zeal, because he had such a pretty female on his arm. He'd been a bit alarmed by them at first, because he thought he'd recognized the lad who clenched his fist, the big one with the shock of tawny hair.

He waited until they were safely past and then he said to Winnie, 'Isn't that the ruffian that I saw accosting you?' Not that he was a coward, really, but you couldn't go making a disturbance, not on the Sabbath day.

But Winnie only smiled at him and said, 'I didn't notice. I was thinking about you. What were you saying about pall-bearers?'

She hadn't noticed other people, because she was with him. That was a new sensation too, and one which put a spring into his step and made him square his shoulders and hold his stomach in.

Mamma recognized his mood, as she always did, as soon as he set foot in the drawing room. She looked up from her letters. 'You're back then, Nathan? Pleased with yourself, too, by the look of you. It wasn't the ordeal that you had supposed?'

He refused to let her rile him. 'I've had a very pleasant afternoon.'

'I'm glad to hear it.' She blotted the writing and put down her pen. 'I told you the girl would be amenable. Now, when have you arranged to meet again?'

Nathan wished heartily that he had thought of it, but in the euphoria of the day he had omitted to suggest anything at all. 'It is a little difficult,' he said in self-defence. 'The weather is already turning cold, so it is hardly fitting to suggest another walk, and in my position I can hardly take her to the music hall or to the moving pictures in Penzance. The next time there's a concert there, perhaps.'

'In that case, Nathan, you are fortunate. Cousin Zachariah wrote me only yesterday. His former mother-in-law is having another of her recitals very soon, in aid of charity. I think that might be appropriate, don't you? It is to be hosted in her house, not in a public hall, and Mrs Boase is family in a way, so there can be no impropriety in your attending it.'

Nathan winced. He had endured Mrs Boase's recitals once before: amateur sopranos of uncertain age and various unwilling baritones, accompanied by Mrs Boase on the pianoforte. The ticket had included 'a cold buffet on the side', meaning a few damp sandwiches and lemonade. It was an evening he would cheerfully forgo.

'You may have my ticket, Nathan, and take Winifred. No, don't thank me.' (It had not occurred to him to thank her.) 'These misty evenings are not good for me. Better that you young people have the benefit – and since it is a family affair you don't really even need a chaperone.'

'But . . .' Nathan protested. 'Supposing Winifred does not want to come?' Somehow he could not imagine Winnie sitting patiently through vibrato renditions of 'Who Is Sylvia' or 'The Wanderer's Song'.

'Of course she'll want to come,' his mother said. 'You'll see.'

Four

Nathan's mother was right. When he summoned up his courage and broached the subject of the recital with Winifred the next day, she not only accepted, she was thrilled. He tried to explain the kind of thing it was, but the more he said, 'It won't be a very grand affair, just a few strangers in a sitting room, listening to one another sing,' the more perversely enthusiastic she became.

'Really, Mr Nathan, I should love to go. I'm sure that sort of evening would suit me very well. I must say it sounds grand enough to me.' She gave him a confiding little smile. 'You will stay close beside me, won't you now? If anyone attempted to converse, I shouldn't in the least know what to say.'

It made him feel protective and oddly worldly-wise. He was uneasy in society himself, but Winifred's experience of life had obviously been even more constrained. It gave him quite a little thrill to realize that and he appointed himself at once her guide and guardian and, adopting a more fatherly and explanatory tone, hurried to offer her advice. 'Since there is a concert, there will not be much occasion to converse – perhaps a little over supper afterwards. People will ask you who are and who your family is. Perhaps it would be wise to mention only that your father owns a business in the town – no need to mention what the business is.'

The last suggestion was for his own benefit. A fisherman's daughter was not quite the prize he wanted to be escorting on his arm, especially if Cousin Zachariah would be there.

Winifred understood at once. 'And Mother was a Jenkins, don't forget.'

He rewarded her perception with a smile. 'Of course; by all means mention that. But keep off politics – you know, the

87

women's suffrage movement, all that sort of thing. Mrs Boase strongly disapproves.'

Winnie dismissed the Pankhursts with a shrug. 'Who cares a fig for that, in any case? I'm sure I don't.' She hesitated. 'What sort of thing do people wear?'

He shook his head. It wasn't a question he had asked himself, but in his role as tutor he must summon some response. He tried to remember the previous occasion. 'The performers will wear evening dress, I expect, but it is not obligatory for the audience. Mother wore her beaded black last time. I'm sure that you'll have something suitable.' He essayed a compliment. 'You looked very nice indeed in what you were wearing yesterday.'

Winnie looked up underneath her lashes. 'How gentlemanly of you! But of course I must find something nice to wear. Oh, thank you, Mr Nathan, it's so kind of you to think of asking me.' And off she went, tripping down the hall.

Nathan watched her go. Obviously Mamma understood the female mind, but he was certain that he never would. What a strange way to react to what promised to be a tedious affair! Well, never mind, it had turned out very well.

He shook his head again. This courting business was unpredictable. He had, however, quite enjoyed the role of instructing her like that, while she looked up to and respected him – almost as if she were his wife. If Winifred was as keen on him as Mamma said – and for some reason it appeared she was – perhaps the sooner he got it over with and made an offer for her hand, the better it would be for both of them. Then they could put all this awkwardness aside and get on with proper married life – show the world that Cousin Zachariah was not the only Zeal who could find himself a bride.

Of course, there were other things that marriage might entail. His profession had given him more than average insight into the details of female anatomy and he had grasped the essential mechanics of the thing, although the little marriage book – which he'd daringly sent away for through the post last week – had been far less helpful than he'd hoped. It had come in plain wrappers and it had cost him an effort to disguise it from Mamma, but when he had opened it with trembling hands it had proved to be a complete waste of 5s 6d. It talked only in the most general platitudes and, apart from urging cold baths and strenuous walks to combat 'ungentlemanly thoughts', it told him nothing that he did not already know.

He wasn't given to 'ungentlemanly thoughts'. In fact his imagination failed him on the whole idea. Himself and Winnie? It seemed impossible. Yet it seemed to be expected when you wed. The prospect filled him with excitement, certainly, but also with panic, confusion and dismay.

Perhaps, as his handbook had suggested, it would come right at the time. It must be so. After all, he reasoned, logically it followed that even Mamma must once have been a party to the act, though he found that too uncomfortable to contemplate.

But he needn't worry about all that yet, he told himself. First there was the question of wooing Winifred. After this morning's conversation he was much more confident, and he started to devise a proper plan.

If he hoped to win her, he'd have to kiss her soon, and that was an adventure in itself. He'd never had a chance to try a kiss before, but she wasn't like the other girls he'd met. If she remained so docile and so keen to learn from him, it might not be so difficult after all. Perhaps on the way back from the concert in Penzance. He would hire a hansom cab, naturally, and that should give him enough time to work up to it. He'd buy some dentifrice and mouthwash especially, instead of using salt and bicarbonate of soda as he generally did.

The recital evening might not be so tedious, after all.

'Just think, Dora.' Winnie was lying face-down beside her on the bed, resting on her elbows and crossing her stockinged ankles in the air. 'A private musical evening in a big house in Penzance. There'll be supper, and a hired cab as well. Servants to fetch it afterwards, too, I shouldn't be surprised.'

Dora looked up from mending Jamie's sock. 'Oh, very grand. You'll be charging sixpence to talk to you, the way you're going on.' She knew she was being disagreeable, and so added in her ordinary voice, 'Honestly, Winnie, I don't know why you think it will be so all-power wonderful. You hate concerts as a rule. When they had the Penvarris male-voice choir down in the chapel hall last year, in aid of the missionary fund, you were the one who fidgeted like fun the

whole way through. And they were really good as well –
national champions. They went up to the Albert Hall and
walked off with every cup in sight.'

Winnie put on her don't-bother-me-with-boring-details face.
'Well, I can't help that. Hours on hard seats in a draughty
hall, it isn't the same thing at all. Anyway, Dora, this is the
thing – what am I going to wear? Mr Nathan says my blue
two-piece will do, but I can't turn up in that.'

'You can borrow my school skirt if you prefer,' Dora said
wickedly. 'Then Cinderella can go to the ball.'

'Oh, don't be silly, Dora,' Winnie wailed. 'Of course I
don't want your horrid skirt. Mother says that there's a dress
of hers I could have – burgundy crushed velvet, nice material
– but of course it's out of fashion now. You've got to help
me alter it, that's all.'

Dora wiggled the needle in and out and neatly finished off
the darn. 'There's no "got to" about it, Winnie. You can take
in a tuck or turn a seam just as well as me. Of course I'll
help you pin it, if you like, but if you're going to insist on
having new clothes every week or two just to consort with
the gentry, you will have to manage on your own. I've got
enough to do with Jamie's socks!' She held up another one,
which had worn through at the heel, and waggled her fingers
through the hole.

Winnie pouted. 'Meanie! You know I've got five thumbs
on either hand. You're just saying that because you're jealous,
or you don't like Mr Nathan as my beau.'

Dora positioned the darning mushroom underneath the hole,
and rethreaded her needle with grey wool, carefully avoiding
Winnie's eyes. 'Perhaps I don't. And I don't believe you like
him either – in that kind of way. If you were desperately in
love, like—' She stopped herself just in time. 'Like I've seen
some people be, I'd do anything to help you, course I would.
But encourage you in marrying a hearse? I couldn't do it,
Win.'

Winnie stared sulkily at her. 'Father approves of him all
right.'

'Well, there's your answer then! Ask Father to let you buy
something ready-made. You're going to need it, by and by,
if you persist in marrying this man.' Some spiteful impulse
made her add, 'Though I don't know what your precious beau

would think, I'm sure, if he could see you now, lying there like a twelve-year-old with your petticoats on show.'

Winnie kicked defiant heels in the air, rolled over on the bed and stood upright. 'Well I might just ask Father for something, too, so there!' She flounced to the door. 'Just wait till you've got an admirer, Theadora Hunkin! See if I'll be any help to you!'

She stuck out her tongue and slammed the door as she went out.

Dora was right, of course, it was the most boring concert possible, though Winnie tried not to admit it, even to herself. There was a balding, bespectacled baritone, a thin, plain, earnest girl with a violin that screeched like twenty cats, and a more-than-ample lady soprano with a heaving chest, who informed the audience in a quivering vibrato that she was a shy little violet hiding in the hedge. It might have been funny if it were not so tedious.

And one dared not even fidget on the brocaded chairs. Every eye was on her, and she was aware of it. The appearance of Nathan Zeal with a young lady on his arm had created quite a stir. That, at least, had been enjoyable, and Mr Nathan had enjoyed it too, positively preening as she was introduced.

But now he was sitting stiffly in his chair, gazing abstractly at the portraits on the wall, while the thin girl with the violin struck up again. The tune went on and on, and Nathan never stirred. Winnie had almost concluded that he had gone to sleep, and was envying him the capacity, when the piece concluded unexpectedly and he joined in the polite smatter of applause. In the end Winnie had to occupy her mind by concentrating on the audience, looking at the fashionable clothes and necklaces and trying to imagine wearing them. Her own burgundy crushed velvet was quite a pleasing gown (Dora had relented and altered it in the end) but if she were to come again, she vowed, she was going to wear something a bit more up-to-date.

Not that she was likely to come again, she told herself. The recital was torture but when at long last the music stopped and it was suppertime, she found that she quickly changed her mind.

She was surrounded by people who were really somebody.

Her hostess introduced her, in an distracted way, to a solicitor, a parson and his wife, and a man from the borough offices where Mr Boase worked. A world away from the kind of common people that one mixed with at the Cove. Any amount of boredom was worth it, just for this. And then when Mr Nathan was dispatched to fill her glass and plate, who should come across to greet her but Zachariah Zeal. He looked extremely dashing in a cummerbund, and to her delight he recollected who she was at once.

'My dear Miss . . . Hunkin, isn't it? How delightful that I should meet you here.' He had a way of looking at you, up and down, which made you feel as if you were the only woman in the room. 'And here's my cousin Nathan! How are you? How dare you bring this attractive young lady into our midst and distract all the gentlemen from the musical artistes?'

Winnie giggled delightedly, but Mr Nathan was inclined to be displeased. She could see from the way he brought over her plate and tried to steer her to a corner by herself, but Winnie was easily a match for that.

'Have you enjoyed the recital, Mr Zachariah?' She gave him her most alluring smile.

'Of course he has. He helped design the programme, didn't you? Dear Zac is such a patron of the arts. I really don't know how Mummy would manage it without his help.' This came from a sallow girl in green, whose mousy hair was wound up in two plaited muffs around her ears, who had been standing unnoticed at Mr Zachariah's side. She had small, even teeth and a simpering smile, and Winnie detested her on sight.

'I don't think you know Susan,' Zachariah said. 'Miss Hunkin – Winifred – this is Susan Boase, my late wife's sister, daughter of the house.'

'Delighted!' Winifred forced a smile.

'And my cousin Nathan I am sure you know.' Zachariah turned to the mousy creature with a twinkling eye. 'Don't be deceived by his inoffensive air. He was quite the knight errant a little while ago. When this poor young lady was being pestered in the road, he went for the fellow with his whip, I understand.'

He was mocking, she could see, though Mr Nathan preened. She looked admiringly at the older man, but Simpering Susan was clinging to his arm and smiling up at him adoringly.

Winnie slipped her own hand through her escort's arm. 'That's not quite the way it was, but Mr Nathan has been very good.'

Susan turned her smile on Winnie, and when she spoke her voice was sweet as sugar, though there was no mistaking the poison in her eyes. 'I don't believe I've seen you in the town?'

'Ah,' Zachariah said, 'Miss Hunkin and her sister live some way from Penzance. Winifred is companion to my aunt, and I understand her sister does a little teaching at the school.'

'Really?' Susan Boase said. 'How quaint. How very modern of you to have a little job and make some money of your very own. Though I have always thought it rather hard on young women who are forced to follow a career. It hardly fits them for married life, do you think?' She turned to Zachariah with a melting smile. 'Especially someone working in a school.'

It was exactly the opinion that Winnie held herself, but she could not simply stand aside and let this odious girl malign Dora in this way. 'You think so?' she said in her sweetest tone. 'I think one might argue quite the opposite. My sister is superb at needlework – which is a very useful household skill – and looking after young children might be seen as a perfectly splendid training for motherhood.'

Mr Nathan looked disturbed at this, but Zachariah said, 'Bravo! I like a girl with spirit. Your sister sounds perfectly delightful too. I look forward to meeting her some time.'

She had the satisfaction of seeing Susan flush before she turned away and allowed Mr Nathan to guide her to a chair, where she could nibble at ham sandwiches while he told her in great detail about all the guests and how many of their relatives he had buried recently.

She did encounter Simpering Susan once again, when she went into the cloakroom to rinse her hands. She gave the other girl an artificially bright smile and would have let the moment pass but Miss Boase came over and said, piercingly, 'How charming to have met you. I am quite sure that we shall meet again.' She leaned forward and inspected her plaited coils in the mirror. 'I understand you are connected to the Jenkinses, too?'

Winnie could only murmur that she was.

Susan Boase turned to her with a frosty smile that did not reach her eyes. 'Then you will forgive me if I honour you with a confidence? I must tell someone, and the moment we met, I felt that that you would understand me perfectly. The truth is – there is nothing public between us yet, you understand – but I know Mr Zachariah is planning to make an announcement soon. Is that not simply thrilling? No doubt Mother will have a little family evening to celebrate the fact. Please, dear Miss Hunkin, do feel free to accompany Cousin Nathan if you wish.'

'How kind of you,' cooed Winnie with murder in her heart.

'A pleasure, I assure you,' Simpering Susan said. 'And now I must go back. Poor Zachariah will be wondering where I am.' She favoured Winnie with that poisonous smile again. 'I'm sure we two shall be the best of friends.'

Winnie was fuming by the time she got outside. Nathan was there, with the other two, and when he took her elbow to lead her to the cab, she leaned towards him warmly, smiled and talked in a deliberately flirtatious way. That would make Simpering Susan understand that she, Winnie Hunkin, was not to be warned off, and that she could find a wealthy suitor of her own.

Mr Nathan was obviously flattered too. He put his hand around her waist as he was settling her into the cab. It was rather wooden but it was a start, and in case Zachariah was looking, she leaned against it briefly as she sat. He did not withdraw it, and that was how they stayed, perched uncomfortably forward and saying very little, for the best part of the bouncing journey home.

They had almost reached Penvarris before he made a move, and when he did it took her by surprise. Without a word of warning he suddenly turned round and planted a dry peck upon her cheek.

She lowered her head and gave him her under-the-lashes look. 'Why, Mr Nathan! I declare!'

'You are not offended?' He sounded as hesitant as the kiss had been.

'How could you suppose so, after such a delightful evening?' His hand was uncomfortable around her back but she did not ease herself. He looked as if he wanted to assay another peck. All at once Winnie realized that she had to take a risk. If she hoped to win him, she would have to egg him on, but at the same time she mustn't frighten him. She leaned towards him,

94

as if offering her cheek, but as he went to kiss it, she turned her head so that he met her not quite squarely on the lips.

As a kiss it was completely dry and passionless, and she couldn't help remembering the warmth and joy of her embrace with Joe. But the recollection only hardened her resolve.

'Oh, Mr Nathan!' she murmured breathlessly, and kissed him warmly in return.

He seemed to like it, though he sat back in his seat. He took her gloved hand firmly in his own. 'You wouldn't mind then,' he said, as the hansom cab turned down Penvarris Hill, 'if I were to appoint myself your beau?' He seemed to have panicked himself by this remark, because he half withdrew it instantly. 'Not that I'm expecting an immediate response. But perhaps, sometime in the future, you might consider it?'

It was everything she had been planning for. And far, far sooner than she'd dared to hope. Why then did she not feel overjoyed?

In fact she had to force herself to press his hand and murmur, 'Dear Mr Nathan, I should be honoured. Surely you must be aware of that.'

He gripped her fingers briefly and then let them go. 'In that case, Winifred,' he said, as if it were the most solemn judgment in the world, 'I think it would entirely appropriate if you were to call me Nathan from now on.'

Five

More and more youngsters at the school were going down with measles, and other parents had starting keeping their children at home in case they caught it too. Soon almost a quarter of the children were away. Miss Blewitt actually considered closing the school, but the remaining families took a different view. 'Better they catch it when they're young and get it over with,' they said and deliberately sent their children off to play with spotty friends, as soon as the sufferer was well enough.

In any case, it wasn't very long before most of the earliest victims had got over it and began to trickle back – looking a bit pale and feeble, one or two of them, but Miss Blewitt made a point of letting them stay in at playtime for a week, especially now the weather was turning cold and sharp. Of Poppy and Harvey Pierce, however, there was still no sign, though they had been the very first to catch the rash.

Dora said as much to Miss Blewitt one November afternoon when all the children had gone home for the day and just the two of them were left, putting things away.

'That will be the mother's doing, I suppose,' she said. 'Can't manage on her own with all the little ones, no doubt, and is keeping Harvey home as usual. It's a shame. Just when he was making such good progress too.'

Miss Blewitt nodded thoughtfully. She rolled up the map of the British Empire that had been hanging on the board. 'Perhaps I should have written to the Board before, making a case for letting Poppy stay.'

That was what Dora had been hoping for – and what Mrs Pierce had obviously been counting on. It was well known that the authorities could usually be persuaded to agree that there were 'exceptional circumstances', provided that the head concerned was prepared to champion the case. She looked up from putting labels on the nature bench to give the headmistress a dazzling smile. 'So, pending a decision, she could come in as before?'

Miss Blewitt reached up to put the map back on the rack, and sighed. 'I suppose so, Dora. Though Poppy and her problems will devolve on you, I fear.'

'Oh, I'll manage Poppy somehow.' Dora arranged the STAMENS label so that the arrow pointed to the proper place. 'It's really Harvey I was thinking of. He's a good deal brighter than he used to appear, you know, when he gets the chance.' She hesitated. 'And you will write and let the parents know?'

Miss Blewitt looked at her. 'Write to them? I hadn't thought of that. Harvey could always read it to them, if you think his skills are up to it. I'd be surprised if either of the parents read. I simply thought of telling Harvey when he comes or letting one of the others take a message to the house.'

Dora flushed. It had not occurred to her that Harvey's parents might not read or write. Most people of that age round here could cipher script at least, though many older folk had never learned, of course. Both of her own parents were literate. Father had only been to Sunday school, but he'd mastered reading there and, though he was not given to doing it very much, he could manage his order books and newspapers and he was like lightning when it came to adding up. Mother had been educated at her mother's knee and – like Jamie – would have spent all day with a book if circumstances had permitted it, although as it was she scarcely read at all.

Dora was anxious not to let the matter drop. She said, almost before she had considered it, 'I could go down there with the message if you like. Otherwise poor old Harvey might not get back for weeks.' She saw Miss Blewitt's look of mild surprise, and added quickly, 'As it happens I have business down that way myself.'

It was a fib. Of course she had no occasion to be going that way at all, except that Tom Trewin lived next door and she hadn't had a proper chance to speak to him for weeks. He still came to chapel when he could, and they'd spoken several times there, but there was never an opportunity for a private chat. Winnie saw to that. She seemed to be determined to hustle off at once and so cut any conversation short. Anyway,

Dora thought ruefully, ever since that kiss there had been a kind of embarrassment between herself and Tom – so much so that she'd even wondered if his new shift-time at the mine might simply be an excuse and he was deliberately avoiding her.

She pushed the thought away. Of course that wasn't true. He couldn't help it if he had to work. He was probably still on the twelve-till-eight shift, which meant he wouldn't even be getting to his class these days unless one of the mine waggoners took him on the cart.

He had managed to tell her, one Sunday, that he'd been promoted. 'Permanent driver on the Duchess now, I am. Even though Bill Handiman is back – you remember, I told you, the chap who broke his leg. Well, Cap'n has moved him over and gave me his shift. Big responsibility, but I'm some glad to have her back. Jack Maddern had me on another engine for a while, to see how I got on. She was only half the bore but, stap me, she was a temperamental thing. One day I had to let off steam three times, and bring her to a stop. Did it 'fore they told me once. I could feel she wasn't pulling right, so I opened up the valve and stopped her, gentle-like – no jerking on the chain and breaking anything. And sure enough there was a problem with the rod. They put it right and after that she ran as smooth as silk. That's how Jack Maddern was so pleased with me. Said I was good as any of them there, and made me up to full engine man at once.'

He had looked at her expectantly, so she'd nodded and tried to look impressed. She realized that he was proud of all of this, but she did not really understand what was involved. She'd done her best, saying, 'Well done, Tom,' but it sounded rather forced and she felt she'd disappointed him a bit.

'Really? You were going towards Penvarris anyway?' Miss Blewitt cut across her thoughts. 'In that case, if you really would not mind, it might be most appropriate if you would call, just to pass on my decision, as it were. But only if you have the time, of course. I should not wish to delay you from your own affairs and it's already getting late. It will be dark before so very long.'

Dora hesitated. That was manifestly true. It was a long walk to the Trewins' house – or rather, to the Pierces', which was what mattered here. If she was not careful she would not be home by dark, and then wouldn't Father half give her what for! So it was a relief when Miss Blewitt said, 'In fact, if you're going to call in there in addition to dealing with your own affairs, Miss Hunkin, perhaps you'd better go at once. We have almost finished here, and I can do the rest myself.'

'Thank you, Miss Blewitt,' Dora said, and she fairly sped out of the school before the head could change her mind. She pulled on her coat and bonnet but did not even stop to do them up; she fastened her buttons and ribbons as she went.

She was not really hoping to run into Tom. Of course she wasn't. Tom would still be at work, worrying about his engine and not thinking about her. There wasn't any chance she'd see him on the road, or on the doorstep of his house as she drew near.

But when she didn't, she was disappointed. Even though she loitered as long as she dared on all the roads where her route might coincide with his, there was no sign of anyone except the butcher's cart, and a tinker mending kettles by his caravan.

When she reached the Pierces' house she stopped. She had been so buoyed up and occupied with her own private thoughts that she really hadn't thought about her errand. It seemed presumptuous, suddenly, to simply knock the door. But, though she lingered outside for a while, no Tom appeared, and none of the Pierce children came out on to the street. In the end she had to undertake what she had volunteered to do. There was no knocker on the door, and so she thumped the flaked paint with her fist.

Silence. In fact, when she came to consider it, the silence was almost unnatural. There were hordes of little children living in that house, and yet there was not a single sound. But there was clearly someone in. There was smoke emerging from the chimney and, though it was still broad daylight, someone had lit a candle in an upstairs room, and set it burning on the windowsill.

She was just raising her hand to knock again, when suddenly the door burst open and there stood a dumpy woman in a faded apron, with swollen ankles and a pale, worn face. Harvey's grandmother, by the looks of it.

'Yes?' One work-reddened hand pushed back the thin hair that was straggling from a net. The greeting was so devoid of warmth and life that Dora felt compelled to strike a hearty tone.

'I'm sorry to disturb you. I'm Dora Hunkin, from the school. Is Mrs Pierce at home?'

The woman looked at her, expressionless. 'I'm Mrs Pierce.'

This must be Mr Pierce's mother, then, come to give the family a hand no doubt – though, Dora thought, she wasn't being very helpful now. 'I meant the Mrs Pierce who's Harvey's mother,' she explained, keeping the smile firmly on her lips.

'That's right,' the woman said astoundingly. 'That's me. Eliza Pierce. Liza Rawlinson, as I used to be. Don't you remember me?'

Dora was so shocked she almost gaped. She did remember Liza Rawlinson. Liza had been a big girl when Dora started school – in a higher class, of course. A pretty, skinny girl with pigtails who liked to boss the little ones about – but only eight or nine years older than herself. Dora would never have recognized her in this woman here, whom she had taken for forty-five at least, though when she looked more closely she could see Liza was not really old, just worn out, like a shoe, and all the sparkle of her girlhood had vanished from her face.

Dora realized that she was staring and hastened to cover her embarrassment with words. 'Well, Mrs Pierce,' It didn't seem right to call her Liza now. 'I've brought a message for you from the school.'

The pale eyes filled unexpectedly with tears. 'Well, you'd better come inside then, 'adn't you?' Liza stood back in the doorway to let her pass.

Dora had not been bargaining for this, but somehow, now that there was that old acquaintanceship, she felt it would be improper to refuse. She walked through, as invited, and found herself in the most depressing room she had ever seen. It was the mirror image of the Trewins' home next door, which had seemed a little cramped and poorly furnished, true, but this room was barren on a different scale.

It was clearly the best parlour, judging by the two big horse-hair chairs, but the stuffing was sagging from the bottom of the seats, and the antimacassars, which perversely still adorned the backs, were frayed and yellowed with disuse. There was a three-legged table by the windowsill, propped up on the other side by blocks of wood, and it was piled high with such an assortment of this and that (old clothes, brown paper, and a child's toy made from a wooden cotton reel were among the objects that Dora recognized) that it was impossible to see the top at all. There was no other proper furniture, but piles of boxes stood around the walls, all of them evidently crammed right to the top. On the floor, which was otherwise bare boards, there was a handmade rug before the empty hearth, but it was worn and faded and someone had been cutting out paper shapes on it. The paper shapes and scissors had all been abandoned there.

Yet there had evidently been attempts to clean. Tracks in the dust in the corners of the room showed the limits of where the sweeping brush had reached, and smeary marks around the mantlepiece bore witness to efforts to polish with a cloth.

Liza Pierce indicated one of the sorry armchairs with a sigh. 'It's very good of you to come. I wasn't expecting the news to reach anyone so soon. It only 'appened two o'clock today. When did you hear?'

'Hear?' Dora was trying to make sense of this. Then a dreadful possibility occurred to her. 'Something has happened to Poppy, is that it?'

'Poppy?' The woman turned brimming eyes on her. 'Not Poppy, no. She's over the worst now, more or less, I'm glad to say. No, it's our 'Arvey, Miss Dora ... Bless his little socks. Just when the spots were starting to go down, he came out a fever suddenly and then ...' Liza spread her hands out helplessly, her voice quavered and she dissolved into tears.

Shock hit Dora like an Atlantic wave, and forced her to sit down. 'You don't mean he's dead?' It was blunt and tactless, but she couldn't help herself. Her mind was too full of images. She had begun to have such hopes of that great, grubby, eager misfit of a boy. Unlikely soil in which she'd seen the first fruits of her teaching just begun to bud. One moment he was full of life and fidget and the next ... 'Not Harvey?' she repeated helplessly.

Liza seemed to take her anguish as reproach. 'I couldn't 'elp it, Miss Dora, 'onestly. I should've fetched the doctor to him earlier, I know, but with Richie working short hours down the mine and all the little ones to feed, I've been at my wits' end for money as it was. Then Friday, when he was burning really bad, I pawned me wedding ring and coat again and fetched the doctor here, though with all this talk of capping off the shaft there's no knowing how I'll ever get them back. And after all that there was nothing he could do. I'd left it far too late to fetch him in, he said.' Tears were trickling down her cheeks again, and she mopped at them impatiently with her pinny. 'I'm sorry to go on and on like this, crying like a witnick, and you a stranger too. You'll be wanting to see Harvey, I suppose?'

Nothing had been further from Dora's thoughts, in fact, but she realized that she was expected to say yes. 'If that's convenient?' she murmured and was taken up the stairs.

The room was just as cheerless as the one downstairs. There was one enormous bed where all the children evidently slept, with what looked like a single blanket over them. Beside it was a coffin, open to view. Harvey was a big boy for his age, but somehow he looked very small in there.

The vision of him lying in that box, pale as death and most unnaturally still, was to stay with her for ever afterwards. None of Mr Nathan's pomp and ceremony here. The coffin was a cheap, home-made affair, although it had been lined with some sort of material, and there was an ornate top to slot in over it.

'We're going to have the iron funeral cart and the miners' band,' Liza's said in a whisper, as though any noise could rouse the boy from sleep. 'The Miners' Welfare have been very good. Even arranged for somebody to have all the little ones today.'

Suddenly Dora could not wait to get away. 'I must be getting home,' she said, and hurried down the stairs. She had very little money of her own, but there was a sixpence in the pocket of her coat, and at the door she pressed it into Liza's hand. Then, just as she was about to hurry off, she suddenly remembered what her errand was. 'I came to tell you that Poppy can come back to school,' she muttered awkwardly. 'The headmistress is going to write a letter to the Board.'

Liza looked helplessly at her. 'Well, tell Miss Blewitt thank you very much, but obviously we shan't be wanting that,' she said. Dora found herself staring in surprise, and the woman added, as if explaining to a foolish child, 'Poppy's the eldest, you see, now that Harvey's gone. I'll have to keep her home to give me a hand.'

'It'll come to it, Tom, you mark my words it will. Capping off North Shaft's only the beginning. It will be the others soon.'

Tom looked at his brother in dismay. 'Can't be as bad as that, Len. Surely not.' They were walking home together from the mine and Len was prophesying doom, as usual. 'Just bought that brand new boiler, haven't they? You heard what Cap'n Maddern said – they wouldn't have done that if they thought it wouldn't pay. Mine venturers don't go pouring good money after bad.'

'Don't they though? You don't read your history, that's what. That's exactly what they do, until they stop. Then they decide they can't do any more, and next thing you know they've capped the mine and turned the workforce off. It's happened round here time and time again. You just ask the union man . . .'

Tom interrupted him. 'That's as maybe, but Jack Maddern says . . .'

Len squinted up his eyes against the rising dark and spat. 'Worse than Father for being stubborn, you are sometimes, Tom,' he said sourly. 'You and your "Cap'n Maddern says". What does Jack Maddern know? Steam engines, all right, I grant you, he's a wizard there, but that doesn't make him an expert, suddenly, on investment capital and the price of tin.' He shook his head. 'No, listen to me, lad. You got any sense, you'll do what I intend to do. Go to Australia while the going's good – afore you have a hundred other men all doing the same thing. Because, as sure as fate, there won't be many other jobs round here – even for an engine driver like your-self. Too many other pits are closing down.'

'Doesn't mean ours is going to,' Tom said stubbornly. 'Stands to reason, the more other mines close down, the more chance there is for us. Somebody has to mine the tin. Prices might go up and down these days, but people have been needing tin for nigh on two thousand years – they aren't suddenly going to stop. And with this new level coming on—'

Len laughed. 'Suppose it ever does. That new compressor boiler you're so keen on hasn't turned out so very clever, from what I hear.'

Tom shrugged and kicked morosely at a stone as he walked past. 'Bit of trouble with the water source, that's all. Bit more than the stream can cope with, seemingly, and got a bit of salty water in. It's nothing much – just had to let her cool down and put a boy inside to clean her out. By tomorrow she'll be right as rain.'

Len gave a mocking laugh. 'But in the meantime they've shut down the shaft – isn't that how you got off early for tonight? And will they pay the men for what they've lost? No fear.'

Len was working round to union talk again, and Tom took the opportunity to lead the way across a muddy stile, and so avoid entering the argument. 'Anyway,' he said, dodging a muddy puddle as he spoke, 'we couldn't both leave home. Mother—'

'We'll send her money home, just like Jimmy does.' Len hurried up beside him, his eyes shining. 'Look, Tom, I've written to him and he's prepared to sponsor us to go – you know they've got this scheme where they'll help with your fare, provided that there's someone out there who will "succour" you, I think they call it, when you first arrive. Well, I got all the forms and I intend to go. There's lots of work, he tells me, and a good man can earn no end out there. Think of it, Tom, a whole new life. A whole new country, too. What do you say?'

Tom shook his head and strode on down the path. He was thinking about Dora, truth to tell, but he wasn't going to tell his brother that. 'You know I've thought about it once or twice,' he admitted grudgingly, without glancing back.

Len came up behind and gave him a playful little punch. 'Well, you want to do more than think, old son, that's what. I've made up my mind. I'm going. I've started putting a bit by each week for the fare. You want to do the same. Here, listen!' He tugged Tom's coat, so that Tom was forced to stop. 'I'm writing off this week. You want to think about it seriously. Mother's got people out there too, up country somewhere, and they'd have one of us for a week or two to tide us over, I'm sure. So we've got two choices there if you're worried that we'd be too much for Jim. It isn't like it would have been for him, turning up in a strange country with nowhere fixed to go and nobody to turn to if your luck ran out. Proper spoiled we should be, by comparison.'

Tom shrugged himself free. 'Well, you go, if you want to. I aren't ready yet.' He walked on determinedly.

Len was still trotting after him. 'On account of that school-teacher you're mooning over, I suppose? Honestly, Tom, I despair of you sometimes. I've told you twenty times. A girl like that! Just 'cause she smiles and is polite to you, what makes you think she'd look in your direction twice?'

Tom had his own reply to that, in fact – a little matter of a kiss or two – but he wasn't about to tell his brother that either. He stomped across the field and paused to free the gate.

'Well there she is, as you're so struck on her!' Len said, pointing down the lane. 'Why don't you ask if you can walk her home, since you're so keen?' He grinned. 'Don't worry. I'll stay here behind the hedge.'

Tom looked at Dora. She was hurrying, head bent, with a look of stricken sadness on her face. It occurred to him that, from the direction she was walking, she seemed to have come from down Penvarris way. Had she been hoping to meet him? His heart soared – she had been quite offhand towards him once or twice on Sunday after chapel, though he'd thought that it was just embarrassment. But if she been down to seek him out . . .

'I will then,' he said gruffly, and set out after her.

She did not look up at all as he approached. She seemed to be deep in unhappy thought. He had to call her name before she noticed him.

She glanced up then, and her eyes were full of tears.

'What is it?' he said gently, and went to take her hand.

She snatched it back. 'Not now, Tom. Honestly. I'm glad to see you, but just leave me be. Something awful's happened. It's Harvey Pierce.' Her voice broke and she turned her head aside. 'You'd better get off home yourself. They'll tell you there. I can't. I'm just too full of it for words.'

He tried to take her hand again. She shook her head. 'No, Tom. I told you. Leave me be. I've got to pull myself together and go home. Father'll have my hide for being this late as it is. I'll see you Sunday p'rhaps.' She broke away from him and hurried off.

Tom was still staring after her in dismay when Len came

sidling up. 'What did I tell you?' he said with a smirk. 'You see?'

Winnie seemed to be home for hours before her twin came in that night. Just like Dora to be somewhere else when there was something important to be shared. And when she did come rushing in, all pink and flustered from the cold, she was more concerned to tell her bit of news than to sit down and listen to what Winnie had to say.

'Sorry I'm so late,' she muttered, pulling off her coat and bonnet as she spoke. Her face looked pinched and white. 'Something most awful's happened. Harvey Pierce is dead.'

'And who might Harvey Pierce be, when he's home?' Winnie challenged. It was not a name she knew. 'Must be somebody important, that's all I can say, to keep you out walking till this time of night. Father would be fuming if he knew.'

Dora glanced over her shoulder with a grimace of relief. 'Father isn't in?'

It was the opening Winnie had been waiting for. 'No, he isn't. He's gone up to Mr Nathan's, as you'd know if you'd been here. Nathan asked him up there so he could talk to him.'

This time Dora fairly whirled around and came to face her twin. 'You don't mean . . . Winnie, he isn't going to offer for your hand?'

Winifred put on her pertest face. 'Well, if he isn't I shall want to know why not. That's what he told me he was going to do.'

'Winnie!' Dora sounded so genuinely horrified that Winnie felt all her own doubts return. 'You can't! You're never going to say yes, for heaven's sake. Tell me that you're going to turn him down.'

'Shan't then, because I'm not a fibber,' Winnie said, over-coming a temptation to stick out a mocking tongue. If she was to be a married woman – Mrs Nathan Zeal – she must learn to comport herself with dignity.

Dora sat down on the stool before the fire and paused in the act of pulling off her boots. 'This is not a joke, Win. Marriage is for life.' She sounded a proper wet blanket, all worn and sorrowful.

106

'Well, why shouldn't I marry him, for pity's sake? You know that we've been walking out for weeks. Besides, he's a good catch – even Mother says so. He's wealthy, with a big house and a steady job; what else do you want? And he loves me – he told me so today.'

'Did he?' Dora said in the special tone she had that meant she disapproved.

Winnie was not to be deprived of her five minutes of happy showing-off. 'Yes, Madam Snooty-nose, he did. He came and found me in the drawing room and said it then. Gave me a kiss to prove it, too – and it's not the first time, if you want to know.' In fact it was the third time, if she remembered right. Once in the carriage that night on the way home, once on the doorstep when he had walked her home, and then again today, after his announcement in the drawing room. It had been an odd sort of announcement, too, as if he'd written down the words and learned it off by heart.

Mrs Zeal had sent her downstairs for a hank of purple thread. 'You'll find it in my embroidery basket in the drawing room,' she had said. In fact, looking back upon it now, Winifred was almost sure that Nathan had told his mother what he hoped to do, and she had left the basket there deliberately.

Winnie was hunting in vain for the purple wool, when a cough behind her made her straighten up. Mr Nathan – Nathan, she must call him now – was standing there, turning his high black funeral hat between his hands.

'Ah, Winifred!' he said, as if she might have turned out to be someone else. 'I thought it might be you.'

There seemed to be no answer she could make to this, so she gave him a bright smile and volunteered, 'I did enjoy the visit to the paintings on Sunday afternoon.'

In fact, it had been a dreary afternoon. The gallery they had hoped to see was shut, and there were only a few paintings on the quay to view – boring subjects, most of them, just ordinary boats and fishermen and girls with aprons on, but Nathan seemed to like them, and so she'd looked at every one.

'Yes,' Nathan said. And then, after a long pause, 'I want to talk to you.'

He was already doing that, as far as she could see, but she smiled again and said, 'Planning another treat?'

He turned a puffy purple. 'Well, perhaps. I hope you think so.' Another pause. 'You might like to take a seat, perhaps?'

She did as he suggested, moving herself past him so her arm brushed his, but he just moved back to let her pass. She sat down on the high-backed armchair. 'Well?' It sounded challenging, so she added impishly, 'What have you to say to me that needs me to sit down?'

And then he did it. He blushed and mumbled, coughed and cleared his throat, but finally the words came tumbling out. 'I feel that I should apprise you of my feelings, Winifred, though I imagine that my actions have made them clear enough. I have grown to be very fond of you – love you, in short – and with your agreement I would like to ask your father for your hand.' At the last words he sank upon one knee.

Winnie had been anticipating an invitation to a gallery or a walk, or perhaps another private recital at the most. This declaration took her breath away, and for a moment she was too surprised to talk.

Nathan too seemed quite nonplussed, but suddenly he leaned towards her, and – as if it was an afterthought – put down his hat and kissed her once awkwardly upon her lips. 'There,' he said, and rocked back on his heels. After a minute he lumbered to his feet. 'So, Winifred, what do you say?'

She was trying to collect her scattered thoughts. It wasn't, somehow, what she'd imagined a proposal would be like, though all of the ingredients were there. Except perhaps, the feeling of excitement that she'd rather hoped to have. However, this was what she had been working for, and doubtless she would feel all that when she'd recovered from the shock. She could feel a sense of triumph, anyway.

She gave her suitor an unsteady smile. 'I would be honoured, Nathan, as you know.'

He nodded. 'Then I will send a message to your father later on, and ask him if he'll join me here for tea. The cook can rustle something up, I'm sure, and there's no time like the present, as the adage goes.' He picked up his hat. 'Well, if that's settled, I will go to work. I've got old Mrs Thornywell to lay out this afternoon. They want the glass hearse and everything.' He gave her a brief smile and squeezed her hand. 'So, I'll be off . . . my dear.'

And that was that. Mrs Zeal was obviously expecting something of the kind, because when Winnie went back upstairs her employer immediately said, 'Well?'

Winnie offered her a stumbling account, to which the response was a sort of brisk harrumphing sound. Then, with what might have been satisfied relief, she said, 'Well, since it seems you are to be part of the family soon, you may come here and kiss me if you wish.'

It was an awkward, uncomfortable affair, and when it was over Mrs Zeal said, 'Well then, did you find the wool?' and the rest of the day passed just as usual.

Even when Winnie returned home, there was little rejoicing at her splendid news. Mother had a dreadful headache and had gone to bed, and though she had said, 'Oh, wonderful,' her heart wasn't in it, you could tell. Gan had gone into St Just to buy some lemons and honey, if she could. Father had sent word that he was going up to the Zeals, Jamie wasn't feeling very well, and blessed Dora had come in so late that there had been really nobody to tell. And now this!

She poured this out to Dora. 'I thought at least *you* might be a bit more pleased for me,' she finished. Her sister had turned away and was putting plates and knives and forks out on the table.

'Well, I'm sorry, Winnie,' Dora said, though she didn't sound sorry in the least. 'I've had a shock, that's all.' She shook her head. 'That poor woman – she's not much older than the pair of us and she looks Mother's age – losing her eldest boy like that because she can't afford to have the doctor in. You know, she had to pawn her wedding ring . . .'

Winnie had suddenly had enough of this. 'Well, what do you expect from a miner's wife like that? Scratching a living out of nothing much. Sick children, drab clothes, cheerless house, not enough to eat, and working all the hours God sends as well. It's just the same with fishermen,' she added, thinking of Joe Pollock for no reason at all. 'That's exactly why I'm going to marry Nathan Zeal!'

She must have been convincing because Dora didn't try to argue back. 'Certainly one can't go rushing into things,' she said. 'Now, are you going to help me with this bit of tea or not? Mother and Jamie may not fancy anything, but there's you and me. Gan'll be back directly, too, and there won't half be ructions if there's nothing set to eat.' She frowned, and for a moment looked grimmer than Winnie ever remembered seeing her before. 'I'm a bit worried about Jamie though, from what you say. I hope *he* hasn't gone and caught the blessed measles now.'

Part Three

November 1909–March 1910

One

As it turned out, Jamie did have the measles. By the next morning he was tossing and turning in his bed, hot as a furnace and unable to bear the smallest crack of light upon his eyes. Dora went in to call him, but he was obviously too ill to think of going to school. The first signs of the rash had come out overnight and when she came to look underneath his vest there were spots all over him.

When Father came down and heard about it he was furious.

'Just when this blessed family had something to celebrate at last,' he fumed, slamming his breakfast bread down upon his plate, 'my son has got to catch these plaguey spots. Almost as if he chose the moment to annoy.'

It was so unjust that even Dora was tempted to protest. Gan was up with Jamie, taking him a drink, and Winnie – all fired up with her new status as Nathan's wife-to-be – had gone off early to the Zeals', so Dora was alone with her father in the kitchen.

'It isn't his fault, Father,' she said, pouring him another cup of tea. 'Lots of the children have gone down with it.'

Wrong answer. Father took an unexpected tack. 'So they might have done, but what difference does that make? This is my son. Mine, you understand? My only son, worse luck.' Father didn't have the time of day for Jamie as a rule, but he could be emotional about the idea when he chose. 'This is your fault, Dora. You know that? Bringing in germs from that confounded school of yours.'

'But . . .' Dora began. She was going to point out that Jamie also went to school, and was obviously in contact with the germs himself.

Father, though, interrupted her with a roar. 'None of your confounded buts, girl! Don't you answer back. Weren't you

113

saying only yesterday that you even went to see a child who died with it? Of course you're bringing the infection home. Who else would it be? It isn't me. You don't get fish with measles. And I'm damty sure it isn't Winfred. I was up there to tea myself last night.'

Dora braced herself to bear another recital of the tale. Father was proud of his reception at the Zeals'. She'd already heard about it several times and could almost have recited every detail by heart, though it really boiled down to Nathan asking to marry Winifred, and Father saying yes and being given a glass of whisky and 'a splendid tea with proper salmon sandwiches and two different kinds of cake.' Now though, Father had something other than his social successes on his mind.

'It's you and that wretched school, that's what it is. Well, I'm not having it, you hear? Bringing all kinds of diseases into the house, and with your mother ill! I've a good mind to send a message to that headmistress of yours, this very minute, telling her that you're not coming back.'

It was so unexpected that Dora cried out, 'Father, you can't!' The words were out before she could bite them back. It was the very worst approach to take with Father, as she knew. It always made things worse when you confronted him head on. 'Not without giving notice, anyway,' she finished lamely, hoping to undo her mistake.

But it was too late. 'What do you mean, I can't? Of course I can. I'm your damty father, aren't I? What I say goes, as far as you're concerned, and don't you forget it! Who's going to want you back in any case, with measles in the house? Didn't you tell me they were sending children home?' She didn't reply, and he reached out and grasped her arm. 'Well? Isn't that right? Answer me!' She was half afraid that he was going to hit her, but instead he punctuated each word with a shake.

She said unwillingly, 'Yes, it's true,' and he flung her hand away.

'Well then!' he said triumphantly. 'We'll send down word that Jamie's sick and that you're wanted at home. And so you are. Your mother's bad and Gan's going to be run off her feet with Jamie sick as well.' He downed his tea. 'So that's that, and no argument. You can go up and take off those fancy clothes, or go into Penzance perhaps and get some meat – make a man a bit of proper stew. We never seem to have that nowadays. Ought to be possible, you'd think, with four damty women in the house.'

Dora wailed, 'But I can't be so-to-say in quarantine, and then go buying stewing steak in town. The school . . .'

He wiped his whiskers on his sleeve. 'You leave that to me. I'll call in, say you won't be coming back. Never did like you going up there in any case.' He jammed his bowler on his head and left.

Dora sat down numbly on the bench. Father would be better than his word, she knew, and these measles gave him an excuse. It was true that Miss Blewitt would not welcome her at school with Jamie ill, and once the break was made, she knew it would be well-nigh impossible to persuade Father to let her go back there again.

She found that tears were coursing down her face. She gave herself a little shake. There was some sense in Father's attitude. She couldn't go carrying measles round the school. Think of poor Liza Rawlinson that was! But it was no use. She couldn't help the sinking certainty that this was the end of everything she loved.

No more Amy Taylor, no more Harvey Pierce – though of course, she corrected her own thoughts, that would have been true in any case. No more pupils at all. Just like that! No more reading, no more sewing, no more object lessons about this and that. No more Miss Hunkin, monitress. She would be virtually a prisoner in the house, a sort of unpaid serving-girl for Gan. And how would she ever see Tom Trewin now?

Tom Trewin. The thought of him was usually balsam in a troubled world, but even that could give no comfort now. She thought back to that moment in the lane when she had brushed him off, too upset by Harvey's death to speak to anyone. How could she have been so thoughtless and unkind? His dear, hurt, baffled face reproached her dreams.

If only she could find a way to speak to him, to explain. But that looked like being quite impossible – she would not even be able to go to chapel now, with this illness in the house. Perhaps when Jamie had recovered she could send him down to the Trewins' with a note, though that would make him come home late from school, and then heaven help them both if Father learned of it.

It wasn't fair, she thought. There was that awful Nathan, positively welcomed into the house, while Tom – affectionate, hard-working, honest Tom – was disapproved of by all the family. She didn't even dare to speak his name out loud. When she had done so once – just once, and nothing special even then, merely to say that she had been offered tea that afternoon when she took Harvey home – even Mother had been moved to say, 'The Trewins? But they're rough miners, dear! You shouldn't go in there.'

Winnie had sniggered knowingly, and Father had lost his temper in a trice. He'd started ranting on and on. 'I won't have it, do you hear? No girl of mine is going off drinking tea with some bloody tuppenny-ha'penny miner's son! What the blazes do you think you're playing at?' And he thumped the dinner table with his fist until the teacups rattled and even Winnie was white-faced and pale.

So Dora could only hug her memories to herself and remind herself that one day, when she was twenty-one, she would be free to love anyone she chose. In the meantime she would see him when she could, even if it was only a few moments on the chapel steps. Though even that was risky, if Father got to know.

It was almost enough to make her envy Winnie.

Stan slammed the door behind him and stormed off down the lane, fired by the knowledge that he was right. So it had come to it. About time too. Dora was getting more like a schoolmarm every day. Just like the wretched Blewitt woman who had put her up to it. Well, this was the end of that!

He shouldered his way past a group of children straggling to school – so roughly that they backed away, surprised. He barked at them and told them to mind out, then strode off ahead of them as briskly as he could. If he was going to tell Miss Blewitt, he would find her quick and get it over with before she rang the bell. He didn't want pesky children listening in.

He wouldn't have admitted it, even to himself, but the idea of confronting the headmistress with the news made

116

him feel a bit uneasy. He resented it. It was not a feeling he was accustomed to, and it made him more determined than before.

It was that Miss Blewitt's fault. She always put him at a disadvantage, somehow. Women of that kind did, with their stuck-up airs and prissy schoolmarm ways. Talking to you sweet as pie, all butter-wouldn't-melt, and secretly sneering down their nose at you, because they thought that they were cleverer than you.

Well, Stan Hunkin was as good as they were, any day. Better. Why, only yesterday he'd gone to tea with people who had servants and a cook. And he'd remembered not to blow on his tea, and to eat the sandwiches in little bites – though heaven knows they were such fiddly little things that any man could have downed three whole ones in a gulp and never notice he'd been fed at all. And, some little demon in his head reminded him, all that fine china and frippery had made him feel all thumbs and, of course, this time Sybil had prevailed so he'd gone trussed up like a fowl, in his weddings-and-funerals suit and a collar which cut into his neck.

Well, one day his daughter would be mistress of that house. That would show Miss Blewitt what was what. Stan Hunkin was someone to be reckoned with. Who was she anyway? Only a blessed schoolmistress, who'd end up one day as a dried-up prune with nothing in her head but dusty books. What red-blooded man would want any part of that? And here she was trying to turn Dora into another of the same. All this nonsense about training school. Well, he'd tell her what for and no mistake.

It wasn't as though he didn't have the right. Dora was his daughter, when all was said and done. He'd been too soft on her, that's what it was. And when he thought of Jamie lying there, all because of that confounded school! Well, it was his duty as a father to do what he was doing. Anyone could see that.

One way and another, by the time he reached the school gate he had worked up quite a righteous little rage. The nervousness was gone and he felt more himself. He went up to the boys' gate, bold as brass. Two lads in the playground stared open-mouthed at him as he stormed up to the class-room and thundered on the door.

117

No answer. But there was somebody inside. He could hear movement. He knocked again.

This time the door was opened, and he braced himself. 'Miss Blewitt . . .' he began.

But it was not Miss Blewitt. This was a tall, thin, grey-haired woman in an ancient pinafore, holding a mop and bucket in her hands. 'Miss Blewitt isn't here yet. You'll find her in the schoolhouse at this hour. Saying her morning prayers, I shouldn't wonder. Always does, before she comes to school.' She squinted at him with pale, watery eyes. 'One of the parents, are you, is that it?'

'No!' Stan said brusquely. Then he remembered Jamie. 'At least . . .'

'Didn't think so,' she said triumphantly, as though she had not just suggested it. 'More like a grandparent, I said to myself.' She peered at him intently. 'But I know you from somewhere. 'Aven't I seen you some place down the town?'

'I'm Stan Hunkin,' he said reluctantly. 'From the fish ware-house. Now, can I—'

She was unstoppable. 'Oh, well I'm wrong then. Don't belong to go out buying fish, without it's a few sprats down Newlyn now and then. My Henry doesn't care for them, says they give him wind—'

Stan cut across this. 'I'm looking for Miss Blewitt.' His tone was dangerous.

The woman must have felt it, because her manner changed. 'Well, she isn't 'ere. I told you. Can't do anything about it, can I? If she isn't 'ere, she isn't 'ere. Can't go cunjurizing her from nowhere, like one of they magicians at the fair.'

Stan longed to shake her, but of course he didn't dare. A noise behind him made him glance around. The audience of children was growing all the time. They had abandoned sliding on the ash pile now, and had formed a semicircle at his back, nudging one another with sly grins. He scowled at them. 'What are you staring at?' he asked, but that just made them snigger more. It made him powerless and uncom-fortable.

He turned back to the woman, and said savagely, 'When will she be here?'

She shrugged. 'I can't say exactly. How would I know that? I'm only the caretaker round here, come to do the floors and get the fires going. This is a bucket, not a crystal ball.' She plonked it firmly down.

Another snigger from the listening boys. Stan tried to keep his dignity. He raised his voice. 'I've an important message about her monitress.'

'Oh, you 'ave, 'ave you?' the woman said. 'Well, you can give it me. I'll see Miss Blewitt gets it.' She was barring the entrance like a guard by now, holding her mop across her as if it was a pike. 'And I 'ope you haven't come here to complain. Real nice girl that young Miss Hunkin is.' She stopped suddenly and stared at him again. ''Ere. Didn't you say you were a Hunkin too? You're never her father, surely to goodness?'

'That's exactly who I am,' Stan said, and was irritated to find that this won him a little more respect.

'Well, shows you can't judge by appearances. Nothing's happened to the girl, I 'ope?' The mop was lowered and she stood aside. 'Want to come inside and wait, do you?'

Out of the corner of his eye he saw Miss Blewitt coming from her house. Suddenly he was anxious to be away from there.

'No, can't hang around all day,' he said. 'I got work to do, if you haven't. Tell Miss Blewitt we got measles in the house and Miss Hunkin won't be coming in. That's all I came to say.' He turned away. The ring of boys fell back to let him through. They were staring at him solemnly.

The woman called out after him. 'When shall I tell them she'll be back?'

'Can't say,' he said with triumph. 'How can I know that? Haven't got a crystal ball, no more than you.' It wasn't what he'd meant to say, and he corrected it. 'Her mother's sick as well, so she'll be wanted home. Probably best if they find someone else and don't expect her to come back at all.'

There, he'd done it and he turned to go. He'd gone a few steps before a thought struck him. 'Oh,' he called back, in a louder voice, 'and tell her Jamie Hunkin will be off and all. It's him as got the spots.'

One of the boys stuck out a tongue at him, but Stan ignored it. He stalked back through the playground gate and out on to the lane, glad to be gone before Miss Blewitt came. Something rapped him on the shoulder, and he whirled around to find the shoulder of his coat was damp and grey. One of the little varmints had chucked a ball of ash at him across the wall. He was sorely tempted to go back and have it out with them, but in the end he just ignored that too.

But when he got back to the fish store later on, he didn't half give Ruby White what for.

Tom's day seemed to have gone wrong from the start. It had started badly, with a row at home – Len and Father going at it hammer and tongs again, about this union thing.

Father had started laying down the law. 'Won't have a socialist under my own roof,' he had said and Len had upped and told them of his plans.

'Well you won't have to,' he said. 'Because I've written off for the paperwork to go out and join Jimmy in Australia.'

Then the roof had really fallen in. Father had stormed, 'Isn't that just like you? Join the blessed union, send the place to rack and ruin and then desert it, soon as times get tough.'

Len had stormed back, 'Typical! Never talked like that to Jimmy, did you? Oh no! Full of how brave and wonderful it was, back then, and how there was so much opportunity out there! But when it's me, it's different suddenly, and I'm just doing it for spite! You only see what you've a mind to see.'

It might have gone on like that for hours, with both of them getting madder by the minute, if Mother hadn't suddenly joined in – on Len's side, of all the unexpected things. 'Well, Dad, you can't blame the boy. Things in this country aren't what they used to be. Look around – shaft after shaft is being capped. It's obvious there's no money to be made from tin these days. People are pulling out their capital and looking overseas, the half of them.'

'And you think they'd be happy to have *him*?' Dad demanded sullenly. 'Lord knows what trouble he'd get into if he went. All this union nonsense – he'll end up in jail. Look what happened at that Eureka Stockade place! They aren't fools over in Australia, boy, whatever you may think. Hard men, that's what they are out there. Building their own houses, fighting snakes and all. You see them giving this socialist claptrap the time of day, can you?'

'Well our Jimmy seems to have done all right,' Mother put

in placatingly. 'And Molly's eldest has done better still. Of course, he was turned off from the mine . . .'

'What did I tell you!' Father said.

'Point is, the government allowed them land – or let them buy it cheap. Two pounds an acre, I believe she said. So he went farming, got a proper farm. Acres of it, with a house and everything. Just think of that, then – all his own. Take you a hundred years to earn that here. No, I'd be sorrowful to see Len go, of course, but if he wants to, I say let him go. Tom too, if he's a mind. Then one day, p'rhaps, they could send home for us, the way my sister's eldest tried to do.'

'Did he?' Tom had been shaving at the sink, taking no part in all the row, but this intrigued him.

Father snorted. 'Only she wouldn't go, of course. Too frightened of the dratted snakes she said – just like your ma would be, if it ever came to it. And she couldn't face that great long journey at her age, if you ask me.'

'Well, no one's saying that you've got to go . . .' Mother began, but Father cut her off.

'I'm sick to death of hearing all this rot. Now, some of us have got to get to work. Let's have a bit of breakfast and some hush.'

Then Len had sat there in a sullen sulk, and it had been a horrid, silent meal. Tom sighed. It wasn't like home at all these days.

Then when he got to work, it went from bad to worse – after he'd walked the mile or more and all. The boy had finished cleaning out the boiler tubes, but there was a lot more damage than they'd thought, and the Duchess still wasn't wanted up to steam. Seemed the new feed stream had too much salt in it, and Cap'n Maddern wanted something done.

'Keep putting that in the new boiler and she'll never do the job,' he declared. 'Have to be stopped down and cleaned out like this every five minutes, and what's the use of that? But otherwise she'll rust through in a trice. Eat away at the metal, see, till it's so damty thin she blows – I've seen it happen once or twice before. Then ten to one somebody gets hurt. One of my engine men most like. For what? Because they haven't got the sense to pipe some water in and look after their own blessed equipment that they've spent a fortune on. Well, I'm not having it. That dratted pit captain can curse and blind, but if they won't get this new level working properly, I'm going down to see the pursar, personal, see if I can make him see sense. Don't you let them force you into getting steam up while I'm gone.'

So Tom had spent an anxious hour or two, just twiddling his thumbs. There was a lot of feeling among the engine men, and matters seemed to be brewing for a strike. Then, mid-afternoon, Jack Maddern came back with a compromise. They'd use the stream a time or two at first, and meanwhile the mine would pay to pipe the water in. It was a huge relief. But getting everything tanked up would take a little while, and it was obvious the Duchess wouldn't be up to steam on this shift, so Tom was sent home. And that was the second time this week. Perhaps Len was right. Perhaps it would be better to get right away and make a new start somewhere else. It seemed a tempting notion suddenly.

Only there was Dora. At least, he thought there was. That meeting the other day had worried him. Of course, she was only anxious about something, wasn't she? Wasn't she? Things had been a bit awkward between them since that kiss. Suppose that, like an idiot, he'd frightened her away? Not at the time – she'd seemed to like it then – but afterwards, when she had time to think.

Well, there was only one way to find out. He'd have to talk to her. At least this trouble with the boiler gave him a chance to meet her after school.

He went down and waited for her by the wall. He stayed there until long after everyone had gone but, alarmingly, there was no sign of her.

Two

Winnie walked home that evening in a sulk. She felt let down and disappointed by her day. Not that there had been anything in particular to put her out, but that was the disappointing thing. It had been just a day like any other day.

She didn't know quite what she'd expected, but certainly not this. A brief, 'Well, Winifred, since your father has consented to the match and you are shortly to be one of us, there is no need to call me madam any more, even when company are here. A simple Mrs Zeal will do. Now, if you would bring those skeins of wool we started yesterday, you can get the rest of it wound into balls.' And that was that. Same chores, same duties, same old everything.

Nathan hadn't even been at home – he'd had a big funeral over at St Ives – and Mrs Zeal had said, 'Well, Winifred, I think that's everything today,' before there was any sign of him, as if there was no reason why the two of them should meet. Not even an invitation to stop and have some tea!

Winifred tried waiting at the gate for half an hour but in the end she had had to give up. By this time she was thoroughly put out, so when she saw Tom Trewin in the lane outside their house she was in no mood to be polite to him.

'Well,' she demanded, 'what are you doing here?'

Tom gave her that shy smile of his. 'I was looking for your sister, actually.'

'What for?'

The smile faded. She had taken him aback. That was probably unkind, but it gave her a sort of spiteful glee.

He mumbled, 'Wanted to talk to her, that's all.'

'What have you got to talk to her about?'

He turned all hot and bothered, as if he and Dora had something to hide. 'Well . . . nothing.'

123

'Oh, so it's private, is it?' Surely, she thought suddenly, there couldn't be anything serious between her sister and this man? Of course not. Dora would have said. They'd always told each other everything. Of course, Dora *had* talked about Tom Trewin once or twice, but only in a joky sort of way. 'Well, you can tell me,' she said impatiently. 'Dora doesn't have any secrets from me. So speak up. What is so important that you want to say to her?'

He would not be drawn. 'Like I said, it's nothing in particular. It's just . . . I was waiting for her after school, but she never came. Hoped nothing was the matter, that was all.'

Waiting for her after school! So all that talk of her 'running into Tom Trewin once or twice' was nonsense after all. Winnie felt furious with her twin. It wasn't that she was jealous – who'd want a common tinner's son? Why, even Joe Pollock was twice as good as him. But it was odd to think of Dora with a beau. Winnie was the one with admirers as a rule. But, she told herself with a wounded sniff, it wasn't that so much; it was the underhandedness that had offended her. Secrets, was it, Dora Hunkin? And with someone so unsuitable as well? Though perhaps it shouldn't come as a surprise. Dora never did have any sense.

She said, in a lofty tone of voice, 'Well, if she didn't come, she didn't want to meet you, seems to me. What do you expect me to do about it?'

'I know she's in there,' Tom said hopefully. 'I glimpsed her going out to the water butt just now. I would have called to her, but then her father came and so I didn't really get the chance. I don't like to knock with him there. He won't approve of me – Dora's told me that no end of times. So go in and ask her, will you, if she'll somehow find a minute to come out? I just want a word with her. I don't mind waiting for a little while.'

Winifred was tempted to retort, 'Against my father's wishes?' and simply send him packing there and then, but Dora was her sister after all, and she was too curious to simply let this go. She turned to Tom. 'I'll see what I can do. But I don't promise anything. Doesn't look to me as if she wants to talk to you.' And without waiting for an answer she went straight indoors.

124

Dora was standing by the sink, peeling potatoes and looking as if the world was coming to an end.

'There's a boy outside to see you,' Winnie said, choosing her words carefully. If Dora could keep secrets, so could she. 'Said he didn't see you at the school.' Now what would her sister do? If she guesses it's Tom Trewin straightaway, Winnie thought, then I shall know exactly what is what.

Dora didn't even turn around. 'No, he didn't see me, and he won't be seeing me again either. Father's put a stop to my going down there, so that's that. You tell the lad, will you, Winnie? It's nice of the children to be so concerned – we had Amy Taylor call round earlier as well – but with one thing and another, I can't face any more of them just now.'

Her voice was so bleak that Winnie almost relented and told her who it was, but Dora said, 'Go on then, if you're going. Father'll be back down in a minute, and I don't want him hearing about this and putting his twopenn'orth in. He'll only make it worse.'

So Winnie went outside. 'She doesn't want to see you,' she told Tom, and saw the stricken look on his face. She really didn't know whether it was sympathy for him or a sudden sense of power that made her add, 'And it's no good you waiting for her up at the school, because she won't be there. Best if you go away and leave her. That's what she says. There's trouble as it is.'

He had turned ashen but he raised his chin and said soberly, 'I see. Well, these things happen, I suppose. Tell her I've got her message, and I won't bother her again. I'm leaving, in any case. Off to Australia, like I said I would, with my brother Len. Tell her that, would you? Not that I suppose she'll be interested.' And he turned on his heel and walked away.

Winnie watched him go. So that was it! He'd come to say goodbye. Well, that solved the problem, and there was no need to feel guilty after all. Clearly Dora didn't care for Tom, otherwise she would have guessed that it was him, though he was evidently sweet on her. In fact, Winnie told herself, she had probably done her sister a good turn by saving her from an embarrassing little scene. Although there was no rush to tell her so: 'farewell' was a message that would comfortably keep and you couldn't quite trust Dora not to do something daft, like going down to his house to say goodbye.

125

Anyway, when she got inside again she found her father there, and Dora sent her signals with her eyes not to say anything at all, so she didn't. She turned the subject to Nathan and Father's visit to the Zeals', and thus was able to thrust Tom Trewin from her mind and forget the whole awkward little incident.

She didn't think of it again for days.

It did not take Tom very long to make his plans. He went straight home and talked to Len. 'If you haven't sent that form off yet about Australia, I've changed my mind. I'll come with you.'

Then Len, of course, played devil's advocate. 'You sure now, are you? You don't want to go rushing into things. Besides, it costs a little bit to go, even with assisted passages. I've been saving up for months.' And so on. It was maddening – as if the whole idea had not been his in the first place.

'Jimmy said he'd sponsor us,' Tom said. 'You get that form away, before he changes his mind. As for the money, you worry about yourself. I'll worry about me. I'll see Jack Maddern about working double shifts. I'll have to talk to him in any case. There was a whole big article in one of the papers down the Institute, all about migrating overseas. You've got to have a letter from your work to say that you are sober and industrious.'

'I know all that,' Len said impatiently, 'but what's Ma going to say?' It was the same argument that he'd previously pooh-poohed. He could be unreasonable when he had a mind.

'Well, I'm going to come with you all the same,' Tom said. 'You're right. Tin's folding up round here. That article in the paper wasn't all that new, but sounds to me like there's a lot of mining work out there. Gold and all sorts – a man could make a mint of money, with a bit of luck. Then, perhaps, in a year or two I might come home again.'

Despite what he said to Len, Tom was dreading having to tell them down the mine, but Jack Maddern was encouraging. 'Course I'll get the powers that be to give you a character, lad, though it's a shame, with you just trained up properly and all. It's a poor lookout for the mine to lose you now, I can't say as it isn't, but if I was younger I'd do just the same – supposing I could persuade my other half. I know a ton of

126

people who've gone overseas – Australia, South Africa or America – and most of them have made a go of it. No, you go, young fella, while you have the chance. You've got a trade now; you'll do very well. I'll give you another bit of letter to take with you too – more personal-like – saying as 'ow we think a lot of you. Sorry to see you go, we'll be – 'cept for Bill Handiman, of course. I'll put him back on the Duchess, he'll be thrilled to death. Though if you ever change your mind, I daresay we could find a place for you back 'ere.' He slapped Tom on the back and slipped him five bob to help him on his way.

Money was a worry, all the same. Tom got his shift changed purposely, worked doubles when he could, and when he couldn't he hung around the school. He would have been prepared to change his mind for Dora's sake, even though he'd signed the forms by now. But it was obvious that Winifred was right. There was no sign of Dora. It was better that he went.

Ma was a bit upset when she first heard, there was no doubt about that, but she rallied splendidly.

'Good thing, if you're going, that it's the two of you,' she said with a brave smile. 'You can look out for one another then. Mind you eat properly and change your socks – and make sure you write me regular when you get a chance. Jimmy is very good with sending wages home, but he's no scholar with a pen. Between you, you could send a letter now and then. There's ships that's coming and going all the time these days, and that quick now, you wouldn't credit it – sometimes they don't take more than eight weeks to arrive.'

Then a few days later Ma was out when Tom and Len came home – a rare event. A mysterious little note was pinned up on the door.

Stew in the pot.
Back on the late horse-bus.

Dad obviously knew something, but would only say, 'Gone to see her sister in Penzance. Lot of nonsense, if you ask me.'

Ma returned that evening, tired and triumphant, with a big parcel wrapped in newspaper. She laid it on the table with a flourish. 'See what I brought you,' she said, unwrapping a battered cardboard suitcase with a smile. 'My sister has been very good. Bought this when she was thinking she might go out there herself, but wrote to say she won't be using it. Almost good as new, it is, and there's a key inside. You can borrow it between the pair of you. Mind you write and thank her, too, before you go.' And after that she busied herself mending clothes and putting things aside for them to take.

Dad was still in a grump about it all – 'sour' Len said, but Tom thought it was more that he would miss his sons – but he was not to be outdone. He went to see the carpenter at the mine, who was a friend of his, and organized a wooden box for each of them, to put into the hold. Never said a word about it, either, until the day they were delivered on the cart. Tom was quite touched when he saw. Dad had painted both of them himself and stencilled their names upon the lids. Mind you, as Len said privately, they were heavy things to lift. Something half the size would have been quite big enough – neither of the boys had very much to take.

As it turned out, it was as well these preparations had been made. Once Len had sent the papers off, the response was astonishingly quick.

'Here,' Len said, waving the letter triumphantly. 'It's come. And they've agreed. You now why that is, don't you? I wrote on the forms that we had agricultural experience as well as mining skills. They're awful short of people for the land.' And then, as Tom stared at him horrified, he said, 'Well, so we have. We've both of us helped out at Crowdie's farm. More than a lot of city folks have done.'

'Picking up potatoes, once or twice, for half an hour after school?' Tom said. 'At that rate everyone for miles could say the same.' It was almost a tradition that local children made a contribution to the family budget by earning a few pennies lifting or planting the potato crop or helping stook the corn. 'You mind they don't catch up with you, that's all.'

'Well, it's too late now.' Len laughed. 'It's done the trick. Twelve pounds each they've awarded us. That only leaves us two pounds apiece to find – leaving aside our fare up to Southampton, of course.' He was exultant now.

Tom read the letter. Inside-bottom cabin, steerage class. It was far from luxury, but it was a ship. Two assisted berths, so cheap that Len could – just – afford to pay both fares from what he'd put aside.

'You pay me when you can,' he said to Tom.

So when the *Silver Star* sailed from Southampton on December 1st and turned her bows into the Channel swell, Tom Trewin was aboard her, being sick.

Jamie had got over his measles long since and had gone back to school, but there was no chance of Dora going back too. She hadn't dared to raise the possibility, as matters were so strained and fraught at home. Someone had been tampering with Father's nets again, and for weeks he'd been walking around like a human thundercloud. Only another invitation to the Zeals' – this time for all of them, after lunch on Christmas Day to meet the family – seemed to lift his mood a bit, and even then it didn't last for long. Even Gan and Winnie had to mind their Ps and Qs.

Then something happened that meant she could not have gone back to work in any case. Mother seemed to have caught the measles too. She had been rather under the weather ever since Jamie went down sick, but she was often off-colour and nobody thought much about it on the whole.

But matters suddenly got worse. Mother developed a raging fever and began to complain of blinding headaches, just like Jamie had, and soon she started vomiting as well. Oddly, she didn't have a rash. There was a sullen sort of flush around her face, but she seemed to have turned yellowish, if anything.

'Trust her to be contrary,' Father grumbled when he heard. 'Why couldn't she get spots like anybody else?' But he did stop sleeping in his bed and move downstairs, to let her have a bit of rest, he said. He even banned Winnie from going into the room, in case of germs and passing the infection to the Zeals. 'Now see what you've done,' he said to Dora. 'Bringing home your blessed germs from school.'

But there was no time to feel guilty and wretched. Dora was kept busy day and night, nursing Mother, bringing up sips of water, trying to tempt her appetite and bathing her forehead when the sweats were worst.

'Tough as old boots, really,' Father said. 'She'll get over it, she always does. Let's hope she's on her feet by Christmas, that's all, otherwise we can't go to the Zeals'. But knowing her, if there's a Jenkins do involved, she'll be right as rain by then.' And really everyone expected that she would.

But the fever went from bad to worse. Dora was getting really worried by this time, and when Mother started drifting off and not knowing anyone, even Gan agreed that someone should be called. She knew how to make it happen, too.

'You don't want it thought that Stan Hunkin can't afford to pay the fees,' she said at breakfast, slicing him some bread. 'Or is too mean to find them. That's what folk'll say. You know what people round here are like.'

Father snorted scornfully into his tea. 'Don't matter to me what people think. Sybil looks all right to me. But if you think she needs the doctor in, we'd better have him, I suppose. You send Jamie off to fetch him, first thing after school.'

When the doctor called he was grim-faced but definite. It wasn't the measles after all. Mother had something the matter with her blood – 'pernickity amnesia', Gan insisted that he'd said. That's what had made her weak and run down all these years, and it was serious.

'Should have been called years ago,' he said accusingly to Dora as she showed him back downstairs, as if she could somehow have prevented this. 'I'd like to have her in the hospital now to test her blood, but I don't think she would survive the journey. As it is there isn't much I can do, except give her some Fowler's Solution – arsenic – and hope that she has enough strength to pull round. It's not unknown in these cases, though usually each recovery lasts a shorter time before there's another and more severe relapse.'

He left some medicine to help the patient sleep and prescribed lots of milk junket, ground liver and beef tea to build her up. It fell to Dora to see to all of this, and it was quite a chore. Beef tea and ground liver both took hours to make – the raw meat had to be rubbed through a fine-hair sieve – but she was glad of it. It was something to occupy her mind and gave her a sense of usefulness at least. Life otherwise was a dull and painful void, through which she was being shunted on predetermined tracks, like a railway train, so numb that she seemed incapable of thought. She hardly saw Winnie, who was in a whirl about her wedding preparations; Jamie was at school, and Gan was her usual unforthcoming, grudging self, busy with the normal domestic chores.

Dora did manage to get to chapel once or twice but to no avail – there was no Tom Trewin in evidence – although it was doubtless good for her immortal soul.

It was her own fault, she told herself. She'd waved Tom away the last time he spoke to her. She had been appalled by what she'd seen at Harvey Pierce's house and, if she was honest, it had crossed her mind that being a miner's wife was no delight. Well, she had her answer now. Tom had obviously given up. She tried to lose herself in making liver broth.

Mother, however, had no appetite. If she was properly awake she would have done her best, but she was drifting in and out of consciousness and it was obvious that she didn't want to eat. When you raised a spoonful of something to her lips she'd spit it out and refuse to swallow it. Dora couldn't get her to take more than a sip or two, even of the sedative and medicine, let alone the liver, which she loathed.

But even that seemed to do her good. After an agonizing week or two the crisis seemed to ease, and by the time the doctor called again – to say her blood was 'less than twenty per cent,' whatever that might mean – Mother was taking sustenance again, and able to sit propped up on her pillows for a bit, though her skin looked thinner and whiter than her bolster case.

She was so weak and listless that it was a struggle for her to talk for very long, but she did manage to take an interest in Winnie's wedding plans.

Three

Nathan clearly wanted to get married straightaway, but Winnie had argued earnestly for June. A date in spring was settled on, as a compromise, and a notice was posted in the newspaper. It was formally announced at chapel the next Sunday, and afterwards people crowded round excitedly, wanting to congratulate the bride-to-be. Winnie spied Joe Pollock on the steps outside and she was preparing to look lofty and composed, but to her dismay Joe looked the other way and ignored her completely. She tossed her head and walked straight past him without a second glance. What did she care, she told herself. She was to be Mrs Nathan Zeal.

Though in truth she was still waiting for the excitement to set in. She couldn't honestly pretend it had. Sometimes the whole prospect seemed so extraordinarily dull that it filled her with a vague alarm. Except for the question of the dress.

She had seen just the thing in White's Emporium one day when she'd accompanied Mrs Zeal to Penzance – a two-piece costume in ice-blue silk with a little white lace jabot at the neck – so while her employer was busy at the bank, she'd been permitted to slip away and try it on. To her delight, it fitted perfectly and she knew she'd look a picture with her blonde hair loose and a wreath of early roses round her head.

'And you could wear a darker blue, perhaps, so it would be useful afterwards,' she said to Dora, self-importantly, as they sat together beside Mother's bed that night, knitting dish-cloths as they kept her company. Winnie had described the outfit several times by now, and was working round to mentioning the price.

'I wish I could come with you to look at it,' Mother said, though of course there was no chance of that. 'Won't be cheap, I'm sure. But I'll make sure that you 'ave it, Winnie, if you've set your heart on it, and never mind what your father says. I've still got a little bit put by that he doesn't know about. I always said I'd give it to you girls, when you got married, if you ever did.'

And then of course, Dora had to go all melancholy and withdrawn. Thinking about Tom Trewin, probably. Winnie was still feeling a bit guilty about him, and that made her impatient, as it always did.

'Oh, don't look so downcast, Dora. If he's gone to Australia, he's gone. There's plenty of other fisher— Fishes in the sea.' She flushed. What was she thinking of? She'd almost said 'fishermen' by accident.

Dora had leapt up like someone stung. 'Who's gone to Australia?'

Winnie could have bitten out her tongue. Why had she gone and mentioned that? Of course, Dora would have found out sometime, that was obvious. There had been some close calls already. Eli Westrill had come out with it Sunday fortnight gone, calling on the congregation to pray for young Tom Trewin who has left for overseas, but fortunately Dora wasn't there to hear, because Mother had been very sick that day. Winnie had been waiting for a time to break the news, but this was hardly what she'd meant to do.

However, now the words were out, and nothing in the world could call them back. 'Tom Trewin,' she said, trying to make her voice sound casual. 'You know – I told you – he called round to say.'

Dora was staring at her like a basilisk. 'Called where? Here, to the house? I didn't know. You certainly didn't tell me anything of the kind.' For the first time in her life her gentle sister sounded cold and dangerous and Winnie drew back apprehensively.

She said quickly, 'Yes, I'm sure I did. It was the night that Father took you off from school. You remember, you were at the sink. I told you there was somebody outside.'

'You never said it was Tom Trewin!'

Winnie wrinkled up her face in a pretended frown. 'Oh, didn't I? I can't remember now. I didn't think it mattered who it was – you didn't ask, and how was I to know?' She played her trump card. 'You've never mentioned Tom Trewin more

133

than half a dozen times, and then not in any special kind of way. You said to send him packing, so I did. In any case, he only came to say goodbye.'

Dora turned white, then crimson, and clenched both her fists. She opened her mouth as if about to speak, but nothing but a heartfelt sigh came out.

Winnie braced herself, waiting for the outburst that she knew she deserved, but Mother saved her by chiming in, 'Tom Trewin from the mine? Dora's not interested in him, for heaven's sake.'

Winnie saw a chance and took it. 'Not as far as I knew, Mother. If she is, she's kept it very dark.'

Dora gave her a bleak look, then turned silently away and left the room.

Winnie tried to talk to Mother about wedding clothes again, but somehow the joy had gone out of it. In the end she gave up and went downstairs as well. She helped Gan damp the ironing while Jamie did his schoolwork by the fire and Dora ground raw beef through a sieve. Father was in the kitchen too, muttering about his nets and glowering behind a newspaper. The atmosphere was not convivial.

Later that night, when they went to bed, there was none of the usual companionable chat. Dora turned away from her sister and faced the wall, and went to sleep without a single word.

The Christmas Day gathering at the Zeals' was always a carefully organized affair. Naturally there were rituals, as in any family, and Nathan was careful to observe them decently just as his father would have done. The house was decorated soberly the night before. No tree – baubles would not be fitting, in his line of work – but there were boughs of holly and other greenery on every mantlepiece, set off by big wax candles, though these were never lit. (They were returned, after the festivities, to the chapel of rest from whence they came.) This year, after some deliberation, Nathan had hung up a single piece of mistletoe in the hall.

The cook had made the cake as usual – the heavy fruit cake that Mother liked, and which kept well if not entirely consumed. It was residing now, white and severely iced, in the centre of the tea trolley, where it kept watch magisterially over the rest

134

of the afternoon's repast. Nothing excessive, Nathan felt, but satisfactory. There were savoury patties – two for every guest – salmon and shrimp paste sandwiches, iced biscuits and mince pies. Three bottles were on the sideboard, reverently arranged. Whisky for the gentlemen, sherry for the ladies and a bottle of ginger cordial for 'all the rest' as Nathan's father always used to say, by way of seasonable jest.

Nathan made the self-same joke himself a little later on, when all the guests had arrived, although nobody seemed much disposed to laugh.

Nathan didn't mind. Nobody had laughed much in Father's time either, but the remark was as much a part of Christmas as the presents for the staff, wrapped in crêpe paper on the piano top and given out first thing – spirits for the gardener, a length of white cambric for the cook and a pair of thick new socks or stockings for everybody else. It was traditional, like going to morning service or eating goose for lunch, and entertaining the family afterwards for tea. Only this time the Hunkins were present too.

He looked around the group of guests again, and felt a glow of pride. Even his father had rarely presided over such a crowd. Apart from himself and his mother, there were Zachariah and the Boases as usual, and Winifred had her father, brother and sister in attendance – though not her mother, who wasn't well enough. Convenient, perhaps. Five males and five females worked out very well. He'd thought at one stage of asking Sammy from the funeral parlour, to even up the numbers, but that had not been necessary in the end. For future Christmases, perhaps, he and Winifred would have to think of it.

He had artfully arranged the chairs in little groups: four at one end of the room for the older people – Mother, Mr Hunkin and the senior Boases – with the younger six down at the other end, with the trolley and the tea stand in between. It was a little crowded in the circumstances, but one couldn't sit at a table for an occasion such as this – it smacked too much of formality.

Mother wasn't terribly delighted by the arrangement – she had hoped to be seated by Zachariah Zeal – but she was doing her best to be the hostess, discussing concerts with the Boases and talking to Stan Hunkin about fish, though he just looked awkward and didn't seem to have a lot to say.

135

Winifred's brother seemed very quiet too, though of course he was the youngest there, by far, and had nobody to talk to anyway. Susan Boase had singled Winnie out, and was talking to her privately – animatedly, with flashing eyes – while Zachariah made social conversation with the twin. It was really up to Nathan, as the host, to go and put the boy at ease, but he was always awkward around children of that age. Anyway, first there was the matter of the drinks – four gentlemen, three ladies, three don't-knows – and instructions to the maid to offer round the food.

And really he could not relax and talk to anyone, even if he could think of what to say. He had a little Christmas game prepared, to entertain his guests. A quiz about the kings of Israel.

He wondered if it was time to play it now.

Dora was counting the minutes until she could escape. The afternoon seemed to hang upon the room more heavily than the dusty velvet drapes which fringed the window seat. She'd watched the hands of the great mantle clock for what seemed positively hours, but they had only inched around a quarter of that massive face, and chimed a dismal single note as if to emphasize the point. If only she could have stayed at home with Mother, as she'd wished, and managed to persuade Gan to come instead.

But Father wouldn't hear of it, of course. 'It's your sister's family-to-be. They're kind enough to ask us, and you'll blurry well oblige, if I have to drag you there myself. Bad enough that your mother and your grandmother can't come. And haven't you got something better than that skirt and blouse to wear? I'm tired of seeing them. Get upstairs and make yourself look respectable.'

And so Dora, who was in her Sunday best, had to go up and put on something else. It was all a nonsense too. Father never really bothered about what she wore, unless he wanted something to complain about, but today he was on tenter-hooks because they'd been invited to the Zeals'. So she was wearing the autumn outfit that she'd made for school. It made her feel quite wistful just to put it on.

Once, she might have borrowed Winnie's clothes, while they had a little giggle about the absurdity of it, but matters

136

between the pair of them were still rather tense. She'd never forgiven Winnie for not telling her about Tom Trewin's call, and with her wedding coming up, Winnie was getting more hoity-toity by the day.

Dora shifted uncomfortably in her seat, and toyed politely with the sandwich on her plate. The food, she thought, was duller than the room, and the company was duller still, however 'moneyed' they were supposed to be. And they were impolite. She had been taught since childhood that it was rude to stare, but it seemed that Mrs Boase did almost nothing else. She was openly inspecting Winnie's family, like someone choosing horses at a fair. She'd even put on her spectacles to get a better view. Dora began to feel like a zoo exhibit.

Susan Boase was worse, if anything. She had not addressed a single word to Dora since she arrived, but instead murmured constantly to Winifred. Even then, from what Dora could catch of their exchange, it was designed to make Winnie feel a frump and out of place. 'I'm sure your Nathan quite adores your dress, but I wouldn't care for such a sober blue myself. Zachariah says that I look best in pastel shades . . .' And on and on.

Yet this was Winnie's family-to-be, and doubtless the invitation would be offered every year. Dora sighed. If this was to be Christmas from now on, she thought, she'd run off to Australia herself.

'That's a heartfelt sigh, Miss Hunkin,' said a soft voice in her ear, and Nathan's cousin was smiling down at her. 'Are you perhaps regretting your mad extravagance in selecting a paste sandwich for your tea? A person can only stand so much excitement, after all.'

It was such a ridiculous remark, and said with such a twinkle, that she laughed aloud. Everybody looked towards her, scandalized.

He kept a straight face. Only his grey-green eyes danced as he murmured, so that only she could hear, 'I am sorry you are having such a tedious afternoon. I'm afraid my cousin Nathan is not the most imaginative of men. However, keep your courage up. There are further treats in store. Nathan always has a little entertainment up his sleeve – perhaps ten questions on the habits of the bee, or something equally fascinating and abstruse. I'm hoping that one day he may vary

137

this, perhaps by dragging us across hot coals, but that's never happened yet, I fear. Perhaps we shall be luckier this year. Ah, there we are, he's got his notebook out. I wonder what enchantments lie in store.'

It was really very naughty. He was making fun of Nathan with these barbed remarks and at the same time flirting quite outrageously with her. She ought to frown to show that she disapproved. Of course, he was nice-looking for someone of his age, but they were almost strangers and he was here escorting someone else. Or at least Susan Boase seemed to think he was!

Then Nathan clapped his hands for silence and announced the quiz. Zachariah looked across at her and winked. Dora found herself grinning helplessly, and suddenly the afternoon was much brighter.

Four

The Trewin boys' voyage had taken longer than expected because of storms around the coast of Africa. Those had meant four weeks of living hell for Tom, tossing and turning on a narrow pipe-frame bunk in a heaving, stuffy cabin at the bottom of the ship, with Len and six other people he didn't know. Anything not actually tied down slid off the shelves and surfaces, and being seasick was a misery.

It was better to get wet up on the deck, his brother said, in the small area where steerage passengers were allowed to go, though it was always crowded to the gills and every wave would soak you to the bone. But Tom was simply incapable of taking that advice. Every time he tried to rise, the ship pitched alarmingly and he could just lurch to the wash-pail in the room (a metal basin with saltwater tank above) or to the absurdly limited toilet block nearby. His stomach would perform distressing somersaults until he staggered back and climbed into his iron cot again.

Len complained bitterly about the food, which seemed to be mostly salt meat and brown bean soup, but Tom ate so little that he scarcely cared. There was a brief respite at Cape Town, where they went ashore, astonished to find that the constant motion of the ship made them stagger when they walked on solid ground. They were there for three days while the ship refuelled and took on fresh provisions for the trip. Three days of fleeting, vivid images – heat, flies, colour, strange fruits and stranger flowers, black men and women and oppressive air. Tom would remember it for ever more.

Things were a good deal better when they sailed again. Tom, who had missed all the excitement of Crossing the Line, now managed to get out and stand about on deck, so he did see a school of flying fish and something that might have been a whale. Mostly though, there was just the sea – mile upon endless mile of it, under an equally huge and empty sky.

Len had found entertainment of his own, in the form of the Butler sisters who were sailing out with their parents to start a new life in Victoria. The elder one was quite a pretty girl, with a thin body and a sharp, lively face. She had made a determined set at Len, which pleased and flattered him, and soon they were spending hours in each other's company. The younger one, Ivy, was thus left on her own and by default consigned herself to Tom.

She was not disagreeable; a bony thing, with long brown hair and a rather simpering smile. Tom did not mind her prattling to him while he watched the sea – it passed the time agreeably enough, but there was nothing in her to admire. Her mind was full of trivial anecdotes, mostly about people whom he'd never met, and Plymouth, which he'd never visited.

When they were getting close to Melbourne though, this arrangement took an unexpected turn. He'd found a quiet spot to sit and watch the coast go by, in the gap between the lifeboat davits and the rail, and presently Ivy came and sought him out.

She squatted down beside him with a smile, letting her eyes close into cat-like slits. 'Next thing to Devon folk, you Cornish are,' she said out of the blue, as though he needed consolation for his birth. 'No wonder we're such friends. What are you looking at?' She huddled close so that her hand brushed his.

It was embarrassing. Tom sat frozen for a minute, too polite to pull away, and was grateful for the intervention of the dinner bell. For the few days remaining of the trip he made as certain as he could that he was not left alone with her. In those cramped quarters it wasn't difficult, but he knew that she pursued him all the same. Every time he turned around he'd find her somewhere near, smiling at him with that cat-like smile.

The day they disembarked he heaved a grateful sigh. There was no sign of Ivy on the quay during the immigration formalities, their surnames thankfully keeping them well apart. Jimmy had come down to welcome them and help them take their baggage to the train. It was a high, hot, brilliant day with a sky of absolutely cloudless blue – Tom had read that it would be summer in January here, but still he found it impossible to believe – and there was a tang of eucalyptus in the air. It reminded Tom of winter and a menthol rub Dad used for colds. The whole new city had a fresh-washed look: neat wooden houses all set out in rows, clocks in towers, painted shops and public offices, all with a smart little railway in front where trains and carriages were puffing to and fro – like a child's model of a town.

'Had a shower of rain that laid the dust,' Jimmy said wryly as he led the way along a thronging pavement. 'What have you got in these here boxes then? Weigh half a ton they do.' He and Lenny were carrying the two, slung between them, using the rope handles Dad had made.

Tom only had the suitcase, but he was struggling. Not with the weight – it wasn't heavy – but the sun. Already he was streaming sweat, and it occurred to him that most of what was in their baggage might be useless here. What good was a thick coat and winter trousers if you were going to melt? 'Does it get cold in winter here?' he pleaded breathlessly, feeling drops of perspiration soak his shirt and run in rivulets into his eyes.

Jimmy looked back to him and grinned. 'Not what you'd called proper cold at home. But it does get a bit nippy now and then. And hail – you never saw the like. Broke the windows of a house near us. Size of ducks' eggs, near enough, they were.'

Tom laughed politely, doubting it, though later he discovered it was true.

'Well, here we are then,' Jimmy said. 'All we got to do is catch the train.'

It was a good train too, bucketing for miles through fields and trees on little wooden trestle bridges, past cows in parched brown pasture, and dusty crops, parrots and waterholes, and streams and shanties and eucalyptus trees. Hundreds and hundreds of eucalyptus trees.

'Look,' Jimmy said, pointing, 'there's a kangaroo.' Something red and larger than a horse went hopping past, ridiculously upright on its tail. Tom had to shake himself to prove he was awake. This was like nothing he had ever known.

It was the same with Jimmy's house. It was a tiny place, just two rooms – a bedroom and a kitchen with a fireplace

141

and a table and some chairs – though, as Jimmy pointed out with pride, it was all his own. There was a sort of shaded verandah right across the front, which Jimmy called a 'porch' and where another mattress had been laid.

'You two will be right as rain out there for now,' he said. 'Watch out for the mozzies, that's the only thing. You don't need to worry about snakes – Rex'll see them off.'

Rex was a rangy terrier that turned up very soon, in company with a small, round woman who was Jimmy's wife. She was hot and red and shiny and so obviously pregnant that Tom felt he had to look away. But his sister-in-law was not embarrassed in the least.

'Too hot for washing, this weather, in my state. But there, it's all hung up and drying beautiful. Jennifer Tresize that was,' she continued, extending a moist hand for them to shake. 'My father used to work with yours. He came here for the gold, but now that's mostly gone. He's moved to Moonta, copper-mining now, over in the east. Jimmy and me are thinking we might go.'

Tom glanced at Jimmy. This was news to him.

Jimmy made a face. 'We're going to need something bigger anyway when the baby comes. We could build on – I got a contract still, with a prospecting company that's after minerals, but Lord knows how long that's going to last. There's lots of work around, mind you. I've arranged for you to see a man tomorrow for a job. 'Tisn't mining, that's the only thing. It'll mean you working on the land. Doesn't pay a fortune, but it'll tide you through, till you can look round for something else.'

It was not what they had expected, and Len looked at Tom. 'Serves me right for putting "agricultural" on my application form.'

Tom said uncertainly, 'Could go up country, where mother's cousin is.'

Jimmy waved the thought aside. 'Better that you hang round here, and come to Moonta with us, if we're going. What do you say, Jen?'

She shook her head. 'Time enough in the morning to think about all that. These poor boys have been travelling for weeks. They must be dying for a bite of something fresh to eat and a bed that doesn't move about all night. Now, have you shown

142

them where to wash, and how to find the dunny in the dark?'

The 'dunny' proved to be a privy out the back. Tom was not perturbed by that – he was used to something very similar at home – until he saw the spiders that inhabited the roof, some of them larger than his hand. He crept back nervously to find his brothers sitting on the porch, and Jennifer frying something on the fire, in temperatures which would have felled an engine man. Eggs, it turned out, a little later on, and more meat than he'd even seen in one place in his life. It was delicious too.

'One thing,' Jimmy said judiciously, tapping his serving with a fork, 'food out here is cheap. Hogget, this is – came from a man I know who's just killed a sheep. I do a bit of work for him sometimes. Lots of people round here run an animal or two. And Jenny's got a garden – you seen what she's grown?'

Tom had noticed on his expedition to the privy and nodded hastily, hoping to avoid another spidery trip. But there was no escaping it. There was a full inspection of her kitchen plot, which admittedly was full of vegetables and herbs, though some of them looked rather parched and thin. 'Water them every chance I get,' Jennifer said proudly, indicating a row of cabbages. 'Never throw a drop of it away. Dishwater, cooking water, anything. I even let the laundry water cool and tip it on them afterwards. That's how they're looking good today. If you're washing, mind you do the same.'

Tom was to remember that, much later on, as he rinsed himself where he'd been shown, in a dip of water from the iron catchment tank. It was clear why Jenny was so careful, too. The tank was almost empty, and what was in it was warm and smelled slightly stale. Not like the barrel outside Ma's back door, always brimming over with cool, fresh rainwater.

He stripped down to his pants and vest and went to lie down beside Len on the mattress in the porch. Len was soon snoring, but Tom was too hot to sleep. Insects buzzed about him constantly. He lay awake for hours, listening to the unaccustomed noises of the night and feeling an aching yen for home, where water and shade were not a luxury and no snakes rustled unseen in the grass.

*   *   *

143

At Hunkin's fish store, Stan was in a rage. Employees stood back warily to let him pass, or busied themselves with gutting fish and kept their eyes firmly on their work. He stalked out, blazing. To think that Ruby – fat, ordinary, stupid Ruby White – should dare do that to him! Just walking out, without a by your leave. Not even that, in fact. She'd not turned up all day and then, this afternoon, an ill-written note fell through the letterbox.

> Deer sir I wont be cummin back my husband says I arnt to on account of threts your faiffull servent Ruby White

The cow. The ungrateful, stupid, thankless cow. Well, she would starve and those brats with her. Serve her right. He'd tell her so when she came crawling back. Which she would do in the end. Of course she would. Where else would she find anybody to give her a job? She wasn't skilled at anything – not even at the fish. Why, he had half a dozen girls who could fillet herring in a quarter of the time. He'd get on just as well without her, thank you very much.

It was her mention of the threats that bothered him. Of course, she could be talking about him. He'd almost struck her yesterday before he stopped himself. He'd roared at her a hundred times before – it couldn't have been that – but this time he'd raised his fist to her when she'd been particularly slow and dropped a fish. Maybe that was what her husband meant.

But supposing it wasn't that at all? What if those young louts of fishermen who hung about the streets and shouted after him had started doing it to Ruby too, because she worked for him? That was a different thing. It didn't matter about Ruby in particular – she wasn't any loss – but if they'd frightened one of his fish workers off, they wouldn't stop. They'd put him out of business, by and by. That was what they had in mind. It was all of a piece with damaging his nets and putting saltwater in his engine oil.

He'd put a temporary stop to that, at least, by paying Charlie not to leave the boat. Even when they came in, dog-tired, from the sea, Charlie would stay aboard and nap under a smelly blanket in the cabin until one of the other crew came back to take his place. It was costly – both in money and the men's

morale – and Stan resented doing it, but it prevented hooli-
gans from tampering with his gear.

Who was behind it was still a mystery. Nobody had seen
anything, or so they said, though Stan was certain they were
laughing up their sleeves. The police were worse than useless
too. They'd keep watch for a week or two and nothing would
occur. Then, sure as they gave up, the interference would
begin again. We'll, he'd called a halt to that. Stan had his
own ideas of who'd been doing it, but of course he couldn't
prove a thing.

But if they'd started threatening his staff . . . He thought
he would explode with fury at the thought. He'd catch up
with them some day, and then let them look out! They were
so stupid, too. Engines were the future, anyone could see.
Fifty years from now, there would be nothing but. If folks
round here couldn't see it, that was their lookout.

He'd jammed his hat and coat on and gone stalking out
and now, without particularly considering where he was going
or why, he found himself storming home along the lane.

To find Joe Pollock lurking around his gate. He stiffened.
He'd long ago decided that those Pollock louts were the most
likely suspects on his list. Every time there was trouble, one
of them was there, and who else had such an interest in the
catch? Though, of course, you couldn't persuade that idiot
police sergeant of the truth.

Stan found his hands clenching at his sides and for two
pins he'd have laid into the youth. But Joe just shrugged his
shoulders and went to slink away. Stan wasn't having it. He
grabbed Joe by the coat and whirled him round.

'What you up to now, young Pollock? More of your dastard
tricks?'

The fellow shrugged him off as though he were no stronger
than a fly. 'Minding my own business, just like you should be.'

Stan's fingers crisped, but the man was young and clearly
much stronger than himself. He contented himself with saying,
'Not outside my gate, you aren't. You tell me what's your
little game, or I'll have the law to you.'

Joe gave an infuriating little smirk. 'Waiting for your
daughter Winnie, if you want to know. Heard she was getting
married and I hadn't wished her well. Nothing the matter with
that, is there?'

145

Stan scowled. 'I don't believe a word of it,' he said. 'What would my daughter have to do with you? Anyway, it's true. She's marrying Nathan Zeal, so kindly beggar off and let her be.'

'I was going in any case,' Joe said, and went, leaving Stan so furious that he kicked the garden wall. It hurt his toe.

By the time Stan reached the back door he was breathing hard, and he slammed it violently as he went in. That's all. Any man in his place would have done the same. It wasn't his fault Jamie was standing in the kitchen with a tray, waiting to take his mother up her tea.

Only, of course, the stupid child dropped the lot. Broke the cup and saucer, cracked the plate and scattered everything across the room. Worst of all, he stood there trembling like a nincompoop, instead of doing anything to clear it up.

Stan crossed the room to him in three long strides and fetched him a backhander that sent him spinning to the wall. Then another and another and another, with all the pent-up fury of the day.

'Father! Father! Stop it. Don't!'

The mist cleared. Dora was pulling him away, and he drew back. He saw the boy's face, white except for the blood that gushed from nose and lip, and the blackening of the bruise around one eye. There was a telltale splash of red against the wall.

'Don't ever lay a finger on that boy again,' said Dora's voice, not wheedling for a change.

He rounded on her, hand upraised to strike. Who did she think she was to speak to him like that? He lunged towards her but she did not flinch, just stood regarding him with steady eyes. He drew back.

'Out of my way, the pair of you,' he said, and stormed upstairs.

It was not that he had been ashamed to hit a woman, not at all, but there had been something in her face that stopped him dead. He wasn't a reflective man, or he might have recognized what it was. A cold, dark anger – the mirror of his own.

Zachariah was not expected as a visitor that day. Nathan would certainly have mentioned it, and his mother, had she known, would have spent the morning debating what to wear.

146

So when Winnie was dispatched downstairs to see who had arrived (such tasks seemed to be devolving on her more and more, now that she was to be Nathan's wife) she was astonished to find Zachariah in the hall.

'I'm sorry,' she said demurely, 'the maid's off today. I'll have to show you into the front room and make you wait, I'm very much afraid. I don't think anyone's expecting you, and Mrs Zeal's not dressed for company.'

He gave her that slow, devastating smile. 'Oh, don't apologize. You'll do very well. Indeed, if I knew I would be greeted in this way, I should be tempted to call more often than I do.' He laughed at her confusion. 'In fact I rather hoped to have a chance to talk to you, though I have my excuses ready for my aunt.'

She smiled, feeling – as usual – a dim resentment that Nathan was not a little more like this. A lot more like this, to be strictly accurate. She had not seen Zachariah since the Christmas tea party, and even then she'd had very little chance to speak to him. That dratted Simpering Susan Boase had adeptly seen to that. Now, though, she turned to him with all the charm at her command.

'It is really too bad, Cousin Zachariah – may I call you that? – that we've had so little chance to get to know each other well. I'm perfectly certain we should be amazing friends. I believe that one can always tell these things, don't you?'

He was watching her with amused grey-green eyes, so wryly that he made her feel confused. 'I am sure, my dear Miss Hunkin, that we have a great deal in common. We are both realists, you and I. We see the world for what it is, and seize our opportunities when they arise.' There was a vase of artificial flowers next to him, and absently his fingers traced the outline of a rose.

Winnie felt a nervous little thrill. Could he be meaning what she thought he meant? She should be hurrying upstairs by now, to announce the visitor to Mrs Zeal. She didn't move. 'I'm sure we should have a deal to talk about,' she said. 'Only last time we met we didn't have a chance. We were both of us obliged to talk to someone else.'

He smiled. 'Ah yes, your sister. A charming girl, I thought. You didn't tell me they had another one like you at home.'

It was not what she'd expected, but she flashed a smile.

147

'Dora isn't very much like me. She's adorable, of course, but very quiet and . . .' She hesitated. It was quite disloyal, but she said it nonetheless. 'Sometimes just a little dull.'

He laughed. 'Much more Nathan's cup of tea, in fact? Perhaps. But no doubt – with the Hunkin looks – she has a score of admirers of her own?'

'Well, no, she doesn't,' Winnie said. 'There was one fellow, but he's gone abroad. Just as well; he wasn't suitable.'

He raised his eyebrows. 'Why not suitable?'

'He was just a common engine driver at the mine, and if I'm to marry Nathan . . .'

'Yes,' he said gravely. 'Yes, I see. It wouldn't do at all.' He seemed to consider for a moment. 'We'll have to find her someone who's a little better bred. Suppose that I, for instance, was walking out with her? That would be more suitable, perhaps. And there would be advantages, as well. I could call on you without embarrassment, and we could talk for hours if we chose. That would be agreeable, I hope?'

He was teasing her, she was aware of it, but all she could say, foolishly, was, 'Yes.'

'Well that is settled, then, between ourselves. Of course, Dora may have to be consulted too.' He laughed. 'And now you'd better let my aunt know that I'm here. Tell her I happened to be passing, and I've brought her that address I promised her.' He smiled again. 'I should go quickly, too, before she calls for you.'

So Winnie went. It did not occur to her till she was halfway up the stairs that Zachariah had 'wanted to have a word with her' and then hadn't told her what he meant to say. But when she went home that evening and learned that he'd called and asked permission to take Dora to a function in Penzance, she realized that perhaps he had said what he'd intended after all.

Five

Tom was getting accustomed to the life in Australia. It was hard work, there was no doubt about that, and thirsty work as well. No wonder half the men around spent most of their earnings every week on beer. Even Len went drinking now and then these days. But Tom was made of sterner stuff. The first time he put a crisp new pound note in an envelope and sent it off to Ma he could have burst with pride.

'Be able to send her one of the new ones, very soon,' Jimmy told him with a smile. 'Now that the Federation of the Australian states is through, they're going to issue their own national banknotes now.'

They still saw Jimmy and Jenny every week, although Tom and Len had moved away by now, and were sleeping in a farm shed where they worked. The farmer was a sick man, and he and his widowed daughter ran the place alone, which is why they'd been looking out for help. The daughter was no shrinking violet. Her name was Cherry – a solid strapping woman with an ample chest and brawny arms – and she could lift a bale of hay as well as any man. She dressed in an eccentric fashion too – in trousers, to Tom's astonishment, with a big shirt, working boots and hat. The first time Tom saw her, he thought she was male.

However, she was kindly in a gruff and offhand way, and had taken care to make the shed as homely as she could, with a lopsided cupboard and a wooden chair as well as palliasses on the floor. They were never hungry either, nor kept short of light, though thrift was a prime virtue on that farm. Nothing was ever wasted. Sardine tins had a second life as patty pans; used cotton reels made handles for the doors. Every piece of wire had to be accounted for, and if you bent a nail you were expected to hammer it out straight to use again. Still, they

149

were luckier than most, as they soon found out from talking to some fellow immigrant lads who had come to work on other farms nearby. Jimmy's recommendation had served them well.

Indeed, as Tom grew hardier and browner in the sun, he began to think that he could settle here. Wombats and kangaroos no longer worried him, and he'd learned that the hand-sized spiders were not the ones to fear, though snakes still sent shudders down his spine. It was a good, healthy, outdoor life: long hours and exhausting days, but there was much about it to enjoy. He had almost determined to abandon mines and engines and adapt himself to this, when something happened to make him change his mind.

He was out in the 'plantation', as they called it, on the field behind the house. It was a long stretch of kitchen garden where Cherry had planted fruit – plums and pears and apple trees and strawberries and something she called raspberries but weren't. It all required constant watering, and netting from the birds (with curtain net from a damaged bolt which Cherry had got cheap after a fire) and protecting with a kangaroo-proof fence. But the plants repaid these efforts by fruiting with such profusion that not even Cherry could keep up with all of it, and the excess was sold at market as a cash crop every year, together with dozens of bottles of preserves.

Tom had been ordered to stake the canes and treat the plants for pests, using a bucket of kitchen soap suds as a douche. It was a back-breaking, time-consuming task, examining each leaf and bud for flies, and he was absorbed in it, when suddenly a voice behind him murmured, 'Tom?'

He straightened up. A girl was standing there, on the outside of the tent of patterned net. For a moment he was totally perplexed, but there was no mistaking that thin form and cat-like smile.

'Ivy?' he said disbelievingly. 'What are you doing here?'

'Me and my sister found a job as well, in the canning factory just down the road.' She named the nearby town. 'They're always wanting hands. We saw an advertisement in the press, and came. We start tomorrow.'

This was too disturbing to be coincidence. 'You knew that we were here?'

The cat-smile faded and her eyes grew round. 'Of course

we did. Len has been writing to my sister, Madge, regularly every week since we arrived. You didn't know?'

Mentally, Tom cursed his brother. 'Never even knew she gave him an address.'

She brightened. 'Well, that explains it, doesn't it? I wondered why you'd never put in a note for me. I thought you might have done, seeing we were such friends on the boat.' She did that smile again. 'Still, no harm done. I've found you now.'

Tom closed his eyes, as if by doing so he could make this apparition go away, but when he opened them again she was still standing there.

'Between ourselves,' she confided, moving closer to the net, 'Len wrote that you two were thinking you might be moving on to South Australia, out to the copper mines. So we thought if we were going to come, we'd better do it now. We talked it over with our maw and paw, and they agreed. So here we are. We've got rooms in a boarding house for now. The woman who keeps it told us where you were.'

He didn't doubt it. Everyone knew everything in this community. He said, accusingly, 'Well, you shouldn't be here, anyway. Can't you see I'm working? My employer will be vexed.'

Ivy laughed. 'She won't. I spoke to her. Said how we were sweethearts, you and me, and hadn't seen each other since the boat, and she told me where to find you. So she knows I'm here. Said we could have ten minutes, in the circumstances.'

'I should think we've had it, by this time,' he said un-graciously. 'You'd better go away and let me work.'

She didn't move. 'I'll see you sometime, then?'

'It looks like it.' He went back to his canes. But when Len called him for his lunch, he went to the shed and carefully unfolded a piece of paper from the pocket of his coat.

'Where's Ek-hoo-ee-ka?' he asked Cherry over his bowl of soup,

She frowned at him. 'Never heard of it.'

'You must have done,' he said. 'It's a big inland port. Biggest in the country, Mother's sister says. They almost made it the federal capital, until they decided on the one they did – Canberra, or whatever they're going to call it now.' He handed her the letter which included the address.

She glanced at it. 'Oh, Echuca!' She pronounced it Itch-oo-ka. 'I've heard of that, of course. Right up on the north border of the state, on the Murray River.' She laughed. 'Never thinking of going up there, are you?'

He said reluctantly. 'Well, yes, I thought I might. I did say when we came here that it was not for long, and I expected to be moving on. I'll serve out the month, of course – I wouldn't let you down. But Mother has relations up there, and I thought I'd go. Only . . . I'd be grateful if you didn't say where I had gone.'

Cherry looked at him and laughed her braying laugh. 'It's that skinny bit of girl who came here after you! I thought as much. I wondered if I should have told her where you were, but she said she had a letter from you, so I thought it was all right. She'd have tracked you down in any case, I'm sure, but I'm sorry I had any part in it.' She looked at Len and grinned. 'Looks like the pair of you are in the same predicament. You going up the Murray too, are you?'

Len shook his head, embarrassed. 'Not thinking to.'

She gave him an approving nod. It occurred to Tom, with some surprise, that Cherry wouldn't mind his going at all if it meant that she was left alone with Len. She said, 'Well then, we'll manage. Tom, if you've a mind to go, you go. There's a train from Melbourne that goes all the way.'

Tom said, 'I thought perhaps I'd walk. It might take me a while . . .'

Cherry's bray of laughter startled the hens outside. 'Walk! You've got no notion. It's a hundred miles. More. And you'd die of thirst before you'd gone a day. There's nothing at all out there except bush, for miles. That was bushranger country till a few years ago. Heard of Ned Kelly, have you?'

Tom hadn't.

'Well, perhaps it's just as well. No, you take the train. And if you're set on going, best if you go before the river floods. It can be terrible up there sometimes.'

Tom was almost beginning to repent of the idea, but the figure of Ivy, hovering around the shed that evening when he got back, was enough to harden his resolve. He had to feign an interest in a wrestling match and sit through that for hours to get rid of her.

Cherry let him off lightly. She and Len could manage now,

she said, and accordingly it was just another week (during which he successfully dodged Ivy, by and large) before Tom found himself, painted box in hand, heading for the town with the unlikely name. He had written his cousins that he was coming, but of course there had not been time for a reply.

Zachariah's visit had created quite a stir. Gan was all of a flutter over him; Mother was delighted and even Father didn't disapprove. Dora herself was flattered – and amazed. She had enjoyed Zachariah's company on Christmas afternoon, but she had not given him much thought since then and certainly had not expected this. The invitation, though, was irresistible.

A supper party in the Queen's Hotel in aid of charity and hosted by some of the most famous names in town would have been an unlooked-for treat at any time. In the circumstances of her present life, trapped inside the walls of home all day, it seemed a miracle. Naturally she had agreed to go.

Winnie, for some reason, seemed to disapprove and acted as though she was secretly aggrieved.

'Oh, for heavens sake, Win. There's no pleasing you sometimes. I'm not to like Tom Trewin, 'cause he's a working man, and when Zachariah asks me out, he is too old for me, though he's not all that much older than your beau. What am I to do? Order a selection of arms and legs and have you make up a man to suit? Is it at all important what I think of him?' Dora was brushing her hair in front of the bedroom mirror as she spoke.

Winnie had turned a sullen red. 'And what *do* you think of him?' She bounced down on the bed.

'That he's a pleasant sort of man, and I'll enjoy an evening out. That's all! I should think that you'd be pleased for me – you are engaged to marry his cousin after all.'

Perhaps it wasn't the right thing to say – her twin knew perfectly well what she thought of Nathan Zeal – but Winnie only sniffed and said, 'Well, it's only your happiness I'm thinking of. I shouldn't like you to read too much into it. Zachariah's a charming sort of man but he's a great friend of Susan Boase's, you know, and more or less expected to propose. She told me so herself. I wonder he invited you at all.'

Dora found herself smiling at her sister's pique. 'I expect

153

she was doing something else that night. And don't worry, Winnie, my affections are quite safe. But tell me, what on earth am I to wear?' And Winnie, who was always interested in dresses, was somewhat mollified. She even offered to lend Dora something of her own.

The evening in question was a great success. There was dancing, which might have been embarrassing as Dora had never really learned (except waltzing round the kitchen with Winnie when the pair of them were young, while Mother hummed a tune and told them where to put their feet) but Zachariah was so kind and helpful that she didn't feel awkward in the least. He partnered her into the progressive dances, like the Gay Gordons, where she managed very well, and when it came to the Valeta or the waltz he led her to a corner table and sat out, and really didn't seem to mind at all.

He fetched her supper – delicious little savouries and a glass of what seemed to be a sort of lemonade, though it was rather bubbly and sour. She didn't really care for it, but she swallowed it politely anyway.

'Would you like another?' He was smiling at her now.

'No, thank you.' But she was grinning back. And then, rather to her own surprise she found herself asking what she hadn't meant to ask. 'Isn't Susan Boase here tonight? I formed the impression that you two were walking out together, more or less.'

He laughed, taking the glass gently from her hand. 'Rather less than more. Oh, Susan is nice enough, I'm sure, and certainly her mother was hoping for a match. But she's a great deal too fiery and determined for my taste. That's all very well in a companion for the evening, but a man wants something different in a wife. Something more gentle and amenable. And witty and intelligent, of course. Believe me, I was married to a Boase, and I know.' He smiled. She tried to think of some witty and intelligent response, but her brain seemed slow to work and before she had the chance to speak, he said, 'Besides, it isn't quite the thing, I think, to remarry into your wife's family like that.'

Dora felt herself turn scarlet. 'I'd forgotten that.'

He laughed again. 'Then let it stay forgotten. No more gloomy and depressing thoughts. I quite forbid it. All cares and sadness, chores and Boases shall be banished from our

154

memories, at least for the duration of tonight. Agreed?'

'Agreed.' Why was she giggling at him helplessly?

He stood up with the glass. 'And you, my dear lady, shall have another drink. And so shall I. No, don't protest. I'm sure that you'll enjoy it when it comes.'

And so she did. The rest of the evening she had a lovely time, though the next day, when she was telling Winnie, she found she couldn't altogether recall the detail. She only knew she'd danced a lot – it seemed to have got easier the more the night wore on – and laughed a lot, and everything was wonderful and fun. And – though of course she didn't mention this to Winnie – when he'd tried to kiss her in the carriage coming home, she hadn't minded it a bit. She even had a vague suspicion that she'd let him stroke her knee, and that she'd rather liked it when he had, though she couldn't now imagine how she'd permitted that.

'In any case,' she said to Winnie, putting that disturbing picture from her mind, 'he must have enjoyed his evening, because he asked me to go out with him again, next time he's visiting Penzance. Though another time, perhaps, I won't drink the lemonade. It seems to have given me quite a head today.'

Winnie looked impatient. 'Lemonade? That was champagne, you goose.' She sounded envious. 'I know, because Nathan had some for his mother's birthday once.'

Dora stared at her. She'd never knowingly drunk alcohol before. 'You think?'

'Course it was,' Winnie persisted. 'You ask him, if he tries to give it you again.'

So she did, and it was, but she drank it just the same. It gave her a sinful little glow. It made her feel witty and intelligent and she didn't think about Tom Trewin once.

Winnie's wedding took place one windy Saturday in March. She looked as pretty as a picture in the ice-blue silk and she was in high spirits now the day had come, though she had been rather subdued and difficult for days.

Dora was helping put the flowers in her hair, when she felt a sudden, dreadful urge to offer one last chance.

'Are you sure you're ... you know ... doing the right thing?' she ventured in a voice that wobbled a little as she spoke. 'Only I'd hate to think of you stuck up there with that gloomy man, if you didn't really want to marry him. I know it would create a dreadful fuss, but it's a bride's privilege to change her mind.'

She was expecting a tirade of reproach, telling her to mind her own business and stop saying such things on a wedding day, but Winnie just went on looking in the mirror, biting her lips to make them red. She made a little face at Dora in the glass. 'Don't fuss so, Dora, I know what I'm doing. I'm very fond of Nathan and he's very fond of me. Anyway it's far too late for second thoughts.'

Somehow that was more sobering than any outburst could have been. And less comforting. 'I'm sorry, Winnie,' she said, with real penitence. 'I don't know what came over me. Just upset at losing you, perhaps.'

'You're not really losing me, you goose,' Winnie said, with something more like her accustomed air. 'I'm only moving half a mile away. I'm sure we'll see each other all the time. Now, if you've finished fidgeting with my hair, we'd better go downstairs. The others will be getting anxious by this time.'

The others were indeed downstairs and waiting. Father was 'done up like a picnic' in his suit, with his hair all short and sticking up where he'd had it cut, and a new shirt in honour of the day. Jamie looked quiet and respectable; Gan was in the beaded black she wore to funerals, and Mother had struggled up and dressed. She was in her best costume, which was almost new, but it hung away from her in folds, and her face was a deeper ivory than her blouse. She looked more old and frail than Gan, and staggered slightly as she rose to kiss them both.

Dora felt the need to cover this with words. 'Doesn't Win look pretty?' she enquired.

'Like a princess,' Mother said with feeling. 'I'm only glad I'm able to make it to the church. I can't stay afterwards, for the sandwiches and cake. I would do if I could, my handsome, as you know. But I'll see my daughter married if it's the last thing that I do.'

It did seem, once or twice, as if it would be the last thing too. Several times, as Eli Westrill droned on and on, Dora stole a look towards her mother, and noticed she was swaying where she sat. But she got through the service

156

somehow and – in front of Zachariah and a small crowd of Boases and the man who assisted the groom with funerals – Winnie became Mrs Nathan Zeal. No one from the village came to watch the bride come out, not even Charlie Cox, who might have been expected to. Father said he was wanted to keep an eye out on the boat, and that if the women at the fish store thought that they were going to get time off to gawp, they could think again.

Mother did go straight home afterwards and took Dora with her, since she clearly wasn't well enough to manage on her own. Susan Boase was heard to sniff at this, and say, 'How quaint. One would think the bride's attendant would have stayed, at least!' But in any case, Dora had no appetite for what Gan called the 'wedding feast' – ham sandwiches and cake which they'd prepared at home and for which Father had hired the chapel hall.

There was a problem getting Mother home. The horse-cab that had been hired to bring them to the chapel had been due to come back in half an hour to take her back, but Father had found fault with the driver on the way and after the service there was no sign of him. Dora was contemplating what on earth to do – Mother was in no condition for the walk – when Zachariah Zeal came up and insisted on driving them himself, in his own carriage.

Dora accepted the offer gratefully. When they got home he helped them in and she managed to get Mother up the stairs to lie down on the bed, not properly undressed but with her best costume off, at least. Dora pulled a blanket over her and went downstairs.

Zachariah was still standing in the kitchen by the door. She'd not expected that. Finding herself alone with him like this made her a little ill at ease. She crossed the room swiftly, picked up the kettle from the hearth, and turned towards him with forced gaiety.

'I haven't got champagne to offer you,' she said, 'but would you like a cup of tea? I'm just about to put the kettle on.' And then, more soberly, 'Mother could do with one, I think.'

'I should be charmed, if you are making it.'

He could always make her blush when he said things like that. She turned away and was very busy for a moment, filling the kettle from the pail and setting it to boil. Still not looking at him, she offered a conventional remark. 'It was a lovely wedding, wasn't it?'

'Quite pleasant, I suppose.' That startled her, and she turned to face him, with the spoon and tea caddy still in her hand. He laughed. 'I am a connoisseur of weddings, don't forget. Yours will be much more memorable, I'm sure. To me, at least.'

She had no idea how to respond to this, so she did not try. She simply went on measuring out the tea, but if she hoped that this would make her look composed, she failed. She put too many spoonfuls in the pot, and had to take a good deal out again. He noticed, too.

'The idea disturbs you? It appears to deprive you of the power to count.'

'Not at all,' she retorted, in defiance of the truth. 'I have no thought of marrying, that's all.'

'Perhaps you should.' He was assessing her with those disturbing eyes, as if she were a painting in a gallery and he was judging it. 'I'm not getting any younger, and someone like you might suit me very well. You're a pretty girl and . . .' His lips twitched. 'What was it? Intelligent? Witty and amenable, we're working on. Though I must say, champagne appears to help.'

Had he really just proposed to her? Or was he only teasing in that way he had? In her confusion she fumbled with the teapot and almost let it drop. She managed to rescue it in time and put it down, but she did splash boiling water on her thumb.

Zachariah came over instantly and seized her hand, but only to force it into the water pail. He held it there a moment, and the throbbing eased.

'A sovereign remedy for burns,' he said, taking out his handkerchief to bind the wounded thumb. 'I know. A blacksmith taught it me, when I went too near his forge. About a thousand years ago, when I was young, like you.' He kissed the sore spot lightly, and added with a laugh, 'I'm sorry that you hurt yourself. Does that mean that you're busy thinking about what I said just now?'

He was still holding her fingers and she withdrew them gingerly. 'Did you mean it?'

'I should not have said it otherwise. Though, I confess, I had not meant to say it quite so soon.'

'Only . . .' She struggled for the words. 'Please don't be offended, but I can't. At least, not now.' She paused. 'I do like you, very well indeed. And I have enjoyed our outings. Oh dear, I sound like Winnie. I'm so sorry, Zachariah.'

'Of course.' The teasing tone had gone. 'With your sister getting married and your mother sick, it was a tactless moment. I apologize. Though we will continue to be friends, I hope.'

She was suddenly stricken with a sense of loss. She had put Tom Trewin off by her indecisiveness and now she was doing the same thing again. She said, hesitantly, 'More than friends, perhaps, one day. I really meant it when I said I hadn't thought of marriage in the least. This is so sudden . . .'

He threw back his handsome head and laughed. 'As they say in all the plays! Of course, my dear Dora. You must have time to think. And the next time I ask you, I shall make sure that I do so with the aid of some champagne. Though that may not be for a little time, I fear. I have business to attend to back at home – though you know where to find me if you change your mind. Now, are we to have this cup of tea, or not?'

She took one up to Mother, and by the time she came downstairs again, Gan and Jamie had got back from the hall and there was no chance for private conversation any more. Zachariah made a few conventional remarks about the day, then drank his tea and left.

She heard next day from Winnie, in a triumphant little note, that he'd gone back up the county and would not be back for weeks.

Part Four

April 1910–August 1912

One

'Morning, Mr Trewin. Managed to find anything today?' The skinny, grey-haired woman, who was dispensing tea from a huge metal urn, smiled at him with her broken teeth. Like everybody else he had met up here, her skin was tanned to leather by the sun.

He put the newspaper away. 'Not yet.' He forced a smile. It would not do to let Mrs Hochenheimer see that he was worried about finding proper work, though it was getting more pressing by the day. He had managed to get by with odds and ends so far – digging the odd garden, loading goods, or standing in as a labourer for a day or two. Once, he'd even helped the baker out. But if he didn't find something steady very soon, he did not know what would become of him – unless he went to work for the Echuca butter works, but that was a legendary last resort round here. The last unfortunate who'd worked there had been up in court for stealing butter – not that he was wicked, but simply to survive, because his master worked him fourteen hours a day and paid him too little to be able to meet the rent. Even the judge had sympathized with him. But it might come to it. Tom hadn't sent anything to Ma for weeks and he had only just enough to meet the boarding-house bills.

He had not intended it to be like this. And it was no one's fault. He'd found his relations easily enough, but it was clear why there had been no reply from them. The family had lost everything in a fire – the house, the crops, the stock – and were living under canvas on the site, trying to rebuild their ruined lives. They'd been very kind to him, as far as possible, but it was obvious their land would not even support themselves this year, let alone a stranger in their midst.

It was easy to see how fire could take hold. If Melbourne

163

had been hot, this place was a furnace. The grass was parched to tinder and the smallest spark could spread – 'like wildfire', you might say, except that that's exactly what it was. And if it got into the trees, watch out! Eucalyptus doesn't burn like other things – Tom had witnessed bush fire by now, and knew. A sort of misty vapour seemed to form and then, whoosh, the whole cloud went up and the fire could spread for miles at a stroke. His cousins had got off lightly, with their lives and what they could carry with them on the cart.

Tom had camped out with them overnight – he was too tired to do much else – but the next morning he had headed back into Echuca town, having reluctantly promised 'not to tell them back at home, it would only worry them.' He was not unduly anxious about himself. In a thriving port, he reasoned, there was always work, and he'd learned of a Cornishman who kept a boarding house.

The boarding house was easy – clean, neat and respectable, and they had a vacant room. It was basic but affordable and Tom took it on the spot. The work, however, proved to be a different thing. The coming of the railway had moved trade from the port and it was nothing like it had been a few short years before. People were drifting from the town, hotels were shutting down, and scores of men were chasing what little work there was.

'I tell you what, my lad,' the harbour-master said, pushing his hat back on his sunburned head and staring morosely at the huge new wharf where a solitary paddle steamer was discharging logs from a barge that it had towed, 'I shall be bloody leaving here myself, the way it's bloody going. Look at that,' he gestured to the wharf. 'Hadn't even bloody finished building it before it was too late. Two hundred boats a year we used to have through here. And now bloody look. Lucky if we see two or three a month. So, no, there isn't any work to offer you.'

And if there were, Tom thought, it wouldn't come to him. It would come to one of the owners of the boats that were lined up further down, waiting to be towed away and sold or broken up. And who could blame the town? It looked after its own first, like anybody would. It was depressing though.

All this was running through his mind as Mrs Hochenheimer took his cup and poured him a second cup of tea. It was hot

164

and sweet and strong – made with the milk and sugar in the urn, not a bit like cups of tea at home – but it was comforting. And sustaining, too. 'Put hairs on your stomach,' Mrs Hochenheimer said. Like most of the non-British newcomers to the town – Dutch, German, Chinese, there were a lot of them – her English was good, but individual.

'I might go over the border for a bit,' Tom said, meaning that he would cross the river into New South Wales. 'I hear there's a farmer over there who's still got hay uncut and he's taking people by the hour to get it in and get his turnips sown.' It would be a long walk, with the prospect of only a few hours' work, at best, and very little pay to show for it, but it was something. There wasn't anything else at all in view.

Mrs Hochenheimer gave a scornful grunt. 'Oh, yes, the Simpson place,' she said. 'I heard of that. Silly begorrah, it is all his fault.' Mrs Hochenheimer was strictly Dutch Reform and did not approve of swearing words, so she made approximations of her own, sometimes with colourful results. 'He's left it far too late. Rented his steam harvester and thresher out to one and everyone, and when he needed it himself, it broke.'

Tom nodded. A steam harvester – just a stationary steam engine, surely, geared up to drive a belt? How could you break a simple thing like that? Burst the boiler, perhaps, or blown a valve. 'Wonder he hasn't had it fixed.'

The woman gave her snaggled grin. 'He had a part sent out for it, I heard, but he can't make it work. Mad as a hatmaker, they say, because he can't find an engineer to put it right. That's his own fault, too. There's plenty who could help him, but they won't. He wouldn't spend a crust of money on advice. There were people tried to tell him, but he wouldn't hear a word, just insisted on doing everything himself and charged the world for it. They told him it would break if he went on like that, but he thought he knew better, when he didn't know a thing. They wouldn't raise a hand to help him now.' She stopped. 'Why, what is it, Mr Trewin? Did I say something wrong?'

Tom was already on his feet, leaving his precious cup of tea half-drunk. 'No, Mrs Hochenheimer,' he said, resisting an impulse to kiss her freckled nose. 'I think you just said something right. I'm going out to the Simpson place right now.'

165

It was not at all straightforward even then. George Simpson was a huge, shaggy, fat and disagreeable bear of a man, with a loud voice, a short temper and a meek little mouse of a wife who went in awe of him. He was evidently widely unpopular as well, since he had difficulty hiring hands in spite of the general lack of work around the area. When Tom mentioned the real reason for his visit, instead of being pleased, Simpson let out a roar which scared the crows, and threatened to throw him bodily from the place.

Tom stood his ground. He had come a long way for this, and after a heated argument, in which both he and the steam engine were called several things that would have turned poor Mrs Hochenheimer blue, he had a flash of inspiration.

'Listen, Mr Simpson, I'll tell you what I'll do. You show me where this part and engine is, and I'll have a look at her this afternoon. If I make her work, you owe me fifteen bob. If not, you owe me nothing. What have you to lose?' Only desperation made him offer such a thing. He knew about steam engines, certainly, but he was not a qualified maintenance engineer. Building and repairing them was not his field, although he had studied and watched men doing it and had a fair idea.

Simpson had simmered down by now. 'All right, it's a deal. But don't come bleating if you change your mind. Fifteen bob is what you said, and only if it works.' He led the way across a filthy yard and pushed open the door of a shed. 'There it is,' he muttered, and aimed a kick at it. 'Ruddy thing. You try to make it work, since you're so keen. Don't give much for your chances, but that's your lookout.'

It was a great deal worse than Tom had bargained for. The engine looked neglected and decayed, although it was only months since it was last used. It had clearly been dragged here on a sort of sledge and dumped, just as it had come in from the field. There was still chaff sticking to the underside and no lubrication in the oil lines at all. Even the fire tubes inside were all clogged up with soot and dust – and insects, probably.

It was blisteringly hot inside the tin shed and he had to strip off to his underpants. No one had provided him with tools, and of course he had nothing of his own, but there was a wrench and hammer hanging from a nail on the wall and a can of unused engine oil underneath the bench. He made a start by finding an old pail. He filled it with water from the drinking trough and sluiced down both the engine and himself. As he did so something black and sinister slithered out from underneath the sledge and vanished, hissing, into the yard outside. After that he worked more cautiously.

Still, it looked a little better for the wash. Next he cleared the tubes, using an old sack and rags he found, wrapped round the handle of a rake for fear of ants and spiders. He brushed out the firebox, too, and carefully fed oil into the thirsty lines. Now that it was properly revealed, the boiler looked discoloured at one end. That led him to the problem. The fire door wasn't sealing properly. It was nowhere near, in fact. The door had evidently been replaced – the piece that Simpson had ordered, by the looks of it – but whatever accident had befallen the original had also bent the flange, and the replacement had simply been crudely hammered on. That made sense – Simpson had no feeling for machines, you could see that by the way the regulator had been set to squeeze every bit of pressure out of her, and never mind the safety of the thing.

Tom moved the door. It grated as it closed and hung lopsided so you had to force it shut, and then it left a gap – it was impossible to organize a proper draught like that. No wonder the poor thing would not get up to steam. And with the regulator screwed right down, as well! That hinge would take some moving, forced on like it was, but if he was right it could be taken down and put back properly.

He was black from head to foot and streaming sweat by now, and it was well past noon, but nobody appeared with the light midday meal that was usually provided on a farm. It surprised him until he realized that in striking this deal he had not stipulated food, and he could tell Simpson was not a man to give you anything he hadn't bargained for. Tom had no lunch with him, only a big bottle of cold tea, and with the heat he had to ration that, but he worked grimly on, sustaining himself with little sips of water from the pail and splashing himself down from time to time.

It was well into the afternoon before he got it free. He went outside into the blessed shade and sank down, panting, underneath a tree. With reluctance, he finished off his drink. He knew he would regret it later on, but he needed liquid like he

167

needed air. His head was buzzing and there seemed to be a sort of tapping sound.

He sat upright. There it was again. They didn't have wood-peckers out here, did they? He looked around. There was nothing to be seen. It wasn't Simpson – Tom could hear him, miles away, shouting at whatever labourers he had. Yet there it was. Tap, tap, tap. Tom staggered to his feet, fearful of some dreadful reptile under him.

Tap, tap, tap. It was the mousy wife, tapping on the window opposite. He walked across the yard to her, a little nervously. She pushed the window open. 'Here,' she said, 'I saw you coming to the trough. You put this in your pail. Be quick – Georgie'll be vexed if he sees me talk to you.' She handed an enamel basin through the gap, filled to the brim with water. Tom looked at it longingly.

'Go on,' she said. 'And then you come back here. I've got a bit of lemonade I made. And a bit of home-made bread and jam. You must be perishing of thirst out there. I wanted to bring you out some lunch, but George said no. Said you'd made your bed, and you could lie on it. Go on now, do it quick, before he comes. He'll give both of us a row if he finds out what I've done. Give me that bottle of yours as well, I'll put the lemonade in that.'

Tom did so gratefully. The lemonade was cool and sharp and more refreshing than he could believe. He took the bread and jam inside to eat, where Simpson couldn't see. It was still painfully hot in there, but thus refreshed, he set to work again. It was easier to get the door on square than it had been to get it off, and he managed to reset the regulator too. By the time Simpson had led his other workers to the yard, a soot-streaked Tom was waiting at the door.

'I think you'll find it works all right,' he said.

For a moment Simpson almost looked perplexed, but then his face hardened in a sneer. 'Prove it.'

'How can I?' Tom protested. 'It's stuck in the shed. But you get it out and try it – or better still, let me. I tell you, I've oiled it and cleaned it and re-hung the door, so it should work as far as I can see, providing you haven't split the boiler by running it with the regulator screwed down as it was.'

Simpson made an expansive gesture with his hands. 'You see?' he said to the surrounding men. 'Claims that he's fixed it, but can't give a guarantee.' He turned to Tom. 'I'll pay you, fifteen shilling, like you said, when I've got it out and stoked and seen it running properly. And not before.'

Tom was as angry as he'd ever been. He squared up to Simpson. 'Listen,' he said with a fury born of despair, 'you've had me working in that shed all day, in the blazing heat, and not so much as offered me a drink. And now you want to cheat me out of what I've earned. You owe me fifteen shillings. You agreed.'

Simpson smirked. 'Not until the engine's seen to work. So just clear off, will you.' He saw Tom clench his fists and added nastily, 'And don't think you can lay a hand on me. I'll have you for assault. I've got witnesses. Proper workers, who've been in the fields.' He gestured towards the men he'd hired for the day.

The largest of them – a bearded giant, bigger and uglier than Simpson himself – stepped forward and said unexpectedly, 'You got witnesses all right. Pay him.'

The farmer gaped.

'You heard,' the man repeated. 'Give the man his pay. Or so help me, I'll break you limb from limb. I know you, Simpson, you're a bully and a cheat. I've watched you. You've had us working here for hours and you've calculated our wages for much less. Well, here's an end to it. You're not cheating us and you won't be cheating him, or you'll have all of us to reckon with. Isn't that right, lads?'

There was a smattering of agreement, not very enthusiastic, it seemed to Tom, but Simpson seemed alarmed. 'Now, look here . . .' he said in a different tone.

'Pay him,' the giant said, and with ill grace, he did.

Tom stopped to wash in the river on the way back home so that he could put his clothes on without spoiling them – Simpson hadn't offered him the chance – so news of this confrontation reached the town before he did. Tom found himself the hero of the hour. Even Mrs Hochenheimer had heard.

More importantly, so had other folk. And when it was rumoured later in the week that Simpson had been spotted in a field with his engine dragged out and up to steam, Tom's reputation as an engineer was fixed. The thing could have burst its boiler three days afterwards and it would not have altered what they thought. From then on he didn't have to look for work; it came to him. Steam did almost everything round here – hauling, milling, pumping, lifting, even dragging loads – and if anyone had a driver – or an engine – sick, the first person they thought about was Tom.

He'd helped put George Simpson in his place. That made him one of them.

Nathan was spreading marmalade on his breakfast toast. He liked a piece of toast for breakfast, not too crisp, with a teaspoon of bitter orange marmalade. That, and a lightly boiled egg on Saturdays, was what he always had. It was part of the routine of life, the way things ought to be, like Mother's breakfast tray and the polished serviette ring by his plate.

The intrusion of another serviette ring opposite his still gave him a feeling of unease – perhaps because it reminded him of mornings long ago when his father had presided over meals. However, he knew that he must adapt. It was one of the adjustments that being married brought, like a bathroom that smelled of a different kind of soap and having someone share your bed with you.

He had been a little disappointed by all that. Not in the mechanics, that had worked out perfectly, but in what his book called 'preliminary steps'. He'd done what they suggested, putting his hand on her chest first and the sort of thing that women were supposed to like these days, but Winnie had been totally unmoved. In fact, he suspected that she'd prefer it if he just got on with it, so that she could turn her back to him and go to sleep. He was coming to the conclusion that you couldn't believe everything you read in books.

He looked across at Winnie and gave her a little smile. 'And what do you plan to do today, my dear?' It was what his father had always said.

'What do you suppose I'm going to do?' she said impatiently. 'I'm going up to see your mother, to help her dress and sort her wools and run round after her, just in the same way as I always do. Just like I did before I married you, only a bit more so nowadays, because I have to do it in the evening too. What else do you suppose?' She sounded so bitter that it quite took him aback.

'My dear, it was only an enquiry,' he said mildly. He folded

170

his napkin precisely into four, then rolled it and put it neatly in the napkin ring. 'Well, I must be off. I have to lay out Mr Clarke today.'

His wife said nothing. She said it so determinedly that he was moved to add, 'It will be pleasant weather for it, anyway.'

'I'd like to come into Penzance with you, Nathan. For a change.'

He nodded graciously. 'I know. You've told me so before. And so you shall. When Mama can spare you sometime, I'm sure we'll manage it.'

He was trying to be helpful but she didn't answer him. She just looked furious and turned away.

He got up nervously and left the room, and a few minutes later he set off for work, with his top hat and kid gloves in his hand. He closed the door behind him with a gentle click, hoping nobody would hear him go. The last thing that he wanted was a scene. It was going to be a problem, with two women in the house – Winnie demanding one thing and his mother something else, and himself caught uncomfortably in between. Married life, he had decided ruefully, wasn't all it was cracked up to be.

Winnie was thinking very much the same thing. She was at the window watching and she saw him go. He raised a hand and waved to her, but she did not respond, just went on staring into nothingness.

Surely to goodness it was not too much to ask, just to be taken into town. Not that she could have bought anything, of course. That was one of life's crueller ironies. When she was just the paid companion here she'd had her wages and – though that wasn't much and she'd given most of it to Mother anyhow – she had usually contrived to keep a few pence for herself, to spend on ribbons or a bit of violet scent. Now she had nothing of her own at all. Nathan made her no allowance – she could apply to him for anything she wanted, he explained – not even for the housekeeping. Because she was not the mistress of the house.

That had been made very clear to her the first morning she came up here to live. She had had notions of what was expected of a brand-new wife, and she had gone into the kitchen to interview the cook. The woman listened to her, sullen-faced, but paid very scant attention, Winnie felt. A little later Mrs Zeal had sent for Winnie in her dressing room.

'I have something a little difficult to say to you. It is awkward, but I felt it best to mention it at once, so that there could be no misunderstanding later on. The fact is, this is my house, Winifred. It doesn't come to Nathan till I'm dead. Until then, if there is any interviewing of the servants to be done, it will be done by me.' She smiled her thin-lipped smile. 'I'm sure you had no intention to offend. Now, if you would be so good as to fetch my combs, you could help me to dress my hair.'

Later, Winnie went back to the gloomy room she shared with Nathan and flung herself in fury on the bed. But it did no good to fume. She was trapped as a sort of unpaid servant in this house and there was no escape. No going home at teatime, no Dora to giggle with at night, only her unwelcome duties to Nathan to look forward to.

She would not have believed how much she missed her twin. They hardly saw each other nowadays. Dora didn't even go to chapel much any more. Mother was too sick. That gave Winnie an excuse to call in at home whenever Mrs Zeal could spare her, but when she did there was no time to chat. Mother needed someone with her all the time – not that she knew much about it; she was drifting in and out of consciousness and thought she was talking to her own mother half the time – so when Winnie came she always went upstairs to sit with her, to give Gan and Dora a chance to do the shopping or catch up with other things. Dora almost seemed to welcome that. Things had never really been the same between them since that silly business with the Trewin boy.

Of course it was quite impossible, the way things were with Mother, for Dora to come visiting her twin. Perhaps it was just as well. Winnie had dreamed of receiving her and serving tea in china cups and generally playing at being the married hostess, but it was clear that if people came to visit it wouldn't be like that at all, and she wasn't sure she could bear for Dora to find out the truth just yet.

She was standing at the window now, still staring blankly out. She had not seen anyone approaching, so she was surprised to hear a knocking at the door. Nathan had forgotten something, probably. She sighed and went to let him in. Answering

172

the door was something that fell to her these days, ever since Alice, the maid, had been dismissed.

Dora was standing on the step. Winnie could scarcely have been more astonished if it had been the King himself.

'Dora!' She faltered. 'My dear life! Do come in.'

But Dora shook her head. 'No, Win. I've come to fetch you. You'd better come with me. Mother's failing – Father's gone to fetch the doctor, but she's conscious now, and asking for you. So please come. And hurry, or we're going to be too late.'

'Who is it, Winifred?' Mrs Zeal's thin voice called down from upstairs.

'It's my sister, Mrs Zeal.' She nodded to Dora. 'You wait here. I'll just get my hat and coat and I'll be back.' She left the front door open and flew upstairs, two steps at a time.

Her mother-in-law was waiting in her room. 'What . . .' she began.

Winnie did not wait to hear. 'My mother's taken bad,' she said. 'I'm wanted at home.'

The older woman sniffed. 'Well, that's most inconvenient.'

Something inside Winnie snapped. 'Yes,' she said, 'I've no doubt it is. Inconvenient for Mother, too. But there it is. So I'm going down there. I'm not sure when I'll be back.' And, leaving Mrs Zeal gaping like a fish, she rushed downstairs, seized her coat and bonnet from the stand and was back with Dora in a trice.

There was no time for talking, and no need. Dora just reached out for her hand and they hurried down the hill together, glad of one another's presence and support. But they were too late. Winnie knew it as soon as they turned the corner of the lane and saw the doctor there, talking to Gan, who was staring at the ground and twisting her apron in her hands.

Their grandmother looked up as they approached. 'She's gone,' she said, and her voice was not ungentle for a change. She nodded at Winnie. 'Want to go up and see her, now you're here? She went quite peaceful in the end.'

Winnie nodded. She felt numb and cold, and though she was full of tears, they would not fall. 'Best thing,' she said abruptly, and together with Dora she went up to the room.

Mother was lying there, as she always had, her eyes closed. Only the lack of breathing showed that she was gone.

173

Impossible to imagine that she would never smile again, that she would never say, 'Why, Winnie!' and reach out to hold her close. Winnie leaned over and planted a kiss on the cold forehead, while Dora took Mother's hand and sobbed. For a moment they both knelt silently beside the bed.

Dora got up and said urgently, 'Winnie, there's something . . .'

Gan came to the door. 'I've made some tea,' she said, and the moment of intimacy was shattered. Together they followed their grandmother downstairs.

Dora looked utterly bereft, and Winnie longed to comfort her. She put her arms around her sister's neck and pulled her close, but though Dora sobbed as if her heart would break, Winnie found it impossible to cry. She felt quite numb, as if something inside of her had died as well.

She stood awkwardly patting her twin's shoulder for a little while, and then offered the only bleak comfort she could find.

'Nathan will see to the funeral, of course.'

Two

Nathan did see to the funeral. Saw to it in style, as well: a big wreath for the door and deep rushes in the street; casket in best mahogany; glass hearse and six black horses dressed with plumes; four matching coffin-bearers, all in black; two mourning carriages for the family, and the St Just town silver band to follow on behind.

It was certainly impressive, though Dora could not suppress the feeling that somehow it was more an advertisement for Zeal's Funerary Services than anything to do with grief for the deceased. A simple service with a scattering of friends, that was what Dora would have chosen, and what Mother would have wanted for herself. Not this. Though it seemed that she was the only one who thought that way.

She glanced discreetly round the chapel. There was Father, pleased as punch by all the show – Dora could tell by the way he strutted like a turkeycock in his best suit and collar, though he kept a sober face and joined in, loud and solemn, in the hymns. Next to him was Gan, in her inevitable beaded black, and Winnie, strikingly fair and pale in her new black bombazine with a fetching little feathered hat and veil. Both of them, at different times, had murmured in her ear, 'Nathan has really done us proud.' Jamie, beside them, was too upset to care.

A reproving little cough came from the seat behind and Dora was aware of the elder Mrs Zeal, whose eyes were no doubt boring disapprovingly into her back, so she turned her attention to the preacher's words – though she could have told him more about her mother's worth than he appeared to know. She sat through the remainder of the service in a trance, and when they went out to the non-conformist burial-ground she watched the coffin lowered, by top-hatted strangers instead

175

of family, with a sense that all of this was quite unreal.

Besides, she had a problem that she could not share and she could not drive the recollection from her head. In one of her mother's last bouts of consciousness, she had gestured to Dora to come closer to the bed.

'Something . . . important . . . want for you to do . . .' The words had cost such an effort.

'Of course, Mother. Anything. What? You want a drink? Another pillow? What?'

Mother moved her head impatiently. 'In . . . big wardrobe . . . In the bottom . . . box . . .'

Dora went to the cupboard and opened it. Sure enough, under the folded summer clothes there was a box, full of old bags and half-worn gloves and outgrown shoes. 'This one?' She took it out, wondering what ancient memory her mother wanted to revive.

The sick woman nodded. 'In the bottom . . . pair of button boots . . . look in the right-hand one.'

She found the boots, still wondering, and slipped her hand inside. Right down in the body of the foot her fingers closed on something wrapped in cloth. Even before she drew it out, she knew what it was. 'Money?'

A faint, triumphant smile flitted across the haggard face. 'Told you before . . . For you and Winnie . . . when you're wed . . .'

Dora nodded. 'You said you'd buy her wedding outfit, I remember. But there's more than that. Much more.' She ran the stack of coins through her hands. 'There must be, oh, forty pounds or more.' It was a small fortune, she realized. More than enough to furnish a whole house.

A feeble nod. Then Mother said, as if the sight of it had given her strength, 'There's fifty guineas there. My mother gave it me and I've kept it all these years. Your father's been a good provider, give him that. And it's all there. Winnie never had her share – your Father paid up for her outfit, good as gold, and she is not in want. I was going to save it till she had a child, supposing she ever did. But now . . . You have it, Dora. For the two of you. Don't tell your father – promise me. He'll see for Jamie – he curses and blinds, but Jamie is his son – it's you girls I worry for. And don't tell Gan.' She fell back, coughing.

176

'Mother,' Dora said, 'I can't. I can't keep this from Father.' She was trying to imagine hiding this from him, and what he'd say and do if he discovered that she had.

Mother's thin hand closed on hers. 'You can. You must. Save it, for my sake, in case you're ever in real need. It's been a comfort to me all these years, to know I had this bit put by – I want the same security for you. Promise me, Dora.' She half sat up again and her eyes were feverish, as if this had demanded all her strength. 'Promise me.'

She pleaded with such strength that in the end Dora agreed and, at Mother's urging, slipped away to hide the money with some old treasures of her own – seashells and a drawing book and a card that Jamie had made – in the bottom of the chest of drawers she'd shared with Winnie until so recently. When she returned her mother had sunk back, eyes closed.

'Fetch Winnie, then.' And those had been the last words that she'd said.

Dora glanced at Winnie now, standing numb-faced at the grave, like a stricken statue. She hadn't managed to tell her about the money yet. On the one occasion when she had tried, the day Mother died, Gan had come in and interrupted them and somehow it hadn't been possible since.

Partly, Dora knew, it was not an accident. If Winnie suddenly had money of her own, you could not rely on her to use it sensibly – and Father would find out at once. Better, perhaps, to keep it in reserve as Mother did herself. But it was a terrible responsibility.

Besides, was she legally entitled to keep anything at all? She had overheard Father bragging to Charlie the other night that everything Mother had owned was his by right, so he was now sole owner of the fish store, boat and house. It had never occurred to her that he was not before. So what about that fifty guineas in her drawer? There was no one she could go to for advice. It was almost comforting to turn her mind to that, so that she did not have to listen to the dull thud of earth on the coffin where the remains of her beloved mother lay.

But the ordeal of the day was not over even then. It was back to the chapel hall again. Father had hired it for the afternoon and Nathan had organized a 'catered tea' – a grand affair of ham and tongue and potted beef, and what Father described

177

as 'fancy bits of things', with buttered splits and iced cake afterwards. Plenty of everything, too, so although there were more people than expected present (Nathan had put a notice in the paper, and Mother had been well-liked in her youth), Father had been able to stand up and say 'we hope that you will all join us for refreshments afterwards' which pleased him, you could see.

He shook hands with people and assumed an appropriately grieving face. Dora, thinking of the times when he had roared at Mother till she shook, felt suddenly furious with the whole charade and turned away. Of course, she was risking Father's wrath. She should have been seeing to it that the guests were fed and given a glass of the blackcurrant cordial that Nathan had laid on, 'in deference to Mrs Hunkin, who was a Methodist.'

'Not eating anything yourself?' a voice said in her ear.

She turned. It was Zachariah Zeal, to her surprise. 'I . . . I didn't know that you were here,' she stammered. 'Winifred . . . that is . . . you did not sit with us.'

He smiled. 'I'm not exactly family.' He did not say 'not yet' but his eyes conveyed the message all the same. 'Besides, I doubt if anybody knew that I was in the area. I hadn't planned to be down west just now, but I saw the notice in the paper yesterday and naturally I came.' He bent down and murmured so that only she could hear, 'I doubt if even Aunt Millicent realizes I'm here. So quickly, before she spots me and summons me imperiously to her side, allow me to help you to some cold meat and a buttered split.'

She shook her head. 'I should be serving you. It's my mother's funeral . . .'

'You're upset, of course you are, but you must eat, you know. I can't have you fading interestingly away.'

She found that he had made her smile with his absurd remarks. Suddenly she was glad that he was there.

'Why don't we strike a compromise? We'll serve each other,' he murmured with a smile. And she allowed him to steer her to the table once again.

'Ah, Dora, there you are!' Her father sounded sharp. 'I couldn't see you anywhere. Mrs Pearson needs another drink.' And so she was obliged to slip back into her role as dutiful hostess.

She looked across at Zachariah. He winked encouragement. Thank heaven he'd been there, she thought. It had forestalled a scene. No one else had noticed her moment of retreat. It occurred to her, with some surprise, that perhaps she could confide in him about Mother's gift. After all, he'd dealt with wives who died. He'd know what to do, if anybody did.

It was a relief to think of it, but she did not have the chance to speak to him privately again that day. The two Mrs Zeals had borne him off and claimed him for their own.

'Cousin Zachariah! How nice of you to come!' Winnie had seen him minutes earlier, but had only now managed to escape from sympathetic friends and make her way over to his side. 'Dora has been looking after you, I see.'

He smiled. 'Your charming sister, yes.' The smile alone could make your pulse race. Why couldn't Nathan ever do the same?

'You still find her charming?' She tried to make it light. 'Well, I am delighted. I know that you escorted her on one or two occasions earlier. You are not about to break her heart, I hope.' She was consumed with unreasonable inward jealousy about those outings, but the connection at least kept Zachariah close.

One eyebrow flickered upward. 'No, indeed. My intentions are quite serious, I assure you. Who could resist a lady of such charms? Demure, intelligent, and dutiful. But your sister won't be rushed.'

'Well, she's a Jenkins, like the rest of us,' Winnie said. She knew that good family was important to the Zeals.

'Ah yes, she's a Jenkins, too. Let us never overlook that salient fact.' He was teasing her again. 'And she is not unpleasing to the eye. Though you, my dear Winfred, look quite ravishing. Black suits you wonderfully. Confess it now, was that not the reason you elected to marry the worthy Nathan as you did?'

She felt the hot blush rising to her cheeks. 'You are absurd!'

'Of course!' He held her eyes with his own mocking ones. 'Now,' he went on without altering his tone, 'Aunt Millicent is bearing down on us. We must be conventional, nibble at a split and pretend to be engaged in social niceties.' As the

179

elder Mrs Zeal approached, he added without pause, 'And how are you settling to married life?'

She could not play his game with any skill. She found herself blushing and stammering, 'Oh . . . it . . . I . . . It suits me well enough.' It was a lie, she thought. A lie. She hated it. It was worse than boring, it was stultifying. She rued the day she'd ever agreed to marry Nathan Zeal. And to think she'd sought it and encouraged it! She looked up in surprise. It was the first time she had admitted this so strongly, even to herself. She met his eyes, and knew he read her thoughts.

Her mother-in-law had jostled through to join them by now. 'I should think it should suit you!' she said, with some asperity, making clear she'd heard that last exchange. 'Not many young women have such privilege.' She turned to Zachariah. 'My dear nephew, it is good to see you here. Pray, take no notice of her nonsenses. Nathan is very attentive and generous to her, I assure you. Indeed – though it is early days as yet, of course – we have hopes of very good news soon.' She stretched her thin lips in a meaningful smile.

For a moment Winnie could not work out what this meant, and when she did so she was mortified. Bad enough to have to suffer Nathan's inept nightly fumblings, without her chances of having offspring being publicly discussed, as though she were some kind of convenient brood mare. Zachariah had noticed, too. He glanced at her with that laconic eyebrow raised.

But her mother-in-law swept on. 'My dear Zachariah, you are too good, you know. Making the effort to come all this way on our account. Though Nathan did not disgrace us, do you think?'

'It was a splendid effort,' he said soberly and added, without the faintest outward hint of irony, 'I shall think of calling on his services myself. Shan't you?'

He was outrageous. Winnie had to bite her lip. But Mrs Zeal seemed oblivious to any mockery.

'And shall you come to tea with us, when we have finished here?' she enquired in the skittish tone she always used to him.

'That would be delightful.' He looked directly at Winnie as he spoke.

And so after a decent interval he escorted them back home.

It was a more agreeable evening than Winnie had spent for weeks. He charmed Mrs Zeal, teased Nathan horribly, and flirted with Winifred till he made her blush. But though she hovered close to him all evening, he did no more than brush her hand with his.

It was only after he had gone that it occurred to her that perhaps it had not been seemly to enjoy herself so much on the occasion of her mother's funeral.

Stan took off his tie and collar as soon as he got home, wriggling his neck free with so much force that he broke a collar stud.

'Curse the bloody thing!' he muttered, as the end flew off and underneath the bed. He did not stop to grovel round and pick it up. He wanted to get comfortable and go downstairs. There were things he needed to get straight.

He undid the top two buttons of his shirt and loosened his braces and the waistband of his pants. That was a bit more like it. How did they expect a man to breathe, stuffed up like a wax dummy in all those fancy clothes? Still, he told his reflection in the glass, it had gone off well enough. Stan Hunkin could hold his head up high. They had given Sybil a good send-off, with a band and everything. Nobody could say he didn't do it right.

He was glad it was all over, all the same. Now he could have a cup of tea and settle down to be himself again. It was a strain, all this shaking hands and listening to everyone going on about what a fantastic woman she had been. They didn't know the half. Nothing but martyred moping and being ill for years, yet worse than useless round the house or anything else you'd want a woman for. 'A merciful release,' one of her friends had said, and it was – though not in the way that stupid cow had meant.

And now there was his idiot of a son to think about. Sybil had made a proper namby-pamby out of him. It was unnatural the way that lad was creeping round today, pale as paste and snivelling like a girl. Perhaps, now his mother was gone and couldn't run round fussing after him, there would be a chance to turn him into a bit more of a man. Something needed to be done, at any rate. You couldn't leave a boat and business to a mollycoddled jellyfish like that.

Stan squared his shoulders and went belligerently downstairs, ready for the tears and arguments he knew were bound to come. His mother was fussing with the tea kettle, but otherwise the kitchen was empty. It seemed unnatural, especially when he'd been preparing for a spat.

'Where is everybody?' he demanded, sitting himself impatiently on the nearest chair.

Gan set the teapot on the table and began collecting cups and saucers from the shelf. 'Dora's gone up with a basket to the chapel hall, see can she bring home anything that's left. Seems a shame to let it go to waste. Jamie's gone with her for a bit of a walk. Do the boy good to get out a bit today.'

'You're damty right it would,' he grumbled. 'Do him good to get out every day. Don't hold with all this sitting round with books, like some daisy girl. Man wants a bit of fresh air in his lungs.'

Gan fetched the milk and sugar and some empty plates. 'He's clever, mind you, Stan. His teacher says he'd win a scholarship.'

'And what damty good is that? Boy's got a living waiting. Here am I – I've set it up for him, all he's got to do is buckle down – and is he grateful? Not a bit of it. How many lads round here have got the chance he's got? You answer me that.'

She nodded, putting knives and spoons around and fetching down a pot of home-made jam. 'I know, Stan. You've been very good. But Jamie's not the type, I s'pose. He hasn't got the strength. Bit flimsy-like. Takes after his mother in that way. You can't turn him into what he isn't, Stan.'

Stan brought his fist down on the table with a thump that made the crockery shake. 'Can't I though? We'll damn well see. He doesn't try, that's all. Afraid of his own shadow, that one is. Well, I aren't putting up with it no more. He's coming fishing, whether he welcomes it or not. Got a good mind to take him out tonight.'

'Stan, you can't do that the day his mother's buried. What would people say? Anyway, it's far too late for that. The boys will have put to sea by now, if they are going at all.'

That was true, but he was not admitting it. He said, grudgingly, 'Well, tomorrow then. And don't go saying as he's got to go to school on Monday morning, 'cause he's damty near old enough to leave. If I say that he's coming out with us, he does, and there's an end of it.'

Gan looked as if she might argue, even then, but Dora and Jamie chose that moment to walk in through the door. She turned to them instead. 'Well?'

Dora shook her head. 'Nathan Zeal had sent a servant down to take the stuff up there. Well, what could I say? He was the one that paid for it, when all is said and done.'

Stan was unreasonably furious. His son-in-law had paid for everything, all right, but whose wife's funeral was it, after all? 'So what are we supposed to eat?' he said.

Dora put four buttered splits and a handful of egg and bacon tartlets on the plate. 'Jamie had a word to them and they gave us these. Make us a bit of tea at any rate.'

Her tone of satisfaction was the final straw. Stan lumbered to his feet. He swept the plate and contents to the floor. 'Oh, they did, did they? We'll I'm not taking charity and that's a fact. Just as well that some of us have learned to bring home fish. That way at least we'll never starve. So you, young fellow,' he whirled round to his son, who cowered like the wretched thing he was, 'you can come out and do it from now on. Starting tomorrow, and no argument.'

Dora said, 'But Jamie . . .'

'And there's another thing – "Jamie, Jamie"', like a blessed girl. Why can't he be James or Jim like anybody else? From now on things are going to be different around here. He's James, and don't let me hear you call him by that soppy name again.'

Dora was on her hands and knees collecting up the food and he stepped over her. He was hungry, but he wasn't going to admit defeat by eating any of that wretched supper now.

'Well, now your mother isn't here to tell me otherwise, I'm going to do what I ought to have been doing years ago. I'm going down to the Miner's Arms. Don't know when I'll be back.' And he stalked out, leaving them staring after him. As he pulled the door shut he saw Dora putting the shattered tarts back on the plate and scraping dirty butter off the spilts.

It was not unpleasant at the Miner's Arms. Nobody was very welcoming – people round here weren't any friends of his – but there was nothing said. The publican even bought a drink for him.

'Out of respect for your sorrow, Stan,' he said.

Three

'Is there a Tom Trewin 'ere?'

The man who lurched into the dining room was a scrawny sort, in tattered canvas trousers and a vest which left his sunburned neck and shoulders bare. He was wearing heavy muddy boots as well, and had not removed his hat, which was old and water-stained and fringed with old corks to keep the flies away. His arms were heavily tattooed, he walked with a decidedly sideways limp, and he gave off a smell of river-mud and sweat.

The half-dozen breakfasting residents all turned to stare at him. Mrs Hochenheimer, at the urn again, made disapproving tutting noises with her tongue.

Tom had been finishing his meal – a hunk of toast and a generous spoonful of congealing scrambled egg – but he pushed back his plate and got slowly to his feet. 'Who wants him?' he enquired.

The newcomer squinted appraisingly at him. 'You Trewin?' Tom didn't answer but the fellow nodded as if satisfied. 'I hear you're a fair hand with steam engines. That right?'

'Maybe,' Tom said. He had learned to be cagey with strangers in the last few months. Ned Kelly and his gang were dead and gone, but there were still people in the district who operated on the fringes of the law. Hard men, who drank and fought and gambled endlessly; who'd steal your boots to buy another beer. People told stories of being accosted and required to pay imaginary debts. Tom did not like the look of this visitor at all.

The man took a step forward. He was scrawny but he emanated a kind of wiry strength. 'Name's Murcheson,' he said. 'I need an engine man.'

So it was business. That was a relief. But Tom had already had an offer for the day. 'I'm not available.'

184

'I think you will be, when you've heard what I've got to say.' It sounded like a threat.

'I told you. I can't do anything today,' he repeated. 'Promised to go down the sawmills later on. They've got a driver short.'

Murcheson looked at him for a minute thoughtfully then spat, leaving a pool of spittle on the floor. 'Tomorrow then. Eight thirty.' He turned as if to leave.

'Hang on,' Tom said. 'I never said I would. Don't know how much you're paying or anything. What kind of engine is it anyway?'

Murcheson pushed back his hat and stared. It was a hard face, Tom thought, but not a stupid one. 'Paddle steamer, of course,' the stranger said. 'That's why I need a man so urgently. Can't keep her tied up, eating money here. I got a cargo, and I got to get upstream before the rains.'

'You want an engine man to come with you?' This was a new idea to Tom. He had become accustomed to living day to day, taking work where he could find it and accepting what anyone would pay. He had got by – paid the rent and even managed to send money home sometimes – but he hadn't had a steady job since he arrived.

Murcheson laughed. 'Isn't that what I'm telling you? Of course I want an engine man to come. Not much use to have one and leave him behind. Now look, young fellow, I don't know you, but I've heard good things of you. You come with me – give it a try, six months – I pay a decent wage. Fifteen bob a week. And you'll have your keep as well. Damn sight better than sitting here, putting cash in someone else's hands – saving your presence, missus.' He doffed his hat mockingly to Mrs Hockenheimer, who had been openly listening to all this, revealing as he did so a fringe of thinning auburn hair. The woman looked away, and he turned back to Tom. 'They tell me you are trying to send money to your ma. This ought to help, provided you don't go drinking what you earn. But you make up your mind. I want to leave first thing.'

Tom found that he was listening. 'What boat is it?' he asked.

'The *Mariebelle*. You ask around. Anybody down the pier will know.'

Tom had already decided to have a word with the harbour

master if he could. But he was reminded of what that gentleman had said. 'I thought the paddle boats were nearly dead?' he said. It sounded a bit insulting, so he added hastily, 'Put out of business by the railways, I heard.'

Murcheson looked him in the eye. Pale blue eyes, with dogged determination written in their depths. 'Did you so?' he said laconically. 'Well, they haven't put me out of business yet. And won't, if I can find an engine man. Last blighter that I had got drunk again last night. I had to let him go. So, there you are, young Trewin. That's the offer, and you won't do better. Ask around. Eight thirty tomorrow morning. I'll be waiting on the dock.' He jammed his filthy hat upon his head again and limped away.

Tom did ask around a bit, and he quite liked what he heard.

'Bit of a rough stick, old Murcheson,' the sawmill owner said. 'But straighter than a red gum, all the same. Been up and down this river twenty years. I've sent supplies upriver on the *Mariebelle* myself. He'll never make a fortune, mind: nothing's too good for that confounded boat, though he never spends a halfpenny on himself. Started in the navy, I believe, then bought that boat of his and came up here. Had a wife and kid as I recall. I know the wife died, years and years ago, but I don't know what happened to the girl. Must be – oh, I don't know – nineteen or twenty I should think, by now. He hoped she'd come back with him on the boat when she was grown, but I don't know if she ever did. Too grand for the river-men by half.'

That evening when he got back to the boarding house he paid his bill, packed his few remaining possessions in his battered box, and at eight thirty in the morning, when Murcheson came limping down the dock, there was his new engine man to welcome him.

'You're coming then. Thought you'd make up your mind to it, from what I heard of you.' Murcheson took the box and swung it from the ground.

'Would you have gone without me if I hadn't come?' They had arrived at the *Mariebelle* by now, her blue paint peeling in the sun, and a barge, loaded with bales and furniture, hanging off astern. Her fires were already partly stoked and a lazy wisp of smoke was rising from her stack.

Murcheson stepped aboard, dodging the paddle chain that

186

ran along the deck. 'How could I go, when I didn't have an engine man?' he said, giving a little barking laugh, leading the way onboard. A blast of heat came out to meet them from the firebox. 'I'd just have come and seen you every day until you did.' He slung the box on to a tiny bunk in the little cabin at the front, which was neat and clean and stiflingly hot, though not as hot as Tom had rather feared – perhaps being near the river helped. 'You make yourself at home, and I'll make us both some tea. Then I'll you show where this engine is.'

That was amusing, Tom thought, since the engine dominated the whole centre of the boat. Murcheson took a heavy metal can and went back astern.

'I've got a Chinese hand aboard, to help us stoke and load,' he called. 'He's fetching stores for us this minute, but when he gets back we'll get her up to steam and make a start. We've got enough firewood to make the Williamses. That's the first wood pile up the stream.'

Tom looked surprised. He was accustomed to engines that were stoked with coal. 'She uses logs?'

'Tons of them, but there are places on the way. We fuel her as we go. Bring that enamel mug that's hanging up. I've got the billy boiled.'

And that was Tom's introduction to the cubbyhole which would, if he had known it, be his home for years.

There was no dissuading Father. He was taking Jamie fishing and that was that, though Gan had succeeded in nagging him out of doing it midweek, at least, because of school.

All the same, it was upsetting for the whole house. They had been out several times by now, and it was invariably the same. Jamie would spend days beforehand, pale and shivering. Father would look like a thunderstorm, and nobody would dare say a word. When the dreaded night arrived they'd go out on the boat, with Father looking grim as granite all the while. Jamie would be sick and miserable to death, and then come home whiter than a sheet and really need to have a day in bed. Father refused to hear of that, of course – 'no mollycoddles here' – so Jamie, or James as Father now insisted he was called, would spend days creeping around the house like an apprentice ghost, trying to make himself invisible. And then the whole business would begin again.

187

It was hard to know how anyone could profit by all this – it interfered with the smooth running of the boat and even Charlie had been up to have a word. 'Boy isn't strong enough. 'Tisn't his fault, Cap'n, it's his health. Some lads are just not up to it.' But that had only made things worse. Father had made his mind up. It was his boat and his son, he said, and he wasn't brooking interference from anyone.

So it was no good Dora saying anything. The atmosphere between them was like Newlyn ice works now, and even Gan couldn't get a civil word from him after she'd done her bit by getting Jamie's fishing trips confined to Saturdays. 'Conspiracy of bloody females,' Father said, and stomped off down to the Miner's Arms again. He was going down there more and more these days, which meant the house was briefly peaceable at night, but when he came home he was impossible.

Mercifully, there'd been no more trouble with the nets. With Father in this mood there was no knowing what he'd do. Take it out on Jamie, probably. The heckling in the street had stopped as well. Dora knew why that was. 'Lost his wife, poor fellow,' people would be saying, as though that was an excuse for everything and Father's drinking and bad temper had been caused by grief. Dora knew different, but she was powerless.

Sometimes she thought of simply running off. She longed to be back working at the school, but that was impossible – and in any case, by now they had appointed someone else. She had become a sort of household drudge, doing the heavy chores that were too much for Gan, though nothing she did was ever right.

She'd do a sight better going off somewhere as a maid. The work would be no different, but at least she would be paid for what she did – and get a half-day off a week! Father wouldn't like it, but he wouldn't have to know. With Mother's money she could catch a train and go somewhere he'd never find her. London perhaps. She could even buy into an apprenticeship, maybe, and learn a trade – though that cost money and she didn't know how much. Sometimes she lay awake at night and dreamed of it. But then she thought of Jamie, and she knew she couldn't leave. She wasn't much protection, but she was all he had. Since that confrontation in the kitchen,

188

Father didn't often strike him nowadays when she was there.

Thank heaven Winnie came and saw her once a week. That was the only bright spot in her life. The awkwardness between them had eased a little bit since Mother died, and Winnie very clearly liked to come.

'It's like a prison up there, Dora, honestly. Fetching and carrying for Mrs Zeal – just like I always used to do. But if I say I'm coming down to see you, Nathan sticks up for me and I can come.'

Dora knew exactly how she felt. She would have liked to get out sometimes too, but she was glad of company and, anyway, Winnie's visit spelled freedom of a kind. Gan always used the time to slip out to Crowdie's for some milk.

So here was Winnie today, sitting at the kitchen table as though she'd never left, sipping tea and nibbling one of the rock cakes she had brought – Mrs Zeal had no objection to her bringing home stale buns, if the cook had no other use for them. She was looking prettier than ever in a deep-violet mourning dress, which made Dora feel as dowdy as a mouse, but she was typically impatient of her sister's compliment.

''Tisn't as if I chose it for myself,' she said. 'It was a piece of silk that Nathan's mother had, and she said that I could use it now I'm coming out of black, because it was "appropriate for Nathan's wife". I sometimes think I'll never be allowed to choose my own clothes again.'

Dora said something deprecating. She always felt a little guilty when Winnie talked like this. She hadn't told her about Mother's money yet – she still intended to ask Zachariah Zeal about it when he next came down this way. Supposing that he did. It seemed a long time since she'd seen his mocking smile.

She said, with pretended casualness, 'Never mind, Win, I'm sure you look very pretty as you are. You must ask your cousin Zachariah when he comes. Have you and Nathan heard from him lately, by the way?'

Winnie turned scarlet, for no reason Dora could perceive. 'Oh, you know Zachariah, he is quite absurd,' she said. 'He writes that there are wildcat strikes among the boilermen in the docks up north and he's afraid that it will spread down here and start affecting his shipping interests. He's even talking about selling up in Fowey and finding somewhere nearer to

189

Penzance, since he has to come and go so much these days.'
She gave a little laugh. 'I should have supposed it would have
suited him the more to move to Plymouth or Falmouth, where
the shipping is – but there! Perhaps he will return to court
you after all. He's coming to the Boases' again, I understand.'
She had gone so pink her cheeks looked half on fire.

'I wanted to consult him about something, that's all,' Dora
said, feeling herself flush scarlet in her turn. 'Though how I
should contrive to do it, I don't know. I hardly seem to leave
the house these days.'

Her twin was instantly contrite. 'I'd ask you up to us, sometimes,' she said, 'Only I'm not sure I'd be allowed to entertain you on my own – Nathan's mother would want to be
there too, being the great lady and taking charge of things.
We couldn't talk. It wouldn't be the same.' She pushed her
cup to Dora, who filled it with more tea. 'I sometimes think,
you know, that you were right. I shouldn't have gone and
married Nathan Zeal.'

Dora was so astonished at this admission that she almost
dropped the milk. 'Why, Winnie! What's the matter? He's
not unkind to you?'

'Oh no, he's not unkind. He isn't anything. That's the
trouble, I suppose.' Her sister gave a bitter little laugh. 'I
don't know why I'm bothering to say. It's just . . . I might as
well be married to a chair, for all the life and romance he's
got in his soul.'

Of course, it was immensely tempting to say 'I told you
so', but Dora suppressed the impulse and managed to murmur,
with genuine concern, 'Well, being married isn't easy, Mother
always said. I'm sure you'll grow more used to it in time.
And you've got plenty to be thankful for. Nathan's not unkind,
you said, and he keeps you in good style. You've got that big
house and everything – and at least you're not rattling around
here.' She didn't envy Winnie her creepy husband, certainly,
but for two pins she'd trade places sometimes, all the same.

Winnie had been stirring her tea with energy. She didn't look
at Dora now. 'Just don't you go making the same mistake, that's
all, rushing off to marry Zachariah, just because he's there.'

Dora gave a rueful grin. 'Don't worry about that. I'm not
likely to marry anyone, though it would have attractions sometimes, I admit. Zachariah asked me once – at least I think he

did – but I told him that I needed time to think. It must have put him off. In any case, he's never asked me out – or even come here calling on me – since.'

'But he likes you,' Winnie burst out, and then seemed to wish she hadn't. 'That is . . . well . . . oh, nothing. Let's talk of something else. Have you seen anything of—'

But whatever she was going to say was lost. Gan came dashing in that moment, so afire with news she didn't even stop to take her shawl and bonnet off.

'Here, have you heard?' she said, panting in a way that made it clear that – despite her bad arthritic knee – she'd run all the way home. 'I heard it from somebody who'd just come back from town. Town crier was hollering the news out in Penzance. Everything is closing down and sending people home. Who'd have thought it? We knew that he was ill, of course, but who'd believe that it would come to this, at his age? What a dreadful thing.'

'What is?' Winnie voiced the question before Dora did.

'Why, the King, of course. He's gone and blooming died. Just shows that money can't buy everything.'

Nathan took a professional interest in the funeral of the King. He bought every newspaper that he could find and studied the photographs with care, and hunted the pages of the under-takers' and embalmers' magazines. Of course, he couldn't offer gun carriages or mounted escorts to his customers, but, following his sympathetic murmurings to the bereaved, there was a brief fashion for having the coffin immediately followed by the family dog, just as the King's had been. Miss Amanda Hartington – a spinster of such enormous bulk that they had to take the coffin down the cottage staircase sideways-on – even left instructions that her cortège should be headed by her white, bad-tempered cat, which one of the paid mourners had to carry on a satin cushion all the way.

'I don't know why people want to do such things,' Winnie said with a sniff when she heard.

They were having breakfast on the morning following that burial, and Nathan had mentioned it to her – partly because he thought that it would interest her (the cat had disrupted the procession to the grave by jumping off its perch and running off), and partly to break the awful silence that seemed to

191

descend over breakfast these days. Nathan had even confided to Mamma that he feared that his wife was not content.

'Nonsense,' his mother had replied robustly. 'Winifred has been rather spoiled, I fear. She's discontented for the sake of it. She misses her family, no doubt, but so does every bride. And of course her mother died, which must affect her too. She's not accustomed to death as we are, Nathan. You must give her time. Wait until there's a family on the way – things will be different then, you'll see.' She gave him a sideways look. 'Things are all right in that department, I suppose? Some young women are ridiculously coy and difficult about these things.'

And he'd been obliged to say, 'No, things are all right there,' because they were. He could not complain. Winnie never actually refused him, though she made it clear she didn't care for 'being pawed', and it had occurred to him that the occasions when he persisted, like last night, corresponded with the coolest silences at breakfast the next day. But, as Mamma said, none of them was getting any younger and they wanted to see the business with an heir before she died.

He took a deep breath now, and tried to improve the atmosphere again. 'These things are good for business, my dear,' he said. 'If I can say to people, "as seen at the late King's funeral", they welcome it. They think we're up to date and they are getting the best service for their loved ones. What is wrong with that?'

'While you make extra charges?' Winnie sneered.

'Well, I had to pay an extra man to hold the cushion, naturally,' Nathan replied. She had nettled him. Why could she not be more interested and encouraging? He had done his best by her, provided her with the new dress she wanted – Mamma had been very good to turn up that unwanted length of silk – and permitted her to go down and see her sister every week, though it was an obvious inconvenience to Mamma. What more could a woman ask?

She looked startled at his sharpness, and he felt ashamed. Two wrongs did not make a right, as Mamma said. He added, by way of offering amends, 'The Boases are giving another concert in aid of charity. Funds to the Boer War veterans, I believe. Mr Boase had a cousin killed. Should you like to accompany me again?' In fact, as he knew, there

192

was very little choice – Mamma had already decreed that they should go.

Winnie knew it too. 'I suppose I am obliged to.' It wasn't gracious, but he took it for assent.

'That is settled then.' He folded up the paper, which he'd had beside his plate, and got to his feet. 'Now, I must go. We've got another body coming in today. I've to measure up his wooden overcoat.'

She didn't smile at his pleasantry. He walked over and kissed her on the cheek, a token which she permitted without saying anything. At the door he paused and tried again. 'You're going to your sister's this afternoon again?'

She looked at him dully. 'Yes.'

Just that. He sighed and left the room. He hated it when she was cold like this, and now it was happening almost every day. Sometimes – and he hated to admit this to himself – he wondered if, despite what Mamma thought, he hadn't been better off as a bachelor. He got himself ready gloomily, carefully combing the strands across his head, and had just picked up his hat and gloves when something struck him. Zachariah was invited to the concert, too, and he'd escorted Dora to things once or twice. Perhaps, if he mentioned that prospect to Winifred, it would improve her mood.

He went back to the dining room. His wife was there. She didn't notice him. She was standing in front of the mirror, making alarming faces at herself and addressing her reflection bitterly. 'A Boase concert! What a crashing bore! Still, I suppose it will get me out of here and I can be bored in Penzance for a change. And, even if I have to talk to that appalling girl all night, it will be a change of company at least. I believe otherwise I shall go completely mad.'

Mad? It was a possibility. Who else would stand there talking to herself and making faces in the looking glass? Nathan glanced around. Supposing the servants were to hear? Fortunately there was nobody around. He watched Winnie for a moment, horror-struck, then tiptoed silently away.

Even Mamma, he decided, mustn't learn of this.

Four

Tom heard about the King's death from the Chinaman who was the deckhand on the *Mariebelle*.

Wing Lo, he was called, but Murcheson called him Johnny Chinaman, and Wing Lo didn't seem to mind. He was a small, stooped man with missing teeth, skinny as a rat, but he had surprising strength and stamina. He could unload furniture and wool bales on his own, sometimes quicker than Tom and Murcheson could manage it between them. He was an expert stoker, an indifferent cleaner and an erratic cook – all of which tasks fell chiefly to his lot – but when they occasionally picked up a load of gigantic red-gum logs to take back downstream to the mills, he truly proved his worth by being as agile as a monkey, and as fearless too.

The biggest logs were always carried half-submerged, held on by chains on each side of the barge – that way the water took the weight, and hugely increased the load the boat could tow – while the smaller giants were lashed in a slippery, rolling pyramid on the deck. Thus loaded, the *Mariebelle* was very wide, and a log would sometimes catch on an obstruction and threaten to slew her round or even bring her entirely to a stop. This was where Johnny came into his own. He would nip overboard from the stern of the *Mariebelle* and – ignoring the threshing of the paddle wheels – shinny like a squirrel across the towing line and edge out on the slippery logs to free the snag. Sometimes he fended them away by casually standing on a log and using his foot to push them off, and at other times he did it with a broom.

It made Tom wince to watch him. The Murray River was often dangerous. There were water snakes and eddies and Johnny had never learned to swim. No wonder when they tied up somewhere that had a public bar, Johnny would disappear at dusk and not come back till dawn. It was wise to avoid him when he did come back. The usually grinning Johnny became obstreperous with drink and had once, it was rumoured, threatened the previous fellow with a knife.

So it was not surprising that when Johnny wandered in at midnight one hot and rainy night, shouting and apparently much the worse for wear, Tom simply pretended that he was asleep. This time, however, the pretence was not enough. Johnny lurched into the cabin and seized him by the arm.

'Tommee, Tommee, waking up,' he said.

Tom half opened an eye. 'What is it, Johnny? Seen those ghost barges again?' He'd heard Johnny's stories about them many times. The Chinaman had seen them, many years ago, and lived in constant terror that they would come back. Tom knew what they were, by now, and there was nothing supernatural in the sight at all. Demand for red gum had been so intense in the glory days that some barge masters used to load their barges up with logs and simply let them loose, to drift back on the current on their own. That way they could load more barges than the boat would tow, and it saved considerably on fuel. It was dangerous: some of the barges had no men or lights aboard, although they did drag heavy chains which kept them to the central channel more or less and helped to slow them down. It must have been alarming to encounter them at night – black, unlighted craft drifting eerily down the river with a clank of chains. Tom had explained all this to Johnny several times, but the Chinaman was still convinced that he had witnessed river ghosts – and evil ones at that.

'No ghost barge Mister Tommee. Listen what I tell you. Mister King he dead.'

Tom struggled upright. 'What?'

'True, Mr Tommee. They tell me in the town. Your Mr King the Edward, he dead yesterday. No sell beers today. Where Mr Murcheson?'

'Gone to see his daughter in the town.' Tom was wide awake by now. 'This township is where she's lived since she left school. Some relative's been looking after her.'

Johnny shook his head. 'Missee Marcia, she come on the boat one time. Before you come. But other engine man he drink too much and make a – what you say? – a grope.' He

195

gave a sudden wicked grin that showed his snaggled teeth. 'He brave man, that engine man. Missee Marcia, big girl.'

Tom found himself smiling at this account. 'So her father sent her back here again, where she was safe? And now he only sees her now and then?'

Johnny nodded. 'Only I think Missee Marcia want to come with him. She tell me last time she not like it here. Want to be on the river. Will be her boat one day, after all.'

Tom stared at him. 'But she's a woman.'

'Have been women on the river. Some got boats.' That wicked grin again. 'Anyway, I tell you. Missee Marcia – big girl.'

Tom's curiosity was by now aroused. He wondered what this Marcia might be like. He did not have long to wait. Next morning, Murcheson was back, with someone who was obviously his daughter on his arm.

'Morning, Trewin, sorry to be so long. Bit of a change of plan, here, I'm afraid. The King has died, I dunno if you heard. No good us moving for a day or two. And when we do, this little lady wants to come. Far as Echuca anyway. This is my daughter, Marcia. Marcia, this is Tom, the engine man.'

She looked like Murcheson. Same auburn hair, same freckles, same piercing, shrewd blue eyes. And she was scowling at him like her father sometimes scowled. But where Murcheson was scrawny, she was indeed a big girl – tall and strapping, with muscles in her forearms like a man's.

'Mornin',' she said abruptly, in a deep voice. She nodded at Tom briefly, then turned away at once. 'Dad, where am I to sleep?'

'My berth, like you always did,' her father said. 'I'll bunk in with Tom.'

Tom winced inwardly. There were two berths inside the cubbyhole, but there was not much room and up to now he'd had it to himself. Johnny preferred to sleep out on the deck, rigging himself an awning if it rained, or – if the cargo they were carrying was appropriate – shinnying across the towline to make a shelter on the barge.

It was awkward, too, with Marcia aboard. There seemed to be no privacy at all. You couldn't do a simple thing like change your shirt without feeling that she might be watching you – although, to do her justice, when he glanced at her she

196

was always looking somewhere else. In fact, she almost seemed to be ignoring him. She kept as far away from him as possible all day, and didn't address a word to him that wasn't strictly necessary, although she prattled on to Murcheson non-stop. Tom did not mind at all. It saved him the trouble of avoiding her.

Johnny and Murcheson seemed pleased to have her there. She made herself useful, you had to admit that. She had soft rags out in no time and, in the few days that they were moored, had polished all the brasses till they shone and scrubbed the decks a good deal cleaner than Johnny ever did. And she could cook. The soup that she conjured up for lunch was excellent – not salty or watery or burned, as Johnny's almost certainly would have been.

All the same, the casual comradeship was lost, and since there was nothing to be done aboard the boat, Tom did what he very rarely did – he went ashore and wandered rather aimlessly around the settlement. It was a tiny place: a wooden church, a general store with a corrugated roof, a butcher's slaughter shed that doubled as a shop, a blacksmith's forge-cum-ironmongery, a bakery, a greengrocer, and a woman who had a notice on her door:

> Being in possession of the latest mechanical sewing machine, I am now able to offer alterations and dress-making at home. Tooth-drawing also undertaken.

That, with a scattering of houses on a dusty street and Johnny's favourite hotel and public bar, seemed to be the commercial extent of the new little town.

It was Sunday by now, and everything was closed, but Tom was amazed to realize that even in this tiny place, half a day from any other town and half a world from London, there were already black banners in the windows of the shops and notices saying CLOSED MONDAY, IN HONOUR OF THE KING. It seemed extraordinary to be standing here, under a merciless Australian sky with red dust blowing in his face and brightly coloured parrots pecking at the trees, and know that at home they would be mourning in exactly the same way. He wondered how the message had been flashed – from ship to ship, perhaps? – around the globe.

197

A horse and cart went clattering by, and covered him in dust. He glimpsed the tangled pile of dead snakes in the back. There had obviously been another hunt – there was a trade in skins for shoes and handbags now, and there were records of thousands being shot in one weekend. Tom was getting used to snakes. Johnny came back with one, from time to time – whether he had killed it himself, Tom didn't know – and grilled it on the fire. Tom couldn't bring himself to try it though.

'You wait, Mister Tommee,' Johnny said. 'You get up the river when he dries. You stuck, for months maybe. You be glad to eating anything. Snake meat very good.'

Apart from the cart there was no sign of life, except for a mangy dog that came and sniffed his shoes. Somewhere a piano was being played, and the sound hung in the heavy air like dust. After a little while he turned away, and went back to the *Mariebelle*. It was cooler on the water, and though glowering Marcia still treated him with suspicion and disdain, she had grilled some delicious river fish for tea.

Tom went to his cabin early. Mercifully, Murcheson didn't snore all night.

'I've brought a bit of sponge cake with me,' Winnie said, producing a small brown paper package which she'd been carrying. 'The cook up there was going to throw it out. It's rather on the stale side, I'm afraid, but if you warm it up and put a bit of something wet with it, it'll make a bit of pudding by and by.' She seated herself on the kitchen settle as she spoke.

'That's good of you, Winnie,' Dora said sincerely, unwrapping the piece of cake with care. It was dry but, as her sister said, it was far too good to waste. There were few treats in the Hunkin household nowadays: anything left over when the basic bills were paid seemed to disappear down at the Miner's Arms. And you couldn't ask for extra; Father just got furious. Dora was at her wits' end sometimes. Jamie was growing like a tree, and needed a new pair of shoes, but goodness only knew how she was going to pay for them. Unless she used the money Mother left . . .

She wouldn't think of that. She said instead, 'So, what about a lovely cup of tea? I've only got bread and jam to give you, I'm afraid.'

198

For a moment she thought Winnie was going to refuse, but her twin said softly, 'Mother's jam?'

Dora nodded. 'Blackberry. One of the last batch she ever made,' and they stood for a moment remembering those days, when they had brought home fruit and she had made it into jam, filling the house with warm, sweet smells – and bees. It was saddening now to recollect how tired she had looked.

'Good jam, then,' Winnie said, so Dora fetched it, made the tea, and they sat down to eat.

Winnie was complaining about the Zeals again. 'Thank heaven Nathan's going to take me to a concert soon. Only at the Boases, but still. And it's likely that you're going to be invited too. Your Zachariah's coming down, I hear.'

'Well, I haven't heard about it,' Dora said. 'And he's not "my Zachariah" anyway.' She felt regretful, though. It would have been fun, she thought, to spend another evening in his company, but obviously, since everything was planned and he'd not been in touch with her, he was intending to escort someone else. Served her right for saying no to him.

'Well, he was going to ask you,' Winnie said. 'He wrote to Mrs Zeal. He said—' She was interrupted by a knocking on the door.

They looked at one another, in one of those moments they sometimes had when each of them knew exactly what the other one was thinking.

'That'll be him now,' Winnie said.

'It can't be.' Dora got up to answer it. But she hoped it was.

It wasn't him, of course. On the doorstep was a little girl, all pink and breathless and so dishevelled that it took a moment for Dora to work out who it was. 'Amy Taylor?'

Amy was too breathless to say anything. Instead she reached out a small hand and tugged Dora's skirt.

'What is it, Amy?' Dora said. Amy was usually fastidious. It must be something terrible, she thought, to make the child come running here like this with her skirts askew and her plaits escaping from their fastenings.

Amy let got the skirt and pulled her hand. 'Oh, Miss Hunkin,' she managed between gasps. 'Come quick! Your father – he's murdering your brother Jamie down there at the quay!'

*   *   *

199

Stan had lost all sense of self-control. The world had turned into a crimson mist and he was holding Jamie back against a bollard and hitting him with anything that came to hand.

'Varmint,' he was hollering. 'Bloody little varmint. Bloody cut my bloody nets, would you?' He punctuated each word with a blow. Even when the boy fell to the ground it did not stem his anger, and he began to kick the cowering form. 'I thought it was the bloody Pollards and that was bloody bad enough, but it was my own bloody son all the bloody time!'

'Stan, that's enough. Can't you see the boy is hurt.' That was Charlie clawing at his arm.

Stan shook him off. 'You clear off out of it. You're bloody near as bad. Pay you lot to keep an eye out on the boat, and what? You let this bugger come along and bloody slit the nets. How much do you think that's bloody going to cost?' He was still aiming kicks at the culprit as he spoke.

A voice said, 'Stan Hunkin?' in a tone that made him pause. He looked around. It was that useless police sergeant from Penvarris, getting off his stupid bicycle and coming over with a self-important air. Stan had a momentary wild desire to knock the fellow down – which he could easily have done – but he realized there was a crowd of people standing watching him. He hadn't noticed them till now. He aimed a boot at Jamie one more time, then whirled around to face them.

'What you all staring at? Man's got a right to protect his property, I hope. And to discipline his son.'

'Not to half murder him, he hasn't,' the policeman said, drawing out his notebook and a pencil. 'There's been complaints. Now, what's all this about?'

Stan found that he could hardly speak for rage. 'I came down here. That fellow,' he indicated Charlie, 'is a member of my crew. He was keeping watch, or was supposed to be. I've had all this before – people slashing nets and putting water in my fuel. I've made complaints to you, but it did no bloody good. Course, then I didn't realize who it was. It was this confounded varmint all the time!' He lunged at Jamie again, but someone held him back.

There was a silence. The policeman said, 'Go on.'

'Point is,' Stan went on, almost speechless with rage at the justice of his cause, 'I come down here and there's no sign of anyone on watch. I go aboard to look, and when I come

200

back out, what do I see but this beggar here, up on the quay, got hold of a knife and slashing at my nets. Well, I'm reporting him, that's what. Criminal damage, that is. Let's see what he has to say to that.' He flung an accusing arm at Charlie. 'And ask him why he wasn't on the boat, and all, when I was paying him to be.'

The policeman turned to Charlie. 'Well?'

'Thing was, I got a message, see, saying I was wanted up the store. Urgent, it said. "Mr Hunkin's waiting for you there." Well, naturally I went. But nobody was looking for me after all – and when I got back, Stan, there you were knocking seven bells out of the lad.'

Stan snorted. 'Message? I never sent a message.'

'Well, I know that now. But I never knew it at the time. And I thought, seeing how . . .' He checked himself. 'Nothing. It's not important now.'

Stan was about to say, 'A likely tale!' but the policeman spoke before he had a chance.

'The boy brought you the message? Is that it? And you believed it?'

Charlie looked abashed. 'Well you would do, wouldn't you? When it came down with his son?'

Stan pieced this together, and let out a roar. 'Jamie brought the message, so the coast was clear for him? Where is he? I'll give him messages!' He whirled around to look for Jamie, where he'd been kicking him, but he wasn't there. There was a bloodstain on the bollard and on the ground as well, and for a moment Stan had an awful feeling in his gut. But then he saw the boy. Not dead at all, but being half-carried to one of the nearby houses by a man. He recognized that interfering beggar too. 'Joe Pollard!' he exclaimed.

'Yes,' said the policeman, putting away his notebook. 'Now, Mr Hunkin, I'm afraid I'll have to ask you to come along with me. You're causing a disturbance of the peace.'

'What?' Stan was seized by incoherent rage.

The policeman was unmoved. 'That's right. That Pollock fellow sent for us with a complaint. And don't you look like that at me. I could have you for assault as well if that young lad would press charges, although I don't suppose he will.'

'And what about my bloody nets?' Stan roared. 'That's all

right, is it? Creeping down here when my back is turned to slash my nets and ruin my engine too. Tens of pounds that's cost me. Who's going to pay for that?'

'We'll have the boy in for questioning as well, as soon as he is up to it,' the policeman said. 'He's in no condition to be talked to yet – he's half-unconscious. Got a broken collarbone by the look of it, and nasty lacerations to his face and head. Of course, causing damage to your nets is an offence . . .'

'It will be paid for,' said a voice, and there was Dora, to Stan's astonishment. She was holding the hand of a trembling little girl and Winnie was behind her, watching him. He was about to say something sneering, but Dora went on, 'I've got money, Mother gave it me.' She turned to the policeman. 'The poor boy only did it 'cause he was terrified. I heard him say so, a minute since, to Joe – and I believe him too. Father made him go out fishing every Saturday night, you see, and he thought that if the nets were cut he wouldn't have to go. He was petrified of going to sea – it made him really ill, and Jamie isn't very strong at the best of times. But Father wouldn't listen. Ask the crew. Jamie did this as a kind of self-defence.'

Stan didn't like the way the police sergeant was looking at him now, as if he was some kind of monster. ''Tisn't the first time, is it?' he burst out. 'This had been going on since before I ever took that wretched boy with me.'

'That wasn't Jamie,' Dora said in an infuriating tone that suggested her father was an idiot. 'That's what gave him the idea, that's all. You're unpopular with other folk than him.'

He took a step towards her, to wipe that sneering smile off her face, but the policeman laid a restraining hand upon his arm. 'I warned you, Mr Hunkin, you'll have to come with me. Now, you coming quietly or not?' And Stan was obliged to accompany him, in front of everyone, and – worse – to spend an uncomfortable night locked in the cells with a drunken fisherman for company. It was humiliating. Stan Hunkin, locked up like a common criminal!

Next morning they let him out, without a charge, but threatened that if he ever fetched up there again, or if there was even the whisper of complaint, he would be 'up in court quicker than you can say Jack Robinson.'

He accepted all this humbly at the time, but all the way home he was planning what he was going to say and do. They'd pay for this, that Dora and the boy.

But there was a surprise in store for him when he got home.

Five

Dora watched her father led away. She was aware of that cold, determined anger she had experienced once before and her mind was working with surprising clarity, as though it had no connection with her body, which was trembling like a leaf. Something must be done, she thought, and soon. Jamie was safe from further harm for now, but how long would that last when Father got back home? About her own safety, she did not care to think.

Joe Pollock had taken Jamie into a nearby house, and Winnie was already following. Dora pulled her shaking self together and set off after them. A group of anxious people was clustered on the street outside, the way there always was when trouble struck, but they stood back as Dora hurried past with Amy still tugging at her hand. It was the child's own house, as it turned out, and it was as neat and spotless as she was herself. As soon as Dora set foot across the threshold, she was struck by the atmosphere of ordered cleanliness. Amy shut the door behind them to keep the curious out.

Jamie was obviously in good hands. He was lying on the kitchen table, pale as flour, with Mrs Taylor bending over him, sponging his battered face. Blood was still oozing from a nasty cut, and the legs and buttocks visible under his short trousers were already turning blue.

The woman looked up as the two came in. 'Ah, Miss Hunkin! Amy's spoken about you. Nice to have you here, I'm sure, though I wish it could have been a happier circumstance. I've got your brother here. He'll be all right, but he's been badly bruised – and broken his collarbone by the looks of it. I've strapped it up, but it wants looking at.' She rinsed the sponge out in a basin on the chair, adding in a heated undertone, 'He's a brute, your father. I never saw the like.

That's what comes of being down the Miner's Arms this time of day.'

Dora nodded and moved past her to the table. 'Jamie, you all right?'

Silly question, but his eyelids fluttered open. 'All right now,' he said, and they fluttered closed again.

Dora dropped back to let Mrs Taylor tend to him again. As she went on sponging, the woman murmured, in that same low voice so Jamie couldn't hear, 'I do think the lad should have the doctor, miss, if you can run to it. I nursed my mother when she'd had a fall – came off a cart once and got kicked by a passing horse that shied. Nothing to see but bruises, but she'd hurt her spleen. I'd hate to see the same thing happen here.'

Winnie was standing at the bottom of the table all this time, clinging very hard to Joe Pollock's arm. He had interlaced his fingers with her own, but Winnie was obviously too shocked to be aware of that – or if she was, she didn't seem to mind. She looked at Dora, with a question in her eyes.

Dora nodded. 'We'll have the doctor to him. I've got a little money of my own. Of course, I promised most of that to pay the nets, but I'll worry about that later. We'll look after Jamie first of all.' She avoided looking at her twin, wondering what Win would think of that.

Winnie burst out, with sudden heat, 'Father'll pay for Jamie – or if he won't, I'll see that Nathan does. I won't have it said that our family are mean as well as cruel.' She was gripping Joe Pollock's hands so hard that they were turning white.

'If Stan Hunkin refuses to have a doctor for that lad,' Mrs Taylor said with finality, 'He won't find a single soul round here to work for him. Not even Charlie – his wife was here before to ask me could they bring the boy to me. Said Charlie was shocked with what he saw this afternoon. As for the women up the fish store, they'll walk out at once.'

Dora wasn't at all sure about that. People had to live, however strongly they might feel about a thing. All the same she nodded. 'I think we should send for somebody at once. Winnie's right. Father will pay up in the end, I'm sure. If he isn't worried about Jamie, he'll worry about people thinking that he can't afford the fees.' If that sounded bitter, she thought, she really didn't care.

'I'll go,' Joe Pollock said. 'I know where Doctor Mackie is. He's up St Evan way this afternoon. I saw his gig tied up there earlier, outside the vicarage. I can be up there in a brace of shakes. And the vicar's got a bicycle, in case the doctor's gone on somewhere else. I'll see what I can do.' He disengaged himself, gave Winnie's shoulders a quick squeeze, and disappeared at once.

There was an awkward silence. Mrs Taylor straightened up and said, 'There! I've done as much as I can do, I think. I'll leave you two together with the boy. I think he's drifted off to sleep – the shock, I 'spect. Better he stays here till the doctor comes. He's in no state to be taken anywhere. Amy can go and tell your grandmother. I'll just empty out this bowl and then I'll go and make up a proper bed for him.'

After the woman and the child had gone, Winnie looked at Dora. 'How didn't you tell me you had money, Dora? Mother gave it you, I suppose?'

Dora felt dreadful and she said, with genuine regret, 'I'm sorry, Win, I should have said before. I meant to, scores of times, only something always seemed to interrupt. There's money for you too – Mother gave it me before she died, and said I wasn't to tell Father that she had. There's quite a lot – more than twenty-five pounds apiece. Only I wasn't sure we could hang on to it. I thought it might really have been Father's by rights. I was going to ask Zachariah about the ins and outs of it.' An awful thought struck her and she said bleakly, 'I suppose Father might claim it even now.'

They had been speaking in low voices so as not to wake the boy, but Mrs Taylor in the scullery must have overheard. She came back with the basin. 'It's no business of mine, of course, but I couldn't help hearing what you said and I can tell you this. If your mother gave something to you when she was living, it's yours, and no mistake. We had the same problem when my mother died. So don't you worry yourself any more for that. Ask someone else, by all means, but I'm sure you'll find that's right. Good thing if you have got a bit of something of your own, it seems to me, with your father the kind of man he is.' She turned and went away upstairs, with a clean pillowcase across her arm.

Dora looked at Winnie in embarrassment. First she hadn't told her sister anything, and now she'd blurted it all out in front of other people. Winnie, though, only seemed concerned that the money might not rightfully be theirs. She said, 'That's right. There was some money. I'd forgotten that. Mother offered to pay for my wedding dress. She said she was going to let me have it when I wed. I only wish she had. Would have been too late then, wouldn't it, for Father to decide that it was his?'

Dora said, apologetically, 'She wanted to wait and give it to you when you had a child.'

Winnie rounded on her. 'Oh, for pity's sake, don't you start on as well. I have enough of that from Mrs Zeal!'

Dora was upset and horrified. 'Win, I didn't mean . . .'

A wan smile flitted over Winnie's face. 'No, of course you didn't. I aren't blaming you. You've had a deal to put up with since I left home, by the look of it, what with Mother dying and Father how he is. I didn't realize it had got so bad. Lord knows what the Zeals will make of all this when they hear. Wish they'd never had to do with any Hunkins, I should think.'

'On the contrary.' A cool voice from the doorway made them start. Zachariah Zeal was standing there with Amy at his side. Neither twin had heard the newcomers arrive. 'We can't be held responsible for what our parents do. And it's just as well. Every family has its private skeletons.' He turned to Winnie. 'Nathan, of course, has more skeletons than most.'

It was appalling, outrageous, making fun of Nathan's undertaking business in that way, but it made Dora smile when she had felt an instant earlier that she would never smile again. All of a sudden she knew what she must do.

He made it easy for her. 'Your grandmother is on her way. I came on ahead. She might be grateful for your company, Winifred. And Amy's too.'

Winnie darted him a startled look, but left, taking the reluctant child away again. He looked at Dora, but she turned away, stroking the damp hair on Jamie's brow.

'You got rid of them,' she said. Her heart was thudding painfully, like the little pulse that now throbbed at Jamie's eyebrow.

'Yes. I wanted to speak to you alone. I came to ask you to a concert in the town, but I suppose with all this . . .' He gestured to Jamie's half-unconscious form.

207

'No. A concert would not be appropriate, I think. Besides, the police have got my father . . .'

'It was not your father that I came to see.'

She turned to face him. 'So you'd have taken me to the concert, despite everything?'

'I should. I am not much given to care what people think. And it would please me – that's enough for me. So you will come, after all?'

She squared her shoulders and did what she had to do. For Jamie's sake. 'Not to the concert, Zachariah, no. But if you were serious in what you said before, then I will marry you.'

He went to move towards her – to hold her perhaps – but she prevented him.

'On one condition only. Jamie lives with us. It isn't safe to leave him with my father any more.' Zachariah was frowning slightly, and she hurried on. 'He'll have to go to school, of course – he's very bright. They say that he could even win a scholarship.'

'We could find a private institution, do you think? The boy could come home to us on weekends.'

She could have hugged him. 'You mean it?'

'I'll make arrangements with a place I know in town – they'll take him straightaway. And in the meantime, till the wedding day, I'll find somewhere for you. You could stay with the Boases, perhaps. It isn't safe for you to be at home, that's clear.'

'I'll be a good wife to you, Zachariah. I don't know how to run a household, but I'll learn, I promise you. I'll fetch your slippers and I'll read to you . . .' Her imagination failed her, and she stopped.

'All this for the boy's sake? No hint of affection for the hapless spouse?' His tone was bantering, and she felt herself relax. He was teasing her again. She blushed.

'You are absurd! Of course, I like you very well indeed.' She couldn't say, 'I love you'. That emotion had been given once for all, and lost, a long long time ago.

He twinkled. 'In that case, how could I refuse? It's not often a man gets an offer of that kind. Ah, Mrs – Taylor, is it? Please come in.' Dora realized with embarrassment that the woman had been hovering in the hall, and must have been listening in again. She came in now, looking sheepish. 'Mrs

Taylor,' he went on, 'you may be the first to know. Miss Hunkin has been kind enough to offer for my hand, and I intend to accept her – if her father doesn't mind. And in your presence, I will seal that promise with a kiss.'

The poor woman didn't know what on earth to make of this, of course, but she said, flustered, 'Well, that's very nice, I'm sure. I'll make a cup of tea.'

Then Gan, Amy and Winifred arrived and there was quite a fuss. Dora was congratulated warmly on all sides, and even Jamie roused himself enough to take it in. When Dora explained what her plans would mean for him, his pale face lit up in a smile, which would have been reward enough – even if she had promised to marry someone that she liked a great deal worse than Zachariah Zeal.

She bent forward to give the boy a kiss. 'Zachariah's very good,' she said.

How good, she didn't learn till afterwards. When the doctor came back with Joe, bringing poultices and liniment and laudanum, and pronounced that Jamie must have at least a week in bed but that nothing else was damaged as far as he could see, it was Zachariah Zeal who – without telling anyone – put his hand into his pocket straightaway and paid the fee.

Winnie heard the news of this betrothal with a sense of disbelief, but somehow it did not make her jealous as it might once have done. When Dora had explained what was to become of James, it was obvious why she was throwing herself at Zachariah in this way, and he if was good enough to have her, that was wonderful.

Gan seemed to think so anyway. The tension between Father and Jamie had been affecting everyone, and she never had cared for Dora much, so it was obvious that she was pleased. Father was her son, and she'd soon have him to herself. Well, Winnie thought, may they all have joy of it.

When she went home at last, reluctantly, she had something to talk about, at least, though Mrs Zeal put her in her place. She was sharp and disagreeable all the afternoon, and kept making barbed remarks at tea. 'Poor, dear Zachariah, what a fate for him! Marrying the daughter of a man like that!' she said.

It was intended to make Winnie feel ashamed.

Nathan took these remarks as a rebuke to him as well as to his wife, and there might have been a little sympathy between the two of them, for a change, but instead she found him impossible to tolerate tonight. Every time he touched her she shrank away from him, remembering another touch – so warm and strong – which she had briefly revelled in that day.

Joe. She could hardly bear to think of him. It had been so long since she had even exchanged a word with him, yet there he was, supporting her, when she was most in need. Like magic. It *was* magic. Why else had she felt so happy and at home with him? Even Dora's underhandedness in withholding Mother's gift had not seemed half so hurtful, because Joe was there.

She had spoken to him for a moment afterwards, when the doctor had gone away again and Jamie was settled down in Amy's room – Amy, to her great delight, was to go home with Gan and sleep in Dora's bed for the night. So Winnie and Joe had stood together on the quay, not touching now, because the world might see and – after all – she was Nathan's wife. They hadn't said a lot.

'Thank you, Joe, for all you did back there.'

'Glad I was there to help,' he said gruffly. 'Always do anything for you, you know that.' Silence. 'Don't you?'

'Yes.'

'You just remember that. I haven't changed, you know. Though I know you've never felt the same. You got what you wanted. I'm just glad of that.'

'I don't know what I wanted.' There were tears behind her eyes. 'Whatever it was, it wasn't what I got, that's all I know. Anyhow,' she turned her head away, 'It's too late now. I made my bed and I've got to lie on it.'

'Winnie,' Joe said, urgently, 'don't be unhappy. I didn't mean to make you cry. It's just, if there is anything – ever – that I can do, you let me know. You're still my 'andsome maid. Nothing will ever alter that.' And with that he left her and walked away.

But he had not left her thoughts. He filled her dreams all night and when, next day, she made an excuse to go home again, it was partly so that she could look out for him on the way. She didn't see him though.

Father was home again by now. She knew by the atmosphere

210

as soon as she got in, though Gan at least was fairly welcoming. Amy had scampered home again, 'to give her Mum a bit of hand'. She had made her escape when Father turned up, that was clear.

He was in a funny state of mind. Not chagrined and ashamed, as you might have thought, but full of how he had been put upon and unfairly treated by the police.

'Stands to reason, a man must discipline his son. Hasn't that wretched child been damaging my nets? Start arresting people every time they raise a hand to anyone, and then where shall we be?' he said to Winnie the moment she came in. 'Nation of namby-pambies and disobedient louts.'

She knew better than to argue. 'Perhaps,' she said, then changed the subject. 'What do you think of Dora's getting married then?'

He scratched his armpit. 'What am I s'posed to think? Come home and find her gone. Well, I wash my hands of her. Glad she's found somebody to have her. Used to think she never would. Just like her mother, she is, all for books and not of bit of use for anything. Still, he'll find that out. Got enough money to keep her in style, if that's what he wants. I wash my hands of her.'

'And they'll give a home to Jamie, too,' she ventured.

You would have supposed, with everything, that Father would be pleased the boy was going, but his face darkened and he hit the table with a thump.

'Desert me too, would he, after all I've done for him? Just because I lost my temper with him yesterday. Wonder I didn't do it long ago. Stupid, useless, feeble lump, he is. His mother made a proper milksop out of him. Well, let him go and all. I don't want either of them darkening my doors again. I'll disinherit him. I will. I've got a good mind to go and see a lawyer on Monday afternoon.'

Father obviously wasn't troubled by regrets. Poor Mother, Winnie thought. It was clear now that all those bruises weren't caused by 'clumsiness' at all, the way she always said. Looking back, she must have had an awful life with him, and even now she was gone she still got blamed for everything. No wonder she wanted to keep the knowledge of that money to herself. It was a pity she hadn't used it to run away some-where, when she was young enough to start again, and never mind what people would have said. Better than staying in a joyless marriage like she had.

Winnie brought herself up sharply with a start. That was a totally scandalous idea. Whatever had possessed her to think a thing like that?

Johnny Chinaman was right. When they got back to Echuca and moored up again, Marcia did not leave them after all. On the contrary, she came back from the draper with mysterious packages and then proceeded to launder all her clothes, hanging lacy bloomers and camisoles from every stay and line, until the boat looked briefly 'like a cross between a Chinese laundry and a Christmas tree', as her father said. It was embarrassing. It was as well that everything dried so quickly in the heat, and that they were tied up at the far end of that impressively long quay, half a mile from where the store sheds were, otherwise the whistles and comments from the wharf hands would have been even worse.

'You flying the bottom-end rag now?' one of them shouted, as Marcia took down the last pair of sturdy bloomers from the stanchion rall. There were hoots of laughter from the other lads. Boats on the Upper Murray flew the 'top-end flag' and there was always a certain rivalry. Marcia turned scarlet and hurried down below.

'Best place to do the washing, where the water's clean,' her father said indulgently, watching all this from where they were loading up the barge. 'Marcia's coming back upriver with us after all.' He gave Tom one of his rare, grizzled grins. 'Believe she's taken quite a shine to you.'

You could have fooled Tom. Marcia still scarcely addressed a civil word to him. He gave a short, embarrassed laugh and turned his attention to the job in hand. They were loading bales of linens and home-made crates of household furniture ready for a new place that had just been built, replacing the original wooden shack, on one of the properties up near Boundary Point, many miles upstream.

He applied himself to the biggest crate of all. 'I swear there's a blessed harmonium in here,' he muttered as he edged it forward to be craned aboard. 'Good thing that's the last.'

Murcheson laughed. 'Could be a harmonium as well. Daughter runs a Sunday school for the workers on the place.

Still, it's well worthwhile. They've got a downward cargo for us too – a load of wool for us to bring back here.' He stepped aboard the barge and helped Johnny lash the load, and then led the way back to the *Mariebelle*. There was no sign of Marcia. 'Now where has she gone? Just like a woman, when it's time to move. River's running high. Against us too, of course, though at least we'll have plenty of water under us.'

'Long as it doesn't wash half the town away, like it did four years ago,' Tom said, remembering the stories of the flood.

Murcheson grunted. 'Not much chance of that again, I shouldn't think. Anyway, here's Marcia. Get what you wanted, did you?' he enquired of her as she stepped aboard.

'Most of it,' she countered. 'Been up to get the post.' She handed him a sheaf of envelopes, and turned to Tom. 'There's one for you as well.'

'For me?' he echoed foolishly. Mother wrote him regularly every month, but he wasn't expecting another letter yet.

'If your name is Tom Trewin, then yes, this is for you. They were keeping it for you up at the hotel.' She thrust the letter at him.

It was from Len, which was rather a surprise. Len wasn't a great letter-writer as a rule, and generally it was left to Mother to keep everyone up to date with news. Tom opened the envelope with some alarm, but he need not have worried after all.

> This is to let you know that me and Cherry tide the not.
> Hopping you are keeping well as this leaves me.
> Your loving brother, L Trewin
> P.S. Ivy and her sister has found another bow.

Len was no scholar. The eccentric spelling made Tom laugh aloud and Murcheson looked quizzically at him.

'My brother's just got married,' Tom explained. 'To the daughter of that farmer I used to work for once. He wasn't a well man, the father, so no doubt he'll be glad. Means there'll be somebody to carry on the farm.'

Murcheson gave another of his grunts. 'Only daughter, was it? Sensible. Perhaps the girl was more amenable than mine.' He looked from Tom to Marcia and back again, and Tom realized with alarm that this remark was aimed at him. It was something of a shock – if Murcheson meant what Tom thought he did. Marcia obviously thought so, because she looked furious, tossed her head and stalked away.

There was no time for further conversation then. There was too much to do if they were to reach the Williamses' wood pile before dark.

Tom went below and got the engines up to steam, while Murcheson took the wheel and Johnny tightened the tarpaulins on the load. Marcia was handy enough to let go the mooring lines, assisted by some of her tormentors from the wharf. Murcheson rang the bell to signal 'ready', and Tom released the valve and let the pistons drive. He gave a blast on the steam whistle to warn other river-users that they were on the move, then slowly the paddle wheels picked up rhythm and they were away.

Tom stuck his head up to have a last look, as he always did, and was appalled. Among the usual urchins waving on the bank there was another figure that he recognized. Already they were too far away to hear, but he could guess what she was shouting.

'Tom! Tom! It's me, Ivy! Stop! Come back!'

He disappeared below again at once, and stayed there, in the parching heat, until half an hour later Marcia brought him down a drink. He needed it. It was so hot down there it dried the perspiration as it sprang and would have parched his throat in seconds – if the sight of Ivy hadn't already turned it dry.

Marcia slammed down the mug of tea without a word and turned to go. She didn't look at him.

'Thanks,' Tom said, and then, 'Look – I'm sorry if you were embarrassed earlier. I didn't realize what your dad was playing at.'

She gave him a contemptuous glance. 'Didn't you? Then you're the only one. Why do you think he keeps on bringing engineers aboard?'

Tom laughed. 'To keep the engines running, I presume.'

She was not amused, but angry. 'So why does he always pick out younger men? They know what he's up to. Course they do. Bet you did too.'

'I didn't,' Tom said.

214

She ignored that. 'All over me like a dust storm, given half a chance.'

Tom, who had experienced a dust storm by this time – and had cowered indoors like everybody else with a wet cloth pressed across his nose and mouth – could not suppress a smile. She had a lively turn of phrase, when she chose to say anything at all.

'Well, I'm sorry,' he said. 'I had no idea. You weren't even on-board here when I joined.'

'No,' she allowed. 'But I know what you engineers are like. Look at that last one – disgusting man, especially when he was the worse for drink. If I hadn't yelled blue murder that night and woken Johnny up, he'd have forced himself on me, and then I'd have had to marry him if I wanted to or not. That's what he was banking on of course – what he really wanted was the *Mariebelle*.' She shuddered. 'Hands like ivy, he had, creeping everywhere . . . What are you grinning at?'

'You speak truer than you know,' he said. 'Did you see that woman on the wharf?'

She frowned. 'I saw somebody. Why, what's that got to do with it?'

'Ivy!' he said. 'Creeping everywhere. Ivy – that's her name. I came up here from Melbourne to get away from her.'

She turned to face him, hands on hips. 'You got some poor girl into trouble and abandoned her?'

'I never laid a finger on her. Met her on the boat when we were coming out from home, and I was civil to her, that was all. I wish I hadn't been. Even at that stage she started following me about. My brother was friendly with her sister at one time, so she worked out where I was and turned up after me. I came up here, and here she is again.'

'I bet you encouraged her to hope.'

He lost patience then. 'I did no such thing. I did have a girl once, back in Cornwall where I lived, but her father had no time for me, 'cause I was poor. So one way and another, that was that. But after her – a sweet, lovely girl with gentle manners and a mind sharper than a knife – how am I going to be interested in a common girl like that? Or any other girl, so rest assured. You're safe from me, for all your blessed *Mariebelle*. Now, just go away and leave me, will you? I'm upset.'

215

She didn't move. 'That true?'

He kicked the fire door shut. 'You think I made it up?'

She put down the empty cup and said, in a softer voice, 'I didn't know. This girl of yours, what was she like?'

He scowled. 'What's it to you? I've told you – leave me be. I've said too much about her as it is.'

For days and days Marcia had avoided him, and now – perversely – she refused to go. 'Thing is, Tom, it was the same for me. There was a boy. He lived not far from the house where Father boarded me. Only, he had an accident. Fell off a horse and killed himself. I've been—'

'Marcia!' Murcheson's roar of anger made the timbers ring. 'Where in tarnation's name have you got to now? Where's my cup of tea?'

She darted Tom a startled look and fled. But she was a good deal more friendly after that. By the time they got to the Williamses' wood pile she was chatting as though they were old friends, and when they'd loaded on the fuel (the *Mariebelle* could burn half a ton an hour) and moored beside the bank, she came to sit beside him on the deck.

It was a hot, clear, windless night. No sound but the ripple of the water and the plop of river creatures round the hull, except when something rustled on the bank or Johnny gave a snore and slapped at a mosquito in his sleep. Murcheson, behind them in the wheelhouse, kept the door open but did not come out.

She looked up at the Southern Cross, which twinkled above them from a sea of stars. 'Is it true that even the skies are different, where you used to live?'

'Everything is,' Tom said, and found himself telling her about the things he missed – bluebell woods, tin streams, country lanes. Soft, cool Cornish rain. Stone cottages that huddled from Atlantic gales, and churchyards where villages had buried their dead for half a thousand years. She listened avidly. These things were as strange to her as kangaroos and snakes had been to him.

After that they sat together every night and talked. She told him about her girlhood, painting pictures with her words: arid bushland crossed by rocky tracks; isolated cattle farms half the size of Wales; flash floods from sullen streams that nonetheless ran dry every summer; bullock trains labouring in clouds of dust; and purple heat haze over eucalyptus trees.

Tom found that he liked her company more and more. He was astonished by her skillfulness as well. When they were through the treacherous rapids of the Bitch and Pups, her father let her take the wheel a bit. She steered the boat with confidence, as well as any man, though she blushed like a woman when Tom told her so.

She was getting fond of him, that much was obvious, much to her father's undisguised delight. Tom, though, did not make a move. He could not love her, though he liked her well enough. She was interesting and lively, and though she was no beauty, she was strong and competent. He thought of Ivy, in Echuca, and wondered if Murcheson's idea might not be a good one after all.

It was a letter from his mother that decided him. They were up at the property at Boundary Point, loading up the barge again with wool in preparation for the homeward leg, when a passing skipper called across to them.

'Hey, Trewin. Heard you were up here. Brought this up for you.' Tom scrambled to the far side of the barge and they came alongside with his letter. He retrieved it from an outstretched hand and watched the other boat move out of sight around the bend amid a fluttering of pelicans and ducks.

Mother's note was chatty as it always was – full of Len's wedding and what the neighbours had said about it when they heard. It was the last bit, though, which made up his mind for him.

> Weddings seem to be the fashion. I see that school-teacher you used to like has just got married too – to some relation of that undertaker chap. Dead lucky, your father says, but he means it for a joke. Hope you are well, and don't go catching cold.

Tom, streaming sweat, went back to loading wool. But that night he did what Marcia had obviously been hoping he'd do. He slipped a timid arm around her waist.

By the time they came back to Echuca, cut the engine, dropped the barge and nudged into the wharf, it was a settled thing. Ivy was too late. Marcia had agreed to be his wife.

217

Part Five

April–October 1916

One

Winnie had taken Christopher for a walk beside the sea. It was cold and windy but she did not care. She enjoyed her little nephew's company, and these days she was glad of any opportunity to get out of the house.

Christopher, at four, was a sturdy little lad and steady on his legs. He was inclined to toddle determinedly away if you let go of him – like now, chasing the seagulls on the quay – and she found that she was hurrying to keep up with him. Ridiculous of course, the way Dora turned him out, in patent-leather shoes and sailor suit. 'Aping the gentry' as Gan would have said if she were still here and not buried beside Mother up in the cemetery.

'Come on then, Christopher,' she called. 'Come to Aunty Win. Time to go home and get ourselves some tea.' That was the unpleasant truth of it, she thought, stretching out her hand for him to take. It would be a case of getting themselves tea. There was a woman came in twice a week to clean, and after a few disasters they had found a cook who waddled in to make the dinner every night, but otherwise Winnie had to do everything herself. Making beds and sweeping floors and cooking breakfast like a slave, and still running up and down the stairs at Mrs Zeal's beck and call. Mercifully, Nathan had agreed to send the heavy laundry out, otherwise that would have fallen to her lot as well. She had to mark and sort it, as it was, and rinse out everybody's smalls.

It was the war, of course. Servants were becoming very hard to find. No girl wanted to drudge away all day when she could earn a better wage elsewhere. Women worked in armaments and factories these days, drove vehicles or went to nurse the troops, or took over men's jobs in shops and offices. There was even talk that the government was setting up a

221

register and unmarried women would be compelled to work in shortage areas like forestry and farms. She would not have minded doing that herself, but instead she was stuck with running that horrid, inconvenient house that was designed for half a dozen staff at least. And of course with all the men away there was no outside help at all, except one decrepit gardener who 'obliged' them now and then, and he was so slow and old that he could scarcely lift a spade.

Nathan, of course, had been no help at all. He'd permitted all the maids to leave, accepted his mother's views on everything, and when life got too uncomfortable at home, he volunteered and got posted overseas.

'Plenty of work for undertakers,' he had said when he joined up, but they put him in the Transport Corps and had him driving carts because he was familiar with managing a hearse. Up to his ears in mud sometimes, he wrote. Well, it served him right. He didn't have to go. Leaving her alone to cope with this, while Sammy – who wasn't fit for active service – ran the firm, and almost seemed to think he owned the place.

She gave her nephew's hand a little tug. 'Come on now, Christopher!' But he escaped her grasp and toddled off again. He could be a disobedient little boy. Dora spoiled him far too much, and as for Mrs Zeal, she thought the sunshine rose and set with him and was always cooing over her 'little grand-nephew, the youngest Zeal'. It was all aimed at Winifred, of course – a reproach that she had no children of her own. Perhaps that was because of the enthusiastic scrub she always gave herself whenever Nathan had been pawing her, or perhaps – as Dora said, thinking to console her – it was just the way things were. Whatever the truth of it, she was free of worry now. Nathan wasn't here to paw her any more.

Dora herself seemed more or less content, living in the new house in Penzance with Zachariah and the child. Of course, that place was much easier to run – better than Father's place had been. Zachariah had seen that no expense was spared. He'd had the latest cooking range installed, gas lighting in all the rooms, a proper inside lavatory and even a hot-water geyser for the bath. And, having no mother-in-law to please, Dora could do as she wanted in between, which was why she was off at the sewing bee today, turning sheets and mending pillowslips for the convalescent home, at what used to be Trevarnon House.

Winnie had volunteered to look after Christopher on sewing afternoons, partly because it afforded her the walk, and partly because she'd hoped at first that Zachariah might come, to bring the boy. But of course, it had not worked out like that. Dora had found a woman who came out on the bus, and she brought Christopher with her and took him home again. Anyway, Zachariah didn't have his dashing carriage any more – the army had requisitioned local horses and only left him one, and that only because he had business interests to attend to round about. In any case he was always up in London now. 'About his shipping business,' Dora said, but Winifred knew differently from that. He was off with Susan Boase – Nathan had once seen them getting on the train.

'Got into a carriage and pulled the blinds down quick, as if they were afraid of being seen,' he'd said, capturing his wife's full attention for a change. 'Though, of course, you can't read anything in that. So mind you don't tell Mother what I said.'

Winnie could still feel a secret pang, although she had long suspected something of the kind. Of course, Zachariah was playful and pleasant to her when they met – he always was – and no doubt he was similarly attentive to his wife, but he was the same with almost any girl. And that Simpering Susan woman had always thrown herself at him. No wonder he was tempted when Dora got so heavy with the child.

Of course, Winnie hadn't told her sister about this. It would not be kind. And it gave her a sort of secret power, besides. She'd never quite forgiven Dora for keeping Mother's twenty-five guineas from her all those months – although of course she had it now, hidden in a bottom drawer upstairs where Nathan and his mother would never think to look. She had never spent a penny of it to this day. She was keeping it, like Mother, for emergencies.

There was almost an emergency in front of her! She'd let her attention wander, and there was Christopher, right out at the quayside, still chasing seagulls. She scurried after him.

'Come here, Christopher, you naughty boy!' Her long skirts impeded her from moving fast. The boy was dangerously near the edge by now.

A fellow examining the nets beside the wall turned and

realized what was happening. He ran, vaulted a bollard and scooped the boy up one-handed from the ground. 'This yours?' he said to Winnie.

Joe Pollock. Large as life and smiling at her in that way that made her heart do somersaults.

'Why, Joe! I haven't seen you to speak to for an age.' Since the day that Jamie was attacked, in fact, close to this very spot. 'Thought you were serving in the army overseas.' Too late, she saw the empty sleeve pinned uselessly across his chest, and the expression on his face. 'Oh, I didn't know . . .' she blurted, making matters worse. There was a pause. 'Thank you for catching him.'

He handed her the boy. 'A pleasure. And don't look so distraught. I'm luckier than some. Lots of the fellows I was with are dead. Caught in the same blast that did this to me. Can't say it's not a trial though. It aches like billy-o.'

There was still a stump above the elbow, she observed. She could not drag her eyes away from it – from him – though Christopher was clinging to her neck, unhurt, and saying, 'Teatime,' in the sing-song voice she used to him.

'Fine little chap,' Joe Pollock said. 'A credit to you both.'

Winnie said, 'Oh, he isn't mine,' with such alacrity that she surprised herself. 'He's Dora's boy – you know, my twin. Nathan and I haven't any children of our own.' Why had she felt it necessary to tell him that at once?

Joe laughed. 'Well you should keep a better eye on him, that's what. Don't know what your sister would have said if you'd had to take him home all dripping wet.' Or drowned, he meant, although he didn't say the words.

Winnie nodded. 'I know. He got away from me. I'm not very used to children, I suppose.'

'Good thing I was there.'

'In lots of ways.' She met his eyes. He understood. She saw it in his face. She said, without apparent connection, 'I come down here every week, about this time, with Christopher.'

He nodded. 'Looks like I might be here myself – though I'm not much use to anyone like this. Can't even mend the nets. However, the army doctors say they're going to fit me with an arm of sorts.'

She could have wept for him. 'Oh, Joe.' Christopher was

kicking in his struggle to get down, but she scarcely noticed. 'I wish I hadn't . . .'

'What?'

'Nothing. I've been a fool, that's all.'

'You're not unhappy, are you, Winnie? I couldn't bear for you to be upset,' he murmured as she set the child down.

She turned her face away to hide her tears. 'I daresay I'll survive. And now,' she went on in her Aunty voice, taking her nephew firmly by the hand, 'it's time to take this little fellow home and have some tea.'

Joe said, 'Till next week, then.'

'Yes.' She hurried off back to the house, where she found the elder Mrs Zeal in raptures because Zachariah himself had come for Christopher. He was as charming as he always was.

'Rode out, since it was such a pleasant day, and I had business in the area. He can sit ahead of me going home. I've let the woman know. Good for the child to get accustomed to a horse. Besides,' he smiled at Winifred, 'I find the views out here are wonderful.'

And so on, all the way through nursery tea. But though he did his best to flatter and tease her, her heart refused to give the slightest skip.

Dora was sitting by the fire, waiting anxiously for her family to come home. She never liked it when Zachariah rode and carried Christopher with him on the horse, although, as her husband said, the mare was such a tired and slow old thing that even the army hadn't wanted her. All the same, she worried, just as Mother must have worried about Jamie years ago. It surprised her sometimes, looking at her son, how much love it was possible to feel. She had not known such sweetness since those stolen moments with Tom Trewin in the lanes.

What would have happened if she had married him? No Christopher, that was one certain thing. Would Tom, she wondered, have gone off 'on business' as Zachariah did, and come back smelling of expensive scent? She doubted it.

She shook her head. It hurt, of course it hurt, although she had known from the beginning what Zachariah was like. You could no more stop him from charming girls than you could prevent a seal from swimming in the sea. He couldn't help

225

himself. She'd seen him charming Winnie – and even Gan. That charm was the reason she'd married him herself. And Susan Boase had always been there, preening and flattering, and making up to him. But now . . .

She bit her lip. She wouldn't think of that. She was not like Mother, browbeaten and afraid. There was still a good deal to be thankful for.

She did not love Zachariah, and he did not love her. That was not the understanding when they married and it wasn't now. She had kept her promises to him – borne his child, kept his house, and been as good a wife as she could be. And up to now he'd kept his bargain too. She must remember that. He had been a thoughtful husband and he never raised his voice.

And he had cared for Jamie, uncomplainingly, given him an education and a home, which Jamie had repaid by doing splendidly and earning a scholarship at Truro School. There was even talk of his going to university next year, supposing that he didn't get called up with this new Conscription Act. He might, with luck, escape that, since – despite good food and medicine – he never had been strong. In the meantime he was helping Zachariah with his work. Just as well. It was hard to find office workers nowadays. Men everywhere were signing up. Quite old men too. Zachariah himself had talked seriously of volunteering once or twice, and even Father had boasted that he'd go – at his age! – if they wanted him.

Of course, they wouldn't. Father was sinking more and more in drink, and had visited the police cells more than once for fighting in the street. He was even falling out with Charlie nowadays. Poor Father. Both the Stephens boys had gone to war, and he was struggling – though he didn't ask for help or sympathy and wouldn't take it if you offered it. She'd done her best – offered to come down and do a few things for him in the house – and had been sworn at for her pains. He wouldn't let her cross the step at all, so now she rarely tried to call, though when she went down to Winnie's she always knocked on the door, just to make sure he was all right.

Though even going to Winnie's was difficult these days. This awful war was changing everything. No staff, no horses, sometimes even shortages of food. Shopkeepers were putting notices in their windows: 'NO EGGS, NO COCOA, NO BAKING

226

POWDER TODAY.' The bread they sold you was disgusting, too, and such a price! Dora sometimes wondered how much Winnie realized of all this – old Mrs Zeal, though feeble and confined almost entirely to a chair – still ruled the household purse, and did it expertly. She had hoarded jars and tins of things for years, had arrangements with farmers and fishermen to buy whatever little they could spare, and sent a shopping list back with Christopher each week for Dora to buy for her in town. Things were often unobtainable, but Dora did her best and, in return, occasionally got a tin of something that had lost its label in the store cupboard.

But, there was no such offering tonight. Christopher came running in and – when he had put the horse away – his father followed him.

'Where's Jamie?' Zachariah enquired, seeing the empty chair.

She looked at him. To hear him speak you would suppose that everything was just as usual and that what she had learned that afternoon was just a shameful dream. Don't raise it now, she told herself. Wait until Christopher's in bed.

She forced a smile. 'Gone out to Eli Westrill's on the bus. I don't know why. He got a letter earlier, but he didn't show it me. One of his pals got killed again, I think. He takes it badly. Anyway, I let him go. He's old enough to walk back a few miles in the dark.'

If she was constrained, he didn't notice it. He said something flattering as he always did, pecked her cheek, then went away upstairs murmuring that he had letters he must write.

It wasn't until much later on, when the evening meal had been cleared away and she was sitting sewing by his side, that Dora raised the matter that had been distressing her. She put away the sheet that she was hemming and remarked, 'Your ex-mother-in-law, Mrs Boase, was at the sewing bee today.'

She saw him stiffen, but he lowered his book and said, in a falsely casual tone, 'Indeed? How was she?'

She threaded her needle carefully, and didn't meet his eyes. 'Very odd, I thought. I went to speak to her, of course, but she cut me utterly. And do you know, her daughter's gone away to look after some elderly relative in Fife?'

He didn't answer, and she went on simply, 'I'd never heard

227

of Fife. I asked the lady sitting next to me if she knew where it was, and she said she'd no idea, but under the circumstances she assumed it was as far away as possible. It all seems very sudden, don't you think?' She could feel her cheeks burning scarlet as she spoke, but he made no move to comment or explain.

She did not tell him any more of it. About the women gossiping in groups when she arrived, groups that fell silent as soon as she appeared. Or about the whisper, purposely loud enough for her to hear. 'It's always the wife who is the last to know.' How the pieces of the puzzle had slotted into place and she'd been forced to face the truth.

She longed to shout at him, 'How could you do this to us? To Christopher and me? Have you no affection for the two of us at all? Couldn't you have the decency to see that your amours were under wraps, and not humiliate your son and me like this? Don't we deserve at least that much from you?' But she said nothing more. It was part of the bargain she had made with herself.

He was very quiet. He picked up his book and glanced at it, but after a little while he put it down and rose. 'I'm sorry that your day was disagreeable, and that I must leave you to spend the evening on your own. But something has arisen which I must deal with urgently. I'll see you in the morning. Don't wait up for me.'

He kissed her lightly, as he always did, and left the room. Dora sat, pressing her hands between her knees and screwing up her eyes to fight the tears. Where had he gone now? Back to Susan Boase? She couldn't bear the thought.

'Don't wait up for me.'

They were the last words she ever heard him speak.

Stan was slumped on the kitchen table, half-asleep, when he heard a faint disturbance at the door. He stirred, aching and bone-weary in every limb. He felt more than a little sorry for himself.

It wasn't just that he'd been down at the Miner's Arms, although he had. It was more that last night's attempt at fishing had been too much for him. All very well for Charlie to insist that, since they were using short lines and hooks instead of nets, they didn't have to take the *Cornish Rose*

228

so far – they had to stay out for hours, and even then they were only bringing in a fraction of the catch. But what else could you do? With the engine, she was heavy to handle under sail. It wasn't his fault you couldn't get the petrol nowadays.

And as for Charlie claiming that he – Stan Hunkin – was a liability, because he fell across a rope and bruised his leg! It was a liberty, that's what it was. He wasn't the worse for drink at all: he was getting old. It was a dreadful thing to be a poor old lonely widower whose daughters had deserted him just when he needed them, and whose son had been a dreadful disappointment from the start.

The contemplation of the cruelty of fate almost brought tears of self-pity to his eyes. No wonder a man sought consolation down the Miner's Arms.

There was that noise again. Somebody was knocking on the door.

'Awright!' Stan mumbled, lurching to his feet. His voice was not quite answering his command. 'Keep your confounded shirt on, will you? I'm coming. Who is it anyhow, this time of night?'

He stumbled to the door, toppling the chair over as he went. Bloody furniture. Nothing was sturdy like it used to be. He took up the candle from the shelf and peered into the night.

There was a young man standing on the step. The sort of well-dressed, lah-di-dah young man that Stan despised, all scarves and gloves and highly polished shoes.

'What you want?' Stan muttered. 'Can't you leave an old man in peace to have a rest?'

'Father?'

Dear God, this apparition was his son! Stan had not set eyes on him since Christmas gone – and then only briefly through a drunken haze when Dora had brought him to the door. The recollection still made Stan annoyed. All those pious invitations to come up to Winnie's house – bad enough when Nathan was at home, but what man would choose to spend his time with a load of women and the son who couldn't wait to get away from him? Well, he'd soon seen them off – though looking at him now, the boy had changed. He was still bony and bespectacled, but he was bigger now, older and more self-confident.

He blinked at the figure on the step. 'What are you doing here?'

'Came to see Eli Westrill,' the young man replied. 'He suggested I should talk to you, and so I've come. You going to let me in?'

Stan stood back half an inch and let him pass. The boy had never been here since the day, all those years ago, when Stan had lost his temper – like any father might – and hit him once or twice. He seemed to fill the kitchen. He was taller than Stan now, and with his fancy clothes he made his father feel uncomfortable.

'Well?' Stan sneered. 'What did you want Eli Westrill for? Going to help him take the light to distant lands are you? Seeing you aren't answering your country's call.'

Jamie didn't flinch. 'That's just it,' he said. 'The papers came today. I've just turned eighteen. Got to present myself next week, or appeal to the tribunal as to why I should be exempt.'

Stan said contemptuously, 'Well, don't let it worry you. The army will take one look at you and sign you off at once. All that weak chest, poor eyesight and knock knees. Folks like you aren't man enough for them.'

The boy was standing very still and quiet. He said, 'Thing is, I'm not going to the medical. I'm going to register objection to the war. I thought you ought to know.'

Stan found himself staring. Why in pity's name would he do a thing like that, getting himself in trouble unnecessarily? 'You're bloody not!'

'I am.'

Stan lost his temper then. 'And I say you're bloody not. You hear me? Bloody not. No son of mine is going to make a fool of me by making an exhibition of himself for cowardice.' He could feel the righteous anger pounding behind his eyes. 'Though I suppose I might have guessed you'd be too scared to fight – great, wet, lily-livered thing you've always been.'

'It's not that I'm afraid to fight. It's just that I don't think fighting settles anything. Three of my closest friends have died. For what? Has it brought peace a minute closer? Not at all. All that promise wasted. Who had the right to point a gun at them and shoot? What gave them the right to do the same, just because the men they tried to kill happened to be born in Germany?'

230

'This isn't pistol practice, this is war,' Stan roared. 'Defending their country, that's what gives them the right. It's what you would be doing too, if you had any manliness at all. But not you, oh no! Can't even do the decent thing and let them turn you down; you've got to go and make a fuss, with this tribunal nonsense.'

'Hoping to fail the medical is just the coward's way,' Jamie said. 'I'm going to ask them for a questionnaire, and tell them what I think . . .'

Stan was no longer listening. 'The coward's way? I'll give you coward, you pathetic, spineless . . .' Words failed him.

'Father, I'm sorry that you're vexed. I understand your feelings, but I thought you ought to know. I spoke to Eli Westrill and he thought so too.' He turned to go.

Stan stepped in front of him. 'So, not content with coming here yourself, you have to make a laughing stock of me with Eli, too? Well, I'm not having it, you understand? Not having it!' Almost without willing it he raised his fist.

Jamie didn't flinch. 'Going to hit me again? Is that it?' he said quietly.

That did it. Stan made a lunge for him. 'Well, you asked for it.' He seized the boy and flung him hard against the wall. Jamie made no response at all, just accepted it like a jelly-fish. That was somehow more provocative than striking back. 'Defy me, would you?' In a kind of haze, Stan picked up the chair and brought it down hard across the young man's back.

Jamie sat there against the wall with blood dribbling from his forehead and his mouth, looking at his father steadily. 'I won't fight the Germans, and I won't fight you,' he said. 'You're the one who taught me how useless violence was.' He got up, shakily, but calm.

Stan found that he was trembling too, with anger and dismay. He watched the boy go over to the door and open it. 'Goodnight, Father, I've done what I came to do. I doubt that I'll be seeing you again.'

'Go, and good riddance,' Stan said bitterly. 'You'd have had my blessing if you'd gone to war like anybody else.' He was breathing heavily. He closed his eyes against the pounding of his blood. When he opened them again, the boy was gone.

231

Two

Dora waited up until midnight, but her husband didn't come home. She had almost decided to take his advice and go to bed. She was sitting, dozing, in the armchair by the fire, when she heard the front door and someone tiptoed in.

'Zac?' she called, but of course it wasn't him.

Jamie put a face around the door.

'My dear Jamie!' She leapt up, instantly awake. 'Whatever happened to your face?'

He shook his head. 'It's nothing, Dora.' And then, since this was manifestly untrue, 'I went down to see Father, that's all, and it came to blows. On his side, not on mine.'

'And you walked home like this?'

'It's all right, Dora, there's a midnight bus these days. Serves that munitions factory they've set up. They're working round the clock. Anyway, it isn't serious.'

'You ought to bathe these cuts and bruises all the same.' Dora took his head between her hands and looked intently at the wounds. He was right. There was bruising, but the damage wasn't deep. She let him go, and said with passion, 'That man wants locking up. What were you doing there in any case? You know what he's like.'

Jamie gave that little shamefaced smile that reminded her of Mother, even now. 'Thing is, Dora – perhaps I should have told you this before, but my army papers came today. I went to let him know.'

'I don't know why you bothered. They'll exempt you anyway. He was bound to make a fuss.'

He looked at her steadfastly. 'In fact, I may well be fit enough these days. Thanks to you and Zachariah, I am stronger than I look. But that's the point. I'm not content to have them turn me down. I refuse to be a soldier and bear arms. That's

232

quite a different thing. I'm going to go to the tribunal and fill in that objector's questionnaire.'

'Jamie!' She was horrified. 'You can't!'

'I can. I spoke to Eli Westrill, and he explained it all to me. He's on the tribunal sometimes, so he knows how things are done.'

'But . . .' She broke off. It was bad enough for those who simply hadn't volunteered – they were sent white feathers and were spat on or had slogans daubed across their walls. Shopkeepers wouldn't serve them, either, half the time. People took cowardice very seriously indeed, especially when their own husbands, brothers and sons were at the Front. But now conscription had begun it was getting even worse. Some of these conscientious objectors, as they called themselves, had been sent to jail, and there were stories of them being attacked by other inmates and harshly treated by the authorities. One suspected 'conchie' was rumoured to have been tarred and feathered by an angry mob.

All the same, she thought, if it were Christopher, she might prefer him to face imprisonment and jeers than have him sent off to the Front and join the ever-growing lists of dead which were being published on the lamp posts every week.

Jamie seemed to read her thoughts. 'It isn't what you think. It isn't funk, although I'm scared, of course – who wouldn't be? I saw Nick Lewis in the town. You remember Nick – he went to school with me.'

Dora nodded, recalling a small, thin, fair-haired boy with adenoids.

'He lied about his age and joined up at the start. He was home on convalescent leave. Something the matter with his feet. He was telling me about the war – or some of it.' He paused.

'Well?' Dora said. Not much information filtered through about matters at the Front. Men who came home didn't want to talk. Newspapers were full of articles about 'our daring boys', but those endless lists of names, and the sight of wounded soldiers in the street – men who had been gassed or shot and who were missing arms or legs or even half a face – suggested an altogether grimmer reality.

Jamie shook his head. 'Nick couldn't bear to talk about it much. Except that he'd seen three of his friends blown up in front of him. But one thing was clear from what he said – how essential stretcher-bearers are. Well, apparently they ask you on these exemption questionnaires if you'd be prepared to do National Service in some other form. I'd be happy to put down for that – saving lives instead of taking them.'

'But, Jamie, you could get the doctor to stand up for you, I'm sure, and then wouldn't have to go at all. If you put down for this, you'd be just as much at risk. With no way to defend yourself, as well.'

'I know. But anyway, what difference does it make? If a shell hits you, you are just as dead, whether you are carrying a gun or not. At least I would be useful.'

She nodded slowly. 'No one could say that it was cowardice. Did you tell Father this?'

That smile again. 'I didn't get a chance. But what will Zachariah say? That concerns me more. He's been so good to me. Where is he, anyway?'

'He said that he'd be out late tonight,' she said, avoiding the question. 'We can tell him in the morning.'

But they never did. Zachariah must have come home, some-time in the small hours, because the spare bed had been slept in and there was a letter on her breakfast tray.

I am sorry about the embarrassment I have occasioned you. You might have expected more of me than that. Believe me when I say I didn't know about the child. I went down to the Boases' tonight, to do the decent thing and offer to make a settlement on the girl, but they refused to see me. I shall make arrangements for her nonetheless. I know how hurtful this must be for you. For your sake it is best if I withdraw with dignity, at least until the possibility of further scandal has died down. I therefore intend to see the recruiting officer first thing in the morning and enlist. I imagine that they'll take me – they are conscripting forty-year-olds now, I understand. When I get a posting, I'll write and let you know. You can decide then what you want to do. Try not to think too badly of me, if you can.

He hadn't signed it.

Ironic, really, that the day her husband chose to volunteer was also the day that her brother formally refused to fight,

234

though he was accepted as a Red Cross volunteer. Ironic too that after training they should both arrive in France the self-same day and – judging from the letters Dora got – be stationed not so very apart, though of course with the censor's pencil it was difficult to know, and neither knew the other one was there.

It would have been the ultimate in irony, if – when Zachariah was struck down by a shell – it had been Jamie who carried the broken body to the field hospital behind the lines, but of course that wasn't the case. A mile is a long way on a battlefield, and Jamie was floundering through mud to deal with other wounded men elsewhere.

But Jamie would have understood the truth: that when the medical orderly came by and saw Zachariah's wounds, he shook his head and put him to one side, tied a label round his toe and left him there to die. Effort and resources in that nightmare place had to be saved for those who stood a chance. All Dora ever knew about her husband's agonizing end was that a letter came, saying that he died in action, and was an inspiration to his men.

In Nathan's absence, they had to ask Sammy to arrange the service of commemoration for Zachariah. Old Mrs Zeal had wanted it, and Dora – who seemed to be walking through life in a dream – did not object. Such services were becoming commonplace these days, since of course there was no coffin to inter. Zachariah had presumably been buried where he fell.

He must have had a lot of friends, Winnie thought, looking round the hall. The place was packed, although, oddly, none of the Boases were there. Father came, red-faced and straining at his collar-studs, but didn't stay on for the supper afterwards – and nor did Mrs Zeal, though she'd struggled out of bed for once, to pay her last respects. The effort made her look so gaunt and pale that, when she sat back with her eyelids closed, you might almost have thought she was a corpse herself.

When Winnie got home afterwards she found that the old lady had gone up to her room and was refusing to come out again. She was taking the death of Zachariah very hard. Up until then she had coped with everything with a tenacity that Winnie could almost have admired, if it had not been accompanied by such acerbity – still sitting up, giving instructions to the cook (when they could get one) and making sure the char swept out the grate. And ordering Winifred about, of course.

Even when Nathan had come home for a week last year, suffering from a flesh wound in his foot – nothing heroic, he had simply trodden on a rusty nail, and it had got infected – his mother 'bore his misfortune stoically', as Zachariah said. But this was different. Over the next few weeks the old lady went into decline, took permanently to her bed and hardly seemed to eat or drink at all.

'Overstretched herself by going out in the cold', the doctor said, but Winnie knew that it was more than that. Her mother-in-law had lost her favourite, and had simply given up the will to struggle on.

It was with no great surprise, therefore, that Winnie went into her room one day in early summer, to draw back the curtains as she always did, and found Mrs Zeal unconscious on the bed. Help was called at once, of course, but there was nothing to be done. The old lady lingered on a day or two, and then slipped away with a quietness she had never shown in life. Another funeral – Nathan had left instructions – and Winnie was suddenly left the sole mistress of an inconveniently large, cold and empty house.

Dora was very good. After the funeral she took Winnie home, gave her a cup of tea, and said, 'Look, Win, I know it's early to think about all this, but I'm on my own as well. No point in running two establishments. Better if you close up the house and come and stay with me. Christopher would like it too, I know.'

'Well, if you're sure you wouldn't mind,' Winnie said eagerly at once. 'It would be lovely to have lively company.'

Dora refilled the teapot from the silver jug. 'And don't worry about Father being on his own. We can still go down together if you like so you can try and keep an eye on him. It's no good my going down alone; he won't let me in the house. Says I enticed his son away, and this stretcher-bearing business is entirely my fault.'

Winnie hadn't thought of Father up to now, but she said, 'All right. Though I don't know why I bother. Since he had that row with you and Jamie, he's cut me off as well. But thank you, Dora, I'd be glad to come and stay. Be just like old times,

236

won't it, just the two of us? And think of the money it would save. One bag of coal could heat one room instead of two.'

There were other advantages as well, although she didn't mention these, and naturally they did not influence her decision in the least. Joe Pollock had been fitted with his artificial arm and, since he could not go fishing any more, had been found constructive employment in Penzance.

'I'm to be working for a boot-maker,' he had said the last time she saw him – weeks ago – when she had slipped away from Mrs Zeal's bedside for an hour. 'Supposed to be serving customers and delivering orders round the town. It isn't much, but they can't get the errand boys these days.' He sounded grim. 'I suppose I should be grateful for the chance. I'll be earning something, anyhow, and at least you don't need two good hands for that. And it isn't charity, although it was arranged. The shoemaker will be glad of me. Even the gentry are sending to the menders now, instead of buying new.' It was painful watching him attempt to salve his pride. He looked at her. 'Only thing is, I shan't be able to meet you like this on Thursdays any more.'

She'd smiled, of course, and said that he must think about himself, but she had missed him dreadfully. Well, the first thing she would do, if she moved in with her twin, was take a pair of shoes in to be heeled.

Dora looked doubtfully at her. 'Only I want to make this clear – this is just for the duration, no offence to you. Nathan will want his own house when he comes home, and you know I've never greatly cared for him. I don't want him moving in with me.'

Neither do I, something inside Winnie whispered fretfully. Sometimes she thought there was a malevolent destiny at work. There was Nathan, out in France, with people dying round him every day – young, lively people with sweethearts back at home who missed them every minute. People like Zachariah Zeal, blown to pieces or shot down where they stood, while dreary Nathan plodded on unscathed. There seemed to be no justice in the world.

These thoughts were so disloyal that she shocked herself. She forced her brightest smile. 'Of course. It would be the one thing that cheered up this dismal war. If you mean it, when can I move in?'

Dora was smiling now. 'Why not tomorrow? You can send down later for your things. I'm sure Crowdie, or one of the other farmers with a cart, would bring them up for you.'

So Winnie went home, in the funeral carriage which had been standing by for her, and packed a bag. Deep mourning clothes again, for Mrs Zeal, of course. Next morning she dismissed the surly cook and the obnoxious woman who came in to clean, though it cost her a week's pay for each of them. After lunch she cleared the store cupboard and put the contents in a wooden crate to be collected when the carter came. She covered the padded furniture with sheets and pulled the curtains closed.

Then she left the house and, with a long, deep sigh that might have been relief, locked the door after her and went.

Tom Trewin was walking down the lane beside the school. There it was, as it had always been, though smaller and greyer and more solid than he'd remembered. The ash pile still not dealt with, although the urchins who were sliding down it now, with grimy knees and boots that pinched their toes, would have been only babes in arms when he left home.

There was the wall, where he used to wait for Dora after school. Where was she now? he wondered. Married with a child, his mother said. He wouldn't dwell on that.

There was the very pennywort that he and Len had picked when they were small, to use for coins when they were playing shops.

Astonishing how strange the country looked, and how familiar, too. Grey, blue and green, were the colours here. Not the bright, searing azure of the Australian sky, but a pale eggshell colour, delicate and sad. Leaves and grass of a lush intensity he had forgotten could exist. And grey – granite, cliffs, sky, houses, everything. Even the people were a little grey, worn down by damp and work and worry and the dreadful proximity of death. It was said that, on a quiet night, you could hear the echo of the guns in France. The war.

He had been there, seen it. Not in France, but on the Eastern Front. Gallipoli. It gave him nightmares just to think of it. Images danced before him in his dreams. Men, swarming like cockroaches between rocks and sea, or crushing determinedly through the prickly brushwood up steep cliffs and into inky valleys, despite the murderous hail of shrapnel, fire and shells. The dreadful sounds of the enemy at night, strange bugle calls and blood-curdling cries. Even the weather was an enemy: the searing heat, the blinding rain, and, later, the biting cold at night that gave men frostbite and robbed them of their toes. Everywhere the dead and dying. And the flies.

Tom had seen flies in Australia. He had learned to live with mozzies, spiders, snakes – all sorts of wretched things. But this was different. Flies that swarmed on food. Raw food, cooked food, dried food, every kind of food. Every time you took a bite you had to wave your hand to move the flies, and if you were not quick enough they would be back and you would find flies moving in your mouth. Any piece of food uncovered would be instantly blotted from your sight by flies. They liked dead bodies, too.

Many of his worst dreams were about flies.

And yet flies had more than likely saved his life. They said it was the flies, spreading disease into the food, that brought the violent pains and dysentery which had so prostrated him that – only half-recovered from a bout and attempting to take part in a foray – he suddenly collapsed, tumbled down a sharp incline and broke both his legs. They took him out by lighter to a ship, and when the rest of the Thirteenth Battalion of the Australian Imperial Force had been taking part in the desperate attack on Suvla Bay, Tom had been on a hospital cot on his way to Egypt desperately ill, but more or less physically intact. More than half of his battalion had been lost that night.

He was better now. His limbs had mended and his stomach had responded slowly to purgatives, good food and soothing clay. He was luckier than most. He heard afterwards that more than three-quarters of the men had suffered from dysentery during that campaign, but in most cases it hadn't saved their lives.

Since then he had been retained in Egypt, at Alexandria, where the ANZACs still had their training camp for new recruits. He was seconded on attachment to the commanding officer, who had taken an unexpected shine to him and – on the basis of Tom's familiarity with managing and loading boats – put him in charge of loading camel trains.

'Ships of the desert, Corporal,' he said airily. Tom had

239

come to hate camels almost as much as he hated flies, but it had been a 'safe billet', as the soldiers said, and he knew that in the end it couldn't last. It hadn't. The commanding officer had been posted on elsewhere, and Tom was due to join his regiment again, in the thick of it this time, in France.

But before they sent him there, they sent him home on leave. Again he was lucky. Most of the ANZACs were too far from home, but now that Marcia was dead, giving birth to the son he never had, his only ties were here, with his ma and dad and Cornwall, and they had let him come. Even the *Mariebelle* was history. He'd kept her running to the bitter end, but river-trade had got so bad that finally there was no help for it and even Murcheson had given up. It had been a sad day, though, to see the old paddle boat stripped down and lined up with the others to be towed away for scrap.

Murcheson had money – not much, but just enough – and he'd invested wisely over years. Tom had nothing. The boat had been his home, and with Marcia gone there was nothing else for him. As soon as the deal for the *Mariebelle* was closed, he went to the recruiting office and signed up. YOUR COUNTRY NEEDS YOU all the posters said, and this was his country after all, although he wore a different uniform.

One of the youngsters on the ash pile had stopped sliding now, and had come out to the gate to stare at him.

'You a soldier, mister?' one of the urchins said.

Tom nodded.

'Funny hat.'

'Now, Billie, don't you be rude to the nice gentleman.' A girl had come out of the girls' playground to intervene: a girl with a mop of startling ginger hair and quite a pretty, freckled sort of face. Tom wasn't good at ages, but he'd guess she was perhaps ten or twelve. She gave him what she clearly hoped was a grown-up, knowing smile. 'I'm sorry, mister, but he's only five, and he don't know any better than to stare . . .' She broke off and began staring at him openly herself. '`ere,' she went on in a more ordinary voice. 'Aren't you Tom Trewin, as went off overseas?'

He was astonished. 'How do you know that?

She grinned at him. 'I'm Poppy Pierce, as used to live next door. I remember you. Used to be friendly with that Miss Hunkin that our Harvey liked so much.'

240

There was nothing he could say to that. He laughed. 'My,' he said, 'you've grown up, haven't you?'

She looked affronted. 'I should think so too. Years and years it's been since you were here. Wouldn't have known you, really, except I heard your ma telling mine that she'd had a letter and you were coming back. Then when I saw you, of course I knew your face from the photograph she's got up on the mantlepiece. It had to be, I thought. We don't get many strangers hereabouts.'

Tom nodded. The child was obviously right. He was a stranger here. Things had changed completely since he'd gone away – not just Poppy, who had transformed from snot-nosed infant to almost womanhood, or this brother of hers who was then not even born. Everything about the place had changed. The mine was full of strangers – he'd gone down there earlier, but hardly saw anyone he knew. Men had been co-opted in from everywhere if they weren't quite fit enough to fight. There were girls in uniform – breeches, of all things – working in the fields. And when he'd walked past the house where Dora used to live, he was shocked to see how neglected it looked, as if nobody had lived in it for years. He sighed.

The children were still staring at him with that intense, bold curiosity that only children have.

'Well,' Poppy Pierce said decisively. Obviously she was the leader of the group. 'Can't stop here all day. Got to go and eat our bit of crowst. Afternoon bell will go before we've had it, otherwise.'

'Goodbye then,' Tom said, and watched them troop away. Then he turned and walked slowly down towards the sea.

Three

Father was in a maudlin mood again. He was sitting in the kitchen, muffled up in a dreadful cardigan, repeating in a woeful voice how terrible it was to be old and unwanted and not visited by anyone.

'Well, it's your own fault,' Winnie said impatiently. 'You won't let anybody in. Anyway, what are you talking about? I'm here!' She swept the dirty dishes from the side and thrust them in the sink. 'Look at all this. I don't believe you've washed-up for a week. Why don't you come to Dora? She keeps asking you.' It did not occur to her how strange it was that anyone could talk to him like that these days.

His florid face hardened, and he raised his voice. 'Well I shan't. I shan't have anything to do with her. Turning my own son against me . . .' And off he went again. Winnie had heard it all a hundred times.

'I don't know why Dora is so good to you. Sending down food and doing your washing all the time. Where is it, by the way? Have you put it in the bedroom ready, like we said?'

He hadn't done anything of the kind, of course, and Winnie had to go and strip the bed and make him change his underwear and shirt. It was worse than dealing with Christopher sometimes. At least the child didn't set out to be obstructive all the time.

She picked up all the scattered objects that were strewn around and put them carefully away, then set to work with duster, broom and pail. 'I don't know what to do with you,' she grumbled as she worked. She'd never done so much housework in her life – even at Mrs Zeal's there'd been a cleaner. This was like having Gan back, at her worst. 'We can't go on like this for ever more.'

'Shan't have to,' Father said, reverting to his whine. 'I'm

an old, sick man, and I shall soon be gone. You'll be glad to see the back of me. But I know what's right. You've found a few minutes to look after me a bit, when no one else has cared. When I'm dead, everything is yours.' For two pins, she thought, he'd find himself in tears.

She said, 'Don't be so silly,' but it was a factor, if she was honest with herself. Of course, she'd see that Dora and Jamie got a bit as well. It was impossible to know, with Father in this state, if he had really done what he proposed and made a will, but otherwise she might really have been tempted to give up and stop coming down here every week like this. He was never a bit thankful for anything she did, though he was drinking himself to death so fast that at least he wasn't frightening any more. His brain had turned to beer, and though he roared and raged, you were in no danger if you just kept out of range. He was in no position to come after you.

'Now you make sure you eat this.' She tipped a great big jar of stew into a saucepan where he could heat it up. 'Good food that is, and food is hard to get. There's people starving for the want of it, and all you do is leave it half the time.' She wondered if he ever realized what sacrifices she and Dora made for him. Dora had queued for hours to get that bit of meat, and she herself had struggled with the heavy jar all the way out here. Of course, he never thought of that at all. Every time she came she found plates of food half-eaten and going bad. Father took most of his sustenance in liquid form these days.

'Charlie's missus sent me down a bit of fish last week,' he said. 'You'd think she was doing something special, the way that she goes on. It should be my fish anyway by rights – though I aren't able to go out fishing any more.' He didn't go out anywhere. Charlie was fishing with someone else these days – lots of boats had been laid up for lack of crew. He wouldn't go to sea with Father any more, after he got drunk and fell into the harbour once, and though Father had tried single-handed once or twice, he really couldn't manage on his own. Of course, it just drove him down the Miner's Arms again.

It was as well he still had money from the fish store or he might have been in a worse state than he was. The government had put in somebody to run that now, 'for the duration' as the leaflets said, buying in catch from others and tinning a lot of it for the soldiers overseas. All the same the business was doing very well: people were getting desperate for food.

'Well, that's very nice of Charlie's wife,' she said.

'Didn't come for my sake,' Father said. 'Charlie wants to buy the boat from me, a little at a time. Well, I might let him do it. Breaks my heart to see her standing there. When I've got a son who might have worked her, too. Well let him 'ave her. Though he'll take that engine out. He's mad. You'll see. Fifty years from now, won't hardly be a boat that hasn't got a petrol engine. But there you are. I shan't live to see it, and who takes notice of a poor old man like me?'

He would get tearful if she didn't move. She hated seeing him like this; it was worse than when he got angry, in a way. At least that was himself and not the drink. She said briskly, 'Well, I'll have to go. Want to go up and look around Nathan's house,' – she couldn't bring herself to say 'my house', even now – 'and make sure everything's all right. We might be able to let it to the army or the government, Nathan says, though goodness knows what they would want it for. And then I'll have to go and catch my bus, otherwise I'll have to walk back home. I'll see you next week then.'

'That's right, you go and leave me on my own. Don't worry about me. I'm only your father after all.' He was impossible. There was no point in saying anything, and she just took her basket and the bolster case, full of his washing, and slipped out of the door. It was a nuisance taking that all the way up the hill and after a few steps she stopped and put it down. There were children playing hopscotch in the lane, the numbered squares all scratched out in the dust.

She went up to them. 'You want to earn a penny?'

The biggest of the children looked at her. A fiercely tidy little girl with plaits. 'What for?' She asked suspiciously.

'Keeping a bit of an eye out on my things. I've got something else to do, and I don't want to carry it or have it blow away. I shan't be long.'

The child considered this. 'All right.'

Winnie was better than her word. Without the awkward bundle she was very quick, and twenty minutes later she was back again. She fumbled in her purse. 'There you are, young lady. Buy yourself a treat.'

The child stopped teetering on one skinny leg and pocketed the coin. 'Saw you come out of Ogre Hunkin's house, a minute since,' she said, and added in a burst of confidentiality, 'You're awful brave. I wouldn't go in there.'

'He's my father,' Winnie said. 'I used to live there once.'

'Oh,' the girl said in a disappointed voice, perhaps because the ogre was human after all. Then she looked up suddenly. 'Used to teach my sister Amy once, did you? She's always talking about Miss Hunkin. Was that you?'

'My sister,' Winnie said. 'Now, let me have that bolster. I've got to catch my bus.'

The child didn't move. 'We had a man come to our school today who was a friend of hers. Poppy Pierce knew him. She was telling us. A soldier.'

'Oh yes?' Winnie said indulgently but without interest, stepping past her to pick up her things. Most young men their age were soldiers now. 'Who was that then?'

'Tom somebody. He had a funny hat.'

Winnie straightened up abruptly, arms full of bolster case. 'Not Tom Trewin, surely? Couldn't be. Was that the name?'

The girl shrugged. 'Something like that. Can't remember now. Lived next door to Poppy once, that's all I know.'

'It was Tom Trewin then,' Winnie said aloud. 'Well I'm dashed. Just wait till I tell Dora about that.' And she almost ran up to the lane to catch the bus, as if that would make it get there sooner so she could go home and share the news.

'No, Winnie!' Dora said firmly, for the fifteenth time. 'I won't have you sending letters down. What would it make me look like? Anyway, who knows, Tom might be a married man himself by now.'

'Why would he come home to his parents, then?' Winnie asked, sullenly but with a certain justice. 'And it isn't 'cause one of them is dead. I asked one of the women on the bus.' She had come straight into the downstairs drawing room and was stripping off her outer garments as she spoke.

'You didn't! Can't you leave anything alone?' Dora was unreasonably annoyed. 'People will think I'm chasing after him.'

'Well wouldn't you, if you knew he was still single? You were always keen on him. Worse than a moonstruck calf, you were.'

'And who put a stop to that?' Dora snapped, with a passion that surprised herself. 'Sent him off without a word to me, although you knew how I felt about him all the time. Just because you wanted to impress your blooming Nathan – though the Lord only knows why. Well, I hope you're satisfied.' She'd said more than she intended and she turned her back, picked up the basket by her chair and started vigorously rolling tablecloths to iron.

Winnie's response surprised her. She'd expected an outburst and an argument, but all her sister said, in a small and thoughtful voice, was, 'Yes, I made a proper mess of everything.'

Dora looked up. Winnie was perching on the arm of the big chair opposite, looking so tired and woebegone that it was impossible to be angry any more. 'Winnie!' she cried. 'What is it?'

'You're right. You were right about everything, all along. You told me Nathan was a dreadful, dreary, dismal man . . .'

'Winnie, I didn't!'

'Well, you warned me off him, and that's what you meant. But I wouldn't listen and I married him. Him and his dreadful mother. And that awful house. I hate it, Dora, but I'm stuck with it. It's my own fault, too, that's the worst of it. And there's Joe Pollock, who would give his arm for me – oh, dear, I didn't mean that – but you know what I mean. You told me once that I should marry him, and you were right – again.'

Dora did not know what to say. She had never seen Winnie in a mood like this. 'Well, I married Zachariah,' she said.

'I know. But you liked him. And you only married him for Jamie's sake. I don't know. You're so . . . upstanding, you two. There you are, with your sewing bees and giving me a home and sending down to Father every week, though he won't even speak to you or let your name pass his lips. And Jamie, facing up to him like that and going off overseas – I worry about him every single night. I'm not like that, Dora, standing up against the tide. I'm a coward. I only think about myself.'

'After you've been slaving down at Father's house all day? And everything you do for Christopher? Don't be so silly.' All this self-criticism was embarrassing, though there was a certain truth in it. 'You're unhappy in your marriage, and I'm sorry about that, but you aren't alone. Hundreds of women must be just the same. I know Mother was. That's why she kept that money all those years.' She added the last of the damped ironing to the pile. 'But that's not the point. You've made some bad decisions in the past, but you aren't going to put things right by rushing off and sending letters to Tom Trewin now on my account. If I want to get in touch with him, I will.'

That wasn't true. She wanted desperately to get in touch with him, to find out how he was, to hear his voice again and hold his hand, but she wasn't likely to. He would think her overeager and she'd embarrass him. Anyway, he was a lovely man; he almost certainly had another sweetheart now. She couldn't bear to meet him and let him go again.

Winnie looked sullen. 'Well, you please yourself.' She was back to her normal self again.

Dora was struck by an appalling thought. 'Winnie, you haven't sent a note already, and not said anything to me?'

'No!' said Winnie so crossly that Dora changed the subject.

It therefore came as a complete surprise the next day to open the front door, expecting to see the milkman on the step, and find Tom Trewin standing there.

Her first reaction was embarrassment. 'Drat Winnie,' she said, knowing she'd turn pink. 'She did write after all.'

He frowned. His face had changed. He was thinner and older and his skin was brown. But his eyes were just the same, and he was still good-looking. Just standing there was making her heart pound. 'I don't know what you're on about,' he said. The old voice, tinged with an accent that made it even more attractive than before. 'Why did she do right?'

It made her laugh, and broke the ice. 'I meant she wrote to you. To tell you I was here, and widowed now.'

That old, slow smile. 'She didn't. Nobody wrote to me. I asked around and found you. It wasn't difficult. I heard your husband had been killed in action – that's an awful thing.'

'You've been in action too?' Of course he had. What a simply idiotic thing to say.

He nodded. 'Yes, in the Dardanelles, and I'm posted back again – to France this time – quite soon. With the Australians. I went over there with my brother Len, you know.'

It was dreadful, thinking of him in danger from the guns, but she forced herself to say, 'Yes, I heard you'd gone out to Australia. You've got a home there, I suppose.'

'Not any more. I am a widower, like you.'

'Oh.' She should have said 'I'm sorry' but it wasn't true at all and, treacherously, the words refused to come. She was suffused with a wild, unreasonable hope. She said, 'Well, I shouldn't keep you standing on the step. Why don't you come inside? Winnie's here and I think the cleaning woman's finished in the drawing room.' Why did she want to assure him it was respectable? 'We'll have a cup of tea, and I'll introduce you to my Christopher.' She saw his face fall at the masculine name, to her unashamed delight, and she added instantly, 'My son.'

'I should be honoured,' he said gravely, and she let him in. Into her house, her heart, and back into her life.

'Here, don't go in there,' the daily woman said. 'She's got a friend in there. A soldier by the look of it – one of they foreign Empire ones.' She gave Winnie an exaggerated wink. 'Holding hands and talking nineteen to the dozen they were when I went in with the tray, so I tiptoed out again and let them be. She asked me to get Christopher, and I will do later on, but they won't have much time together, will they, with him only home on leave? Does my 'eart good to see her smile like that. Had a lot of sorrow in her life, poor soul, and she don't deserve it if anybody don't.'

Mrs Purdy never used one word where twenty-six would do. She had a good heart, but despite her words there was a look of wicked satisfaction on her face, and she had obviously been listening at the door. This would be all around Penzance within an hour.

Winnie edged around her to the drawing room. The door had been left ajar, probably by Mrs Purdy and the tray. She looked inside. Yes, it was Tom Trewin, and from the look of it he would be there a little while. That gave her time to do what she had planned.

She turned to Mrs Purdy. 'I won't disturb them for a minute then. I'm going down the town. I've got a pair of Father's boots to sole.' Somehow she felt compelled to add, 'It is all right, you know. We've known the man for years. She used to go to school with him. They were sweethearts once.'

Mrs Purdy gave her a little nudge. 'Never supposed otherwise, I'm sure. Wouldn't begrudge a bit of 'appiness, in any case, even if it wasn't what you say. Life's too short, especially with this war. Mightn't be here tomorrow, that's how I look at it. All of us going to end up dead one day.' She leaned across to Winnie. 'There's one girl I know, husband at the Front, made friends with a sailor who was home on leave. Well, who can blame 'er? She was young, and so was he – can't wait forever, can you, at that age? Anyway, this Jack tar, he went back to sea, and got blown up by one of those summerine things. Well, she was cut up of course, but she says who cares what people think; she gave him a bit of pleasure while he lived. Nice girl too. Not the sort you would expect, at all. And she's not the only one. Things aren't what they were when I was young. Mind, her husband won't half give her what for when he finds out.'

Winnie wondered what version of today's events would reach Mrs Purdy's listeners by and by. 'Well,' she said, 'I'd best be off. Christopher is upstairs in the nursery with his toys. I'll send him down to you.'

She did as she had promised, and then wrapped up the shoes. The soles still had a lot of wear in them, but it gave her an excuse to call on Joe. He had found a way to use his useless hand to hold things on a last, and was doing simple cobbling jobs these days.

But when she got back to the front door with the parcel, she stopped. Mrs Purdy had disappeared and from the open drawing room there was the sound of laughter and Christopher's small voice saying earnestly, 'Come and see my soldiers. I've got one like you, but his paint's rubbed off a bit.'

It made her heart turn over. Tom would be off again, of course, but Dora had found a brief, sweet happiness at least. Why couldn't she and Joe have that? Of course, if Nathan didn't come back from the war, she would be a wealthy widow. No problems then. But if he did come back?

What was it Mrs Purdy said? 'Who cares what people think?' Upstairs among her things, she still had Mother's twenty-five guineas hidden in a box. Enough to run away somewhere and start again. Looking after Father, she had learned to run a

249

house, and Joe might make a living mending shoes. What would he say if she suggested it? Sweep her into his one remaining arm and shower her with burning kisses, as he always did in her dreams? Or turn away and never speak to her again? There was only one way to find out.

She tiptoed back upstairs, took out the money and wrapped it up in a piece of newspaper, like the shoes. Then, taking a deep breath, she went down into the town.

He was in the shop alone, tapping brads into a heel. The doorbell gave a little tinkle as she went inside.

He raised his head and smiled.

'Joe?' she said.